DON'T MESS WITH MY Relic

MADELYNNE ELLIS

First Published in 2024 by Incantatrix Press.
Original Version Published in 2005 by Black Lace, Virgin
Books Ltd.

ISBN- 978-1-917284035

www.madelynne-ellis.com

Join my newsletter!

Don't Mess with my Relic

Lust in the dust of the Egyptian desert.

Adie Hamilton's lifelong dream of joining a prestigious archaeological excavation in Egypt is finally realised when she lands a spot on maverick professor Killian Carmichael's team. However, Adie quickly realises her brilliant but grumpy boss has little patience for her youthful enthusiasm and intuitive approach to the dig. Luckily, she forges a connection with fellow archaeologist Anton Kelley, who is more than happy to indulge Adie's passions – both professional and personal. But as Adie navigates her increasingly thorny relationships with the two men, she learns they have an equally complicated history.

Once, Killian was driven by the same thirst for discovery that fuels Adie, until his youthful enthusiasm cost him everything he held dear — his career, his friends, and the love of his life. He's still haunted by those past mistakes, even as he finds himself inexplicably drawn, against his better judgement, by Adie's drive and keen spirit. Both of which leave him itching to guide and possess her in equal measure.

As the excavation progresses, the three archaeologists must combine their talents to locate a missing relic before Killian's bitter rival, a cult leader intent on cashing in on their efforts, gets to it first. With grave robbers, fanatical groupies, and pesky feelings complicating the mission, the team competes in a high-stakes race against time. For Adie, failure is not an option – she'll stop at nothing to unearth the relic, even if it means making some ethically questionable choices.

Scandalous Seductions
A Gentleman's Wager
Indiscretions
Phantasmagoria
Three Times the Scandal
The Viscount, His Lover & I
The Ghosts of Christmas Past
The Serpent's Kiss

Romps & Rakehells
Capturing Cora
Seducing Sophia
Taming Taylor

Forbidden Loves
The Kissing Bough
Pure Folly

The Black Halo Books
Come Undone
All Night Long
Off the Record
Come Together
All Fired Up
Come Alive
Reflex
Replay
Refrain
Toxic
Reckless Beat

Anything But...
Anything But Vanilla
Anything But Ordinary

Stirred Passions
Cherry Bomb
Black Velvet
Soul Kiss
Mint to Be
Screw Driver

Standalone titles:
Tempted
You, Him, & Me
Don't Mess with my Relic
Sharing Adam
Gabriel's Naughty Game
Confessions of a Greedy Girl
Crazy Love

-AUTHOR'S NOTE-

Which Includes Spoilers. You've Been Warned

Once upon a time, quite a long time ago, I wrote a book. It was an erotic book, and an adventure story set in Egypt on an archaeological dig. It was the second novel I ever completed, and it was fun. Roll forward twenty years and times have changed. My focus and my writing have changed. In 2022, when I got the rights back to Passion of Isis, my intention was to give it a tidy up, re-title it and put it back on sale. However, it quickly became apparent as I delved into the details of the story that it was going to need more than a bit of polish to bring it up to date. Turns out that twenty years is both the blink of an eye, and a very long time indeed.

So, here we are. Passion of Isis is now Don't Mess with my Relic. It still has the same characters, they're still searching for the same relic, and there's still quite a lot of shagging going on. But there are a lot of changes too.

Killian wasn't explicitly bisexual in the original, and it wasn't a ménage à trois. (Actually, let me correct myself here. It was conceived as one, that part just never made it to the published version.) Nor could you ever have truly labelled the original as a romance. It was pure smut, or erotica by and for women as the publisher liked to categorise it at the time.

Now, it's definitely a romance involving three people. It's also still smutty. In some ways, more smutty. Killian's still a grumpy professor, Anton's still your quintessential smouldering bad boy, and Adie remains young, adventurous and a maker of profoundly dubious decisions, but we can't all be perfect. It's been fun rediscovering them and dragging them into the modern age.

If you read and loved the original, I hope you love this version of the story too. If you're here for the first time, I hope it hits every one of your lust in the dust fantasies. Happy reading,

Madelynne Ellis. September 2024.

Note: This book is written in British English and uses British spellings, slang, and idioms. Of notable mention, as Google is sometimes confounded by it too, is the dialect word lozzucked, which means to lounge/idle about being unproductive, and is mostly restricted in usage to Shropshire, Staffordshire, Cheshire, and Lancashire. There are also a few Arabic phrases.

-PROLOGUE-
Esther

20 years ago

"—and then from Giza we'll go across the desert to Saqqara and see the Step Pyramid."

"Precisely."

Her niece rode across the rug as if steering her camel across its shaggy pile, before turning back to her great aunt's high-backed armchair. "Will we cruise down the Nile, Auntie Esther? I want to see Thebes too, and the Valley of the Kings." The girl was dressed in her very best adventuring gear: cargo shorts, and a dark pink T-shirt, with a small brown backpack and her all-essential leather fedora perched on her head. The tail of her neatly plaited long brown hair fell down the centre of her back, and on her feet, she wore a smart pair of lace-up boots she'd only recently learned to tie for herself. It made the old woman smile to see her so enthused, to see her eyes light up with the possibility of adventures she'd once too dreamed of going on.

"You'll do all those things, Adina. All those things and many more. Your adventures will be endless.”

“Show me on the map again, Auntie Es.”

Indy was still playing silently in the background as Adina climbed into her lap. They spread the map over the surface of the jigsaw table, momentarily covering the Sphinx’s broken nose. Then traced a route from Alexandria in the north all the way down the Nile past Luxor to Abu Simbel on the banks of Lake Nassar, approaching the border with Sudan.

“And we’ll stop lots of times and see all the tombs, won’t we? I want to see all the tombs.”

“What, every one? That might take a while.”

“Every one,” the child said in all seriousness. She was a serious little thing, when not caught up in the thrill of an adventure, but that was to be expected, given she’d been barely out of nappies before her mum and dad were gone, and now her grandparents too. “All the important ones, but all the others too, even the ones of the people we don’t know the names of. Maybe I’ll find something and be able to work out who they are.”

“That I’m sure you’ll do.” Esther’s breath grew tight in her chest and became a wheeze as it too frequently did these days.

“Here’s your mask, Auntie Esther.” The girl put it over her mouth and nose.

Things hadn’t always been this way. Once upon a time, adventures had been outdoor events involving fields and haystacks, puddles, and ponds, mountains, and merry-go-rounds. And though she’d never trekked as far as Egypt, in fact, no further than a day trip to Ostend, she’d lived life wild and free as the birds she only admired from the window now.

Kathy appeared from the kitchen. "Perhaps it's time you let your aunt rest now, Adina, love. I can put you a DVD on in the little study."

"All right," Adie agreed, far too soberly for a six-year-old. She snuggled against Esther's side before riding her camel down the hallway.

"You shouldn't let her tire you out, so," Kathy admonished.

She hadn't the breath to reply, to say that the girl was the only true joy remaining to her. Instead, she rested her head against the chair wing and listened to her niece battling thieves on the stairs and squealing with laughter as she whizzed down the banister.

"She's gonna come a cropper one of these days," Kathy tutted. "I'll bring you a cuppa and your meds, then we'll settle you down for a nap, eh? The little adventurer's off to a friend's this afternoon, so you'll be able to get a decent bit of shut eye for once. Right then, back in two ticks."

She turned off the TV and folded the map before bustling out again.

Esther shut her eyes and dreamed.

-1-

Adie

"Damn it!"

Doctor Adie Hamilton slammed her fist into the desk, causing the dodgy lamp to flicker and blink out. It was past nine, and she was still no closer to deciphering the dog-eared hieroglyphic manuscript than she'd been six hours ago. It was probably time to call it a night. She'd catch Joe in the morning and get his take on it. While she hated admitting defeat, especially to the gruff, bushy old professor who'd taken her under his wing during her doctorate, she was never going to progress if she couldn't crack this damn code.

Adie glanced again at the paper before tucking it away in her satchel. She'd attained her PhD two months ago. All her fellow students had moved on, mostly to clerical jobs. One or two had scraped in as archivists or curators, but she was still lingering about the place, conducting the odd seminar, and holding onto the dream of a gig on an excavation team. Sooner or later, she was going to have to give it up and bury that dream. There just weren't that many positions, not for the number of graduates the universities turned out, and everyone wanted reams of experience, or the promise of funding attached to your name. She could try for a lecturing position, except teaching wasn't her forte. Her mind had a habit of wandering. They'd start out discussing one thing, but she'd lose track of the topic and end up somewhere else instead.

"Night, Rob," she called to the caretaker, doing his sweep of the building before locking up.

"I thought everyone had gone but Professor Levine."

"Joe's still here?"

He gave her a nod.

Adie about turned. Pushing seventy and ripe for retirement, Josef was a workaholic, who'd confided more than once that if he was forced out, he'd be dead within a year. Still, it was unusual to find him here at this time of night. "I'll check in on him."

"Sure chicken, whatever you say."

The building was in semi-darkness, the primary source of light courtesy of the outside security lighting and the emergency exit signs. It painted stripes across the floor as she backtracked up the stairs and along the top corridor. The door to Joe's office stood slightly ajar, light spilling from the interior.

"J—" She halted, her intention to knock and march right in, amended by the sound of voices. Who the devil could he be talking to at this time?

Adie peeped through the gap. Joe was sitting behind his desk. No mistaking that shapeless brow suit sleeve. All that was visible of the other figure was a neatly pressed trouser leg. Male, based on the socks and feet.

"—I question your sanity over being back at Saqqara. Why on earth would you think I'd have someone I'd send out there with you?"

Saqqara! Her ears perked.

"I had to face it someday. It is a rather large necropolis, and the prospects for the new site are good. They're really good, Joe."

"So, you say, and yet you're here."

"Out of necessity. That's the only reason. Come on, Joe. I know you've got someone."

Yes, me! Adie damn near stopped breathing. A chance to work on an excavation at Saqqara was her dream come true, but also likely hotly contended.

"Just advertise like a normal person or employ someone already out there."

"Tsk, I've not time for that. Nor do I want to risk being swarmed by tourists and amateurs. If I advertise internally at the university, that's exactly what'll happen."

The furrows in Joe's brow deepened. He took a long swallow from his stained coffee mug. Adie had once made the mistake of washing it, believing she was doing him a favour. She'd not made that mistake twice.

"Come on, who've you got? I know you've got someone. You always do. You only take the best. As do I. Just as you taught me."

The reflected praise brought a smile to Adie's lips. Oh, my, God! This was so perfect for her. She'd no close family, no specific job, a flat that the lease was about to expire on, and she'd worked on a dig in Cyprus the previous summer along with every dig in the UK she been able to volunteer for that'd happened in the last six years. She dragged her teeth across her bottom lip, waiting for Joe to say her name. Instead, he further hunched down in his chair and scratched a hand through his wiry hair.

"Someone competent, plenty of potential to shape, and that no-one will miss. It's not a huge ask."

"Hoping to slide under the radar?"

The man gave a cough. Damn the angles. She wanted a look at him but wasn't about to barge in. If Joe mentioned her, then... then she could conveniently arrive and speed things along.

Was mystery man someone she'd met? Not based on that voice. Well to do English, she thought, but probably multi-lingual, his inflections melodic in a way that conjured images of stealthy beauty. Most likely, he spent a lot of time speaking Arabic if he was working in Egypt.

Josef shook his head. "There's no one."

What! She stared at her former professor, outraged. What did he mean? There was no one? Her. There was her. Here. Right here. And he knew she was looking. God, he'd written her reference after reference.

Joe sat back in his chair, bring him full into view. He folded his arms across his chest, his expression grim. "I'm sorry, Killian. I really don't think I can help you."

Adie clamped her hands across her mouth to contain a squeak. Killian? Oh, fuck!

Doctor Simon Killian Carmichael was the leading authority on the Early Dynasties, and had headed high profile expeditions to Giza, Abu Sir, Dahshur and, most recently, Lisht. He was her goddamned idol. There weren't many famous Egyptologists about anymore; the days of Howard Carter were long past, but Doctor Carmichael certainly made her list, and those of many of her peers. He'd been the most requested guest for the end-of-term lecture for the last five years. Not that he'd ever given one.

Wow! And he was here, looking to recruit.

Rumours had traversed the department in the past that he'd been a former student of Joe's, but she'd never given them any credit.

"Why do you need someone, anyway?"

"I've had to send Bill Harris home with a broken leg. He slipped down some steps at the dig and won't be on his feet again for months."

Joe's lips thinned into a tight line. "Assuming you'd want him back."

To that, Killian made no audible response.

"Come on, Josef. Do you really expect me to believe that all of your recent PhD students have walked straight into their ideal jobs? I'm not buying it. I know you've reservations, but can you at least admit that I can offer them something most of them will only ever dream of? It's potentially a salaried position too, not a short-term contract."

Josef pushed a stray paperclip towards the small silver mountain by his work-tray. Why hadn't he said her name? She was the obvious choice! An acidic tang crawled up from her stomach. *Say my name, Joe.*

"Fine. I'll think about it, but I'm not making any promises. I'm really not sure I've got anyone for you."

Tempting as it was to burst in and shriek, "I'm here, pick me," Adie contained herself.

"And I don't believe you, but I'm sure after you've thought..." Killian stood, which still only gave her a glimpse of his left-hand side from shoulder to toe before she was obliged to step away from the door. "You can contact me at my hotel. I'll be around for the rest of the week. Don't keep me hanging around, eh? I'll be waiting for your call."

~Ж~

The following morning, Adie sidled into Joe's office while he was marking papers. She placed a fresh mug of coffee at his elbow before settling in the same seat Doctor Carmichael had occupied the previous night.

"I suppose you've heard," he huffed gruffly, not looking up. "News certainly gets around fast."

"You're going to put me forward, right? I mean, it's perfect for me. And, no one has told me. I overheard you last night, Joe. He was actually here, Killian Carmichael was here, and he wants someone for his project at Saqqara."

"Hush you. Keep your voice down." Joe set down his pen on the essay pile, which he still insisted on printing out and marking by hand, despite the departmental policy of submitting work online via the university portal. "Adie, I know you're hungry, but... I can't, in good faith, put you forward for this."

"Can't or won't? And why? He wants a PhD and some fieldwork experience. I've got that, and nobody's going to miss me. Or are you saying I'm not good enough?"

"Adie, you're plenty good enough. I am not saying that. If anything the opposite's true. You're too good for him." He rose and began to pace, taking himself over to the office window and back.

"That doesn't even make sense. You know how much I want this. How important it is to me. Why would you not support me?"

He turned, putting his expression into shadow. Even so, it was impossible not to detect his frown. "You've never even been to Egypt. I'm suggesting Murphy and Longford."

"What?"

"They both worked on the Luxor project last year, and—"

"Joe, that's not fair. It's bullshit." She slapped her palms down on his desk, causing an ornament and pen to jump. "Chris Longford hasn't even submitted his thesis yet. How is he better qualified for this position than I am?"

"I didn't—Adie, you don't know what you're asking. You don't know—" He raked a hand through his thinning hair. "I'll help you find something; I promise I will, but Killian's team is not for you."

"Why not? You need to back that up with a reason if you're going to be like this. Does he want a man? Is that it? Is he a rampant misogynist?"

Joe recoiled. "No, of course not. It's just... Adie, I don't think you and he are a good fit. You're too intuitive. It's not his way. He'll stifle all your best instincts. He'll drain all the heart out of you."

"So will being forced to work in Tesco's." A prospect that was becoming increasingly likely. She might have a little nest egg of an inheritance, but it wouldn't keep her going for long.

Joe winced again, so she knew he'd acknowledged her point.

"Adie, I've already given him my recommendations."

"And I'm sure he won't mind if you add another. Please, Joe. All I want is an interview... a chance. Do I not deserve that? He might not even want me. If our ways of thinking are so alien, then..."

"Oh, he'll want you."

He scowled when she shot a curious glance at him. Damn it, if he didn't give in soon, she'd have to do something dramatic like run crying from the room. The tears would be genuine.

She bit her lip. There was one other thing that might nudge him from his position. "I'll leak the news of the site to the press."

"Adie, don't be ridiculous. I don't believe for a second that you'd go to the press. Some of my students, yes, but not you. Don't demean yourself, please."

"I might," she insisted, her tone even less persuasive than before. "Even a couple of emails to some of the more sensationalist websites would do it, or one of those lunatic fringe writers. You know, Cadillacs of the Gods, that kind of thing."

A heavy silence fell.

Joe flicked a speck of lint from his corduroy jacket. The furrow between his bushy brows deepened.

For a moment, Joe looked genuinely worried. Had she touched on a sore subject?

"If you did that, you'd ruin your career."

"What career? I'm going nowhere. What is there to lose?"

The crow's feet around his eyes softened, then his lips twitched as he shook his head. "Dear God, don't make me regret this. Fine, I'll call him."

"You will?" Relief dissolved her tension.

"Yeah, yeah, get on with you."

She scampered around the desk and flung her arms around Joe's shoulders. "You won't regret this. I promise." She gave him a peck on the cheek.

As she skipped out the door, she heard him mutter, "I already do."

-2-
Adie

Doctor Carmichael didn't waste time. He conducted the interviews that very afternoon. Adie, the last of the three was patiently waiting her turn, leaning against the photocopier outside Joe's office when Callum Murphy came out, red-faced and sweating around his shirt collar. "That bad?" she asked, clasping his elbow to stall him. He looked at her like he might puke down her front.

"I was told to tell you to go on in."

"Straight away?"

"Yeah. Brace yourself."

"Tough nut, eh?" she said, forcing cheer into her voice. She might not feel confident, but she could fake it.

Callum snorted. "Nothing fazes you, does it?" His head bowed, and he pulled away from her muttering to himself something that sounded a lot like "My God! Oh, my fucking God."

There was nothing for it but to obey the summons.

Adie knocked and entered the office, not knowing what to expect. Joe hadn't given her any pointers. In fact, he'd refused to discuss the project beyond what they'd already said. Thus, she didn't even know what the job was besides being part of an excavation team in the desert. Killian himself was another mystery. There were no pictures of him online, and while her friends in the department had described him as a daring, darkly attractive Indiana Jones type, realistically, he was more likely to look like one of the guys off Time Team: weather-beaten, wiry, and a bit grizzled, but, well... a girl could dream. And she'd take her dream job over her dream man any day.

The man who rose from behind Joe's desk to shake her hand couldn't have shocked her more if he'd donned a clown mask.

Killian Carmichael was so unlike anything she'd expected, that when he held his hand out, she stared at him, dumbfounded.

His hair was startling white. Not blond, but fully white, which was crazy, because if he was a day over thirty-five, she'd give up chocolate forever. His eyes were grey like crystal, sapphire tinted around the limbal ring. His jaw, carved of granite...

He cleared his throat, prompting her to wipe her sweaty palm down the side of her skirt before accepting his handshake.

Strong. A quick sense of pressure against the back of her knuckles that she felt in multiple seemingly unconnected places. There was a strange chill to his touch accompanied by a fizzle of static charge. Then the contact was over, and she stood bereft.

"Please, take a seat."

"Thank you." She smiled. His reciprocal one didn't reach his eyes. He folded his hands in his lap as he waited for her to settle.

"I don't intend to keep you long, Doctor Hamilton. Josef informs me you threatened to go to the press."

"I... Er..." She gave a sharp cough. Joe really didn't want her to get this post. Frankly, she was astonished Killian had invited her to an interview at all. Maybe that wasn't what this was. Rather, he intended to give her a thorough chewing over instead. "I wouldn't really have done it. Joe knows that. I just wanted a chance."

For a moment, Killian's hard expression faded. His lips twitched into something that approximated a smile. Then he leaned forward conspiratorially. "Yeah. That's what I figured. Josef wouldn't recommend someone he didn't consider trustworthy. He likes you, I think, Doctor Hamiliton. Likes you a lot. Has a lot of time for you, is that not so?"

"Yes, I suppose." How was it he left her feeling so wrong footed with such an observation? More importantly, why did it matter?

"I understand if you don't want to interview—"

"I want to." He stretched out a hand over the desk as if to press her back down into her seat, and in so doing, revealed the face of an expensive watch. She instantly felt shabby in comparison. Though really, she ought not to be surprised. Archaeology had always been the pursuit of the rich.

"Shall we get to it?" He glanced at a leather notebook open on the desk. "Why do you want to go to Egypt, Doctor Hamilton?"

Why? What sort of mad question was that?

Because she'd dreamed of it since she was a child. Planned adventures, lived a thousand iterations of them. And she wanted the thrill of unearthing treasures, to feel the desert wind blowing through her hair, to sleep beside a desert oasis...

"Egyptian culture and society fascinate me. I want to see the foundations that the theories are built on."

"I dislike theories," he said intensely. "Facts are what matter. Adventure stories and daydreams don't interest me."

"Of course." Evidently, he wasn't an Indy fan.

Adie swallowed the lump forming in her throat as he made some notes. Then the interrogation began. He delved into obscurities. Forced an opinion out of her on several ancient controversies. Made more notes. Taxed her in a way no exam had ever done and grilled her harder than the panel had done when she was called in to defend her thesis.

He was a monster.

Her heart was pounding nine to the dozen by the end of her twenty minutes in the hot seat, also hopelessly turned on and wet for him.

"Shall we try an easy one? Can you give me the names of four of Ramesses II's thirty-odd sons?"

"Ah...ah..." Her mind blanked.

"Not one?"

Not one, and dammit if she hadn't learned them

in the past alongside the alphabet. "I could look them up. I'm very good at that sort of thing. Google. Search engine stuff..." What the hell was she saying?

He gave her another of his curious half-smiles that turned up the very corners of his lips and made her want to reach out and touch his mouth. The man had beautifully soft looking lips.

"Is that your thesis?"

Adie handed over the leather-bound copy. Killian began to flick through the heavy volume, pausing to ask the occasional question, but mostly *hmming* and nodding. It gave her the opportunity to really focus on him. The tan-line just visible below his collar, the surprising glint of a stud earring through one ear, and that startling white hair like the colour had been shocked right out of him.

Eventually, he handed the tome back to her. "I've one last question for you. Assume yourself in my position, needing to recruit a team player. You'll interview dozens of recent post-docs, some graduates and, at best, their experience is of polishing exhibits and glueing pots. What could possibly interest you about any of them? What distinguishes one from the other?"

"Depth of knowledge."

Killian gave a decisive shake of his head. "They all have that, Doctor Hamilton. Try again."

"Team spirit."

"This isn't an IT company. One last try."

Oh lord, she needed to think. Think, Adie. Think. What was he looking for?

Then, for a split second, she was back in the

dingy classroom of her first A level History lesson. "Never forget," her lecturer had said, as he wrote a word in big chalk letters on the whiteboard and underlined it twice.

"Objectivity," she blurted, in full awareness that it was something she frequently lacked.

Killian observed her calmly for a second or two, then nodded. "That's it. We're all done, Doctor Hamilton. I'll let you know."

"Wait."

He was already out of his seat, heading towards the door. He opened it for her. She followed him as a matter of course. "Don't I get to ask you any questions?" That was normally how job interviews worked.

That disarming half-smile reappeared again. What would it be like if he ever broke into the full version given this one knocked her so off kilter. It made her ready to accept whatever he said as gospel, even apparently being ushered out of the room without a chance to find out a thing about the job offer.

"If I decide to employ you, you'll be provided with all the information you need. The salary is non-negotiable."

"There is a salary, though, right?"

"For the right person."

Killian shook her hand again and showed her out.

-3-
Killian

Killian Carmichael prided himself on being a decisive man. While he abhorred idle speculation and facts that couldn't be properly verified, there were some areas in which he still relied on his instincts. Or at least, the instincts of others that he knew to be honed and sharpened by years of experience. It made the decision over whom to employ that much simpler. Adie Hamilton was the only one of the three Joe Levine had said a damned thing about. It was clear the old bastard adored her.

Sure enough, when he returned to his office, Joe's craggy face was all scowl and ire. "Don't," he pleaded.

"Don't be absurd, Joe. We both know she's the standout candidate."

He got a grouchy growl in response, followed by a deal of *hmming*.

Killian wandered over to the bookcase by the window, where a row of dusty photographs occupied one shelf. "You're being overprotective."

With some reason, admittedly. Killian's past was a constant lingering threat to his future, and anyone else associated with him.

"Am I? She's not the right person for your team, Killian."

"How so? She's young, bright, self-assured, knowledgeable—"

Joe's eyes shone with fury as he marched over to where Killian stood. "She's impetuous and romantic. Desperate to leap fucking snake-filled pits and unearth secrets and treasures—"

"Don't we all," he replied laconically. "At least the last part." Snakes he'd happily pass on.

"You used to." The old man snatched a photo frame from near the back of the grouping. Killian did not need to see it to know the contents of the picture it contained. Every line of it was etched into his brain. Hell, he remembered every moment of that day and was never likely to forget it.

Joe thrust it into his hands. "She's exactly how you were back in the day. Full of hopes and idealism. Do you remember that? What it felt like? How desperate you were to get to Egypt? What you were willing to sacrifice? You were ready to dig up the whole Sahara with your bare hands if you had to. The young Doctor Carmichael and his faithful sidekick."

"People change." He did not need this sort of reminder of his youth. "They move on." Killian replaced the photograph of the two graduates and their professor back in the indent in the dust.

"Have you seen him recently?" Joe enquired, refusing to give up.

Killian sighed. "You know damn well that I haven't." Nor would ever seek to. You couldn't live in the present if you were constantly tethered by your past. Sometimes you had to shed the baggage and not look back. "She'll be a good worker, Josef. That's what I need, and if she's as ambitious as you claim, then she'll be heading her own projects in a few years. A place on my team is exactly the sort of head start she'll benefit from."

"A place on your team is a dual-edged sword and we both know it. You have the respect of your peers at present, but we both know that's not always been the case, and what's to say—"

"You worry overly much."

"What's to say your past doesn't crop up and skewer you again?"

He kept the exasperation from his voice. It was a fight, but he did it. "Josef, for God's sake. That business is long over. Long, long over. I wouldn't employ her if I thought it would harm her. I wouldn't employ anyone if I thought the association would do that." He drew a heavy breath to try to still the anger roiling inside him, then slowly, steadily he breathed his irritation away. "I promise you, there's no cause for alarm, and I'll try not to ruin her with my cynicism."

"Promises are like kisses. Easily given and all too forgettable."

Killian might have said something about the old bachelor never having been kissed by the right person if he genuinely believed that to be true, but that would be like handing out an invitation to rifle about in his personal life, and that wasn't something he ever invited anyone to do. And frankly, Josef knew more than enough about him already.

His old professor bowed his head sadly. "I suppose you won't be reasoned with. That at least hasn't changed."

Killian shook his head, whereupon Joe sagged into his desk chair. "Very well. Then I guess I'm going to have to acclimate myself to the fact that my best student is poaching my second best and find myself a new protegee. Just look out for her, eh? She doesn't really have anyone, and I'm going to be pissed as hell if you lose her in the desert."

He'd watch Adie Hamilton with the same vigilance he watched over the rest of his team. "I haven't mislaid anyone yet."

Leastways, not unintentionally.

"Will you let her know, or shall I?"

Killian found his coat. "I'll leave you that honour. Change of plans. I'm flying back to Egypt tonight. I need to check in for my flight in an hour."

-4-
Adie

Freshly through customs, Adie waited outside Cairo International Airport for her ride beneath a canopy providing a meagre bit of shade. The world was so very bright here. The sky uninterrupted blue. Around her taxi drivers in dusty Peugeots were clamouring for their customers, while scores of international visitors milled past, destinations determined. Just over a week had passed since Professor Levine had called to give her the good news. Her arm and bottom still ached from numerous cautionary vaccinations, and her nose was still a bit red from her parting with the grumpy old fool, but she was finally here in Egypt. Finally making steps on her journey she'd been planning since childhood. She'd thought of Esther a lot these last few days, how thrilled her great aunt would have been to know her dreams were finally being realised.

Speaking of dreams, she'd been having some interesting ones about her new boss. Doctor Carmichael had woven something of a spell over her. It never seemed to matter what she was doing this last week; he'd kept sliding into her thoughts. He was a near nightly visitor. And some of those dreams—well, they weren't precisely dreams, more visualisations—had been pretty spicy.

She'd been studying all his papers to harvest the tiniest of clues about him, but all she'd learned were decidedly dry and impersonal facts. He was thirty-six, Oxford educated, PhD from Durham—not a surprise, Joe had once lectured there until he'd been lured away by the promise of his own department—now attached to the University of Cairo, where he sometimes lectured, but his excavations were largely funded through private individuals.

To her left, a crowd of people milled around a dirty coach. Their milky tourist complexions, so much in contrast to the darker skin of the locals, had attracted a plague of guides and street vendors. A tall Nubian woman pushed a luggage cart through their midst, followed by a line of wide-eyed children whose lilting voices seemed to hang in the air. Adie clutched her overnight bag for comfort. Suddenly home seemed very far away and the present a little too vivid. She shifted her feet uncomfortably. Her clothes were already damp, beads of sweat rolling down her back into the crease of her buttocks, and her skin felt gritty. She'd been promised someone would be here to greet her, but the stream of people was slowly thinning, and Doctor Carmichael had yet to show his face.

Weary, she closed her eyes and fell back into the fantasy she'd been entertaining herself with during the flight.

"Can't you concentrate, Ms Hamilton?" Killian

flashed her one of his intriguing half-smiles. They were back in her interview, only she was stripped down to her underwear and he was in his shirtsleeves with his hand inside her knickers. "Such a disappointment."

"I can... I can remember them. Khaemwese... Merenptah. That's two of them."

"So, it is. So, it is." He rewarded her with the flick of his index finger over her swollen clit. "But I wanted four. You can manage four for me, can't you?"

"Yes." Desperate to feel more of his touch, she dredged her memory for more names. If she succeeded, would he thrust those fingers inside her, fuck her with them so that she was ready for his cock? "Amunhotep. Mery-Atum."

"Well done, Doctor Hamilton. Well done." This time he caressed her with the pad of his thumb. "But you can do me one more. Josef's favourite is definitely up to that."

"And I'll get the job if do?"

His pale eyes flashed, like lightning over the desert. "You'll get something. Something we both know you're desperate for."

Pleasure coiled within her nub, became intensely focused. One more. She only needed to think of one more.

"Just a single name." His breath whispered against the side of her throat. She held her breath waiting for the pressure of his lips that didn't come.

"I don't know." She reached out to him, frantic, and clawed the front of his shirt. "Ramesses... That's it, Ramesses, after his father."

"A good guess, Doctor Hamiliton. A very good guess." His tongue-tip tickled her earlobe, then his fingers slid deep into her sex. "That's it. Good girl. How well you take them." She preened at the praise. "I know another. No. Another three... six."

"I bet you can name me all thirty."

She proceeded to do just that. It was as if his fingers splitting her, thrusting, and filling her had opened a lock inside her mind, so that all her rote learning was released. It made her gleeful and giddy as a goose, as Aunt Esther would have said. The names rolled off her tongue, while her body thrilled to his touch. He pumped them in and out, a steady accompaniment to her words. Burying them to the fullness of their length, then drawing them out shiny with her arousal, while his thumb bruised her clit. The sight of it, of him so casually penetrating her while he stood there so handsomely dressed had her ribs straining to draw air into her lungs. He was all crisp white shirt pulled over strong shoulders and eyes of pale fire, while she... she was a mess of need.

"Stand up now and bend over," he said once she was done reciting. Adie draped herself over the wide oak desk so that her burning cheek was pressed against the grain and her arse was aloft.

Killian pulled the damp cloth of her panties down her legs, so they sat like a hobble around her upper thighs. "I think Josef's good girl deserves a special reward. That's if you think you're ready for it. Are you ready for it, little dove? Are you ready to be my good girl instead? Ready to take your professor's thick, hard cock?"

"I am," she groaned. "I definitely am. Give me it."

"Adie? Doctor Adina Hamilton?" The tap of a hand against her shoulder broke her reverie.

"Yes. Yes, that's me." She startled to attention, opening her eyes to find a blonde, slender as a lily with triceps a professional athlete would envy standing before her, two perfectly plucked eyebrows quirked upwards. "Erm. Hello?" Unrealised arousal simultaneously zipped around her body, making her desperate to rub her legs together. The result was an awkward jiggle, she prayed the other woman interpreted as a desperate need to pee.

"Hi. I'm Doctor Lawrence, Siân. Doctor Carmichael sent me to collect you." The woman offered her a hand, which Adie shook. Then, she seized Adie's heavy suitcase and lifted it as if it wasn't only five grams under the luggage allowance. "I'm sorry you had to wait. The traffic's appalling at this time of day." She set off through the lines of cars and donkey carts towards a battered old Land Rover leaving Adie to waddle along behind, following the swing of her neatly plaited hair.

Well lady, you can forget any ideas you have about seducing Doctor Carmichael with *this* goddess-like creature around.

Just as well, she was here to work not flirt.

"Climb on board, it's open," Siân called as she hefted Adie's suitcase into the back. "The drive's not too long. Feel free to wind the window down. You'll want to, the air con's kaput."

From the airport at Heliopolis, they sped south towards central Cairo, past the exhibition centre and the outskirts of the Northern Cemetery, with the dry dusty wind whistling past the open windows.

"I never expected it to be like this," Adie admitted, gazing in awe at the sprawling majesty of the city and its mixture of modern architecture and ancient minarets.

"Nobody ever does." Siân said. "They think it'll all be stuck in the past. Cairo is the sixth largest metropolitan area in the world, the third largest city in Africa, and largest in the Middle East. Believe me, it has everything any other city has, including the traffic." To prove the point, she leaned on the horn and shot through a red light.

Adie winced and grabbed for a hand hold, but nobody on the street or in the other vehicles seemed even slightly surprised. A few of them even chased them through.

"Don't worry about it." Siân hit the horn again as she slalomed between the two lines of traffic.

"Fucking Christ!" She'd expected a slow tour along dusty roads bordered by mudbrick houses, not a ride with Steve McQueen's reckless kid sister.

"Where the hell did you learn to drive like this?"

"From Vin Diesel." She laughed. "Nah, I'm self-taught. Passed my test and everything. My Egyptian driving test, that is." Her grin stayed maniacally huge. "That's six metres forward and six metres backwards if you're wondering."

They skidded around a corner. "Oh, fuck! Is this normal?"

"Absolutely normal, yes."

They sailed past two huge bronze lions and out on to a bridge over a vast stretch of glittering water. Along the banks, date palms and flame trees flanked blue stone walkways bustling with people. She was looking at the Nile, the lifeblood of Egypt since pre-dynastic times.

Siân nodded as she leap-frogged the car down another lane of traffic.

Adie curled her fingers around the edge of her seat and held on tight. "Where are we heading?"

"Oh, the team's apartment. It's on Gezira. That's one of the two islands Cairo spilled onto during the nineteenth century. It's mostly leafy residential, not very touristy, but don't worry, we'll take you to see some of downtown Cairo tonight. We've a table booked at Fishwari's."

That was somewhere she'd heard of. "You're taking me somewhere touristy?"

"It has to be done."

They passed another pair of lions and reached dry land.

"Who's we exactly?" Right now, she wasn't sure she was going to live long enough to eat supper.

"Us. The rest of the team. They're all desperate to meet you."

The buildings were less crowded here on the island, though taller, and the landscape had become more predominantly green.

"Doctor Carmichael?"

"Hah!" Siân seemed to find that notion amusing. "Fat chance of that. No, he's very, very busy, don't you know. You don't honestly think he slums it with us muck shovellers, do you?"

"Oh, I..."

Siân slapped her across the thigh. "I'm teasing you. He's busy at the university. Departmental meeting or something."

"Right. Okay." She fought not to let her disappointment show on her face.

"It isn't anything personal. He did plan to meet you, but something came up and it couldn't wait since we're back on site tomorrow morning." Siân's eyes glittered in a knowing way. "You've taken a fancy to him already I see."

"What? No."

Heat streaked across her face to contradict her.

"Sure about that? You must be the only bloody woman around who hasn't. Even lesbians love him. Actually, they adore him."

"I do find him intellectually fascinating," Adie croaked.

"Well, it's for the best. People have died of old age waiting for him to make a move. He only gets it up for mummies. And you can forget all the romantic crap the media write. It's just not him. He's all discipline."

"Does that mean I can expect a bullwhip being cracked across my arse?"

Siân drummed the steering wheel in delight. "What an image. I like you. You can stay." She grinned wide, clearly picturing it. "Sadly, unlikely. No, Captain Workaholic will just give you the look."

"The look."

Siân delivered her best stern-faced Killian imitation. "And then he'll tear a strip off you. But overall, he's a not bad boss, as long as you only speak when you're spoken to, and never speculate, and denounce Hollywood make-believe at every opportunity."

"Oh!" she said, sagging into her seat. This might be a tougher assignment than she'd thought. "How about the rest of the team? What are they like? Modelled in Doctor Carmichael's image?"

"Nah. Leastways, none of them keep their cocks in cold storage like he does, but that's probably not what you were asking."

Adie shook her head.

Outside, someone was listening to a strange synthesis of eastern and western music on a tinny cassette player: wailing Arabic vocals layered over a Balearic beat.

"It's not a big team. Full-time, besides me and you, there's Matthew and Lucas. Matthew's the dark, pretty one, and Lucas is the blond with the glasses. Matty's good for a laugh, and Lucas will bore you to death after one conversation. His speciality is ancient texts. I always thought linguists would be stimulating. If you know what I mean." She stuck out her tongue and wiggled it about. "Until I met him that is. Anyway, there's also Jason and Samīh, but you probably won't see much of them. They're Killian's doctoral students based at Cairo University. They do a lot of the cleaning and analysis and rarely come out to Saqqara, which honestly is for the best, because when they do, Lucas always, always gets his kecks in a knot."

"How come?"

"Oh, you know, they breathe mostly. They rarely take anything seriously and Lucas doesn't approve. You'll see."

"So, Lucas must be totally outnumbered, then? I mean by Matthew, Samīh, and Jason?"

Siân shook her head. "The three of them have never quite gelled. Not much in common, plus Matty looks down on them a bit. Thinks he's the bee's knees since he's started getting first line billing on various research papers." She shrugged and turned the car through a gateway and on to a white gravel drive.

"And Killian? How do you all get along with him?"

Siân turned off the engine. "He's the boss, Adie. We do as we're told. Do the same and you'll get along fine. Come on now, and you can finally take that bathroom trip you're obviously desperate for."

-5-

Killian

Killian usually avoided his office at the university, which made it all the more unusual that he'd spent the whole afternoon there when he had no actual reason to be present. He was not expected to give a lecture or mark papers, or worse, attend a departmental meeting. All the paperwork for the dig had long been filed and approved. The maps in his possession were the very latest ones, and his doctoral students weren't even around to test his patience with infantile humour. He could have been doing something useful like organising equipment. Instead, he was staring at a stone-cold cup of tea and ruminating over the sort of ancient history that one never wanted to write a paper on, when he ought to be collecting Adie Hamilton from the airport.

He'd sent Siân instead.

Because, apparently, he was fucking avoiding her, which was dumb, given he'd insisted on hiring her. The voice of his old professor was still grumbling away in the back of his brain, making him question his choices. Joe Levine had a knack for that.

That had to be it. Nothing to do with the way she'd lit up from within when he'd grilled her about Egyptology. The way her passion made him excited to get her in the field, and absolutely nothing to do with the way her hair framed her face making her look ever so studious and simultaneously up for an epic quest.

It was professional excitement he'd felt when he'd shaken her hand, not the sizzle of anything else. He'd hired her because she was the superior candidate.

Joe knew it.

He knew it.

Even Adie herself knew it.

Nothing to do with the fact he'd been half-hard when he'd walked out of that interview and was sporting a semi again now from thinking about her.

Jesus. Shit!

He took a mouthful of the tepid cardamon tea and swallowed it with a grimace.

It was her potential turning him on, that's all.

Uncomfortable in his current position, Killian rose and poked around his office straightening things that didn't need to be straightened. The afternoon sun was reflecting off the passing traffic outside, creating a flickering effect across the shelving. He crossed the room to close the blind but ended up poking his head outside the window instead. Below, a group of students crossing the road spied him and waved. His wave in response set them twittering amongst themselves. Had he really become such a dour stick-in-the-mud that a wave prompted giggles?

He guessed, to his teenage students, he was a dreary old man. He snorted because he was hardly old, barely into his thirties. The impression of dry studiousness, though, that was cultivated. Everybody who knew even a little of his history knew his path to his current position of reverence was hard won. What should have been a measured, steady ascent had in fact incorporated several bone-breaking tumbles.

Shit! This was dumb. He had nothing to fear from returning to Saqqara. Bill Harris' fall was not a bad omen. The bad eggs in his life were long gone, and if he was slightly uneasy, that was only to be expected when on the verge of introducing a new member into a carefully chosen and established team. And his hard-on? A predictable inevitability of prolonged abstinence.

He returned to his desk and flicked through his appointment diary: nothing until the next semester. He'd cancelled them all to give the project his undivided attention, but now he wished that he'd agreed to the lecture at the American University in Cairo. It would have brought some much-needed respite from his whirring thoughts.

Of course, he could just head over to the team's apartment and join them for whatever evening plans they'd made.

Yeah. And no.

Better he kept his distance and gave them all a chance to bond without him around forcing them to be on their best behaviour. He knew they'd be talking about him. Could even predict what was being said – ice-cold, grumpy workaholic with a stick up his arse, fair, but frugal with his praise.

At least that's what he hoped was being said. Better that than any of the alternatives—stories from his history that really needed to stay lost and buried.

He hoped he hadn't made a mistake.

Fuck it! He slumped forward and pressed his forehead to the desk. Roll on tomorrow, when he'd know exactly where he was with everything again.

-6-
Adie

The scent of harsh tobacco mingled with that of the bitter coffee in the overcrowded walkways of the Khan El Khalili. They'd eaten at a hotel overlooking the Nile before moving on to Fishwari's – Cairo's oldest coffee house. Three quarters of the way through her second cup of the thick sugary beverage, Adie was buzzing.

"Poor Bill," Samīh mused about their old work mate, as Adie's glassy gaze returned to the rickety table around which they sat. "He was all set for his next race when he broke that leg. And I had money on him."

"Sucks to be you," Matthew said.

Bill, it turned out, was the black sheep of the team. An architecture graduate who'd ended up in the Middle East designing skyscrapers, wound up working on a few projects with the Egyptian Antiquities Organisation and thence wangled a permanent position on Killian's team.

"I mean his skyscrapers are things of wonder," Jason said, "but his camel wrangling sucked. I don't know why you kept betting on him. He never won a thing."

The two young Cairenes, she was rapidly learning, were a double act.

"You're not any good at camel racing are you, Adie?"

"I'm afraid not. I've never even been near one."

Lucas's seat creaked as he leaned over. "I'd keep it that way if I were you. They're unscrupulous beasts, and their owners aren't much better. If you want to go exploring, hire a horse, or better still, get someone to drive you."

"Boring," Jason sang, while Samīh nodded in agreement.

"If you want to visit somewhere, just let me know," Siân offered. "I'll be happy to take you."

"Thanks." Although after her first experience of Siân's driving, she wasn't entirely convinced that camel riding wouldn't be safer.

"On a related topic, I wouldn't recommend going off anywhere alone. Western women have an undeserved reputation among some men in these parts. Cairo's pretty safe, but—"

"Too many Hollywood exports," Lucas embellished. "The image they're fed is that all western women are promiscuous and available. Some of the tourists don't help either, so be careful how you dress. Save your skinny fits and shorts for underground at the dig, where there are fewer wandering hands."

"Which reminds me." Siân dug into her pocket and pulled out a small box. "Killian asked me to give you this." She slid the box across the table to Adie.

Adie opened the hinge and was startled by the sight of a gold wedding band. "I don't—"

"I've one too." The other woman held her left hand aloft and give her fingers a wiggle. "It's a safety thing. You're less likely to be harassed by strange men if they think you're married. Present company excepted. You're stuck with this lot."

Adie stared at the ring thoughtfully, then snapped the box shut and shoved it in her pocket. She couldn't bring herself to put it on. Too weird. It made for a novel interpretation of being married to the job.

"And on that note, we ought to head back." Lucas shoved his chair back, provoking groans from everyone else.

"Really? It's not even midnight yet." Jason shuffled his chair closer to Adie, closing the gap Lucas had left.

"It's an early start tomorrow."

"Yeah, but it's her first night."

Lucas merely folded his arms.

"Don't listen to him," Jason put an arm around her shoulders. "You need to bleed every second of fun out of tonight. I'm telling you, once you get out to Saqqara, that's it. No fun. No smiling. And definitely no alcohol. It's work, work, work. Killian's a real slave driver."

Samīh imitated the lash of a whip. "If you think Lucas here is misery, wait until you experience the boss man. Why do you think we have the good sense to stay in the city?"

Jason nodded in agreement.

"I'm pretty sure it's not work twenty-four seven. There's bound to be some downtime, even if it's only at the hotel."

"Hotel?" The group said as one.

"What hotel?" Matthew asked. He'd been quiet all evening. Siân hadn't been lying when she'd described him as pretty on the car journey from the airport. Matthew was slender and fine-boned with a long straight nose and star-lashed azure eyes. He looked like an artist or a refugee from a Hugo Boss ad, but certainly not an Egyptologist.

"That we're staying in at Saqqara?" Adie looked sceptically at each of them, taking in bemused grins and shakings heads. "There's not a hotel? Camping?" she asked, dubiously.

That set them all guffawing.

Siân eventually relented.

"*Dahabiyya*. Killian owns a houseboat that's currently moored close to the site. He claims it's more convenient than living in a hotel or commuting from Cairo or wherever we end up being based, so I hope you like water."

"And company," Matthew added. "It can be a bit claustrophobic. But then, he likes us all in one place. That way he can keep better tabs on us. Just you wait and see. It's all early night and early mornings. The man doesn't have a single natural urge, and yet for some bizarre reason everybody loves him."

"Yeah, including you." Siân patted him on the back. "So don't make like you're not equally devoted to his ass."

"It is a very fine ass."

"Truth."

"Just the right amount of perky—" Jason elbowed him in the ribs. "What, I'm only saying what we've all thought."

"I haven't thought it," Lucas said.

"Me neither." Jason shook his head. Samīh too.

Siân gave him a one-shouldered shrug. "I mean, I may have thought it, but I'm not such a fool as to waste my time and energy on pursuing it. We all know he's only interested in older women. Much older women."

"Running joke," Matthew explained to Adie as they headed back through the canopied streets. "What's the surest way to get Killian's attention? Paint yourself gold and get someone to bury you in the desert."

~Ж~

Back at the house on Gezira, everyone piled into the kitchen, which Adie considered a pleasing mix of Islamic design and Western gadgetry. The appliances were all high-end, and while the furniture, such as the large dining table, was scuffed and pitted with age, there was nothing cheap or flatpack about the place.

"Is this house Killian's too?"

"I'm not rightly sure," Siân replied. "Probably. It could belong to his sponsor."

"Yeah, his elusive silent partner."

Lucas slapped Matthew around the head. "Hardly that elusive. He signs your pay cheques."

"Pay cheques?" Matthew rocked onto the back legs of one of the dining chairs. "What century are you in? Do you not do direct deposit? Next, you'll be telling me you don't know what a bank card is."

"Oh, shut up! Let's draw lots, so we can all go to bed."

"Yeah, lets," Siân said.

Lucas opened the dresser drawer and took out a handful of tapers. "All right, pick your sticks." He presented the bundle. Each of the team took one. "You too, Adie. You're part of the team now. That means you get the same deal as the rest of us."

"What are we drawing for?"

She drew. Her spill was several inches shorter than the rest.

"Ah, bad luck." Matthew squeezed her shoulder. "Looks like you're greeting the boss."

"It's fine, Adie. You'll enjoy it. He's radiant first thing."

"Siân Lawrence. And you tell me off for tormenting people." Matthew scruffed her hair, which also gave her a whiff of his spicy cologne. "Sleep well, new girl. Babe?" He held out his hand to Siân, which, to Adie's astonishment, the other woman grasped, only for Matthew to reel her in to an embrace and start nuzzling her neck.

"Oh, get out of here," Lucas complained. "No one wants to see it."

"Speak for yourself. I'm enjoying it." Samīh leaned across to her and added in a conspiratorial whisper, "Live floorshow. You have to pay good money for this in most places." His dark eyes gleamed, pupils as wide as saucers, while a delicate flush warmed his olive skin. Meanwhile, Jason blithely stirred a third spoonful of sugar into his tea.

Matthew and Siân lingered a few moments longer, then shuffled off towards the bedrooms, Lucas following close behind.

"So, how early do I need to be up to greet Killian?" Adie asked.

Jason drained his cup in a couple of long swallows, then carried it over to the sink and swilled it before placing it on the draining board. She followed, watching his movements.

"Well, he'll be here around five."

"What? A.M? Seriously?"

He about turned and tidied the spills back into the drawer. "The door's bolted from the inside, so you have to let him in. He'll probably want a hand moving things, too. We've equipment stored in the backroom, and he won't be impressed if you're not zinging with enthusiasm."

"You're really serious? You want me to be dressed and ready by five A.M?"

He rested his hands on her shoulders and gave a nod, suddenly all seriousness, "Adina Hamilton, welcome to your new life. Like we've all been telling you, the fun ends now."

"Yeah." Except it was hard to take them seriously when they all said it with such enormous grins on their faces. "I think I'd better get to bed." She wasn't, if she was honest, a morning person.

-7-
Adie

The sun shone red through her eyelids, while warm sand clothed her naked body. Adie blinked her eyes open to find herself in a square stone room whose ceiling was open to the sky. The rasp of something soft caressed her thigh. It tickled. She tried to wriggle, only to find her body didn't respond. It was as though she was pinned or restrained, but she felt no weight above her, nor cuffs around her wrists.

"Extraordinary," an individual at her feet claimed. "Absolutely exquisite, and perfectly preserved. Why, you must have lain here for over three thousand years, and there's not a scratch on you."

The soft caress continued, meticulously sweeping sand away from the skin on the underside of her breast and causing her nipples to tighten.

Was he talking about her?

The whisper of the desert breeze tickled her toes. She tried to wriggle them, but still couldn't move. Strangely, this didn't panic her.

"If you weren't made of gold, one might be

forgiven for believing you to be a real woman."

I am a real....

Wait. Gold? Whatever did he mean? She peered down the length of her body and discovered that he spoke the truth. Her skin shone with a metallic lustre, bouncing the sunlight in every direction.

The man at her feet was none other than Doctor Carmichael and he was staring at her with heat in his gaze. His brush swept across the plain of her midriff again, then upwards to trace around one areola.

Adie swallowed, the attention wakening something deep inside her. She waited in fevered anticipation for the next touch, and then the next. Each one peppered her skin with goosebumps and made her senses tingle.

"I should, of course, report the find. Yet—" His mouth stretched into a closed-lipped grin. "Well, it'll wait a bit. I don't think I need to hurry the matter. It might be fun to enjoy you all to myself for a while. You are my discovery, after all."

He knelt, discarding the brush as his knees hit the sand. Then his palms splayed over her belly. "Absolutely, astonishing, you're even warm to the touch." He cupped her breast and caught her nipples between fingers and thumbs. "It's like you're alive, and so mesmerisingly pretty. Every detail, every curve, so painstakingly rendered. The craftsman who created you certainly knew his business." His exploration encompassed her hips, the grooves above her collarbones, and then angle of her jaw. "Perfect lips." His thumb swept across the lower one. "A body a man could worship." This time, after caressing her breasts, one palm snaked downward to the apex of her thighs.

She'd dreamed this dream before. His fingers thrusting inside of her, readying her. The trace of his thumb along her split kindle a fire in her womb and heated the rest of her to an anticipatory simmer.

"Ah, what's this? Anatomically rendered too." He made a soft sound in the front of his mouth. "Not just a pretty thing to be admired from afar, are you, but something to be appreciated at closer quarters."

That teasing digit found her clit, and her lower lips parted for him as she released a gasp.

"I bet you were this pharaoh's favourite toy. Did he use you frequently? Slide himself between these lovely golden thighs and drive himself into you? I bet he used you well. Fucked you until you were both hot and peppered with his sweat. Such a pretty, pretty thing. It's hardly a wonder that he'd want to."

He shifted onto all fours, so that she lay caged beneath him. His skin smelled of cinnamon and sandalwood, and he was so shockingly handsome. All suppleness and defined lines. He peered down at her, gazing straight into her eyes, then laughingly stole a kiss.

It was no more than a butterfly brush of his Cupid's bow pout to hers, but then he was in an instance, stabbing his tongue deeper and reaching between her thighs again.

"I think I need to know the pleasure of you too. You don't mind now, do you, my dear?"

She didn't. She wanted him. This man with his chiselled cheekbones and swoop for thick white hair, with his strong shoulders and lean hips.

Balanced in a one-armed press-up, Killian reached down and released his zip. "Keep still for me now, my good girl. I've got something for you. It might be a shock, given it's been a little while for you and we've only just been introduced, but you really are a temptation that's impossible to resist."

His hand was there again. Right between her thighs, strumming at her now swollen nub and spreading some sort of slippery fluid. His fingers filled her first, testing out her limits. "I think I might get all eight inches in there." Then his cock. Slowly, his body trembling, Killian possessed her. He put just the tip in first, before driving deeper. A cry tore free of his throat as he bottomed out. "Ah, fuck, yes! That's just the right amount of squeeze. Is it good for you too, my treasure?"

It was better than good. The heat in her core raced towards her extremities. Her skin tingled and came to life. She was transforming. He was transforming her. Bringing her to life. The air above them shimmered.

Killian cradled her face and kissed her golden lips. Paint flecks stuck to his skin. Made him shiny as if he too were golden.

Say that I'm yours again. Call me your princess. Call me your angel... your good girl!

"Praise slut," he whispered instead, and fucked her harder. Fucked her in a way that made her pulse roar like thunder, and her nerves crackle as if powered by lightning. Until every cell in her body was enlivened by it.

She'd never come from being used, but she would shatter for him. If he just said it.

Say it. Say it, please.

"Oh, oh," he groaned. "Oh, here it comes. That's it. Take my come. Good girl."

She jerked into life. Into wakefulness, right as his balls released their load into her core.

~Ж~

The sound of their combined heartbeats didn't stop hammering once they were done. They continued to pound with increasing vigour, before transforming into the belligerent thump of a knocker. Adie squinted groggily into the dark of an unfamiliar room. The sheets were tangled around her naked sweat drenched body, which was thrumming from a recent explosion of bliss. "Fuck! What?" As she raised her hand to her head, the face of her watch lit, flashing the time at her in luminous green digits. Five past five.

Horrifically early. Her eyelids drooped again, only to snap open at once, the moment her brain engaged.

Five past five. Oh, shit! Not only had she slept through her alarm on her first morning at her new job, that incessant hammering was clearly her boss waiting to be let in.

After a deal of swearing and stumbling about, Adie managed to extract some clothing from her suitcase. Shit! This was her bathrobe, not her hoodie. It would have to do. And of course, the belt was missing, forcing her to clutch the edges together as she staggered through the building.

"All right, all right, take a chill pill. I'm coming."

The heavy bolts slid back with a metallic thud. Adie turned the key.

"About time," Killian griped as he swept past her into the house, shutting the door behind him. He flicked the light switch wakening the entry hall with a soft orange glow. His eyes found hers, and his irate expression softened infinitesimally. "I see they have you answering the door already, mean buggers."

"I drew the short straw."

She folded the edges of her robe more tightly around herself, aware now that he was staring at her, and how thin the cloth of her dressing truly was. Not to mention, how short.

Killian was leaner than she remembered. More chiselled too. It was no wonder every woman loved him. How could anyone gaze on him and think him anything other than handsome? And those eyes— they were like twin diamonds glittering around the edge of black holes.

He'd... She'd imagined him... Oh dear, lord! And she'd come because of it too. The silk of her arousal remained gathered between her thighs.

"Perhaps you'd like to put some clothes on."

"Yes." What an excellent idea. She about turned and fled back to her room. Once inside, she pressed her brow to the doorframe. God, he must think her an idiot. He was probably wondering why on earth he'd employed her. She found the end of the bed and sat heavily with her fist clutched to her mouth. Get it together, Adie. You're better than this, and he can't see into your head.

A firm rap rattled her door. "I've made some coffee. It's waiting on the table once you're ready. I'm going to start loading the equipment."

"Be right there."

She pulled on a pair of lightweight cargo pants and a vest, then set about lacing her boots. She was at the door before she remembered the wedding band Siân had presented to her the previous evening. Having reclaimed it from the nightstand, she carried it with her to the kitchen and set it down on the countertop to claim her coffee. He'd made it black and tar-like. Adie stirred in sugar. Hell, she needed the energy burst. Five o'clock was pre-dawn and in her mind still the previous day.

"You'll be needing to put that on," Killian remarked of the still boxed ring when he entered the kitchen a few moments later. He'd already worked up a sweat, so that his skin was dewy. He swiped his forearm across his brow before filling and then draining a glass of milk.

"Got it. Just feels weird, you know."

She opened the box and stared at the gold band. Killian prized it from its cushion. "Left hand."

She obeyed instinctively, holding out her hand and spreading her fingers to allow him to slide the gold band onto her finger.

"Congratulations, Doctor Hamilton."

"Oh, yes. It was very sudden," she said, playing along. "Spur of the moment, really. We barely know one another, but it's a match made in heaven."

"Good to hear."

Why did it make her tingle inside to hear him say that? She'd meant to make a joke of it. Instead, she seemed to have ramped up the latent tension.

"Should I expect a pre-dawn start every morning?"

"Believe me, you'll prefer it to working when the sun is at its hottest."

Yes, she likely would. Even slathered in factor 50 she'd burn to a crisp.

"Is there anything I can help with?"

Killian shook his head. "Car's all loaded. All you need to do is grab your stuff. Once you have your case, we can get off."

Get off! Lord help her, but she already had once to the fantasy of this man.

"That was a hint, by the way."

"What? Oh, right." She drained her cup and headed to the sink.

"Leave it, one of the others will wash it up. It's time we were on the road. I want to get set up before the tourists start swarming the place."

"Is the dig in a tourist area?"

To this he responded with a dry, humourless laugh. "Adie, every blinking pile of rocks in the desert is a tourist trap. They're everywhere. They literally swarm the place like cockroaches. We're thankfully positioned a little further into the desert than they normally venture, but that doesn't mean I want to be standing about attracting attention."

"Got it. I need to get my arse in motion."

Unlike Siân's beaten-up vehicle, Killian's

gleamed like it was fresh from the showroom. There was just enough room in the back amidst the equipment to slide her suitcase. She settled upfront in the passenger seat. Above them, the moon hung over the city like the left eye of Horus. The light from which played in the silken strands of Killian's white hair. Perhaps, she ought to pinch herself to make sure this was all real. Twenty-six years of dreaming was finally coming to fruition. She was about to see pyramids up close.

-8-

Adie

They reached Saqqara at quarter to six as the sun peeped over the horizon turning the desert landscape into a vast golden ocean. The necropolis was not as she'd imagined it and was markedly different to how it appeared on TV. Civilisation was much closer, they'd driven past numerous cafes and a carpet school right before entering the necropolis, and it was all so vast. Off to the right, Djoser's pyramid rose to the heavens in six gilded steps, surrounded by the mounds of other crumbling pyramids and ancient mastabas, and over it all the khamseen wind raced in great hot gusts, blowing up dust clouds like swarms of incessant midges.

Killian stood silently beside her. At first glance, he appeared unaffected by the weight of history around them, but as they set out towards the excavation, she detected a subtle gleam of emotion in his cool grey eyes.

They left the trunks in the car and walked past the eroded pyramid of Unas – the last king of the 5th dynasty- and the pit-like entrance to Sekhemkhet's unfinished tomb, towards an uninteresting mound of rubble.

"Impressive, isn't it. You can see why it's been ignored for the last hundred years." He scraped away some of the ochre-coloured earth with his hands and rolled away a couple of small boulders to reveal a solid iron door and a thick padlock. "We had the door put in when we realised there was something interesting down here. It keeps the wildlife and the tourists out. Mostly."

"And presumably, the tomb robbers," Adie added cheerily before lapsing into a cough, surprised by the dry taste of sand in her mouth. Still, she was grinning again the moment her throat cleared, both for adventure and the prospect of exploring the ancient ruins with her enigmatic new boss. He really was a study of the forbidden. All sculpted lines and aloofness. There was the palest hint of stubble along his jawline.

Killian gave her a tight smile in response to her scrutiny, then fished a key from his back pocket. It drew her attention to his arse. And wasn't that a delight all of its own? Adie stared more than she ought to as he unfastened the padlock, imagining grabbing a feel, but apart from the cold rebuke she'd get, there was a risk that he'd straighten up and knock himself out on the lintel, and she'd have a hard time explaining that to the team.

The door opened onto a small antechamber at the top of a broad stairway. Adie sought to steady her galloping pulse as she took the offered torch and followed him into the swaddling darkness beneath the sands. This...this was what she'd come here for, not a man, but history. Years of work, of striving, of defying the odds had all been for this. Finally, the chance to stand inside an Egyptian house of the dead. If only Esther could have been here to see it too.

Killian pulled the door closed behind them, blocking out the morning sun and the roar of the southerly wind. No deathless mummies lurched out of the gloom, no giant boulders rolled into view, and no wonderful treasure glinted at her. In the black stillness, Adie's excitement ebbed. She hadn't really expected any of those things, but she still felt slightly disappointed by the plain stone antechamber. She shivered. The sharp odour of animal excrement filled her nostrils and made her gag. Killian's torch cast half-formed shadows over the walls and seemed to declare them as trespassers.

Which they were.

The submerged tomb was the final resting-place of an ancient pharaoh, and whatever their motive, they were unwelcome.

"Careful of your footing," Killian cautioned, his voice echoing dully. "We've already had one accident; I don't want another."

"Got it." She allowed herself to be guided further inside.

Stairs, the walls of which were powdery with white limestone, ran down to a stone doorway inscribed with hieroglyphs. Killian ushered her into a square room. One corner had partially fallen in, but the left-hand wall was virtually intact, its surface decorated with an extensive, intricately coloured relief of animal-headed beings, engaged in some kind of ritual. A section of the frieze appeared to have been hacked out, corresponding to the groin area of the central figure.

"Wow!" She reached out a hand to the vividly coloured surface, but Killian jerked her back.

"Beautiful, isn't it," he said into her ear, and she felt his breath buffet her cheek. The sensation sent a dart of lust straight down her body leaving her temporarily lost for words, capable of only nodding dumbly.

How had anyone missed this for so long? It was in almost perfect condition. And how was she going to cope with working with him? He made her senses tingle purely with his presence. In the closed space she was brutally aware of his presence, the heat, and scent of him, and the slow stirrings of his breath.

"The entrance was lost under a rock fall," he said pre-empting her first question. "We rediscovered it while engaged on a mapping project of the area. Tourists had been climbing on it and knocked some of the stones away to reveal a gap, but until we cleared the entrance we had to scramble through with just basic equipment."

By basic, she took that to mean with a torch held between his teeth. Possibly not accurate, but the image in her head was vivid.

"And this is what you found." She made a point of keeping her gaze on the mural as if wholly transfixed by it. It was incredible, it just, surprisingly, didn't hold quite the same lure as the living man standing beside her.

"Well, we were hardly the first to come down here. As you can see from the graffiti." He pointed out sections in both the northern and western walls. "And there had been previous reports of a tomb here."

"What...Who does this represent?" Adie took a hesitant step forward, wishing but not daring to run her fingertips over the ancient painting. "Do you know whose tomb it is?"

Killian shadowed her movement. "It's hard to say for definite because of the missing fragment, but the figure on the right seems to be Pharaoh as a manifestation of Horus, undergoing some form of ritual performed by the kneeling slave. The priestly figure in the background is Osiris, possibly imparting his worldly powers to his son."

Adie nodded, recognising the distinctive features of the figures, Horus the sky god with his hawk's head and Osiris in his mummy wrappings, holding the symbols of kingship - the crook and the flail.

"Some believe this a depiction of fellatio." The ghost of a smile briefly softened Killian's chiselled features. "Others think it's a washing or embalming ritual, due to the presence of the jars. The team's divided. You're welcome to make up your own mind, but please refrain from broadcasting it outside these walls."

Adie swallowed, imagining Killian as the pharaoh, herself as the slave, lips parted to receive his cock. He was standing very close to her, close enough for his scent—mildly spicy underpinned by the faint smell of his own body—to tickle her nose. She'd never been remotely interested in how a man smelled before. What was it about him that was turning her into such a mushy puddle?

It had to be the place. She'd finally got where she wanted to be. It was simply the emotions of it.

"Are you all right?" Killian placed a firm hand on her shoulder, which sent excitement licking through her insides. It took every ounce of willpower she possessed not to lean into the contact.

"Adie?"

"I'm fine. Just sleep-deprived, that's all. What's your opinion of the mural? Which side do you fall on?"

"Neither. Such speculation is a waste of energy. There are other issues that are far more pressing, like discovering what happened to the missing piece."

"Right." Adie took an uncertain step back, surprised by the chill realism of his last remark. "And are there any clues to that?"

"A few. A mid-nineteenth-century explorer called William Jacobs hacked it out. The story goes that after a successful season at Giza, he came to Saqqara in late December 1881, accompanied by his nineteen-year-old daughter and their native companion. He entered the chamber ahead of the pair and censored the image to protect her innocence. Hence the glut of theories suggesting a sexual nature to the content." He shook his head sadly. "The Victorians had some very strange values.

They made some incredible discoveries, but they did a lot of damage, too. No doubt you've heard of similar examples of mutilated statues, and severed genitalia, all to protect the eyes of the innocents."

Adie nodded. "Josef used to use one as a paperweight until it was stolen."

"Who knew there were so many cock thieves around."

Was that a joke? She stifled a laugh, unsure, given his delivery was so humourless. "So, it does show fellatio?"

"It shows a penis. That much is clear from Jacobs' diary. It's only a pity he didn't take the time to sketch it. The diary, incidentally, is in the Cairo Museum library if you wish to look."

She would. Most definitely would the moment an opportunity presented itself.

"What did he do with the bit he chipped out?"

Killian's broad shoulders lifted. "Who knows? It might turn up here amongst the rubble, but it's more likely that he sold it to a private collector back home. Really, we ought to consider it lucky he didn't remove the whole scene and ship it back to England. The Victorians were thieves to a man. Whatever they wanted, they took regardless of to whom it belonged. But that's enough about them for now." He turned his torch over the other walls. After the brilliance of the mural, the rest of the chamber seemed altogether drab. "Through there, the corridor continues for a short distance before it becomes blocked by rubble, probably from a cave-in. Before that, it branches off into another corridor leading to a network of storage magazines. You'll see them later. To start with, you'll be working in here until you've shown me what you can do. See these plaster fragments scattered around? I'd like you to work on reassembling them, so I hope you've a talent for jigsaw puzzles."

Adie stifled a sigh. More broken pots. Still, there was the prospect of some exploration and the chance of finding that fragment.

"Get some breakfast before you start. It's going to be a very long day."

~Ж~

By evening Adie had learned that her new boss should be taken literally. The rest of the team had arrived shortly after six, and the five of them had worked a twelve-hour shift with very few breaks fixing the lighting rig. It'd been hot, thirsty work, the tomb warming like a slow cooker to broil them. Killian seemed tireless and inured to the heat. Disappointingly, he hadn't taken his shirt off, though perhaps that was for the best. Siân had caught her looking more than once and swished a finger at her and made accompanying tut tut noises.

That evening they moved on to the houseboat. Killian's *dahabiyya* turned out to be a converted passenger boat. Built in the 1920s to carry wealthy tourists down the Nile between Cairo and Luxor, it had been refitted with every convenience, including a modern workroom. Adie tried to picture Hercule Poirot pacing the deck, but he would have tripped over the crates of equipment.

They ate communally after they'd all showered. That part wasn't communal.

Lucas made *fiteer*, a sort of stuffed pizza with a flaky pastry base, which tasted like the most divine food ever invented she was so ravenous. Killian occupied the head of the table. He seemed more relaxed here, surrounded by verdant grassland and chattering wildlife than in the heart of the necropolis. His white hair was slowly drying in the last of the evening sun, and there was a distant look in his eyes as if his mind dreamed while his body ate. Hers was so full of wonder that she was struggling to process what was being said. Her muscles ached too, but she prided herself on not having slacked. She'd kept up with them all.

Lucas gave her a pat on the back. "Hey, well done on getting through your first day without breaking anything."

"Thanks."

"Certainly beats my first day," Siân leaned in conspiratorially, while Matthew dished out coffee. "I was so excited, I managed to put a pickaxe through my foot."

"Please tell me you're joking."

"Oh, no, it's for real. I've the scar to prove it. I spent three months recovering and missed the rest of the season. I haven't made that mistake again."

"What was your first day like?" Adie asked Killian.

He seemed to come to himself. "Insignificant."

"You must have dreamed of it before though. Speculated about what it would be like to be here."

What she earned in response was a cold sneer. "I don't waste my time dreaming. I plan. I investigate, and let the facts speak for themselves. Joe warned me that you're more intuitive than that, which is fine." The way he emphasised the point suggested quite the opposite. "But I don't have time for ifs and maybes. By all means, speculate inside your own head, but kindly keep your opinions to yourself until you can back them up with evidence."

She nodded dumbly. Success with her was often more down to instinct and following her guts than logic. Joe had recognised and encouraged that. Had frequently complimented her ability to see patterns where others couldn't. He'd seen it as a valuable skill, Killian evidently was not convinced. No wonder Joe had mumbled all that stuff about Killian crushing her eager spirit before she left and trying to get her to reconsider taking the offer. The thing was, she had a gut feeling about Killian and this project.

-9-
Killian

"What was that about?" Siân lingered at the table after the others had departed.

He wasn't in the mood to have his actions dissected, being irritable this evening in a way that defied reason.

"You didn't need to lay into her like that. She'd done nothing but work fucking hard all day."

"It's the same lecture I've given you all."

"It's the same lecture I've given you all," Siân mimicked. She left her seat and approached him from the side. Placed a hand on his shoulder so that her fingers dug into the muscles there and began working the tension out of his shoulders. "You like her."

Trust Siân not to beat around the bush. She'd known him too long. They'd worked side by side in cramped conditions for too many seasons for her not to be able to read his moods, almost better than he could. He did like Adie, despite his better judgement. But she irritated him for precisely the same reason he felt all soft-centred over her. She was damned excited to be here and sift sand through her fingers. He remembered feeling that zeal, that passion; all it had ever done was get him into trouble. These days, he measured his responses.

No, he wasn't jaded. He still loved his work. He just didn't walk around with his head in the clouds, expecting to find the treasures of Tutankhamun under every rock.

Siân worked her thumbs into the tightness at the back of his neck, and he released an appreciative groan. There were some aches even a decent rainfall shower couldn't work out.

"Just there, huh?" Her fingers continued to work magic, releasing the bunched muscles, and getting his shoulders to relax.

"She likes you, too," Siân said, putting the knots straight back.

"Fool her."

There'd been a time in the past when Siân had looked at him the way Adie Hamilton had done today, all starry-eyed like he was some sort of messiah. It hadn't lasted. Such infatuations rarely survived working for him. Siân had quickly figured out that he came with more emotional baggage than she was looking for. She liked her relationships to be simple transactional affairs. And he... he didn't screw around.

Actually, he didn't do interpersonal relationships for that matter, leastways not above the level required to run a decent team, and definitely...definitely never with a person on his team. Some mistakes in life, you just didn't repeat.

Been there. Done that. Had the mental scars to prove it.

Hopefully Adie would figure that out quickly too. "I'm not interested, Siân."

"You say that—"

"Because it's true."

"Right." She injected the word with enough of a drawl to sound dubious. "Because you're a total automaton."

They both knew *that* wasn't true. While he usually bottled up his temper and his passions, occasionally that resulted in a messy flare-up. "I brought her here to work, not to flirt with her, or whatever other sordid nonsense you're imagining."

"I'm not sure it's me who's imagining it. And the two things don't have to be mutually exclusive."

Except they did.

"I mean, Matthew and I have never had an issue."

"I don't want to hear it." Frankly, the boat wasn't big enough for him not to be aware of the arrangement the pair of them had going.

And this conversation needed to cease before the stirrings in his groin became something that couldn't be countermanded with a slurp of cold coffee.

He stood abruptly with an announcement that he was going to turn in. Since he'd been up since four, that was reasonable. "Early start again tomorrow. We've lost time to make up." He chucked the remains of his drink overboard, mumbled a goodnight, then stalked off towards his cabin near the prow. Siân shadowed him to her own door, but remained on the deck like she was waiting to see him U-turn to Adie's cabin.

That was never happening.

-10-

Adie

Adie's first six days in Egypt passed in a blur of sand, sweat, and sex dreams. Matthew flirted with her and overshared. He claimed it passed the time. As the two junior members of the team, they had the tedious job of sorting the fractured pieces of plaster from the antechamber floor, which wouldn't have been so bad, except it was hard on the knees, and it meant she barely got to see Killian at all.

"What's it like out there?" Siân asked, coming on her during a ten-minute rest break Adie was taking perched on the rocks outside the tombs narrow entrance.

"Windy." The same as it had been since she'd arrived, the sand whipping across the landscape and softening the outline of the step pyramid over the horizon to a blur.

"Marvellous. I'll look forward to another choppy night on the river and dinner that tastes of sand. I hate this season. Damn wish it'd hurry up and blow away."

"Isn't the khamseen supposed to last fifty

days?" She'd been picking her way through the Lonely Planet guide of an evening, figuring out what she wanted to see once there was any real downtime to speak of.

"Is it?" Siân shrugged and took a perch on the adjacent boulder. "Storms usually blow themselves out after a couple of hours. You must be trouble or something. This has hardly eased up since you arrived." She lowered her penny shades and gave Adie a wink.

"Hey, don't blame me. I don't control the weather faeries...sand genies...whatever they are." They watched a few brave tourists battle the swirling sand. "How are you getting on in the depths?"

Siân held aloft her hand and jogged it from side to side. "So-so. Suppose I ought to get back to it." She took a long draught from her water bottle allowing some of the contents to spill and soak into her navy T-shirt. "You too, mate. The big boss man wants that floor cleared."

Adie sighed. There was still no sign of the missing fragment. Most of what she'd put together so far were bits of hieroglyphs. Matthew was reconstructing a crocodile.

Killian had his back to them as they entered the mural room. His white hair curled against the back of his neck, just above the tan-line from his shirt, the back of which was wet through with sweat from digging and clung to his musculature.

And that, my friend, was how he seduced the media. It was all stage-managed. If they wanted Indiana Jones, he appeared dust-streaked and grimy from the tunnels. And if they wanted the immaculate scholar, he turned up cool and professional in a suit. Honestly, she couldn't choose between them. She just wished he wasn't so distant. She'd been hoping to hear stories of his previous digs and the adventures he'd enjoyed, but idle conversation was apparently another item on his no-no list. Or at least idle conversation with her.

Siân gave her a friendly prod, then slipped past into the tunnels. "Go on, he doesn't bite... much."

"Hi."

Killian turned ninety degrees in response.

"Ah, good, you're here. I was explaining to Matthew that I want you both to concentrate on clearing the north-west corner. From what you've put together so far that seems the most likely area we'll find a cartouche, and it would be a definite boon to find out whose tomb we're in."

"Right," she said and sucked her bottom lip. Of all the areas, that's where the largest concentration of tiny fragments were scattered. "But what about finding the missing willy? I thought you wanted us to try and find that."

Matthew chortled and failed to mask his amusement with his hand. "Willy?" He mouthed at her.

"I believe I said it was highly unlikely that you'd find that. Concentrate on the search for a cartouche, our sponsors will be happier once they have a name to drop."

Killian's soft yet crushing tone stung like a hand slap.

"Cartouche hunting it is then. I'll get right on it."

"Not me. Not tonight." Matthew rose and brushed the dust from the knees of his trousers. He checked his watch. "The shift's almost up, the sun's going down, and I have a hot date tonight."

A date! That was the first she'd heard of it, and after the stories he'd spun her the last few days, she was well versed in his private life. Also, she'd yet to see any member of the team leave the houseboat of an evening for anything more than a coffee run. The notion that they were allowed social lives was novel. On the other hand, Killian did not look impressed.

"I...I don't mind staying late," she offered.

Cue a further eyebrow raise. "You do realise you don't get paid overtime?"

"I'm aware, but this is important, right?"

Behind Killian's back, Matthew made arse-licking motions and pointed at her. Killian thankfully didn't seem to notice. Instead, his mouth squeezed into a thoughtful pucker. "I'm not sure about leaving you alone out here. It's not ideal. I wouldn't recommend anyone working alone. Let me talk to Siân and Lucas."

He wandered off into the magazines.

"Somebody's a sucker for punishment. You didn't have to volunteer. It's not necessary. Those fragments will still be there tomorrow dawn."

"Yeah, but he obviously wanted us to, and what's the harm in me trying to make a good impression? I'm still on probation, remember. I want this gig full time."

Matthew ran a hand through his sand-stiffened

hair. "Adie, if he'd wanted you to work late, he'd have plain up said so. In case you haven't noticed, he doesn't beat around the bush, not in relation to work. The fact he didn't have a plan worked out for who else would be staying, says you just volunteered unnecessarily."

"Except he did have a plan. You."

"Back-up plan."

"Are you actually going on a date?"

"I am now. Not sure who the date is yet, but I'll definitely be enjoying someone's company."

"You're going on the pull?" she asked incredulously.

Matthew gave her his best sexy pout. "I am going dancing, Ms Hamilton. There is a fairly high chance that some of that gyrating will happen in a horizontal position—or not. I'm equally up for a dirty screw in an upright position."

"Won't Siân object?"

"Oh, honey, you're so straight. I've told you, that's an entirely no strings affair. Besides, I was thinking I might pick up a guy, to mix things up a little."

"That's crazy talk." Cairo was hardly liberal when it came to LGBT+ rights. "For God's sakes, be careful."

"Yes, mum." He rolled his eyes, then levelled with her. "Adie, I'll be fine. Believe it or not, I know how to keep myself safe, and out of trouble. You on the other hand, are a sucker for punishment and are going to be sore, sore, sore tomorrow, and have knees like a ninety-year-old by the end of the summer."

Adie grabbed her trowel and rammed it into the earth floor, sending sand and dirt flying. It made Matthew laugh.

"Hey, gently." He reached out and stayed her hand. "The chances are you'll be home in bed by nine as usual. I can't see either Siân or Lucas grabbing the opportunity to work late for free. They don't have anything to prove."

"Maybe Killian will stay."

"Oh, God!" Matthew clutched his thighs as he bent forward laughing. "There's actual delight in your eyes at that prospect. Babe, you have it bad. Do you think staying late with Captain Workaholic will be fun, Adie? Are you imagining playing find the willy with him?"

"Cartouche. We're looking for a cartouche."

"Yeah, right. Whateves. It might be what he's looking for, you," – he waggled a finger at her – "you, not so much. But I'll tell you what, I'll give you a pointer over where to look... Just reach out and slide his fly down." He mimicked the action. "Then voila, willy. Do that, and you might not have to spend all night on your knees. Although maybe that's where you want to be. I've a feeling you wouldn't mind choking on his cock."

"God, you're rude." She slapped him across the thighs.

"Yeah, but right. Babe, you're red as a beacon."

"Of course I bloody am, you're talking about our boss's"—she dropped her voice to a whisper—"cock."

Matthew wet his lips. His mouth still stretched

into a maniacal grin. "Ah, you're so sweet. Come on, admit it. You've thought about unbuttoning those sensible shorts of his and taking it like a good girl."

"Fuck off, Matthew."

"I've thought about taking it like a good boy."

"No, you haven't. You're just digging."

"It is my job."

"Yeah, well if you're not going to do it, piss off."

"Oh, I'm going." Indeed, he collected his water bottle and headed towards the exit. He stopped shy of mounting the stairs, turned back, something obviously on his mind. "Reckon you're more passive than that," he said. "You're more into the idea of him unbuttoning you and eating you out from behind before shoving his—"

"Matthew!" She covered her ears as the heat in her cheeks spread to fan out across the tops of her breasts. "Go. I don't need you planting visions."

He turned on his heels, chortling. "Pretty sure your brain has already been there. See you tomorrow. I'll look forward to swapping deets."

Yeah, and no. Adie wetted a cloth and wiped her burning face once he'd gone. Then, she crawled over to the north-west corner and settled by an already marked out quadrangle. It wouldn't hurt to get started, even if she only managed to catalogue a couple of pieces before the shift ended. Barely a moment later, Siân and Lucas wandered through, with Killian on their tail, still sweaty and stupidly handsome. She didn't know why he caused such a ricochet in her heart, but he did. There was just something about him that drew her like a magnet. To her astonishment, he dropped into a squat by the quadrant next to hers.

"It's nice to see someone with a decent work ethic. However, it'd be irresponsible of me to leave you working out here alone into the evening."

"Does that mean—"

"It means pass me a trowel, Adie."

Pass him... "Wait, you're staying behind with me?" Until this moment, she hadn't given the notion any real credence.

"Problem?"

"No. No, it's unexpected, that's all."

Oh, my! She was actually getting to work with him, not just for him.

"Do you think I'm above getting my hands dirty?"

"No. I've never thought that." She knew from Siân that he spent plenty of time with a shovel in his hand doing what many would consider grunt work, backbreaking digging, shifting rubble, and the like. She'd seen him sorting fragments too, and painfully attempting to reconstruct them into larger pictures. And it wasn't because he had to. He could have left them to do all the labour-intensive stuff and purely overseen the operation.

She handed him a trowel, and he started on the patch next to hers. His pace was much quicker than hers, and she took notes of how he achieved that, watching him from the corners of her eyes. He didn't speak to her, so they worked in near silence for a good portion of the first hour.

She tried. Every ten minutes or so, the lack of

conversation would get to her, compelling her to make a remark. Matthew was right, chatter did make the minutes pass faster. Killian, however, never answered with more words than were strictly necessary. He didn't divert off onto conversational side-quests, which made for stilted interactions. She tried a variety of topics, both leading and non-directive questions. None of it made a difference.

"Do you need some knee pads?" he asked when she started raising one knee then the other off the floors from an all-fours position. "We can call it a day at any point."

"It's fine. I'm fine."

"Adie, if it's too painful—"

"I don't mind a little pain mixed in with my pleasure."

His brows scooted up towards his hairline.

Adie dug her teeth into her lower lip. "I didn't mean it like that. Though I do."

What the hell was she saying?

"I just meant that—"

"I know what you meant."

"Sorry. Forgot who I was talking to for a moment then. I've just been—"

"Working with Matthew."

"Yeah." She moved another fragment to the crate. "Him. He—"

"Does he distract you?"

"No, he's... It's fine. I like...love working here. I'll happily work with any of the team on any task you wish me to."

"Good to know."

"Do you..." She felt his focus fix on her. "Does it still excite you to be here? I don't want it to ever feel old. It's such a privilege, I don't want to lose the thrill of it."

It took him so long to answer, she began to think that he wouldn't, but eventually he swept the longer strands of his hair back off his face. "I'm not sure anything is ever as thrilling as the first experience of something, but I'm still here, still fascinated by the ancient world, and all the things we can learn about it. But let's not pretend that this is the stuff of dreams. It's drudgery, Adie. Hard labour. Not glamorous or exciting. If you're looking for those things, I fear you've chosen the wrong career. Perhaps acting would've been a better choice. It's the only way you'll experience the public perception of Egyptology. Those of us here in the field know there are no lever puzzles or curses, no giant swinging rocks, or spinning saw blades, and no enigmatic tattooed horsemen riding about desperate to preserve the secrets passed to them down through the generations."

"You're not battling sphinxes and leaping ravines down there in the tunnels, then, to reach the treasure?" She asked nodding her head towards the passageway he, Siân, and Lucas disappeared into every morning.

"Obviously that's what we're doing," he replied dry as dust.

"Yeah, figured so. You're doing the fun stuff while Matthew and I play in the baby pool."

He dropped his trowel and rose to his feet. "Do

you want to see what's down there?"

Would she? Hell, yes, she would. She'd been waiting for him to say it was okay and finish the tour he'd promised her that first morning. In fact, she'd been churning ideas of why she'd need to venture further on her own, but so far, whichever person she'd intended to seek had miraculously appeared before she'd even stuck her head into the tunnel entrance.

Stiff-kneed, she got to her feet.

"Leave the trowel behind, you'll need your hands free, and grab a head torch. Sure, we've a lighting rig set up, but that doesn't guarantee it won't go out at an inconvenient moment, and there's no light down here at all. It's rather like venturing into a mine. Also, watch out for your head. The ceiling gets rather low."

All kitted out, Adie dogged Killian's footsteps, taking care to tread exactly where he did. Before long a cave-in blocked their forward descent, however, a side passage turned west, and a little further on, north again.

"Up ahead, running east and west there are a series of magazines." He used his torch beam to show her where he meant. "We're not entirely sure how many yet. There are currently sixteen in that direction and nineteen in the other, but suspect we'll unearth a few more. This is where we're conducting much of the current work. If you look here, there's a vertical shaft to the surface. Or at least that's where it led in the past. It's been partially filled in and buried under the desert.

"Access?"

"Possibly, or ventilation."

They wandered deeper into the storage area, most of which were empty as far as she could see.

"No evidence of a burial chamber?"

"If there is one, it's most likely on the other side of the cave-in, and clearing that'll likely take years, and some serious feats of engineering. It's relatively sound at present, but all that changes if we start trying to fashion a way through. It's what Bill, your predecessor was working on."

Adie wandered to the end of the western magazines and back, shining her lamp into the various chambers. There was little to be seen. They weren't decorative rooms, merely storage chambers. After a short while, it became apparent that Killian was waiting to turn back.

"Whose tomb do you think it is?" she asked once they'd returned to the mural room.

Killian shook his head. In the dim light, his white hair shone like spider silk. "Based on the layout, and the positioning here at Saqqara, it's likely 3rd dynasty. It shows commonality with both Djoser's pyramid and Sekhemkhet's, both of which you should take time to see, if you've not done so already."

When had she had the time?

"I'll do that, maybe this weekend."

He nodded his approval. "I'm sure you don't need me to tell you there's a wealth of history on the doorstep. Direct observation is always preferable to pure textbook learning. I came out here immediately after graduating and did most of my doctoral research in the field. Real Egyptologists go to the source."

Ouch!

"I'd have liked to, but—" He wasn't listening, having already turned his back and taken several long-legged strides towards the exit.

"I'm going up for five minutes. Stay here and avoid wandering. Just because the tours are done for the night, doesn't mean it's safe out there."

She might have retorted something about him venturing out alone but doubted that would win her any favours. Instead, she sank down to work again.

The tomb lost all its heat with Killian's departure. The lights seemed dimmer, and the air infused with a chill she'd never noticed previously. Adie looked to the four corners of the mural chamber. Nothing had changed, but she was suddenly conscious of the weight of sand above her, and the laborious, repetitive nature of what she was doing. She'd known this was what being here would like, but at the same time, that reality had never quite pierced the fantasy. "I wonder what you'd have made of this, Esther? And what you'd have made of him. I'm not sure I'm going to discover anything, not even Osiris's missing willy. Still, I'm here."

Maybe she wouldn't unearth golden treasure, but equally maybe she would. What wasn't to say the burial chamber on the other side of that rockfall wasn't crammed with treasures to rival Howard Carter's find when he opened Tutankhamun's tomb? Or if she dialled things back a bit, what's to say her next scoop of earth wouldn't yield the cartouche Killian so desired her to find.

She'd like to see his face then. Would he still be frosty, or would his eyes ignite with fever, and his wan half-smiles broaden into full-bodied grins?

"You're amazing. A real asset to the team." In her fantasy, he lifted her off her feet to swing her around in delight. "I'm excited to officially make you a permanent member of this team. We should go out to celebrate." This being her fantasy, out was a euphemism for a meal and wine followed by a lot of crazy hot sex. "Yeah, because he's totally into you, Ades." The man hadn't given the slightest hint to that effect. Why would he be interested? He was Doctor Simon Killian Carmichael, the closest thing Egyptology had to a rockstar these days, and she... she was fresh out of school. A wide-eyed innocent— not really innocent—to his dirty professor.

He *was* dirty beneath all that ice-cold veneer? He had to be, right?

Just so long as he wasn't submissive and turned out to be one of those men who commanded total authority over most things but was eager to shed all that in the bedroom. While that might be fun for a few minutes, Matthew was right, she'd like Killian to nail her into oblivion and then tell her what a good girl she was afterwards.

-11-
Killian

Killian had a two-fold reason for staying late. One was down to a preternatural instinct honed from experience for trouble brewing. The other... the other was trouble already arrived. He didn't want to be intrigued by Adie Hamilton, but he was. Since her first morning as part of his team, when he'd begun the day, thanks to her sleep-deprived early morning softness, with a semi that refused to go down, he'd avoided being alone with her.

He wasn't tempted. Not really.

He knew better than that.

It was her determination to impress him that was doing it for him this evening. Sure, many tried, but most wrote him off as a grumpy old bugger in short order. She wasn't letting his realism strip her of anything. He could see the stars twinkling in her eyes. Intuit the fantasies she was concocting of treasures and adventures, and likely curses and the walking dead too. That ought to have killed his interest, instead, it seemed to be fuelling it. Hence his sprint into the encroaching twilight.

He needed to get his head on straight before he did something out of character.

Killian loved this time of night in the desert. While he'd happily live without the chill that threaded through the air the moment the sun descended, he appreciated the stillness evening brought to the necropolis. The endless parades of tourists that blighted the landscape during the daytime vanished to their hotels and the plethora of bars and restaurants that encroached further with every passing year. Then, it was just sand and stars and the occasional bit of wildlife. Everyone imagined the pyramids occupied remote areas of desert. It was the lie they were fed via carefully angled images. In truth, the city coiled around the monuments like an enormous Nile crocodile waiting for its moment to swallow everything up.

He found a secluded spot in which to relieve himself. Only the moment he was done, his cock perked up all excited, the call of his bladder no longer overriding the burr of arousal irritating his senses.

When was the last time he'd got laid?

Too long ago. No matter. He wasn't going to do anything as dumb as seducing a colleague. He'd learnt that lesson and learnt it well. Back in his youth, Killian had done plenty of dumb as fuck stuff. Like making out in tombs. Hell, it'd practically been de rigueur for him and his then partner. Every new site, bonking ensured.

God, they'd been fools. They ought to have known better. Had in fact known better. It just hadn't stopped them.

It was odd thinking back to those times. He never did anymore. The memories were like scenes from someone else's life. He didn't see himself in that young man.

He'd grown. Changed. Hardened.

A few critters skittered across the horizon, while a vulture wheeled overhead.

He shivered with unease. For such a scholar of history, he had little time for dwelling on his own past. Was it Adie, or this place forcing him to recollect?

The sound of a motor humming caught his attention. A car coming along the access road towards the car park by Unas's pyramid. It shouldn't have made the hairs on the back of his neck stand up. People sometimes trekked here after the ticket office closed for the night, kids mostly, or romanticists that wanted to watch the sun go down behind the pyramids. Though mostly they went to Giza for that.

Possibly it was just that he was expecting trouble. Joe Levine's portents preying on his mind.

A quick sprint took him over the sandy ground to where he could get a better view. He arrived in time to see the car pull up.

Two men stepped out, one of whom he recognised instantly, and whose presence dropped boulders into his guts.

Fucking unbelievable. In all the world, why would he be here now?

Killian ducked behind the mound he'd used as a vantage point before he was seen, then made a sprint back to the submerged tomb. If he was out here, there could be only one reason for it, but he was damned if he was going to let that rat-arsed bastard anywhere near his find, no matter how many officials he bribed.

They were not repeating the past.

-12-
Adie

The longer Killian remained absent, the more oppressive the shadowy chamber grew. Adie finished the quadrant she'd been working on and moved on to another. This one tight against the wall. It only took a few moments to realise that while chunks of the plasterwork had cracked and fallen off the higher portions of the wall, which wasn't the case for the lower portions. More importantly, they continued below the current level of the floor.

She tested another area, and found the same held true there too, and for the section in between.

Damn, she needed some better light on this. The head torch and the lamps weren't enough. There was something here, she was sure of it. Butterflies were flapping in her chest. Below the top few centimetres of compacted dirt, the earth was loose. She dug deeper still, following the lines of the relief.

Holy shit! There was something here... She'd found something.

"Killian!" she called. Her voice echoed back at her in the empty sepulchre, but she was too excited to worry about it. She traced the pattern again, then scrambled to her feet, and raced up the stairs in search of him.

The desert wind was slowly shifting the sand dunes northward. The twilit sky was full of dust that stung as it hit her face. "Killian!" she called, one arm raised to shield her eyes as she ran wide of the excavation to get a better view of the surroundings. Where the hell was he? "Doctor Carmichael."

Frustrated, she kicked a rock, and something wakened beside it.

"Shit!" Scorpion.

It advanced, tail held high, prompting her to scurry backwards. The sand gave way beneath her, landing her on her arse looking skywards into the iridescent blue of the heavens. On the crest of the nearest dune stood a horse. Its rider, swathed from head to toe in light-extinguishing cloth. It was as if Rudolph Valentino had ridden straight out of The Sheikh.

She gulped. Blinked, and he was gone.

Mirage?

The shuffling motion of the scorpion tugged her vision downwards again. It was almost level with her toes, which instinctively curled inside her boots. Horrified, Adie leapt to her feet and fled back to the excavation.

Killian stood waiting by the door; his mouth drawn into a sour frown. "I thought I told you to stay below."

"Yes," she agreed, aggrieved by his snappiness. "But I came to find you. I know this is going to sound crazy, but I think I've found something. Let me rephrase. I have found something. I started working on a new quadrant, and the reliefs continue below the current floor level. Look, let me show you."

She grabbed his arm and tugged him towards the stairs, only to misjudge the step and stumble.

Killian caught the back of her shirt, sparing her the same tumble as Bill. "Adie, slow down. Whatever it is you think you've found, it isn't about to up and disappear. You said something about the reliefs."

"Yes, the current floor level is higher than in the past. I think I've found a door to the burial chamber."

He made a dismissive noise in his throat, then shook his head at her. "I'd expect to find the burial chamber at the end of the descending passageway that extends from the south wall, not the north-west corner. That would be more typical, wouldn't you agree?"

"Right," she echoed, irritated by his logic. Sure, he was probably right, but did he have to sound so patronising about it? Couldn't he manage to be a little impressed... a bit excited about the fact she'd uncovered something.

"All right. Show me."

"It's here." Adie led him straight to the area she'd dug out and pointed out how the design extended downwards in all three places.

"Yeah," he said after a moment or two. "You're right. The floor level's been raised. But it's as likely to be because of a robber's tunnel as a side chamber."

"Robbers," she echoed, horrified that her find might already have been carried off.

"We'll take a closer look tomorrow. I think we're done here for tonight. Gather the trays of fragments, we'll take them with us and work on them on the boat."

"Couldn't we—"

"Start on it tonight? No. We don't rush things, Adie. Regardless of what it turns out to be, all these fragments still need cataloguing first. It's time for us to leave. I'm done hanging about in this graveyard full of ghosts for the night.

-13-

Killian

Killian couldn't remember the last time he'd remained in bed much later than daybreak, but the following morning, while he woke as usual to the first rays of light filtering through the slats between his cabin blinds, he contentedly lazed. And why not? Even though the day would be busy, it was still only twenty past five. And he'd been dreaming.

He'd been twenty-five years old again, bursting with energy, and desperately in love both with Egyptology, and with his best friend in the whole universe. They'd been inseparable. And unstoppable. A dream team destined for greatness.

Better still, his recollection hadn't been soured by the events that followed. Time hadn't whittled the memories down to the knotty stumps they were in the waking world.

He'd felt so damn alive.

Invincible.

Turned on.

No wonder he'd woken with morning wood.

It certainly wasn't anything to do with the

team's newest recruit, who'd probably still been bouncing around the deck until the early hours, she was so hyped up over what she'd unearthed.

A knock on the door startled him into a sitting position. "Come in."

Lucas stuck his head around the jamb. "I'm off to join Mark Leyham this morning. I thought I'd just remind you."

"And I'm now reminded." Killian pressed his steepled fingers to the bridge of his nose, regretting his decision to lend Lucas to the team working in Unas's pyramid. "How long does he want you for?"

Lucas entered the room proper. He took off his glasses and started cleaning the lenses. "I'm not sure. He wants me to look at some inscriptions they've uncovered in the valley temple."

"Fine, well tell him I can only spare you today. Make sure he knows that. Lucas, I need you."

"Okay." He backed towards the door, hands raised.

"Wait. Take Matthew along."

"I thought you said we're busy." Lucas perched his glasses back on and squinted though the lenses down his long nose, clearly less than pleased to be saddled with a hanger-on.

"We are, but it'll be good experience for him." Also, he'd have to suffer through the hangover he was no doubt nursing under the stony gaze of Mark Leyham, rather than by distracting Adie from her work. It was time he started seeing what she was truly capable of, and from what he'd witnessed last night, the first step of that was separating her from gossip guy.

Lucas gave him a salute. "As you command, boss." He glanced at his watch. "I'd better go. Don't want to keep Mark waiting."

"No, better not. Send Adie along once she's finished her breakfast, will you?"

Killian sank back into the pillows, already planning the day's activities in his head. With Matthew and Lucas gone, that left himself and Siân to stabilise the intact portions of the antechamber wall, while Adie cleared the rest of the floor. Only then could they start digging down, to see what was under that raised floor.

His cock gave a twitch as his thoughts turned in Adie's direction. Jeezus, what was the matter with him? It made no sense that she moved him, but every time she gazed up at him with wonder in her eyes and a smile on her lips, his heart, and more annoyingly his cock, got perky.

Hell, it was perky now, which was not good, given he'd just summoned her.

Irritably, he slid a palm down his torso.

It wasn't her. It was this place... Saqqara. So teeming in memories. It had to be. His head was never turned by students. Not that she was quite that anymore. He grasped his cock and gave it an idle stroke. Hissed through his teeth at the instant rush of pleasure chemicals to his brain, which lit images, one after another, like fireworks going off in his brain.

Adie in his office at the university, upended over his lap, skirt up and panties down. Adie in the desert, bound at the wrists and ankles, helpless to resist whatever he wanted to do to her. Followed by Adie naked in his bed... in his shower... kneeling and choking on his cock.

No.

He threw off the sheet and padded across the wooden floor naked towards his makeshift dressing table, where his erection mocked him in the mirror. He ignored it in favour of a faded square of red cloth that lay crumpled on the surface. It was an old memento. He couldn't even say why he'd kept it, but he lifted the faded cotton to his nose and breathed in its scent.

A lifetime had passed since that dig in England. The cloth was part of a banner planted by his undergraduate mates in an attempt to fool him. Except he'd spotted it for a twentieth century wall-hanging purely from the reek of incense that wafted off it. The faint trace of sandalwood lingered even now.

He recalled too, the black-haired girl to whom it had once belonged. The many nights he'd spent in her dorm room, back when he had a social life, when he was the first on the guest list for parties because people enjoyed his company, not because he was some archaeological superstar.

She'd smelled of sandalwood too.

Adie Hamilton smelled of jasmine talc.

God why was it so hard to keep her out of his head?

He stepped under the shower spray with the cotton still in his hand, where he circled it against his abs, before wrapping it around his cock.

"Is that a pair of my panties professor?"

Fuck! He was a dirty sod, who needed his mind bleaching. On the other hand, maybe a good wank would sort him out. He firmed up his grip and began a steady stroke, eyes closed, the shower spray raining down on him.

"I did wonder why I couldn't find them. I don't mind if you use them. That erection does look very painful."

"It is. Very. Perhaps you'd like to kiss it for me, Adie?"

In his vision she was as she'd appeared that first morning in Egypt, hair tousled, sleep tugging on her eyelids, and the outline of her curvy body all too visible through the silk of her dressing gown.

"Wouldn't you like me to?" She flashed him an impish grin. "I think even professors ought to say please."

"Please kiss it for me."

The way she moved caused the edges of her robe to gape apart, flashing him glimpses of creamy skin. Killian dislodged the silk from one shoulder with two fingers, whereupon the whole garment slithered south into a pool at her feet. He slid his hand around the back of her neck, pulled her to him, and claimed her lips, before pressing her onto her knees.

She didn't open her mouth for him. She puckered her lips and dotted chaste kisses along his shaft driving him ballistic. He turned the temperature of the water down. It didn't help. A thin thread of pre-ejaculate clung to the cloth he held, like spider's silk hung with raindrops.

Did Adie own panties in the same muted shade of red? He pictured her on all-fours, arse raised, a thong-like strap peeping between her heart-shaped cheeks.

Saw himself plucking at the string, then angling his cock down towards her cleft. Hauling her hips up and then sliding smoothly into her heat. Fucking her until she squealed, until she cried out his name, and broke apart.

Until he teetered on the edge of breaking apart too.

"Yes," he murmured, lifting her auburn hair in a tight grip, then biting at the back of her neck. "You can take the whole of me, can't you? That's my girl, my clever girl. My good girl, taking her professor's needy cock like the hungry brat you are. I'm going to possess every inch of you."

"Yes," she screamed in reply. "Yes. Please fuck me, professor. Fuck me. Fuck me hard. Make me yours."

"Make me yours," a voice echoed right out of his past splitting the fantasy asunder.

No, his mind screamed. But his body... his body it soared.

I'm yours. I'll always be yours.

His orgasm caught him like the bite of a whip, sending streaks of pleasure through his tensed muscles and out through his cock.

Killian froze, watching the shower water washing away his seed from the cubicle wall.

"Fuck!"

He was so fucked.

Was it not enough to have to contend with having Sadler prowling around?

No, he had to start getting horny for a woman who was off limits. She wasn't even his type. She was all gilded sunshine and chirpy excitement. If they were together, he'd want to throttle her as often as he'd want to fuck her.

And that just planted a vision of his hand around her throat while he fucked her senseless.

"Fool." Bloody imbecilic fool.

-14-

Adie

Adie paused before Killian's cabin door chewing her lips. Although it was tempting to imagine he'd summoned her to an erotic liaison, that seemed unlikely.

She took a deep breath, knocked, then when there was no answer, tried the handle. "Hello? Lucas said you wanted to see me."

Within the cabin, the air sat heavy with water vapour. The blinds were still drawn, so the light was bronzed. Killian was standing by the chest of drawers, towel-drying his white hair, dressed in nothing but a towel.

"Oops! You're not ready. I can come back in a bit."

He glanced back at her over his shoulder. "It's fine. Take a seat. I'll only be a moment."

"Um, okay." Well, he wasn't a prude.

The only place to sit was the bed. Awkwardly, she perched amidst the rumpled linen, and attempted to keep her eyes averted. The cabin was depressingly identical to hers. There were a few knicknacks scattered about, and a wall of books, but it was depressingly unrevealing about its owner. No framed treasure maps. No leather-bound heirloom journals, or maps marked with flight paths.

Killian wrenched open a drawer in the dresser, and raked through the contents, eventually pulling out a pair of black boxer-briefs, that he tugged on beneath the robe with his back turned to her. He did the same with his trousers, inadvertently flashing her a glimpse of his arse, two shades whiter than the rest of him. He turned about and snatched up a shirt from the end of the bed, only to relocate it rather than put it on.

"Would you mind?"

"Huh?"

A bottle of suncream landed on the bed beside her.

"Okay. Sure. Right." Yes, she could totally help him with that.

Killian turned his back again, "Shoulders, and the back of my neck, please."

Was this real?

Was the fantasy going to proceed from her massaging suncream into his shoulders to her using it as a lubricant to give him a stealthy handjob?

He coughed, prompting her to leave the safety of the bed and her sordid imaginings behind.

Damn, but the man was built like a gymnast, all honed muscle, and shoulders and biceps to die for. She'd noticed he had those lines too, angled down from his hips towards his groin. The suncream was weirdly cold, when she squeezed it onto her fingers, as if he'd been storing it in a refrigerator. His body though, that was all heat and deliciously tanned skin.

"It's not necessary to be quite so gentle, I'm not made of glass."

"Sorry, right." She cleared her throat hating the way she sounded so mouse-like. She wasn't timid. Had never been timid. She was brave. Fearless. Her palms made more solid contact. God, she wanted to do more than massage his back. She wanted to reach around and slide her hands over the ridges of his abs and push her hands under his waistband. Also, turn him about and trace the penny-like discs of his nipples with her tongue. His every breath, each thud of his heart radiated through her palm. Neither quite steady, but both less raggedy than her own.

"What was it you wanted to see me for?"

"Are you done?"

"Almost." She traced a few more languorous, and largely unnecessary circles.

Killian impatiently shifted his bare feet.

"Would you like me to do anywhere else?" She picked up the bottle again, but Killian claimed it from her. "I'm good, thank you." He daubed a blob on her nose, where she'd previously caught the sun. "I just wanted to let you know that things will be a little different today and going forward. I'm going to rotate you through working with each member of the team. That way you'll pick up a variety of skills. Today though, you're still on clearing those fragments. Lucas and Matthew are off site, so I need you focused. Remember, the quicker you clear that floor, the sooner we get to dig."

"Will you and Siân still be working in the

magazines?" She didn't much fancy working alone.

"No, it's important we secure the intact portions of the mural. We'll be concentrating on that. And Adie, I don't want you talking to anyone outside the team about what you may or may not have found. It's too early to say if it's anything. It could be literally nothing. I don't want the press getting wind of things and blowing it out of proportion. For one, if it really is nothing, then we end up looking like fools, and conversely, if it is something, we don't need a hoard of interested parties dogging our every move. Do you understand me?"

"Yeah, I get it. Zipped lips." She mimed the action and throwing away the key.

"Good. Let's get moving then."

~Ж~

By lunchtime, Adie had cleared almost two-thirds of the fragments from the earth floor, but her enthusiasm for the task had withered completely. Killian had gone to take some measurements at the far end of the southern corridor, where the ceiling had collapsed, leaving Siân to work on the delicate mural. Adie's shadow leapt across the chamber wall like a demented moth as she came up behind the other woman.

"All finished?" Siân asked cheerily, without taking her eyes off her task of inserting a long syringe full of epoxy resin into the wall.

"No. I'm giving my joints a rest. My knees have had enough." She rubbed at the scuffed patches on her trousers for emphasis.

Siân shot her a sympathetic glance. "Hasn't Killian noticed? I'm sure he'll give you something else to do for a bit."

"Nope, and I'm not about to beg. I'm itching to know what I've found, and the only way I'm going to find out is by picking all these bits up. Besides, whinging is hardly likely to impress him."

"And you think flogging yourself will?"

She frowned uncertainly.

"Babe, all the work in the world won't melt his icy heart. I've known him for years, and all I have to show for it is a Christmas card and a Sharpie that he leant me. And believe me, I've spent more days on my knees than I can easily count. So, unless you're prepared to jump him and tie him down, you've more chance of finding this missing bit of wall than of getting into his—"

"I'm not trying to get into his pants," she protested, perhaps a little too virulently.

"—good graces."

"Oh, right." Abashed, she bowed her head.

"Hey, there's nothing wrong with wanting either." Siân lowered her tools and shuffled along the floor to the next spot. "As long as you're realistic about the prospects. The fact is he's a grumpy ice-hole. Are you sure you want to do the horizontal mambo with that? You might get frostbite."

"He felt plenty hot earlier. Oh, God, Siân. He had me smother him in suncream this morning. I thought I was going to spontaneously combust."

"Yeah, I did notice you looked a bit cooked when

you emerged from his cabin. Dare I ask where he had you rubbing him?"

"Just his back," she said, failing to process the innuendo in Siân's voice. "Not that I'd have minded doing elsewhere. The man is insanely ripped. You know that, right? You might have mentioned it."

"And why would I do that? I'm pretty sure I warned you not to get your hopes up. I'm hardly going to then tell you things that'd fan the flames. Just like I'm also not telling you he has a ten-inch dick."

"No, he doesn't. Does he?" How did Siân know?

"Purportedly, but that's nothing on old pharaoh here, who must have at least twelve." She tipped her head in the direction of the gap in the plaster.

"There's such a thing as too big, you know." Her eyes threatened to water at the mere prospect of being drilled with anything that huge.

Siân clapped her on the butt. "Not in my experience, baby girl. I like them well hung, and with dancer's hips. You know the best way to grab his attention, don'tcha? Find this missing cock."

"He says it's unlikely—"

"Precisely. But unlikely isn't the same as impossible, and if I'm not mistaken, I'm looking at a girl who likes a treasure hunt."

She did, and while it was looking increasingly unlikely that she'd find the missing fragment among the rubble, Killian had already pointed her at Jacob's journal. There were bound to be some pointers in it. She bounded back across the dingy chamber to her work pitch.

"Thought of a plan, have you?"

"Nope."

"Liar. You're grinning like a lunatic."

"I'm grinning like a woman on a quest."

"His cock isn't really ten inches long. Just in case that's what has you perked up. I've seen him sporting wood, and it wasn't poking from his waistband."

"Siân!" Adie threw a wary glance towards the tunnel Killian had vanished down. She really hoped he couldn't hear them from wherever he was currently working.

"What's that? Who are you talking about? Who doesn't have ten inches?" Matthew plodded in from the stairwell. He was coated from head to foot in a thick layer of white dust. "Oh, let me guess. Is it a certain white-haired eccentric?"

"You're back early," Siân replied. "I thought you'd be gone for the day."

Matthew sniffed and wandered over to see what she was doing. "Nah, my services are no longer required. They sent me back once the spadework was done. I was happy to stay, but Lucas couldn't wait to be shot of me." He snorted and began to ineffectually brush at the dust on his trousers. "I don't know who they're trying to fool. It's bloody obvious that Mark's trying to poach him, and Lucas is ready to jump, providing the price is right. Christ, look at me. I look like I've been sandblasted."

"Wouldn't that make you look clean?" Adie remarked, which diverted Matthew over to her work pitch. He clacked his tongue, clearly impressed by how much she'd got done. She'd have had half the number of sample trays if he'd been around to distract her.

Probably Killian knew it too.

Matthew hovered over her for a few minutes, before circling back to Siân. "What do you ladies think, eh?" He aligned himself with the depiction of the pharaoh and adopted the same pose. "Is he having his cock sucked, or what? Lucas reckons not. Says it's going to be a crook or something in his hand that he's using to bestow life or a blessing on the kneeling figure, but that's bollocks. You can see it's bollocks. Even pharaohs don't have three hands."

On her knees, Siân shuffled closer to Matthew, so she was mirroring the position of the kneeling woman. "What do you think, Adie?"

Adie stared at the pair of them puzzled. "About Lucas?"

"No." Siân laughed "The mural. Is she being blessed or face-fucked?"

"Hm. I'm not quite…" She drifted closer, trowel still in her hand. Matthew's loucheness didn't really lend itself to the arrogance of the pharaoh, and Siân wasn't nearly servile enough. "Your positioning isn't quite right. You're too far apart. Also, given all the inbreeding, isn't him having three hands actually more likely? I mean, there's not exactly an extensive catalogue of ancient Egyptian pornography about."

"There's the Turin Erotic Papyrus," Matthew interjected.

"True. Good point." Siân nodded.

"Never heard of it."

"Haven't you?" The other woman seemed surprised. "It shows twelve positions, some highly acrobatic, at least one involving a chariot, and another featuring hair pulling. That one is my favourite. It'd be cool if it didn't bear an uncanny resemblance to 1970s porn."

Adie's frown clearly communicated her confusion.

"The guys are all hairy, bald, and unkempt and the women highly idealistic. Oh, and they all have at least foot long schlongs."

"Well, shit! Consider me informed."

Matthew, perhaps realising that he was no longer the centre of attention, began unbuttoning his fly.

"What the fuck are you doing?" Siân asked him.

"Staging a proper reenactment, obviously."

Adie gulped, as he hooked his thumbs under the elastic of his underwear and pushed it down far enough to expose himself.

"Matty," Siân cautioned, and shot both him and Adie significant looks.

"What? I'm sure she's seen a dick before, and this is a proper scientific investigation." He started tugging himself to coax an erection. "Get the camera out, Ades. Now what do you think?"

"Um." Her focus zoomed in on the red tip of his cock and how damn close he was to Siân, who didn't seem at all perturbed by the fact she was inches shy of blowing him. Matthew handed her his phone to snap them, which she obligingly did on autopilot. "I'm still not sure. You're not quite posed the same way."

"Yeah, well it's quite hard to twist my shoulders one way and my hips the other."

"And Siân needs to open her mouth."

Siân looked up and dropped her mouth open, only to give a startled gasp and veer away from him. It caused them all to turn their heads.

Killian was standing in the archway that led to the south corridor. His grey eyes smouldering.

"Fuck!" Matthew hissed.

"What in God's name do you think you're doing?" Killian brought the steel ruler he was holding down into his open palm with a smack that must have smarted. He didn't flinch. The three of them did. Killian's nostrils flared, prompting her to brace herself for a string of expletives, what he said instead came out as chill as frost. "I thought this was an excavation, not a peep show. Give me one good reason why I shouldn't dismiss the three of you on the spot?"

"We were just—" Matthew began feebly, waving one hand at the mural while he simultaneously tried to zip himself up.

"I can see perfectly well what you were doing, thank you, Matthew."

"Yeah, but it's my fault. I started it." He anxiously drew a hand through his dust-stiffened hair.

"We all joined in," Siân admitted.

Killian's attention swung to her, and his pale eyes narrowed to two flinty steels. "Make yourself scarce," he said. "And Matthew, assuming you still wish to work here, pick up those crates and take them back to the boat. Then, you stay there until I bloody well say otherwise, do you hear me?"

"Got it." He zipped up, snatched his phone from Adie, and started stacking trays.

Siân lingered on the stairs.

"And Adina—"

Oh, Jesus. Full name. She hardly dared meet his gaze.

"How exactly should I express my disappointment? According to Joe Levine you're one of the brightest he's ever taught, but that counts for nothing if you behave like a teenage delinquent."

She swallowed the lump of anger and injustice growing in her throat. "Sorry. We were just trying to figure out—"

"Killian, it wasn't her fault," Siân said in her defence. "Don't pin this all on her."

"Out!" He slammed the rule into his palm again, which sent both Siân and Matthew scurrying. "It seems to me, Miss Hamilton that you're not very good at taking instruction. I told you to concentrate on clearing this floor. I told you to put the notion of fixing this mural and speculating about it out of your head. Instead, I find you doing precisely the opposite, just as I found you outside last night, when I'd told you to stay indoors."

"I was just—"

"I don't care what you think you were doing. What you're here for is to do the job I tell you to do and nothing else. You're not here to think. Or speculate. You're not even here to randomly shovel shit when you're not supposed to be. You're here to be obedient."

"I can't believe you're criticising me for making a discovery."

"You haven't found shit yet, Adie. Not a goddamned thing. And you won't if you continue to behave as you have been. Now get back to what you're being paid to do, and keep your head down, or you'll be on the next flight back to England."

~Ж~

It took another three days of tense and painful labour to clear the remainder of the anteroom floor. Matthew was confined to the *dahabiyya*, grounded like a teenager who'd broken curfew. Killian, it seemed, had no sense of humour. Lucas had laughed like a drain when he'd learned why they were all running foul of the boss's temper. And, of course, they'd all seen the photos that Matthew refused to delete.

They broke the soil on the fourth day. Killian wielding the shovel, while Adie and Siân stood by ready to sieve the sand. It was the sort of hot sweaty work guaranteed to leave tempers frayed, and as it was conducted largely in uncomfortable silence, so that the minutes dragged by interminably.

They had to dig three feet down before the wall relief gave way to a lintel, and then a dark sliver of opening.

Killian mopped his brow with the cuff of his glove. "Give me a torch."

Siân passed him a baton mounted one, which he slid into the opening, before widening the hole sufficiently to poke his head through the gap.

"Is it a chamber?" Adie asked hopefully.

He knelt back, shaking dirt from his hair. "A tunnel. Low, windy, seems relatively clear, but I can't see very far. Let's get the entrance cleared and we can send the rover down." He pulled himself out of the trench and disappeared into the depths of the tomb to fetch it.

"Nice one," Siân congratulated Adie once Killian was out of earshot. "I don't mind digging if you're okay to sieve. We can swap over in a bit."

It was nearing sundown by the time they'd properly uncovered the low, ragged tunnel, but none of them were ready to quit for the night. They'd each taken shifts at digging, and Killian had sent the rover in, which beamed them back a few pictures, but he'd had to pull it back when the terrain was too uneven for its treads.

"Does this mean one of us will have to venture in?" Adie asked, itching for the chance to volunteer. She'd found the odd trinket before, Roman coins and Viking weapon shards, but this was different. Bigger. Who knew what lay at the other end of that tunnel. They could be on the verge of a major new discovery.

"It does," Killian confirmed. "But that won't be you. Siân, get kitted up. You first, I'll follow you."

"But that's not fair." She might be the lowliest member of the team, but this was her find. They wouldn't have even found the tunnel if not for her.

"Fair has nothing to do with it. Do you have any

experience potholing, or working up a new area? No. Siân and I do. Adie, we have no idea where that tunnel goes, how long it extends or anything. There's no way I'm taking a novice down there blind. You'd be a liability. We'll do this safely, thank you. Following standard protocol. Lucas, find her a job."

"I don't want a j—" Heat filled her cheeks. Damn him. While he was right, she was the least experienced member of the team, that didn't mean he had to be such a prick about it. The only way you got experience was by doing things, and she was way smaller than he was. It made sense to send her down along with Siân for that reason alone. She'd less chance of getting stuck.

"Adie, to the magazines," Lucas commanded.

"Oh, come on. Why can't I at least stay here? I mean, someone has to keep watch, right, in case they need anything, or one of them gets stuck or something?"

Killian's second in command exchanged a glance with their boss. "She makes a good point."

"Fine. You can keep watch, but do not follow. Start getting some better lighting set up. If this actually leads somewhere, we're going to need to run cabling through it. Check we've the supplies to do that."

-15-
Killian

"**W**hy the hell are you being so mean to her?" Siân asked. He was nose to boot with her in the tunnel, only a few metres in. Siân was slightly ahead of him, her movement restricted to an awkward sort of army crawl. The lack of wriggle room practically confirmed to him this wasn't part of the original tomb. What was intriguing was the fact it angled downwards and left, rather than up towards the surface like he'd initially anticipated. It suggested the thieves who'd dug it had done so from inside the antechamber.

"How am I being mean? She still has a job. The three of you shouldn't, after that stunt the other day."

"God, are you still fixated on that? No one was hurt. Nothing got damaged, and in any case, you can't hold her responsible. It was me on my knees, Matthew with his fly undone. She just happened to be there."

"She was directing you," he replied stubbornly. That whole incident had put him in a foul mood that he'd been unable to shake.

Siân groaned in response and put a concerted effort into moving forward. The churning of her feet as she tried to create some leverage sent puffs of dust into his face. It felt deliberate, like she was expressing her annoyance with him in the only way she could that he couldn't countermand.

"You know perfectly well why I didn't bring her down here."

"Yeah, I do," she retaliated. "And it has fuck all to do with her experience. I think you just prefer not to be alone in a tunnel with her. I think she freaks you out with her excitement for the job. What's the matter, Killian, are you afraid she might remind you that you enjoy this stuff?"

"Keep moving. It's hot as hell in here. Let's not prolong it."

He barely had the words out before Siân slithered away from him.

"Fuck!" Her curse was accompanied by a landslide of loose earth and stones and the dance of her torch beam overhead, lighting ancient support beams before it dramatically winked out.

"Siân? Are you okay? Siân?"

"Fine. I'm fine. There's some loose shingle where the incline sharpens. Careful how you come down."

"Do you need my torch?"

"I'm good. I still have the one on my helmet, and I don't think it's rolled far. There seems to be a wider area ahead. Besides, you'll need yours to get down safely."

He listened to her struggling onward for a moment, giving her space to get ahead, before tackling the incline for himself. At the bottom of the head-first descent, the tunnel opened out enough for him to rise onto all-fours. Then followed a series of sharp steps, and an even sharper turn into a circular burrow large enough for him to kneel upright inside. Siân was waiting, a newly acquired scratch across her chin. "Are you all right?" he asked again.

"Fine."

"Did you find your torch?"

She showed him it. "Either the bulb's gone or the batteries have fritzed."

"Here," he mopped his brow, then passed Siân a flask of water. The closeness made the air feel heavy, and him vividly conscious of the weight of earth above them. They'd easily descended another five or six feet.

Siân grateful accepted his offering, and took a sip, wiping her mouth with the back of her gloved hand before passing the canteen back.

"Where do you think this is going? It's obviously a robber's tunnel, right?"

Killian ran his hand over the wall as if he could read its history like Braille. "It seems a valid assumption. If it was meant to be part of the tomb, the walls would be smooth. This was cut in a hurry, and it'd be useless for bringing tools in and out."

"Do you think they're still down here? The robbers? I'd hate to think we'd been beaten to the prize."

"If they are, they're long dead."

"Probably been promoted to tomb guardians by now. Oh, Killian, don't pull a face. It's a joke. I'm not seriously expecting to find a band of supernatural beings at the end of this rat run, same as I know the only objects that we're likely to find are a few broken pots. It doesn't mean I don't hold out hope of one day discovering gold. After seven years in this business, it'd be nice to get a glimpse of something with a bit of wow factor. Tell me truthfully that you never dream about unearthing something so fucking breathtaking it steals the air from your lungs."

"I'd prefer the air to stay in my lungs," he replied testily.

"You know you should have brought her."

"Yeah, well I didn't." He brushed the dust from his nose where it was beginning to tickle. "The passageway continues that way. I'm going to go on." He crawled past her and shone his torch down the next stretch of inky tunnel. "If I'm right about the direction we've come..."—a quick check of the compass in his pocket confirmed it—"this should take us the other side of the cave-in in the southern corridor."

"Is that your way of saying she might actually have found you a burial chamber?"

His jaw clenched so hard his teeth ached.

-16-
Adie

Adie was sitting on the bottom step of the main staircase when Siân pulled herself out of the pit. "Find anything?" she asked glumly.

Siân shook her head. "Not yet. I came back for more batteries, and a decent lamp. He won't admit it, so don't expect a clap on the back, but this might actually get us to the burial chamber, or at least near to it. The tunnel slopes down and then veers south." She climbed out of the pit and opened the lid of one of the storage trunks to rummage the contents.

"Is it just safety protocol that means I'm stuck out here?" Adie asked, she'd been mulling that thought while they were down there.

Siân upended a sack. Brushes and dental picks spilled everywhere. "Where are all the D cells?"

"Siân?"

"Babe, what do you want me to say? If he says it's about protocol, then it's about protocol. He's the boss. Do I happen to think he's being an ass? Yeah. There's no real reason why you can't go down there. That's assuming you aren't claustrophobic."

"I'm actually fond of small dark spaces."

Siân slammed the lid of the trunk. "I can't find these damned batteries. I think I've some in the car. Also, this scrape on my chin is itchy as hell. I'm going to find the first aid kit. Meanwhile, someone ought to take this lamp to Killian."

"Me?" Adie meeped.

The blond woman made a point of looking around as if to confirm the absence of other volunteers. Then she raised her shoulders in a shrug.

~Ж~

Two minutes later, Adie shuffled into a circular chamber with her torch tucked down the front of her top, held in place by her bra. There was no sign of Killian yet, or of anything more interesting than the shingle-like floor which dug into her knees and palms, grazing skin and scuffing fabric. Not that it mattered. She'd dreamed of doing this ever since she was old enough to read about lost and buried treasure.

Pressing onwards, she crawled into the second half of the tunnel. Here the going was more difficult. First, she had to arch her back uncomfortably to manoeuvre around a bend, and after that, the only way to move forward was to wriggle on her stomach while pulling and pushing with her feet and hands. Thankfully, it was only half the length of the first section, and she soon pushed her head into the inky, airy space of a much larger chamber.

"Siân." Killian's soft voice echoed off the walls like the wind rushing across a desert lake.

Adie reached out for a purchase on the floor below, for she seemed to have entered the room at waist height. The chamber was strangely quiet, out of range of the belligerent chatter of the *khamseen*. Presumably, this part of the tomb was a lot deeper than where she'd worked before.

A puddle of light bobbed towards her.

"Adie!" Killian's torch lit up her face. She squinted up at him, an appeasing grin on her face. "What in God's name are you playing at? Where's Siân?"

"She sent me with the lamp." She held it out to him.

"Fuck!" He snatched it from her hand and turned his back to her. "Well, thank you. Now you can about turn and go back."

"Or I could stay and learn something." She continued to wheelbarrow forward out of the tunnel. It wasn't as if there was space to turn about.

"How about learning to do as you're told?"

Adie's hopeful expression twisted into an equally disappointed one. She shifted her hand for balance, hoping to bring her leg out of the tunnel so that she didn't land in an ungainly heap. Instead, something cracked beneath her, so that she tipped off balance and yelped.

A searing pain shot up her arm as her hand plunged into something slimy.

Killian was immediately on his knees by her side, igniting the lantern so that it illuminated the shallow pit. Her hand had plunged straight through a large clay urn, leaving her elbow deep in jagged shards.

Panicked by the damage she'd just caused, Adie gave an anguished moan and recoiled. Somehow, she managed to stagger to her feet, whereupon she collapsed against the nearby wall. Killian followed her, his expression flickering between concern and annoyance.

"Keep your arm raised," he instructed.

Adie peered hesitantly at her forearm where a series of deep scratches crisscrossed her skin. Sticky, red blood was running between her fingers, and her skin was coated in a yellowish viscous paste. Killian clasped her arm around the wrist and poured water from his bottle over the cuts, sending a spray of red droplets over the floor. "They seem clean," he said. "And thankfully not too deep. Are you okay?"

"Yeah. I guess." She didn't sound sure, and honestly, the hurt was making her eyes well up.

Killian peeled off his shirt and tore a strip from the bottom of it which he bound around her arm. "Not exactly sterile, I'm afraid, but it'll keep the worst of the dirt out until we can get it cleaned up properly. Siân shouldn't have sent you down here."

She nodded, chastened, while staring at his naked chest. He was hot and dusty but smelled pleasantly of heat and skin. "I only wanted to see what I'd found. Weren't you the same over your first big find?" She wasn't sure she even knew what that was.

She expected icy denial, instead his expression softened for a fraction of a second. "Congratulations," he said. "You found a canopic jar and destroyed it. How are you enjoying your first feel of ancient entrails?"

~Ж~

"He actually said that?" Siân asked a few minutes later. "Dick." Despite the remark, she was grinning as she swabbed stinging antiseptic over Adie's cuts. The viscous liquid appeared to be honey and not ancient body organs.

Siân peeled the wrapper off a large sterile dressing and positioned it over the largest of Adie's cuts. "On the other hand, he tore his shirt off for you. He must be fond of you, really." He'd also followed her back through the tunnels, making sure she was safely passed over into Siân's care, before heading back down with Lucas as a companion.

"He probably despairs of ever hiring me, you mean."

"Nah, he likes you. So quit with the dour face." She tutted and swept the cotton wool swabs and bits of packaging into a rubbish sack. "Don't I keep telling you he's a cold bugger? He doesn't let people in, Adie, and with good reason, given his past. The fact he hasn't sent you packing is the equivalent of a gold star from anyone else."

"Wait! What do you mean given his past?"

"Nothing," Siân replied in a way that made it an obvious substitution for 'it's a long story, and you won't believe it even if I told you', so I'm not going to bother. "Also, none of your business."

She leapt down from the back of the vehicle.

"Siân!"
"Let it rest, Adie. It's not his ancient history we're here to investigate."

-17-
Adie

Siân's cryptic remarks continued to play on Adie's mind well into the evening. She'd spent the afternoon washing bits of pottery in the sunshine, having been banned from doing anything more adventurous until her scratches scabbed over, and that'd given her far too much time to think.

Joe had been weird about her coming to work for Killian, and now Siân had hinted at something, and Killian was obviously wary. While his attitude could easily be put down to him being uptight, maybe there was a reason for that.

It was obvious that while he was giving her a chance, he also considered her a liability.

It had become her routine of a night, to take a stroll around the deck before turning in. Once the sun set, the world beyond the *dahabiyya* faded into obscurity, sounds faded to the purr of the khamseen and the gentle lapping of the river around the boat's hull. It became easy to imagine things as they'd once been. Lonely. Desert stretching for miles, just beyond the irrigated plains bordering the river. In reality, the jewelled blanket reflected in the dark river was from the lights of urban residences not a star-spangled sky.

She headed along the deck. It was gone eleven. Matthew and Siân had both turned in, and Lucas had gone south to Dashur for the weekend to meet friends, which meant the light in the workroom indicated Killian's presence. Adie hung in the doorway, outside the pool of light created by the desk lamp. He was hunched over a collection of wall fragments, his head propped on one hand as he studied the piece held between his forefinger and thumb. He seemed softer somehow in the dim light. Not so care-worn. The young man he was, rather than the musty professor he pretended to be. He drew his fingers back through his hair, gathering the snowy strands together.

He wasn't old. She knew he wasn't old. He was what...ten years her senior? At the most. A man in his prime, really. It was only his snow-white hair that created the illusion of venerability. It was curious how attractive she found it.

Killian glanced up. He must have caught the shadow of her movement. Their gazes met, and she was instantly transported.

Five years old, she ran along the beach. Seagulls screeched overhead. She was swinging a gaudy plastic bucket full of rocks and wearing a pink gingham sun hat. Her two cousins and great aunt Esther were playing by the water's edge, a game of catch with the incoming tide, while she helped her father fish treasures from a rock pool.

"Look Adie," he said, holding out a dirt-encrusted, misshapen metal pin. "A Saxon brooch."

The memory was so vivid it rooted her to the spot. Her father, the amateur archaeologist, Esther's first student, the man who'd encouraged her love of the past, and the only man who'd ever loved her unconditionally. It should have been a happy memory. Except two weeks later, she had stood in the rain at his funeral. A heart attack. She'd buried that prized pin along with him.

"Did you need me for something?" Killian asked, straightening in his chair so that his shoulders pulled into their usual stiffness.

For several somethings, but none that she was going to admit to his face. She didn't know what it was about him, but something drew her. Maybe it was the glimpses of himself he showed in odd moments, like when he'd been right there for her when she'd injured herself, and maybe it was old-fashioned hero worship, but something about him struck her in the viscera. Something about him whispered to her, drew her in.

She shook her head. "Sorry. I didn't mean to interrupt. I thought everyone had turned in. When I saw the light, I thought it'd accidentally been left on." Looking more closely now at what he was doing, it wasn't bits of wall fragment he was trying to mend, but the pot that had smashed beneath her.

"Will you be able to reconstruct it?"

He lifted his shoulders in a stiff shrug.

"I'm sorry my ineptitude resulted in a breakage."

His eyes narrowed infinitesimally at the

admission of fault.

"I should have done as I was told."

"Yes."

She bit her lip. She truly was sorry about the pot, but on the other hand, she hadn't come all the way to Egypt to perform tasks she could equally have done back in England. "Does it mean I'm banned from working in the new area?"

"I don't know, Adie. Honestly, I don't know what I'm supposed to do with you. You feel like a liability. You're disobedient, but you're a hard worker. You've a brain, yet you don't think. And I haven't forgotten that little tableaux you were involved in a few days ago."

"Does it mean anything if I say I'm ashamed of myself for that? Although really, I wasn't the one doing anything. Matthew and Siân were posing, not me. I just... They asked me for an opinion."

"I heard you," he said, and tapped the fragment between his fingers into the incomplete puzzle before him. "You practically told her to suck him off for your entertainment."

She had not!

She'd only told Siân to open her mouth.

"My interest was purely academic."

"The fuck it was," he drawled, all prickly fury.

"If I wanted to watch Siân and Matthew, then I would hang out in their cabins with them of a night." Everyone knew the pair of them hooked up at least three nights a week. Sex wasn't silent, and the walls of the houseboat were thin.

Killian stood, forcing his chair back abruptly so

that it scraped loudly on the wooden boards. His jaw was locked so that it protruded, and his teeth were clamped together. "You're unbelievable. I should have listened to Joe. He didn't want me to bring you out here. He tried to warn me about your overactive imagination."

"Well, I thought I was coming to work for a gifted thinker, not an academic nazi and a prude. What's the matter, Killian, are you scared of naked bodies? Is the thought of sex terrifying? I'll admit that Matthew was mucking about, but the question of what's going on in that mural is of genuine academic interest. At least to me it is, and to everyone else working on this project. I don't see why it's such an issue that I might be interested in figuring it out. I'm more than happy to stage and comment on all the other possibilities that have been suggested, too."

Killian's pupils widened and the beat of his pulse fired in the side of his temple. "That won't be necessary," he snarled, his usual restrained, icy inflections replaced by something infinitely more primitive and explosive.

It seemed she'd hit a nerve.

He got to his feet and turned towards the door. "I really need to consider if you're the right person for this team."

Oh, shit! She'd let her mouth run away from her. "I don't understand why you're blaming me. Smashing the pot, sure, but the reconstruction... All three of us were involved, but I'm the only one you're mad at. Why is that? Why do I deserve your wrath, and they don't?"

His jaw clenched into an even more painful grimace.

"Please," she said, lowering her voice, and reaching out to him, as if she might sooth his inexplicable anger.

His eyes burned with steely ferocity.

"I apologise. I spoke out of turn. I don't think you're a nazi or a prude. I don't know you at all. Not really. I'd like to though. I want to learn from you." Her hand was still outstretched. Killian slapped it away.

She winced, made to draw her hand to herself to rub it, but his fingers locked fast around her wrist.

Adie stared at the point of contact, then up at him. His expression hadn't changed. It was still angry and brittle. She heard the grinding of his teeth.

"You're a distraction," he barked. "I don't need distracting. I can't fucking be distracted."

She tugged a little, testing his grip. He refused to release her.

"Have me work with Siân or Lucas. I'll stay out of your way."

He shook his head and laughed, though there was no mirth in the sound.

"If it was that easy, we wouldn't be having this discussion."

"Are you saying you want me to go? Are you dismissing me?"

He raked his free hand through his hair again. "No, Adie. I'm saying—" He gave another of those dry reproachful chuckles, then pulled her fast against the iron-heat of his body. "Tell me not to."

Adie gaped at him in shock. Pressed this close, there was no mistaking his meaning.

"Say no to me. Tell me to back off."

She made a noise in her throat, a whimper, but not a protest.

"Fuck," he muttered. "This is a bad idea."

But he wanted it. She could see that now. Could feel the evidence, and maybe she leaned into his heat deliberately, or it could've been the natural sway of two bodies in proximity. It made his breath rush out from between his teeth. Made him curse.

She liked the sound of his agony.

"You don't want this, Adie."

Wrong. So...very...wrong. She wanted it. Had been fantasising about it from the moment she'd first seen him in Joe Levine's office. "You only get to speak for yourself," she said. "If you want to back off, then just let go of my arm."

His grip tightened so much it pinched.

Okay.

"What comes next? Should I touch you?" She trailed the fingers of her free hand over the bulge behind his fly. The effect was electric. Killian claimed her mouth. He devoured her. Stole her breath and breathed fire into her veins. Her head swam. Dizzied by his actions, Adie strained against him, taking his tongue, reciprocating his hunger, meeting him in a furious clashing of tongues and teeth.

He wanted her. As she wanted him. It seemed improbable, but here they were, wrestling with one another, her hands inside his clothing, fingernails scratching the muscles of his back, while he continued to hold her wrist as if they were manacled to one another.

It wasn't enough. They both needed to get closer. She wanted to feel him bare. He was still waging a war. Holding her fast, and destroying her with his tongue, while simultaneously seeming on the verge of pushing her away.

Adie had been passed from person to person for most of her life. She wasn't going to let him take a bite and then leave before consuming the whole feast. One handed, she loosened his fly, pushed her hand between the edges of the fabric and squeezed him through the cotton of his underwear.

Possibly he wasn't a full ten inches, but he was a big boy. The flared tip of him, red and angry, poked above the elastic waistband. She drew a crown around its head, so that he groaned into her open mouth. Adie freed him of the binding and ringed her fist around his shaft. "This what you need, huh?"

More groans. More breathtaking kisses.

"Teach me what you like," she said. "Teach me how to take it. Would you like me on my knees, professor? Is the reason you're so worked up that you want to reconstruct that scene with me?"

-18-
Killian

It was utter madness. Of course it was. She'd been getting under his skin for days now, ever since he'd seen her in that damn semi-transparent dressing gown. No, even before that. Right since the first moment he'd clapped eyes on her back in Joe Levine's office. She reminded him of something. A youthfulness and passion that he'd expunged because it had led to all his biggest mistakes. He'd learnt to temper his exuberance, his passion. He expected her to do the same, yet it was her naïve enthusiasm, her ridiculous fantasies of finding treasure that inflamed him.

Their tongues sparred. Adie matched his fire with a dizzying fervour of her own. His attention moved from her lips to her throat and then to her breast. She smelled strongly of jasmine talc. He'd never realised he had such a thing for the scent. Then again, he'd never smelled it entwined with the warmth of her body before.

"Teach me what you like. Teach me how to take it. Would you like me on my knees, professor? Is the reason you're so worked up that you want to reconstruct that scene with me?"

Goddamn her.

He'd imagined pushing on her shoulders, bringing her down onto her knees before him. Her looking up at him, all bright-eyed enthusiasm. Everything about the image was wrong, but he wanted it, nevertheless. And she was offering. Virtually begging him. He could've said the words, and she'd have done it. She'd have scuffed her already bruised knees for him. Taken his hard cock into her throat. Taken all of him, perhaps—a feat, for most—or at least as much as she was physically able. That was the sort of person she was. A pleaser. He knew she wanted his approval. He'd seen her working relentlessly trying to make up for the missteps she'd made. Trying to be the person he wanted her to be.

Killian didn't want her to be those things. He didn't want the fire in her to die in the way it had in him.

He'd killed it. Smothered it. Deprived it of oxygen, and heat when he couldn't deprive it of fuel. The desert yielded the fuel. Treasures from its history. Unearthing them was his calling. He'd known that all the way back as far as he could remember, but all the things about the journey that had once made his blood sing, he'd ruthlessly snuffed out.

He'd snuff the life out of her too, if she stuck around.

They stopped kissing for a moment. Stopped touching. The heat between them intensified, nonetheless. It grew so hot he could feel it like tongues of fire against his skin. His cock ached. He wanted her mouth. Wanted the heat of her pussy around him.

And then she knelt.

From that moment, Killian accepted he was doomed.

Fuck. Fuck and holy goddamned fuck.

It no longer mattered that he was treading headlong into folly. Raw need had taken precedence.

A look passed between them. It was almost shy on her part. However, there was nothing shy about how she wrapped her lips around his cock. Then, her mouth was firm, her tongue silk against his too hard shaft. He couldn't help but take and glory in the taking.

The way she sucked was perfect. The right degree of worship. The perfect degree of pressure against his over sensitive flesh. "That's right. Such a good girl," he coaxed, stroking her hair, then cupping the back of her head. It wouldn't take long for him to become undone. Already, he felt the singing in his veins, the tightening of his bollocks.

He panted his next few breaths. Four years of abstinence were about to end.

The glacial armour he'd encased himself in was melting now. It grew thinner with each suck, with each lash of her tongue. He fisted his hands in her hair. Moaned when she moaned, grunted when she hummed in pleasure around her mouthful of cock.

The first spasm coursed along his shaft.

"Adie," he tried to say, but no sound came out.

Instead, he pumped jet after jet of come into her throat, and she, delicious, darling angel of a woman that she was, swallowed every damn drop, allowing nothing to spill. In that moment, at least, he was entirely hers, body and soul, his mind crying from the sheer fucking relief of having come.

It wouldn't last. He knew it couldn't last. It didn't stop him clinging to the fantasy of it. To that end, he held her fast against his groin, her nose pressed against the smattering of hairs there, while he made a few extra strokes in and out of her mouth. He didn't want it to be over. Didn't want this moment to end. For the intrusion of reality back into the present utopia. Eventually, they had to part though.

"Killian?" she looked up at him, still on her knees, expression dazed and dreamy, so open and full of admiration. He didn't deserve it. Had done nothing to earn her devotion.

"Fuck," he croaked in response as his surroundings came into focus, and the weight of what he'd done hit his shoulders.

A gentleman would return the favour, but he was wrung out, and this was so fucking wrong that the wrongness of it was there in his throat choking him. What the hell had he been thinking? He couldn't take her back to his cabin, eat her out, fuck her in the way she obviously wanted him to.

Christ, as if things weren't complicated enough!

"I'm not..." He tried to explain, but he couldn't get his tongue to cooperate, to tell her that a relationship was out of the question, or that while he was grateful, this could never happen again. That it'd been a mistake to let it happen at all.

Killian dragged a hand down his sweat-chilled face, then released the grasp he had on her hair.

She let go of him and rolled onto her feet.

Without her support, he almost toppled. His legs were jelly. He had to clutch at the worktable just to secure his balance. The pottery fragments still lay scattered, a four and a half thousand-year-old jigsaw that no one would thank him for fixing. People wanted gold and treasures, not ancient crockery.

The look she gave him, shrewd, cautious told him she knew he was going to bail.

He couldn't not leave. Staying would make things infinitely worse.

"Arsehole." She sniped at his retreating back, and he deserved it. It wasn't enough to make him U-turn though.

-19-
Adie

"Run it by me again, please. Why have you dragged me out of bed at six o'clock in the morning on a weekend?" Siân gave a hippo-like yawn as she fumbled with the ignition key. The Land Rover sputtered into life, stirring the long grass around them, and sending a pair of black kites wheeling into the sky.

Adie had been up since before dawn. She'd lain awake half the night, trying to figure out what the hell had happened, and how to fix it. Not that she'd done anything wrong, but she didn't understand Killian's reaction. How could someone blow so hot and cold in the space of minutes?

"I told you already. I want to visit the museum."

"Adie, the Egyptian Museum doesn't open for another three hours, so don't feed me that sightseeing crap. And what have you done to your lip?"

She flicked her tongue over the cut in her bottom lip. It was one of several battle scars Killian had left her with, along with a ring of bruises around her wrist, and the taste of him on her tongue that even toothpaste and a good gargle of mouthwash couldn't seem to erase.

Turned out that mister ice-cold wasn't really a glacier, more like a tsunami contained by a thin wall of ice. They hadn't come together in remotely the manner she'd envisaged in her ludicrous fantasies. She'd imagined an emotional connection, romance. Whereas what she'd got was the clash of two wildcats, one of whom stalked off as soon as it was over. He hadn't even been gracious enough to get her off too.

Prick.

She'd had to do that for herself. Frantically. Twice, standing in the shower, just to level her emotions a little after his dramatic flounce.

"I bit it."

Siân rolled her eyes as she popped an extra strong mint in her mouth. "Yeah, course you did. You know I'm not a complete dunce, right? Start talking, Adie, or I'm going to find every rut in the road between here and Cairo." To emphasise her point, Siân sped over a particularly uneven stretch of ground.

After her previous experiences of Siân's driving, Adie figured she was better off capitulating now, rather than risking life and limb over something that was bound to spill out, eventually. Christ, maybe it'd even be a relief to tell someone. At least then, it would feel real, rather than some horror fantasy she'd concocted due to heat stroke.

"I blew Killian."

"You blew him!" Siân slapped the wheel and

roared with laughter. "Oh, that's a good one. As if... What really happened?"

She grimaced, drawing her teeth over the nick in her lower lip.

"Oh!" Siân sobered. "For real?" She spluttered an awkward chuckle. "Oh, that's... Wow! Dare I ask how and when?"

"Last night, after you all turned in."

"Was he drunk?"

"Siân!"

Her friend shrugged. "What you're describing doesn't sound like the icy professor I know, staying up after hours to break the newest team member in. So, obviously something chinked his armour, and alcohol does it for the best of us."

"Neither of us were drunk. He was in the workroom, and I just... I don't know. I guess I challenged him. He was still being pissy about the other day, suggesting that he might dismiss me, and I told him that wasn't fair. That we were all involved, but he wasn't being arsy with you and Matthew. And then... I...I don't know, Siân. It was like something snapped in him. And he was all hot and gruff, and 'Tell me to back off.'"

"Which of course you didn't."

Adie raised her hands in surrender. "I fancy him, okay. I admit that. It's a thing. He's hot. I guess I like grumpy professors. So, no, I didn't tell him to back off."

"You sucked him off instead."

That was about the gist of it. "It was fucking amazing while it happened."

"I'll bet."

They passed under the motorway heading north of the Aswan Western Agricultural road.

"I'm assuming, and correct me if I'm wrong, that it didn't result in you winding up tucked up beside him snug in his bed."

Adie winced and put on her sunglasses, heat already radiating off her cheeks. "Actually, he didn't even say thank you."

"Oh, God!" Siân chuckled to herself. "I'm sorry, Adie. I shouldn't laugh. He's being an—"

"Arsehole."

Siân wiped her eyes. "I was going to say ass, but arsehole works too."

"You warned me what he was like. I just don't want to spend the weekend on the houseboat with him, you know, trying not to bump into one another and such. At least if I'm in Cairo it puts some distance between us, and I can check out Jacob's journal." Also, hopefully by the time she returned she'd be able to look Killian in the eye without wanting to scream at him and demand a fucking apology for being a selfish twat.

"So, you can impress him?" Siân asked.

"No." She was done trying to do that. "Because I'm genuinely interested in the journal. It might have some useful clues."

"That you can impress him with."

Adie scowled. That wasn't the purpose at all.

"8th of June 1868," Siân mimicked. "Today I took that pharaoh's cock I hacked off the other day down to the auction house off the marketplace and sold it to a collector for a wodge of cash. Funny fella, totally into cocks. Apparently has an entire case of them in his house in Sussex. Greek ones, Roman ones, a couple of Persian ones too. He was thrilled to add an Egyptian to the mix. Apparently, he's after some Japanese cock next. We exchanged the names of a few contacts and wished one another luck. I promised to contact him first if any more appendages turned up."

~Ж~

Three hours later, after an Egyptian breakfast at the Ibis Cafe, Adie pushed her way through the crowded entrance hall of the Museum of Egyptian Antiquities. The place was packed with visitors so that hot sticky bodies pressed into her from all sides and filled the entrance hall. Towering colossal figures overlooked the crowd. Adie battled through their midst with her brand-new guidebook clutched firmly against her chest. Siân had warned her the place was a tourist trap and to stay clear of the main exhibits until late afternoon, but this was so much crazier than she'd imagined. There wasn't a clear bit of floor between her and the exit in any direction.

Jacob's journal was held in the museum library, but looking at the map in her guidebook, that was precisely where the crowd was converging. She tacked towards the stairs instead.

"Have you seen him already?" The potent scent of patchouli infused the warm air, heralding the arrival of a woman with heavily kohl-lined eyes.

"Um, him?" Adie ventured, digesting the woman's ankh earrings, and the profusion of bangles that stretched up her forearms and chimed with her movements.

"Dareth Sadler. You're not here to see him?" Her incredulity showed in the rounding of her eyes and the tenor of her voice. "Oh, God, he's so hot. I've been waiting an hour already. How can you be here and not know who he is?"

It seemed she'd unwittingly arrived during the visit of some film star or rock god. She didn't pay much heed to the worlds of cinema and music. "I'm here for the exhibits. I study Egyptology."

"Then you must know him. How could you not? Everyone does. You should pick up his books." She pointed towards the gift shop. "I've picked up all the new editions to get them signed. I hope they're not restricting us to one signature apiece. I go to all his events, and sometimes they do. That'll be such a—"

"Who did you say he was?"

"Dareth. Dareth Sadler. He's the most famous archaeologist in the world."

Adie did a double take at the crowd. An archaeologist was responsible for this throng of people? No way! Even Killian couldn't command this sort of excitement, and his name was whispered with awe in university faculties across the globe. If this Sadler bloke was the genuine article, she'd have heard of him.

"Here." The woman thrust a leaflet into her hands. "It's all about him."

Adie glanced over it. True to her guess, Dareth

Sadler was a populist writer and part time dilettante. "I'm not sure he's really my thing." She tried to give the leaflet back.

"You know, I think he probably would be if you'd give him a read, or better still, listen to him speak."

"Well, maybe once the crowd thins. I'm not a big people person."

"Oh, me too, me too." The woman insisted, patting the back of Adie's hand. "But I tell myself, sometimes you just have to put your big girl pants on, Nadine. We could hang together, if that would help."

"Um... I do have a couple of things I need to go and see." She pointed vaguely, oblivious to where any of the relevant exhibits lay.

"Right, for your job, I guess."

"That's right."

"Well, I tell you what. I'll just jot down my number here." She scrawled a phone number on the back of the leaflet. "Then when you're done, you can give me a call and I'll hang with you so that you can see Dareth."

"Oh-kay," Adie's toes curled in her boots. She inched back a step. "Yeah. I'll... We'll totally do that. I'll just get on." She scurried up the stairs, making no noises at anyone who looked like they meant to speak to her.

Adie, she imagined Josef saying. *Seriously, you lasted all of a week before being co-opted into a cult.*

The upper galleries were dotted with casements and statuary. Huge granite blocks, sycamore carvings, and alabaster figurines chipped by time. Skylights fed in light from above, and the stone floor echoed in a properly museum-like way. The crowd thinned significantly too. Adie started her tour with the animal mummies. The battered, dusty assortment of cats, birds, and jackals stared accusingly at her from their cases, prompting her to hurry on. She'd never managed to escape that childish notion that their preserved forms wouldn't suddenly burst into life again.

In room 45, the only ghosts were out of her own past. The ivory pieces of an ancient board game that reminded her of the draughts set Esther had owned, and hours spent leaping pieces over one another to capture them.

Maybe it'd been a mistake to come to Egypt. Like most things in life, reality couldn't match the adventures of her imagination, and now she had the additional awkwardness of facing Killian again to contend with. What was his problem, anyway?

Why did he have to behave like a prick, instead of a rational adult? What was so wrong about the two of them getting off together? He'd made it seem like he was offended by the fact she'd managed to unravel him.

She remembered his words too, though. The praise he'd lavished on her. Good girl, he'd said, and it'd filled her up from within, made her want to preen, and grin from ear to ear.

She'd always been a sucker for reward, everything from a sticker in primary school for acing her spellings, to the student of the year trophy at uni.

She'd liked being Joe Levine's prodigy, but she fancied being Killian's star scholar more. And yes, sure, maybe she was a fool for that considering he'd already proved what a dick he was, but it was what it was.

"Senet. The forerunner to backgammon. Do you play?" a masculine voice asked.

Startled from her thoughts, Adie turned to meet the speaker. He stood to her right, between the casement of playing pieces and a figurine of Anubis, dressed in a traditional long black cotton *galabeyya* embroidered with cross-stitch at the hem and cuffs. Long dark hair framed his startling handsome face. Was this the man everyone else was here to see? A lot of things would make sense if it was.

"Sadler's popularity must be waning. He'd be disappointed to know there was an attractive woman in the building who's never heard of him," he said, disabusing her of the notion that he was the star attraction. "I'm sorry, I couldn't help but overhear you talking to the woman downstairs."

"Are you his publicist?"

"I'd be a particularly bad one, considering he's the worst sort of fraud." He offered his hand, which Adie cautiously accepted. "Anton Kelley."

"Doctor Hamilton," she replied, not yet ready to offer up her forename. She couldn't quite figure if Anton was a local or a westerner who'd adopted an Egyptian guise, and his colouring wasn't enough to sway her opinion either way.

"I think we're probably the only two people in the building who aren't giddy to see him."

"Yeah, well, I'm more interested in the exhibits than some pop pseudo-archaeologist warbling on about things he's likely no qualifications in."

"I can't disagree. I wondered if you'd perhaps appreciate some company, a guide to—"

"No. Thank you." Evidently, she'd attracted the attention of a better-spoken, and rather better-looking version of the pushy tour guides that plagued Saqqara. "I'm all set." She waved her guidebook at him.

"With that?" he scoffed and pushed the guidebook gently aside. "It only covers a fraction of the exhibits. The grandiose and the gold, whereas I am familiar with the secrets tucked away in the corners. The things that only serious scholars care to hunt out."

"And which you'll happily show me if I'll only hand over an extortionate amount of cash," she retorted, anticipating the inevitable demand for baksheesh.

Anton's near black eyes narrowed. "I'm not a tour guide, Doctor Hamilton. I'm a fellow Egyptologist, and I was trying to be of help to a colleague. You're one of Dr Carmichael's crew, aren't you? But no matter, my mistake. I will make myself scarce." His loose clothing made a faint swish as he turned away from her.

Shit! The sting of his rebuke heated her cheeks.

"Wait. I'm sorry. I'm just overcautious, and sick of people trying to sell me things and services. It was kind of you to offer."

He turned his head to look back at her, and gave

a nod, as if her explanation were completely reasonable. "I shan't demand your coins in payment for my services, only your attention, and the pleasure of your company."

"Thank you," she conceded, still wary. On the other hand, providing they stayed within the museum, what harm could he genuinely do? Plus, it was true that the museum was vast, and alone, she'd likely wander about for the rest of the weekend without ever stumbling on its true riches.

It wouldn't hurt to be escorted about by a cinematically handsome man for a few hours either. It might even take some of the sting out of Killian's rejection.

"Are you a friend of Doctor Carmichael's?"

"Our paths haven't crossed in a while. We've been in different places. What can I show you?"

"Actually, I came because I wanted to get into the library, but there doesn't seem to be much hope of that happening today."

"Not unless you're eager to listen to a good dose of drivel. There are plenty of other things to see here though. Perhaps some items related to your current project?"

"Well, I'm based at Saqqara," she said, figuring the desert necropolis was extensive enough that didn't give too much away.

"The Early Dynasties collection is downstairs."

-20-
Adie

"Rahotep and Nofret," he said several hours later, as he encompassed the two seated figures with a sweeping gesture. "It's all about her nipples. You've got to love how perky they are."

"Perhaps she was cold while she was modelling," Adie suggested, admiring the exemplary piece's craftsmanship. The details of the limestone figures had been picked out with precise skill, the colours still bold and vibrant, and indeed, perkily rendered. Anton strode on past the ostentatious display to some dusty half-hidden cases in the corner. "Now these are interesting." The objects within were decorative but clearly functional objects. "They tell us much more about society than that pompous pair. Although, I bet he was playing with her tits beforehand to make sure her nipples stood out like that under her white dress."

"God, don't." Tears welled as she laughed. "Now I'm picturing it. And her groping him back."

"Them exchanging sly caresses while the sculptor sets up to do his drafts."

"Trailing her finger along his beautiful moustache."

Anton cocked a brow. "Odd thing to focus on. Like a bit of hair above a man's lips, do you?"

She shook her head, "Not especially. What's in this case? Are they some sort of weapon?" The cabinet was old, dark wood framed, and the glass clouded at the corners. The tiny labels were written in an indecipherable spidery script, on yellowed card, that looked as if they may have been in situ since the 1890s when the museum first opened.

"They're hunting boomerangs." His breath stirred the hairs on the back of her neck as he leaned in to look at them and raised an unexpected shiver of delight. That was followed by a bolt of lust a moment later, when the hem of his *galabeyya* brushed her calf. Adie's gaze shifted from the exhibit to Anton's reflection in the dark glass. He really was something to behold: enviable cheekbones, a high forehead, thick brows and dark, impossible long eyelashes that shadowed inky pupils.

Damn, the heat was getting to her. Had she drunk enough water today? First lusting after Killian, now entertaining lewd thoughts about a man she'd only known a few hours. She pictured running her finger along his upper lip, the taste of his mouth. Pushing him into the corner and bunching up his robe to find out what lay beneath. Traditional sirwal? Western shorts? Nothing at all?

She'd wager he wouldn't run off the moment they'd finished bumping genitals. Not that it'd got quite that far between her and Killian, and now never would. She had some measure of self-respect. Her boss owed her a fucking huge apology... and... and an orgasm. Two even, to make up for his transgressions.

But what if she just forgot about Killian altogether and concentrated her romantic leanings in another direction? What if she shuffled her fantasies of being his good girl off into a box and got on with being the independent adventurer both Esther and her father had encouraged her to be? She didn't need Killian's praise to be fulfilled, nor was it necessary to dwell in his shadow.

"Are you okay?" Anton asked. "You've gone strangely quiet."

"Thinking, that's all."

"About something you'd like to see?"

"Kind of."

"Intriguing. Something I can show you?"

"Something you probably shouldn't."

"Ooh, cryptic. Now I'm intrigued." He mulled the thought for a moment, fingers pattering against his jawline. "Let's see, could it be that you want to do something naughty with me?"

Oh, Satan! She heard thy herald's call.

"I never do anything naughty."

Anton's dark eyes twinkled. "Of course you don't." He grasped her hand. "Come with me."

She could have said no, but naturally she didn't. They zipped through a couple of chambers, and under a rope cordon, then through a staff only door onto a staircase. "Where are we going? Oh my God, you're going to get us into so much trouble. We can't be here."

He grinned broadly. There was a rumble of mirth in his throat as he spoke, "You're such a good girl, aren't you?"

If she was, she wouldn't be heading down an out-of-bounds staircase into the unknown with a virtual stranger.

Anton led her down, down, down, into a dingy storage area that stank of bleach and other cleaning products, none of which quite erased the underlying musty aroma of artefacts.

"What is this?"

"The best bit of the museum," he said evenly. "The bit every decent scholar's eyes light up over getting to see." He hurried her along, through racks of boxed up items, and Egyptian curios from the ancient to the modern. It was like the grandest of grand bazaars. The sort she'd dreamed of exploring in her adolescent adventures, chock full of magic lamps, and lucky scarabs. The sort of place where relics of long forgotten civilisations whispered their histories to you if you stopped long enough to listen. It was exactly the sort of place where one expected to stumble on the likes of Jacob's journey, or even a wayward mural fragment.

Was it possible it was in fact here, nestled among the flotsam of countless excavations? What if she looked?

Would Anton know where to start? She was weighing the possibility of discussing it with him and finding out versus Killian's wrath over her discussing the matter with someone outside of the team when the clip of approaching footsteps brought them to an abrupt halt.

"Shit!" Anton said under his breath. "It's normally deserted at his point in the day. This way." He tugged her into a parallel aisle, from which they slipped through the stacks, two shadows running on tiptoes, raising puffs of ancient dust as they passed, until they reached an area where the lights didn't blink on automatically at their approach, and thick shadows cloaked them in inky darkness.

The pair of chatting curators walked right past the damaged limestone statue they huddled behind. Adie screwed her eyes closed and prayed. The last thing she needed was to wind up being arrested. Killian would obliterate her like a nuclear winter. Thankfully, the two members of staff remained oblivious to their presence. One by one around them sections of lights dimmed.

The moment she was certain they'd left, she turned to Anton.

"What?" he said before a word left her mouth. He didn't look concerned. His heart didn't seem to be leaping about as if it were trying to escape.

"How much trouble will I get in for being down here?"

"Lighten up a little, eh? It's not as if we're stealing anything."

"Oh, you're a bad boy."

That made his grin broaden and poured dark mischief into his eyes. "Are you seriously only figuring that out now?"

"Are you sure you're a legitimate Egyptologist?"

He laughed. "Need to see my doctoral certificate? I can assure you it's authentic."

"Why have you brought me down here?"

"Because you wanted to come. If you didn't, you wouldn't have slipped under that rope when I lifted it."

That might be true, but that didn't mean he didn't have an ulterior motive.

Anton swept his tongue across his lower lip, wetting it. Unconsciously, she mirrored the action, only to feel the sting as she licked the cut in her own lower lip Killian had caused. Anton was looking at her with a barely constrained hunger in his eyes that suggested he'd really like to savage, not just her lips, but her whole body.

Adie's heart sped. Damn, she was tempted. Hadn't her imaginary adventures through Egypt always involved her getting the man? Just like Indy always got the girl. It didn't matter whether her companion for the excursion was a rugged mercenary or a bookish scholar, whose glasses constantly slipped down his nose, she always screwed them senseless. It was practically a requirement for the mission's success. So why not let herself live a little. Enjoy a quick and dirty fling. With any luck it would cure her of her ridiculous infatuation with her boss too. A boss who was frankly unworthy of the attention.

You didn't come to Egypt to be a side character in someone else's story, she lectured herself. It was time she started authoring this adventure the way she wanted it rather than letting others dictate her moves. Time she stopped waiting for permission and acted.

She raised a hand and slid it around the back of Anton's neck, prompting him to bend forwards. "No strings, right?"

"If that's the way you want it."

She rose on her toes to meet him, and their mouths collided in a hot, breathless kiss that within seconds had them rolling sideways against the shelving, clawing at one another's clothing as tongues warred in the battlefields of their mouths.

"You have condoms, right?"

"One kiss and she's already hankering for dessert."

"Just getting the paperwork in order before we begin," she muttered into the heaven of his mouth.

"We're set." He patted what she took to be an invisible pocket. "But maybe a more private spot might be better."

Anton lifted her, so that she was sat upon the waist-high display case. His lips hovered over the sensitive skin of her neck, breath buffeting the hollow of her collarbones as he settled between her legs.

"I'm curious to know what you've got on under here." She tugged at his *galabeyya*.

"I want to know if your nipples are as perky as Nofret's." He dragged a thumb over her left, which eagerly steepled in response. Then he lowered his mouth and sucked, causing her breath to catch in her throat and tingles to shoot from her breasts down to her pussy.

She hadn't quite acknowledged the depth of her frustration until that moment and her need set her clutching at his clothing. Anton was Killian's opposite in so many ways. Giving where her boss was resistant. Gentle where Killian had been rough. Adventurous, rather than restrained.

Adie bunched up Anton's *galqbeyya*, revealing loose trousers, easily unfastened and pushed aside. His cock was ready for her. It filled her hand with its velvet heat. The tip ripe and weeping opalescent pearls that she spread over his crown. He was circumcised. Markedly different from Killian in that way.

"You're not dressed for this," he remarked, tugging down the zip of her trousers. "Lift up."

Adie pressed her palms to the glass surface of the cabinet as he pulled off her trousers and panties. The cold press of the glass against her bum cheeks seemed to stoke the heat between her thighs. She rubbed her clit while watching him one-handedly roll a condom on.

"You should let me do that."

"Yeah. I mean, I wouldn't mind feeling your mouth there."

He closed the gap between them again. "And I wouldn't mind putting it there," he said right against her lips, before sinking down and eating her out in exactly the way she'd asked him to. He was good at it too, making her writhe against the glass, her fingers tightening and releasing around his long hair. "Fuck, yeah! Oh, God, that's good."

His tongue tickled her nub, stroked downward

into the wet avenue between her lips, then back up. It turned her burning insides to jelly, and set her panting, eager for more. She wished this didn't have to be so rushed. That she could savour him, take her time with him. Explore him properly, rather than making do with a few stolen moments.

They probably wouldn't see one another again, right? And she'd confirmed it was no strings before they kissed. Shame, because the man had a way with his tongue. One that was going to get her there all too soon if he kept it up.

He did. And he didn't. Turned out, he was a monster, purposefully driving her right to the edge, then holding her there, until she was a trembling wreck, the muscles in her thighs jumping around and making her kick and her throat hoarse from moaning.

When he rose to kiss her, mouth shiny from her arousal, she grasped tight his *galabeyya* and wriggled forward to the edge of the countertop. "Fuck me." She hooked her legs around his waist, opening herself to receive him.

"If that's your wish, this desert genie is very happy to oblige."

She clawed at his shoulders, as he joined them, then fluttered her inner muscles around him, making him groan equally loudly. Anton steadied himself, then bent at the waist and lowered her back to the glass. He fucked her slowly to begin with, sucking her nipples as he did so, through her clothing at first, before wrestling up her bra to suck her bare.

"Like things a little rough, do you?" he asked, when she groaned in response to his pinches. "

"You're as gentle as a snowflake."

"That right?" He stretched to reach an object off a nearby shelf. Adie whined as the cold press of a large bottle settled against her mons. Its liquid contents sloshed in time with their thrusts as he rubbed the thick neck against her clit. The weird fusion of cold glass and hot cock made Adie tear at her hair and surroundings.

"Yeah, okay, hot stuff, got it, you've got some moves."

"Oh, more than a few."

He upped the pace, and Adie surrendered to the rhythm of their slapping flesh. Everything about this was naughty, and would no doubt land her in trouble, but she didn't care and wouldn't regret this. Rather, she revelled in it. Just because Killian wanted her to be a paragon of virtue and professionalism, didn't mean she had to live according to his wishes. She didn't owe him anything.

This was her adventure.

And he'd fucked up.

"More," she demanded.

He gave. And he gave. He was everything Killian wasn't. Willing. Eager. Not a whisper of corded restraint. He fucked like the only thing that mattered was making them both feel fucking fantastic. And it did feel fucking fantastic. Really fucking insane.

She turned her head to press one flaming cheek to the cool glass surface beneath her and her heart instantly leapt into her throat, "Mummy," she gasped, her tongue catching up with her brain as the nature of the cabinet she was spread across became apparent. "Fuck!" She crunched into a sitting position and flung herself against Anton's firm body. His prick flexed eagerly in response to the sudden motion.

"Easy there, honey. It's okay, it's not coming for you."

Not coming! "Anton, it's a fucking mummy. We're doing it on top of a goddamned corpse." Staring up at them from its eternal rest were the partially unwrapped remains of a man. Its teeth and the bridge of its nose poking through the crumbling bandages.

"Yeah." He dug his fingers into her bum, until she eased her grip on his shoulders, but never stopped the rolling of his hips.

"You knew!"

"Course I knew. I'm facing it." He leant into her, slid deeper, lighting all the right nerves, and reminding her exactly how turned on she was. "You're not really creeped out, are you now?"

"You don't think it's a bit weird?"

"Not really, we're in the bowels of the Egyptian Museum. It's where lots of mummies hang out. Frankly, it's a miracle there's only one dead fellow observing us."

"Yeah, but..."

He huffed a laugh, "Never before shagged someone amongst the artefacts and you call yourself a serious Egyptologist."

"That's not the usual definition. Pretty sure the aim is to study them, not the other way around."

"He's dead, honey. Pretty sure he's not studying anything. I'm guessing you're not into the idea of being watched?"

She didn't know about that. Perhaps. In certain circumstances. It certainly wasn't hard to imagine. In fact, the fantasy of her spread out for Anton's enjoyment while a shadowy figure—suited, refined, white-haired, watched, was all too easy to conjure. Damn, if the notion of having them both focused on her didn't light her up like a Christmas tree.

"Not yet." Anton smacked her across the thigh as she teetered on the verge of coming. He pulled out and flipped her over, pressing her face down against the glass, so there was no hiding from their observer. "Not yet, Adie." He pushed back into her, then hitched her legs up off the floor, leaving her precariously balanced as if in flight.

Adie closed her eyes, but a sort of morbid fascination soon prompted her to open them again. Anton got his hand beneath her so the heel of it dug into the base of her belly, as his fingers worked their magic on her clit. Her senses flared, and this time there was no stopping it, she came with a cry, while a three-thousand-year-old mummy stared her in the face.

He chased her to completion a couple of thrusts later, reaching his release with a nameless cry.

Adie lay flat against the case once they were done, catching her breath while Anton cleaned up. He helped her back into her knickers and other clothing, before combing the tangles from her hair with his fingers.

"Should we take a bow before we exit?" He cast a nod at their silent spectator. "It was a royal performance."

"Royal?"

"This is Seti I. They must be doing some work on him."

"Yeah." She held a finger up, squeamish again after the fact. "We didn't need to do introductions."

Anton tugged her against his body and smooched a kiss across the side of her face. "Have you really not indulged in any sneaky shags out at Saqqara yet?"

She wasn't sure what that had to do with Seti I. She guessed Saqqara was one huge necropolis, but any mummies there were buried deep beneath the sands, not leering from the other side of a pane of glass. "No, of course not. If you know anything about Dr Carmichael, you'll know he's a stickler for discipline and proper procedure."

"That right?" The way he cocked a brow as he said it made it seem less of a question and more of a refutation.

"How well did you say you knew him?"

Anton shrugged, then took his sleeve to the glass to remove the bum print she'd left behind. "It's been awhile since we've spoken. Can I take you to dinner?"

"Oh, um..." That was unexpected. She'd half suspected he'd dash off. "What about lunch for now? That's assuming you can get us out of here without getting us arrested?"

"Follow me. I know the perfect route."

He led her into a corner of the basement, thence into another stairwell. Adie stalled him on the bottom step. "Were you serious about having dinner?"

"Surprised that I want to see you again?"

"A little," she admitted.

"It's been fun, Adie. I think we could have more fun together you and me, in a whole variety of ways and positions."

Okay, so it wasn't about being friends. They were talking future hook ups. What was it Esther used to say? All work and no play dulls the mind but broadens the behind. "Okay, sure." They exchanged numbers over coffee in the cafe. The queues of women waiting to see Dareth Sadler had hardly thinned.

"Who the heck is this dude?" Adie asked.

Anton swept his long hair back off his shoulders. "Everything you imagine him to be. A hack. A peddler of pseudo-scientific sorcery. A lary middle-aged git with a god complex. The miracle is that people buy into it."

"Maybe they just want something to believe in."

Anton speared an olive with a pick. "Maybe. But I could wish them to be more discerning about whose narrative they buy into. There's plenty of wonder and inspiration to be found in the world without having to resort to phoney theories fed to you by a wannabe cult leader willing to bend folklore and fact to fit his narrative and to hell with the consequences."

She was beginning to wish she hadn't asked given the vitriol he ploughed into his response.

"If he's such a fraud, how come he's signing books in the Museum of Egyptian Antiquities?" A woman on the next table asked. Her four companions turned and shot dagger-filled glares in their direction.

"Because he gave some official a walloping backhander." He forced his chair back with a loud scrape and stood. "But by all means, worship him like a god, hand him your cash, and drool over his feet. I'm sure it'll guarantee you an elevated position in the afterlife."

The woman bowed her head, momentarily cowed, though she took to grumbling under her breath, while her friends gawped over his rudeness. Adie wrapped her arm around Anton's and guided him from the restaurant. "Let's not cause a scene, eh?"

"Sure." He threw off his ire. "Let me help you secure a taxi."

-21-

Killian

"You're up late." Lucas peered at Killian over the top of his glasses. Killian's second in command was lazing in a deck chair sipping something lurid through a straw. "It's guava juice, did you want some?"

He shook his head. Juice wasn't going to cure his sore head. The only thing capable of that was a sodding genie bursting out of a lamp and reorganising time and space.

"Matthew's gone to the gym. The ladies must have taken off before dawn. They'd left by the time I rose," Lucas said, as if Killian standing there obviously required him to provide a rundown of the whereabouts of the entire team, exactly as if this were a workday.

Having barely slept, Killian knew exactly what time Siân and Adie had slipped ashore. He'd been staring at the ceiling at the time, wondering if he ought to be making a ritual sacrifice to some god or other, so they'd stop shitting on him so much, but unable to motivate himself to make the necessary movements to rise.

Late night thoughts. He knew perfectly well the only gods that mattered were the ones in charge of the excavation purse strings, and they didn't give a hoot about his reputation or who he fucked, providing he found the goods. Just as well really, because his name was going to be dirt, again, if the fact he was fooling around with one of his underlings got out.

He might be Mr Archaeology these days, but the trouble with dirt in the internet age was that no amount of scrubbing ever truly got rid of all the specks.

"Rough night?" Lucas asked, glass poised to take another sip.

Killian shrugged and reached for the coffee pot. He wasn't in a sharing mood, and Lucas, at least, had the sense to button it when that was blinking obvious. Siân would have hounded him with questions. He poured and took refuge in the bowl of the oversized mug.

Coffee, one of life's few perks. His brows eased a fraction as the caffeine hit his bloodstream.

"Rumour has it a certain person is in town."

Okay, take that back. The fool had no sense at all. Couldn't he see there was a ritual going on? "Which person would that be?"

"Oh, you know, your arch-nemesis..." Lucas lifted a magazine off the chair situated to his left and spread it open across the table revealing a picture of the one person in the world who Killian would have no trouble punching until he was reduced to a bloody smear. "Dareth Sadler."

His arch-nemesis. Pur-lease! It was impossible to keep the scorn from bleeding into his expression. "As if anything that fool does is in any way relevant to me."

"I just said he's back in town."

"By town do you mean he's in Cairo? Along with the other twenty-two and a half million people. How is that relevant to my day?"

"I just thought you might…"

Killian's glare silenced him before he finished the sentence. No, he did not want or need to know. He already knew. Had already clocked him eyeballing the dig site from a distance. He could smell that particular rat from a mile off.

Lucas swallowed the rest of his juice, then stood. "I'm going to head over to Saqqara."

"Why? We're not digging today."

The blond man already had his back to Killian, heading along the deck in his sports socks and sandals combo.

"Said I'd give Mark a hand with a couple more things. It's on my time. I assume that's not a problem. Means you'll have the boat to yourself for a bit."

That would be a welcome novelty. Though, he wasn't thrilled to hear Lucas was dedicating his weekend to helping Mark Leyham. In his experience, any sort of schmoozing of that ilk was down to one of two things. Either they were shagging, or Leyham was looking to poach his crew, and that was an inconvenience he really didn't need.

"I'll be back around six."

A full day of schmoozing, Jeezus wept! It sure did sound like they were sucking one another's dicks. He took another gulp of coffee and failed to unknot the furrow in his brow. He was going to have to pray that Adie hadn't decided he was such a monumental prick that she'd had Siân drive her to the airport. If that was the case, he could expect an irate call from Josef Levine later, and absolutely zero help with recruiting two potential replacements.

Would she bail?

He clutched the back of the chair Lucas had vacated. Probably not. She wasn't the type. She was too eager, too starry-eyed and obsessed with the notion of finding the next Tutankhamun-esque treasure hoard to let the fact she'd sucked her boss's dick and not received any reciprocity get in the way of her adventure.

Sucked it beautifully too. Gone for it with exactly the right degree of zeal. He closed his eyes, and his nerve endings awakened at the recollection of her breath against his bare skin.

His fingers curled, clutching the chair back, in precisely the way he'd clung to her hair last night. Immediately, his cock began to stiffen.

Don't think about it, you fool!

You behaved abominably. This isn't a memory you should be getting frisky over.

Curiously enough, telling himself not to obsess over it had precisely the opposite effect. Ergo, not five minutes later he was in the workroom, staring at the trays of mural fragments, lost in the memory of Adie perched amidst them like a holographic overlay.

"Is there anything you'd like me to do for you, professor?"

"Well, there's this very large plaster jigsaw puzzle that needs piecing together."

"Yes, of course." She flashed him an enormous grin, then hopped off the table she'd been perched on and about turned. She bent to order the pieces, so that her curvy bottom stuck out towards him and her very short shorts rode up revealing the edge of her panties.

For fuck's sake. He was a grown man. The sight of a sliver of white cotton and the seam of her shorts pressing against her pussy shouldn't make his pulse race or cause a needy groan to rumble around his chest. And it definitely had no business causing his cock to thicken into a state that would slide perfectly into the groove those two bits of fabric were so inadequately covering.

Shouldn't didn't seem to have much to do with it. Fact was, he'd been torturing himself like this since the moment he'd run out on her. Churning thoughts of what it would feel like to slide into the silken heat of her pussy and what sounds she'd make as a result.

All night...in endless circles. His hand fisting around his cock. His wrist working him into frustrated agony, only for him to think better of himself before he reached climax.

Instead, he'd halted, and lain there riddled with remorse, while frustration burned through his nerve endings.

He wound up in exactly the same loop again now. Stroke, and retreat. Stroke and retreat.

Edging could be fun and all, but this was like lighting dynamite and then pinching out the fuse right before it blew. In short, it was only ever going to end in tragedy.

Or rather, with him being tragic.

Killian hauled off his T-shirt and came into the cotton of it. Then he huffily went and found something clean to wear.

KC: Where've you taken her?

He texted Siân three hours and another clean shirt later.

She let him stew for forty minutes before replying.

SIÂN: The museum, because despite the fact you pulled a monumental dick move, she still wants to be the good girl that impresses her professor.

KC: She said that?

SIÂN: Of course she didn't say that. It was a dick move, though. And she is at the museum.

SIÂN: Why? Are you going to come chase after her?

KC: I'm taking the boat downriver a bit. Tell the others. I'll be back at the usual mooring by six ish.

If he was sailing, then he didn't have time to think about Adie, or Sadler, or whatever other nightmares might be heading his way. Three hours wouldn't get him far. The usual Nile cruises took twelve days to travel from Cairo to Luxor, but it would get him to a section of the river with a myriad of inlets that he particularly loved. The verdant greenery was always a welcome sight after the unending plains of sand he was surrounded by most of the week.

SIÂN: No plans to come back tonight, so feel free to hide among the reeds as long as you like.

Lucas and Matthew would likely have something to say about that if he did.

KC: Back 6ish.

-22-
Adie

Siân was waiting for her on the gravel outside the Gezira apartment when Adie arrived. "Quick change." She hustled her indoors and through to the twin bedroom Adie had used her first night in Egypt. "I thought you'd be back hours ago. I agreed we'd meet Samīh and Jason for dinner. Their treat. We're due to meet them in twenty minutes."

"What? Siân, I need a shower." She could smell Anton on her, even if Siân couldn't. Not to mention she'd been traipsing around all day in the heat. "Why didn't you call me and let me know the arrangements?"

"Didn't think of it." Siân offered her a shrug. "What? I didn't think you'd be this long. I mean, I know the place is full of exciting artefacts, but... You know what, never mind. Just get changed and spritz some perfume, or something."

"Uh, yeah, and no, and excuse me." Adie pushed Siân out of the bathroom, where she'd just followed her. "I don't need an audience. I'll be two minutes. Promise."

It took five, but that included drying time. Siân

was sitting on the bed, Adie's phone in her hand when she emerged. "Uh, excuse me? Are you spying on me?"

"Who's AK?"

Adie took the phone from her and shut it down. "An acquaintance. Not that it's any of your business."

"You don't have any acquaintances here, other than the team."

"Invasion of privacy, Siân. How did you even unlock the screen?"

Her friend shrugged. "So, what's he like? You met him today, right? Rebounded right off Killian straight into his path."

"Shut up!" she huffed and pulled on some clean underwear. "That's not—" Okay, it was totally what had happened. "It's not serious..."

"Hm, I'd hope not after one afternoon." Siân waggled her fingers in a come hither way. "Spill."

"He's hot, okay. Really fucking handsome and hot. And he's not an icy fucking dildo."

"Did you just call our boss a dildo?"

Adie screwed up her face.

"It's fine. He is one, at least in the context of this scenario. I'm just amused you said it. Go on, you were telling me how nice, AK is."

"He's more naughty than nice."

"Ooh," Siân crowed. She flashed Adie a sunshiny grin. "So, genuine competition."

"There's no competition. Killian can go fuck himself."

Siân raised her hands. "Amen to that, sister.

Glad to hear the message is finally getting through."

Right. "I need something to wear. Can I borrow something?" She'd only brought a single suitcase of stuff with her to Egypt, and most of that was on the houseboat and consisted of work clothes.

Siân turned her towards the closet. "Rummage to your heart's content, hun. Meanwhile, tell me the name of this paragon of sexy fun and deliciousness who's stolen your heart. I'm curious to know more."

"My heart is still firmly in my chest, and there's nothing much to tell." She found a shift dress and a pair of wide-legged trousers to pair it with. "His name's Anton Kelley. He's working in the Valley of the Golden Mummies. Do you know him?"

Siân shook her head. "Nope." She scrunched up her nose.

"Not good?" Adie asked of her outfit.

"Nah, babe, you look great. I was just thinking, Kelley. I think I might have heard the name before. Don't think we've met though."

"You've probably read a paper by him."

Siân considered a moment. "Yeah, that's likely it. Small world. You set now? Cool, because babe, we are late and need to hustle."

~Ж~

They escaped from the overcrowded bus into the benzene-choked air at the Midan Tahrir. The early evening traffic raced around them, buses and cars competing with donkey carts for lane space. Adie's nostrils flared at the greasy smell of burgers and the cloying aroma of spilled tomato ketchup.

"Fast food avenue," Siân said, pointing out the line of take-aways facing the university buildings. They followed a group of students into the interior of the Aly Baba Cafeteria and found Samīh and Jason by the window on the first floor.

"Ladies." Samīh rose and bowed in mock salute. "We were beginning to think we'd been stood up. What took you so long?"

Siân dismissed the question with an eloquent shrug of her shoulders, then stole a mouthful of Jason's beer.

"I'll get a round," he said.

Four tall glasses of icy Stella soon arrived at the table. Adie took a long draught and propped her elbows on the scuffed wooden table. "Needed that, did you? Boss working you too hard?"

Siân gave a snort. "According to Adie, the boss isn't working her hard enough. She went to the museum to look for Jacob's journal."

Samīh dragged a hand through his close-cropped hair. "Shit timing. I've heard it's been a bad day. Enormous crowds for some signing or something."

"Yeah." She sighed into her glass. "Didn't get to see it." She wasn't even too peeved about it, not considering she'd spent the hours in Anton's company. "Some dude by the name of Sadler. The whole place was heaving with fangirls."

"No sign of the missing piece of mural in our pyramid, then?" Jason asked.

There was a collective shaking of heads. They all

knew that was highly unlikely.

"Not so far." Siân picked up someone's discarded newspaper and began to flick through the pages. "Lucas reckons that Jacob sold it to some collector to use as a paperweight."

"What does Killian think?"

"Duh! Dumb question. He doesn't. Leastways, if he does, he'll never admit it." Siân shot a sly glance at Adie, then returned to the paper. "Wannabes," she added a moment later, tapping her finger to the print. "You've gotta love 'em." Adie leant in to look at the blurred photo she was pointing at. Three enthusiastic amateurs had been captured posing before the Great Pyramid, holding a banner emblazoned with a grey-skinned alien.

Samīh scratched his brow. "I reckon it's in that damn museum." They all turned to stare at him, prompting Samīh to self-consciously scratch his head. "I'm just saying. How many boxes of stuff do they have stashed away? And the place isn't exactly organised. You'll back me on this right, Adie? You were there today. It's a shambles. Leastways, a lot of it is. If they went through all the stuff they've got properly, they'd probably find most of the missing treasures of the art world. And I know they've been working hard to improve things, but still..."

"That's true," Jason agreed along with Adie. After the tour Anton had given her, she'd realised the place held enough material to furnish five massive museums, and the storerooms, had been eye-opening in more ways than one. Colour flooded into her cheeks as she recalled her earlier brush with a stray exhibit.

"Isn't there any way to find out? Don't they have a reference catalogue?"

That notion was met with a succession of derisive snorts, and Jason shaking his head so hard he was in danger of it wobbling clean off his shoulders. "You must have realised after today that labelling isn't exactly the museum's strong point. Their catalogue is hopelessly out of date and missing most of their inventory. Believe me, it's a miracle they keep tabs on anything, let alone expecting them to know the potential whereabouts of a bit of plaster with a hand and a willy on it. You've more chance of finding the Ark of the Covenant in there."

"Or Menkare's Sarcophagus," Samīh suggested.

"Nah, I'm pretty sure that's at the bottom of the ocean," Siân said.

"But is it? Isn't that just the point we're making? Just because it allegedly went down with a ship on the way to England doesn't mean it actually did."

Adie frowned. "Someone must know." Anton had seemed familiar with the layout. She ought to have asked him. Could text him. Killian was probably being OTT about the risks of spilling details of the dig outside of the team. Besides, sometimes you had to weigh up risks versus potential rewards. He'd forgive her if it led her to making a find, right?

-23-
Adie

Monday rolled around all too quickly. Despite having returned to the museum the following day, Adie still hadn't seen Jacob's journal. Apparently, it was missing, temporarily misplaced during a recent audit. She wasn't convinced, but the museum official that she spoke to became rather aggressive when she persisted in her questions, so she gave up before he had her removed.

Killian continued to avoid her. He'd kept to his cabin on Sunday night after she and Siân returned from Cairo. Then, Lucas had come to her first thing with the news that she'd be working in the magazines with him and Matthew going forward. It wasn't fair, but there seemed little point in protesting. At least she wasn't on a flight home to England.

The hours passed slowly in the depths of the magazines. They'd unearthed an additional chamber since Killian had first given her a tour of them, but there wasn't space for more than two people to work in there together, so while Lucas and Matthew concentrated their efforts in one chamber, she was on her own in another.

It was late afternoon when the sound of raised voices echoed along the passageway and reached her corner of the excavation. "What's happening?" she called to Matthew, as he passed the entrance to her chamber. The echo made it hard to pick out individual voices, but she swore one of them was Killian's.

"I'm not sure, but it sounds serious. I'm going to head up and see. He's been acting weird all weekend."

She guessed Siân hadn't shared the details of how Adie had managed to upset him. Honestly, one blowjob shouldn't have caused this much angst.

"I'll come too." She dropped her tools into her hard hat and wriggled out of the corner she was wedged into, relieved to straighten up for a bit. The blood returning to her legs created pins and needles so that she tottered after Matthew wincing over the tingles. The closer they got to the entry, the more obvious it became that it was Killian doing the shouting. He sounded furious.

Adie caught up to Matthew at the base of the stairs, where he'd stilled. "Changed your mind?"

He apprehensively bit his lip. "I know better than to walk straight into the firing line. Are you sure you want to do that?"

She wasn't, not since their boss was already tearing his hair out over her. On the other hand... "Might he not appreciate some back-up?" Besides, she wanted to know what had him so riled. Raising his voice wasn't usually his thing. Killian was generally forceful, but softly spoken. He had a knack of getting his point across without the need to shout, purely based on his use of inflection.

Matthew shook his head at her as she squeezed past him. "I highly doubt it, sugar-plum."

She liked Matthew, but he was a bit of a wimp, especially regarding confrontation. He dealt with things by nodding and smiling, and saved his grouching for when Killian was out of earshot. "Don't worry," She ruffled his hair, sending a shower of dust into his eyes. "If I can't handle it, I'll come straight back and hide behind you."

From halfway up the stairs, she spotted Killian's tense frame silhouetted against the blue of the desert sky. When his voice dropped to a dangerous whisper, and then he lurched forward. While she didn't see the collision, she certainly heard it. The smack of his fist hitting flesh and bone knocked her heart out of her chest and into her throat. The heftier thump of a body hitting the sand translocated her stomach to her feet.

What the hell?

She took the remaining steps two at a time. "Killian!" She presented herself at his side and looked down at the flattened, unfamiliar figure. He just looked like an everyday Joe. A tourist, with an admittedly expensive camera, and a now reddened eyeball, who blinked up at her uncertainly. Killian didn't take his gaze off him for a second, not even to acknowledge her. Instead, he grabbed the camera and began deleting images while muttering to himself, or the guy, she wasn't quite sure, her limited

Arabic failing to keep up with the swiftness of his dialogue.

Eventually, apparently content with his destruction, Killian dropped the camera into the sand by the terrified guy's side.

What the fuck?

"Get the hell out of here, and do not disturb my dig again."

The man snatched up his possessions and made a hasty retreat. "Sorry," she mouthed at his retreating figure, before turning to Killian, so many questions in her head, they were jostling for position. "What was that all about?" She pursued him back into the tomb's interior. "He was just a tourist, wasn't he? What did he do that was so bad?"

Killian turned sharply, blocking her descent. "He was not a tourist. What he is, is trouble. A journalist hired specifically for the purpose of making it. It seems word has got out that we're here."

The coldness of his gaze caused her to back pace. "I'm not responsible for that, if that's what you think."

"Did I say that?"

He hadn't, but it was reasonable to assume he'd been about to. He was certainly ready to blame her for most mishaps.

"Why aren't you at your post?"

Damn, he was infuriating. She was really starting to loathe the fact that her heart sped just at the sight of him. One man shouldn't be able to upset her equilibrium so much. It wasn't as if he was even the best option available. She had Anton's number sitting like a nuclear armament code on her phone, and she knew he could explode her world.

"I was looking out for a colleague, making sure they didn't require assistance, as I'd heard shouting, in the same way I'd hope they'd look out for me."

His expression softened a little around the mouth. "Okay. Thank you. Well, everything's fine, so you can get back to work."

That was it? No explanation, just a stilted thank you that felt like a chastisement. She dutifully trooped down the steps behind him, but inwardly her vexation grew. Matthew had already slipped back into the depths of the tomb, so the mural room stood empty. Killian bent to lower himself into the pit.

"Wait. We should talk," she said. One of them ought to be a grown-up about what had happened on Friday evening.

"About what? If you're about to advocate for you working down here alongside me again, forget it. I've already given you my reasons. Nothing's changed."

Most of those reasons were bullshit, and everything had changed, and besides, that wasn't what she'd meant, and he knew it.

"Prick," she muttered as he knelt to enter the tunnel.

His head whipped around. "Watch your tongue, Doctor Hamilton." His steely gaze landed like a lance blow.

"You know, I don't think I will. I've done nothing to deserve your ire. You're the one who's acting weird. You're the one who initiated whatever the hell the other night was. I'm not going to apologise for that or pretend it didn't happen. It happened, Killian. What's more, you wanted it."

He blinked, so that his eyes closed for a fraction too long. Long enough to let her know that her words had both smarted and sunk in. His lips puckered into a scowl too, but he nodded. "I'll admit, that wasn't my finest hour."

"No kidding." She sighed and swung her legs over the lip of the pit, before rubbing at the building tension around her eyes.

"Adie," he said uneasily. "What are you doing?"

"Talking to you," she said. "On a level. It's weird staring down at you kneeling in a pit."

"I should imagine you'd like to bury me in one."

She snorted, surprised by his humour. Sometimes, it was hard to credit him with emotions. Then again, dry, self-deprecating humour did fit his personality.

He got to his feet again as she lowered herself into the pit. It wasn't large, so they wound up with no more than a foot between them.

"I don't know what to think. One minute you're burning inferno-hot and so fucking into it, then the next you're shirty as hell and making me feel like dirt. Then you're Captain Avoidance... Then you're punching people..."

"That has nothing to do with us."

"I met someone at the weekend," she said. Honesty was hard-wired into her. "I like him. He was cool. We got on well. He doesn't confuse the hell out me." Telling him wasn't just about openness, it was a test of sorts too, she guessed.

Killian crossed his arms, and he seemed to be sucking over that knowledge. "I'm glad for you," he said at last.

"Glad?"

"Yes."

"Sorry, what?"

He sighed and swept a hand back through his white hair. "I'm glad you've met someone you like. Look, Adie, the other night shouldn't have happened. It was a..." His tongue swept over his teeth as if to remove an unpleasant taste. "It was a mistake. I'm sorry for my part in it. It won't happen again. So it's best you forget it ever happened."

"Okay." That wasn't the reaction she'd hoped for, but at least it was something. At least he was acknowledging that it had happened. On the other hand, she didn't much like how eager he was to write the idea of them off and pair her up with some random stranger.

The sensible part of her recognised that he was building barriers and giving her an out. The rebellious part, meanwhile, insisted on putting up a fight. It hated hearing the word can't. *It's not possible, Adie. You can't do that, Adie. This thing... that thing... they're not for you, Adie. Stop dreaming, Adie. Work hard, keep your head down. Don't rock the boat, Adie.*

"I suppose what that amounts to is a reason to ban me from working on the interesting parts of this dig."

"All of it's interesting, and all of it is valuable."

"Sure, but I still want to work in the tunnels."

"Adie... That's just not... It won't work. Frankly, my temper is frayed as it is. I can rely on Siân to do her job and not have to supervise her. With you, there'd be endless contact. I don't think us working in constant proximity is a good plan."

"Frightened I'm going to jump your bones?"

He didn't answer, just flicked his tongue back and forth over his incisors. What was going through his head? Memories of Friday night. His husky praise. His hand on the back of her neck. The feel of her lips around him?

She took a step towards him, and he stumbled over his feet to retreat.

"Don't, Adie." He raised a hand to keep her at arm's length. "Please, just let this go. Get to know this man you've met. He's probably far more worthy of your time, and far less of a prick."

That was a point they could agree on. Pity then that she still got prickles when she looked at him. That when she met his pale eyes her insides melted, and her heart sped. Too bad she could too easily recall the taste of his lips, feel the rough and demanding heat of his kiss, the grip of his fingers on the back of her head, and the smooth velvet heat of his cock in her mouth.

"You have to stop looking at me like that."

"No," she said. "I don't. It's not my fault if you can't control yourself, and I don't deserve to be punished because you're afraid that if you let me in those tunnels with you that your cock will end up in my mouth again."

-24-
Killian

She was right. And that smarted. Killian liked to think he had some control over his emotions.

Good Lord, he'd kept himself in check for years. Learned to rein in his instincts, smother all the shitty urges that had got him into trouble in the past. He'd lost too much. Fought too hard to claw back his reputation to risk it all again over a relationship that would burn hot, and likely enough burn out, before the season ended.

Besides, he didn't need the distraction. He'd seen the papers over the weekend. The two-page spread in the Middle East Times about the signing at the Museum. Coming back to Saqqara was supposed to lay the ghosts of his past to rest, not resurrect them. But here he was, two days later, having just punched Sadler's hired paparazzo.

He'd known looking at Adie, that if he ventured down that robber's tunnel, she'd have pursued him no matter what he said. She was so full of questions. Too eager to prove her worth and for his praise. And he... he was too emotionally volatile at present to be anywhere near her.

So, he'd left the dig. He'd suffered through an ice-cold shower, and then buried himself in paperwork that no one, least of all him, gave a shit about.

Five hours later, he still wasn't remotely calm. Moreover, he'd started wondering who the heck this man was that she'd met. Whether it was someone genuinely interested in her, or someone just using her for information. He didn't put anything past Sadler. The depths that devil would sink to were unprecedented.

Killian didn't join the rest of the team for dinner, or the usual daily debrief, letting Lucas handle it instead. In fact, he didn't venture out of his cabin until he was sure they'd all retired for the night. Only then did he scoff a few leftovers. He wound up sitting in the dark on a deckchair staring across the water.

Insects fluttered around the deck lanterns, and now and then, he'd hear birds fishing among the reeds.

It was well after midnight when Siân sank into the chair next to his.

Siân had a knack for getting him to talk. She did it by maintaining silence, the sort of silence that became so uncomfortable, it made him want to fill it.

"I suppose she's told you what happened?"

Several large moths had joined the aphids fluttering around the lights. One of them singed its wings and flopped onto the deck.

"Clearly you're regretting it."

"It's a complication I can certainly live without."

"What's so fucking wrong with fancying her, Killian? You like her. She likes you. You're both grown adults. If you want to do fun sexy things with one another, then it's your business and has no bearing on anything else."

Not true. He'd never truly mastered the art of severing his emotions from the rest of his psyche. He'd just got really good at avoiding situations that were likely to cause a flare.

He could mention the fact that he was Adie's boss, that he was too fucking old for her, but he knew neither argument would wash, so he stuck with his usual line. "I don't have time for a relationship, Siân. There's too much else going on."

"Sadler," she said, and let the name hang in the air.

That was a conversation he really didn't want to have. Adie was a way safer topic, and he wanted to discuss that about as much as he fancied a dose of dysentery.

Siân tucked her legs beneath her as she turned to face him, so she wound up sitting side-on in her chair. "I've read the book, you know. The original one, not all his subsequent cash-ins. It did the rounds while I was at university. Utter drivel, of course, but fun drivel. It was all anybody talked about that term. People thought I was crazy when I first applied to work with you. Now they're a deep shade of green."

"I was young, and an idiot," he admitted.

"Yet you're still punishing yourself. We all do shitty things when we're young. Making mistakes is how we learn."

"The book was only the surface of what went on," he elaborated, and it tore a wound open in his chest to admit even that much.

"Careful," she warned, stroking her hand down the length of her long plait. "You'll pique my interest."

He contemplated making a pithy reply, but what would be the point? If she wanted to dig, she would. Siân always did as she pleased, quietly, without making a fuss about it in the way Adie did. She'd listen, then disregard anything he said that didn't align with her core beliefs. He'd always respected her for that. Truthfully, he'd built a team of closet mavericks. Adie only broke the mould because she hadn't learned how to mask her worst traits yet.

"I always wondered how the hell you ended up involved with a guy like that."

Killian shook his head. "I was an open book back then."

"That's pretty hard to believe."

It didn't matter what she believed.

"What happened, Killian? I don't mean the stuff I know. The stuff any fool can look up and deduce if they're inclined to. I mean—"

He crossed his arms, already defensive. Then he rose. "I know what you mean. What happened doesn't matter. It was a long time ago. It's late, Siân. I'm going to bed. You should too."

She rose and called after him as he trudged along the deck. "Someone broke your heart."

He put his head to the wood of his cabin door before opening it. She wasn't wrong, but she wasn't right either. Nobody else was responsible for what he'd suffered through. Only him. He'd broken his heart. Everything that had happened was down to him. He'd taken a scorched earth approach to the situation and blown everything up. Everything. It was only after the dust settled that he'd realised exactly what he'd sacrificed to save face. Namely, everything he'd given a remote damn about. He left the light off in his cabin and folded himself on to the bed with his clothes on as memories assaulted him.

Dark hair and dark eyes. A smile that could paint rainbows across a rain-drenched street. Sex, sweaty and grimy, the sort that left you grinning so much your face ached all day. An arm around him in the dark. The heat of another body cocooned against him. Shared dreams and plans. A thousand million moments, each one a splinter wedged into his skin. There was no ridding himself of them, and no way to turn back the clock.

Hell, he wouldn't even do it if he could.

He'd been a fool back then, and he'd needed to learn a lesson, and boy, had he learned it.

At least, until Adie Hamilton arrived, he'd been convinced he had.

Now, now he wasn't so sure he hadn't been fooling himself all this time, and he was still the same dumb as fuck impetuous dreamer he'd always been.

-25-
Adie

Days passed; work continued. Killian continued to avoid her.

"Babe, you need to get your kicks elsewhere," Siân advised. Sensible advice. "What happened to Mr Sexy from the Museum? He hasn't ghosted you, has he?"

He hadn't. Matter of fact, Anton had called. He'd texted. He'd sent pictures of things he'd dug out of the sand. And yes, okay, he'd sent a dirty pic or two, but they'd been artful, and she'd kind of invited him to send them, and they were both hot and inspiring, but...

He seemed too good to be true.

"He wants into your pants, Adie. I think that's a more likely conclusion for his interest in seeing you than him being a dig saboteur or a part of an international network of relic thieves, or whatever it is you're imagining. I think the problem here is that you're so fixated on what you can't have that you can't see the good thing that's offering to rail you like the world's about to end."

"It's not like that—"

"Oh, yeah? Show me the last message he sent you."

Absolutely not! It was an artful shot of a fantastic set of abs, complete with a teasing glimpse of the latest relic he'd unearthed at Bahariya that just happened to be positioned so it concealed a bit of him she was enamoured of.

"Yeah, that's what I thought. Face it, Adie. The problem here is not him, it's you. You got a teeny tiny smackerel of an appetiser from Killian, and now you're not going to be satisfied until you get the main course plus dessert. It doesn't matter how many handsome eager men you have pursuing you—"

"One."

"—offering to give you mind blowing orgasms."

"I never said—"

"Oh, please! Why else would you be dithering? You know he's a good thing, but you were pissed off the day the two of you hooked up and now you've calmed down, you've realised your epic crush on our aloof but totally hot boss hasn't lessened one little bit, and you're so desperate for another round of playing 'Yes, I'm totally your good girl, professor!' that you're probably going to wind up missing out on shagging the other hot and extremely willing professor dude."

"I don't think Anton's a professor." Leastways, she couldn't imagine him in a classroom. Also, at no point had she dropped any sort of hint that that was what had happened between her and Killian. Apparently, Siân was psychic.

"I'm sure he'd pretend to be if you asked," her

friend said, a broad grin stretching across her face. "Did you crush this badly on your university lecturers too?"

"Joe's nearly seventy." He was also her substitute grandad, in lieu of having any living relatives. "I was not like that. Ever. I'm not like that about Killian either."

Siân laughed in her face. "Cute. Delusional, but cute. Face it, sugar-plum, you've got it bad. I think we can safely say it turns you on that he's so fucking aloof and hard to get."

He'd been neither. She'd hardly had to do a thing—besides breaking a damn pot—to get him to loosen his fly and shove his cock in her mouth. It was securing round two that was the difficult bit. "He's a git, and I don't appreciate being treated like dirt." His semi-apology hadn't made her feel better. It stung.

Siân sighed and patted her on the shoulder. "No, but you do like begging for his attention."

"I don't."

Siân gave her head another weary shake and left Adie to grizzle over her own shortcomings. She didn't like begging or taking orders. Nor did she go mushy over being praised. Although, Siân was right, about one thing. She would still drop to her knees in an instant if their boss so much as smiled at her in a way that hinted at possibilities. There was just something about Doctor Simon Killian Carmichael that made her sit up and pay attention. It was bone deep, or soul deep, or something else visceral and poetic.

Either way, it was probably a good thing Killian hadn't been her tutor, not because of all that knocking her instincts out of her bollocks Josef had fed her, but because she'd have been too preoccupied with him to have got the grades she'd earned if he'd presided over her studies.

The sexy git walked past not two minutes later while she was on her knees with a trowel in one hand and a brush in the other, and her mind went straight there to where it had absolutely no sane reason to go, namely to him about turning, and grabbing her by the hair, and telling her to open up and suck his dick like the good girl he knew she was.

Adie choked on her own thoughts as her imagination painted a visceral image of Killian's cock hitting the back of her throat. She felt the invasion and swirled her tongue around her mouth as if she could taste him.

In reality, Killian simply walked on and all she got was a glimpse of his tight arse in his sensible cargo trousers as he hurried down the main tunnel like there was a succubus in pursuit.

She was never chasing him. Not never ever!

"There's a parcel for you," Lucas announced, when she arrived back at the *dahabiyya* that night, sandy and sweaty and still equally frustrated. "It was delivered to the Gezira apartment, Samīh sent it on. It arrived with the groceries."

"For me?" Adie squinted suspiciously at the plain cardboard box he handed over. She hadn't ordered anything, and she didn't know anyone who would send her a random gift.

Adie stepped into her cabin to open the box, away from prying eyes, and thank heavens she had, for the plain outer wrapping concealed a more decorative inner box, and within that, beneath a layer of tissue paper, lay a dark blue harem-girl outfit. It was all paper-thin silk, with decorative embroidered lilies picked out in black and silvered threads. The fabric sheer enough that she blushed at the thought of wearing it. Okay, so it wasn't lingerie, but it might as well have been.

"Oh, my!" Siân remarked, walking in on her unannounced. "I heard you'd had a parcel."

"Try knocking." Like that would ever happen. Siân thought nothing of barging in wherever, and no one ever seemed to stop her.

Adie held the trouser part of the ensemble before her against her legs. "I'm not sure what to think."

"You'll look amazing. I'll loan you my kohl, you can prance along the deck—"

"Siân, I didn't buy this to woo our boss. It's... It's a gift."

"Killian sent you—"

If only. "From Anton."

Siân reached for the note, but Adie snatched the envelope before she could grab it.

"He wants to meet up."

"Hook up, you mean. This is totally an invitation to a booty call." She cleared her throat. "Where and when?"

"Tomorrow. A silken desert palace."

"The whole fantasy sheik thing, nice. Providing

it doesn't involve rolling you up in a carpet and throwing you over the back of a camel. If it does—" she shook her head and made a horizontal slicing gesture with her hand "—you might want to pass. Camels are a hard no. Carpets, I mean, sure if it's your kink."

"Neither are mentioned. I think it's more of a figs and fucking scenario."

Siân nodded sagely. "You gonna go?"

Adie pulled the bobble from her hair and scratched her scalp. "I don't know. Despite what you might think, I don't really do random hook ups. The museum thing was out of character."

"Sure it was." Siân raised her hands. "On the other hand, it was fun, right, and this is an offer of more of the same. Plus, it's technically a second date and therefore doesn't count as a random hook up."

"I guess." She wasn't sure that was entirely accurate.

"Go. Seriously. Why wouldn't you? You came out here looking for adventure, didn't you? Well, here's your chance to drink nectar from the navel of a hot desert prince, lick honey off his nuts, and fuck until you can't remember your own name."

"You know the sort of adventure I was seeking was of the digging around in the dirt variety not—."

Siân was now reading the accompanying card. "Babe, this is going to be plenty filthy enough to satisfy. He has a nice way with words. If his tongue's this sweet in person—"

"It's not bad. Also, your mind is filthy." She snatched back the card.

Siân stroked a long finger over the sheer fabric of the outfit, her expression becoming whimsical. "Well, if you're not biting. I just might."

"You've not even met him."

Adie turned and started packing the outfit back into its box. "Siân," she asked, heat rushing to her cheeks. "Have you ever had a threesome?"

"Shit!" The other woman reached for the note again. "Is that what he's offering? Where does it say that?"

"No." Adie stuffed the note deep into her pocket. "He's not. I just... It was just a passing thought."

She looked again at the outfit. It was utterly beautiful. The sheer fabric would surely tease as it swished against her skin, while the argent threads would shimmer in the sun and reflect like rivers of silver in Anton's hypnotically dark eyes.

"Siân, I can't really go to a place that's just a set of co-ordinates. It's practically asking for trouble."

"Adie, girl,"—her friend slumped onto the bed— "I can't keep up with you. One minute you're asking about threesomes—and by the way, the answer is yes—then in the next breath, you can't go somewhere because all you have are GPS co-ordinates. If that's not the definition of an adventure...of a 'treasure hunt', then I don't know what is. The guy's clearly appealing to your sense of wonder. At least take a peep at a map before you decide to be Adie 'oh-no-I'm-such-a-good-girl' McBoringville."

Thus prompted, she reached for her phone, only to find the battery was virtually dead again. "I swear my phone only keeps a charge for about forty seconds in this heat."

Siân shrugged. "It's a fact. It's because all the little chemicals get too excited. I feel the same thing. Its why we all end up horny as fuck every time we're stuck in the desert too long on a dig."

"I'm not sure that's to do with jiggly chemicals."

"Ades, it's everything to do with them. So, where is it?"

Adie plugged the phone in to charge and opened google maps. "It's the literal middle of nowhere."

"It's not the middle of nowhere." Siân's chin dug into her as she peered over Adie's shoulder at the screen. "It's a perfectly accessible bit of desert that no one is going to pay any attention to, thus allowing for all manner of sexy fun times to take place within the walls of a sober black Bedouin tent. You'll be in this little piece of nothing." She lifted one corner of the harem outfit. "He'll be swathed in his black robe, with barely a stitch underneath."

"It'll be hot and sticky."

"Yes, one hopes."

"That is not what I meant."

Siân rolled her eyes. "Please don't tell me you like the whisper of air con over your behind as a preference to sweltering grimy fun." She rolled her tongue against her teeth and waggled her brows suggestively. "Just what sort of archaeologist are you?"

Adie sank her head into her hands. She turned away from Siân and found herself a bottle of water. After taking a few slugs, she planted her butt in a chair and nursed the rest.

"Look, it's simple," Siân said, hands on her sylph-like hips. "Either you get this kit on and hook up with Valentino for an orgasm fest, or you sit around here mooning over Professor unavailable-and-he's-never-going-to-bonk-you Carmichael. The wise woman in this situation, realises there's only really one choice."

"Mooning," Adie said, shooting Siân a cheeky grin.

Her friend swatted at her. "No! Orgasm fest. Look, in the interests of female solidarity, I'll drive you there and pick you up from this fuck fest when you're done."

"You can't drive me there. It's in the middle of a sand dune."

"I can drive you to within a mile of it." She scrolled south a little and pointed out a road. "The only thing I'm not doing is sitting by the roadside waiting for you, because a) it's the desert, b) it'll be boring and c) I do not need every second vehicle stopping to check I'm okay and getting offended when I reject their manly help. So, we're sorted, and you're doing this, right?

"Hmm."

-26-

Adie

The following evening, Siân dropped Adie by the roadside with a fully charged phone, a compass, a water canteen, and a set of geocaching travel bugs hanging around her neck like dog tags. Adventuring with due diligence, Siân called it. Adie would have to walk about a mile to reach her destination, hence she was also swaddled in a robe-like dress, courtesy of Siân's comprehensive travel wardrobe. It was loose and floaty enough to fit over the top of her harem-girl outfit without leaving her feeling too hot and restricted. Of course, her boots didn't exactly fit with the aesthetic, but she wasn't adventuring without proper footwear. She'd learned that the hard way via a jellyfish sting, during an ammonite hunting expedition at Lyme Regis.

The sun was rapidly fading as she set off at a brisk pace.

Distances in the desert, she soon learned, were deceptive. She'd been walking for a good twenty minutes, without so much as a glimpse of another living thing, no sign of any silken palaces, and then a sand bank gave way to a hidden valley and a verdant band of emerald surrounded by flocks of birds.

Date palms edged the mirrored surface of the oasis, and on the bank stood a single Bedouin style pavilion.

Anton, she mouthed. A grin stretched her face.

She'd never been a big fan of princesses, but she had liked the idea of riding around on a magic carpet. The bathmat had shown promise, it was prone to curling up at the end, likewise the ancient rug that Esther said a man had flown with all the way from Turkey. She'd been ten, and heartbroken when it occurred to her that it'd reached the UK by regular old commercial plane and hadn't soared across sea and land under its own power.

"Hello?" Adie called, nervously raising her fist to knock on the fabric, only for a hand to shoot out between the door flaps, fasten around her wrist and drag her inside.

The inside was illuminated with scores of coloured lanterns, and the soporific scents of sandalwood and myrrh infused the air. The pavilion was carpeted underfoot and along most of the walls. At one end lay a raised sleeping area decked out with a myriad of coloured cushions and surrounded by voile-like curtains.

Anton wrapped an arm around her waist and pulled her in close, her back to the wall of his chest. Adie turned within his embrace to look up at him. He was swathed from head to foot in black robes that seemed to make the pits of his eyes that much darker. She gasped in recognition. It was him, the man she'd seen at Saqqara as she fled from that scorpion, the night she'd found the tunnel entrance.

"You were at Saqqara before we met at the museum. I saw you."

He replied with a string of incomprehensible Arabic.

"I'm sure I told you my Arabic's not that good."

He said something else, which would have been vexing, if the language didn't make his voice sound so sexy.

Anton traced the embroidered edge of the dress Siân had loaned her.

He tugged again, prompting Adie to shed the dress. What the hell. She was here to have fun.

A light lit in the centres of his onyx eyes, and he circled her slowly, admiring the way the sequined cups of her outfit captured her bosom, before grinning at the way the silk skirted over her rear.

"Fair's fair." She tugged at the sleeve of his robe. She'd not seen nearly enough of this man the first time around.

His lips curled at one corner, then he lifted the robe over his head, and let it fall behind him. Wow, he was ripped. Lean, with washboard abs, and two tightly perked nipples. He had on only a pair of simple cotton trousers held in place around his hips with a drawstring.

Again, he spoke, issuing what sounded like a command. Then, imploring her with his best Valentino stare, he pointed towards the cushioned bed.

Adie held a finger up to him. "One moment. I

need to take my boots off for this." She bent double and tore at the laces, wishing she hadn't triple knotted them.

Anton traced his palm across her upthrust rear before moving completely behind her and butting up against her cheeks.

Adie groaned, feeling exactly how excited her presence had him. Damn, yes, she wanted some of that.

Knots unravelled, she kicked off her footwear and about turned, entwining her arms around Anton's neck and leaping so that she straddled his hips before reeling him in for a kiss.

"And here I was thinking I'd actually keep my cool and remain all imperious, but damn, girl. You look amazing, and you feel it too, perched there."

"Here?" She wriggled, which wedged his covered cock more thoroughly against her slit.

The husky groan he gave was another incentive to keep it up.

"Keep doing that and the adventure might be short-lived."

"But Anton, I'm so wet, and you have such a nice hard wedge in your pants."

"Well, if you let me walk you over there." His head tilted towards the cushions. "Then you can get it out and admire it."

"Can I?" She lowered herself from his hold. "I hope you're going to let me do more than look." She curled a couple of fingers into his waistband and led him over to the bed, where she reclined.

"Wait! Off," she said when he made to follow

suit.

"Off?" He looked down at his trousers.

"Off. I want you naked, big man."

He tugged one end of the drawstring so that the knot slowly unravelled. Adie kept her lips pursed and her gaze levelled at him as he slowly, teased the fabric down a millimetre at a time.

"You know a girl only has so much patience." She leaned forward and tugged on his trouser leg, so that they dropped to his ankles. "Now, would you look at that." Adie came onto her knees. "Why Doctor Kelley,"–she breathed in the delicious scent of him—"Is that wood all for me?"

He turned his head making his long hair swish about his broad shoulders as if checking for other persons. "Could be."

God, his eyes were pretty, all dark fringed, and darker centred as he gave her another smouldering look.

"What I want to know is what you're going to do now you've got me all naked and excited."

She knew exactly what she wanted to do. It started with tasting him, but definitely didn't end there. She hesitated only for a moment. Only a handful of days had passed since she'd gone down on Killian and then he'd summarily rejected her. What better way to put that episode behind her than to wrap her lips around someone far more willing and giving?

"I thought a kiss or two. Possibly some licking." She did both those things, drawing more evocative groans from his throat. "And I'm really rather fond of pushing the limits of what I can fit in my mouth." She swallowed around him as the tip of his cock hit the back of her throat.

"Ah, little desert sprite, I'd gladly lie back and let you have your way, but I fear what you'll do to me if I allow you free rein to bewitch me so thoroughly."

She released him with a smack of her lips. "I mean only to please you."

"Is that so?"

"Of course. I'm yours to command."

"Lie back, then. Enjoy the hospitality. Have some fruit." He lifted a piece from a bowl standing on a low table alongside an assortment of beverages. He held it to her, stopping short of touching her lips, so that the juice dripped onto her tongue.

The taste was both spicy and sweet, and made her tongue tingle from the burn of alcohol, as he fed her the piece, then lifted another. This time, the juice hit her chin and rolled down her neck into the hollow between her breasts.

"Ah, my apologies. That was clumsy. Let me..." He lowered his mouth and followed the liquid trail, burying his nose in the crease between her cleavage. His fingers sought the fastenings of her top and relieved her of its constraints, baring her breasts, which he then claimed with hands and mouth.

His lips closed around one nipple, and lavished it with praise, while his fingers teased its twin, before swapping sides.

This man was such a contrast to her boss. Giving, demonstrative. There were no limits, nothing that felt out-of-bounds. It was both easy to give and receive. To bask in the moment, but to direct too, without ever fearing a rebuke or rejection.

Anton lifted his head and claimed another piece of fruit. This time, he aimed the sticky sweet liquid at her navel, where it pooled, and from which he then lapped it.

"That tickles," she protested, nevertheless lifting her hips eagerly to meet each touch. When his tongue-tip poked rudely into the depths of her belly button, lighting rarely stimulated nerves, it sent a shiver through her body that connected with the lightning fork of pleasure arching outwards from her clit.

"Come up here."

"You tasted me. It's only fair I taste you too."

He placed a black grape, like a jewel, in her navel. Then his attention roved lower, skirting over the sequined waistband of her pants, and the sheer silk. The first touch of his tongue was delivered through the fabric, soaking it, moulding it, until it clung to her form, outlining the shape of her mons, lips, and pearl.

"I'm going to touch you bare in a moment. Take this silken mask away and suck you until you scream my name."

"Will you fuck me until I scream it too?"

"Perhaps, little sprite. If it's your desire. But there's no rush, is there? Time is irrelevant here. Leave the world behind. Open yourself to me."

She spread her legs wider, which made him laugh.

While Anton coaxed her with fingers and

tongue, Adie luxuriated in the attention and let the bliss of it envelop her. Her scent mingled with the citrus zest of the fruit, and the muggy fragrance from the oil lamps. Each touch was a surprise. Every lash heightened her pleasure until she was writhing against the cushions, lost in a delirium of need for him to enter and claim her.

"I need you free of this nonsense."

She expected him to lift her legs and peel away the remainder of her clothing. Instead, he stretched over her, and reached beneath the pillows at her head.

"Anton!" He'd drawn a wickedly curved knife. Ornately fashioned, perhaps ten inches long, the blade clearly sharpened.

"Scared, sprite?"

Alarmed, she nodded.

"There's really no need." He dragged the flat of the blade down the side of her throat, setting her heart pounding. Then lower, between the twin mounds of her breasts, following the path he'd trailed with the juice earlier, then along the seam of her pants to where the sodden fabric was rudely moulded to her pussy. "I'd never harm my sprite, but best hold still now. You wouldn't want to get pricked." He sliced straight through the stitching, creating a large gash. "And now... now, you and I are going to have some fun. Have I mentioned that I like that this puss isn't bare."

"You hadn't," she squeaked. She kept down there all neatly trimmed, but she'd never gone in for waxing, or creating some sort of weird landing strip.

"Well, I do." He cut away a curl of her pubic hair and lifted it to scent.

"You're insane." She couldn't take her eyes off him. "Please put the knife down."

But he just kept looking at her with those glittering dark eyes. "Anton?" she said again, nervously curling her fingers into the nearest cushions. "You're scaring me."

"And you're loving it. You're so wet I could drown in it. Shall we play a game, Adie?"

"What game?" She hoped she didn't sound as tremulous as she suspected she did. "Not one that involves cutting."

"Not one for blood play." He teased her with the flat of the blade.

Adie shook her head.

He let her sweat another few seconds, then cast the knife aside. "Very well, none of that, but the game... It's a simple one. You're the captive. A treasure I found abandoned in the desert all lost and lonely, so I brought it home."

"To do what with?"

"Fuck," he said simply, before flashing her a smile. "Because despite how the old proverb goes, ecstasy doesn't involve watermelon."

"I feel I ought to ask how you know."

His eyes crinkled with his smile. Then he lowered himself over her, taking hold of her by the wrists as he did. "That's a story for another time. But believe me when I say that nothing compares to the heat of a woman enveloping you. Nothing. And I've sampled all the wisdoms of the ancients. Thinking sex is in any way about duty is where it all goes wrong. It's about pleasure. It's about survival. Look at me, Adie. Look at me, while I enter you. I want to see what you feel, and I want you to feel every inch of me."

She was already feeling it. The crown of him was tormentingly lodged at her entrance. Her heart pounded so hard, she felt it in her temples, and the shroud of his hair surrounded them as their mouths met.

Adie gasped into those tresses as Anton delivered on his promise.

She'd made the right choice coming to meet him. Her icy boss couldn't hold a torch to this man, who was all passion and danger, and who playfully nipped her earlobe, before rearing back and lifting her legs to rest on his shoulders so he could bed himself right to the hilt.

Damn, that was an angle to remember.

As was the play of light and shadows across his muscles as he fucked them both into synchronous releases, before making her come again with his tongue.

Sticky and too warm after the fact, Adie nevertheless gasped at the loss when he pulled away. She sank back, watching him. His eyes were the mesmerising black of the Nile waters reflecting the night sky. Sweat sheened his skin. And they were so attuned, they were even taking breaths simultaneously.

"I haven't..." She coughed to clear the thickness from her throat. "I've never come simultaneously with anyone before." The admission made her blush.

"That right?" He disposed of the condom, then settled himself on his side beside her, so they could cuddle like spoons. "Well, since we're sharing, I haven't been able to get you out of my head since the museum. There's something here worth exploring, don't you think, Doctor Hamilton? You feel it too, don't you?"

"Have you?" she said, avoiding the question. "I mean with someone else."

Anton settled his head on a pillow, leaving her to roll over to watch his face. "A few times," he said, in a way that suggested it was of no consequence. "Not recently.... It was quite a long time ago, actually."

"With someone you loved?"

He reached up and cupped her cheek. "You never stop digging, do you?"

"It's kind of my profession."

He snorted. "Yeah, but... most of us don't treat everything as a puzzle. You don't need to map out my history, Adie. I'll tell you anything you want to know."

"Can you remember their name?"

"Yeah, I can remember their name. It's not something I'm likely to forget. We were engaged for a bit."

"Oh!" She found herself looking at his hands. Relief swelled in her chest when there was no evidence of a ring. "Shit! I'm sorry. A while? What happened?"

He brushed her hair aside before returning his

hand to her cheek. "Turned out we weren't as compatible as we thought. It's water under the bridge. Let's move on. Can I offer you some refreshment before I attempt to bonk your brains out again?"

"Are we not done?"

"We're not done."

"Then yes, a drink would be lovely."

-27-
Killian

"Where is she?" Killian demanded, emerging from the shadows as Siân crossed the gangplank onto the houseboat. He'd heard them sneak off. The roar of Siân's Land Rover engine was unmistakable, and their idea of stealth had been giggly whispering that carried for miles.

Siân pulled her shoulders back. "Out having some fun. She has my number, so I can fetch her when she calls. And before you get weird about it, she's a grown adult, and she signed on to be a member of an excavation team not to give up her autonomy and sexual freedom."

She had told him she'd met someone. Someone unlike him. He'd thought she was just throwing words around though, hoping they'd sting.

"Have you met him? Vetted him? Is he for real? Is it her he's after or—"

"Killian, listen to yourself," Siân said, cutting him off. "Sure, there are plenty of skeevy blokes in the world. Including unscrupulous ones who would consider coming on to an archaeologist purely to gain access to their treasures, but between you and me, I think he's more interested in what's inside her knickers than the collection of broken pottery we've unearthed."

"You don't find it suspicious that he's just popped up out of nowhere?"

"You think it's incomprehensible that an attractive young woman might attract the attention of an equally hot young man?"

Well, no, if she put it like that, but it was irrelevant.

"Where is she, Siân?"

"Seriously," Siân rolled her eyes at him fishing his car keys from his pocket. "You're going to be that crass? What are you going to do, Killian? Rock up and drag her home? You've made it perfectly clear that you're not interested in fucking her, so why is it such a big issue that she's out fucking someone else?"

His blood ought not to be boiling just from hearing the words fucking and someone else in the same sentence. And it wasn't that he wasn't interested, only he knew it was a bad move. It'd serve both of them ill.

"You had your shot with her, now stop messing with her and put your fucking keys away."

"Sadler's prowling about. I can't believe you're on board with this... aiding this... Siân—"

"She's not meeting Sadler. She's not talking about the dig. Right now,"–she glanced at her watch—"I imagine she's having her pussy ploughed by a charming fellow with a nice big dick, and hopefully once they're through, I won't have to talk any more sense into her over lusting after your ridiculously tight arse."

"My arse is not that tight."

She snorted.

So did he when he realised what he'd said.

"Want to extrapolate?" Siân crooned, from behind the hand she had covering her mirth. "I'm sure I'd love to hear about how your arse isn't quite so—"

"You say that like I've never been ploughed before."

Her jaw dropped. Then she gave him an accessing squint. "But you're not..."

"I'm not what, Siân?"

"Shit!" she said and gave her head a shake. "Is that why you turned her down? Except, that still doesn't make sense of the snog fest. What, were you just seeing if you liked it?"

"I'm not gay, Siân."

"You just said—"

Christ! "The world isn't black and white. I can't believe I'm having to tell you this. There's an entire spectrum in between."

"Oh! Okay. Yeah. So, you're what? Bi? Pan? Christ, you've kept that quiet."

"I hardly think my sexual preferences are relevant to our professional relationship."

The expression on her face suggested otherwise. She clasped her hands together and thoughtfully tapped her thumbs against her lips. "So, just to clarify...the other night when you said I didn't know the half of what went down between you and Sadler… Does that mean you were shagging him?"

"The hell!" he swore loud enough to scare some river birds into flight.

"It's a reasonable assumption."

"Excuse me, while I go and bleach my brain." He turned as if to head to his cabin, only to recall his purpose. He was genuinely concerned for both Adie's safety and the security of the site and its relics. The rules he made were in place for a reason. And sure, he'd never enforced them particularly religiously, but that's because he worked with professionals, not students with more ideas than sense. Usually, they were perfectly capable of policing their own behaviour, with notable exceptions—Bill. There was a reason he wasn't on the team anymore. That leg break had been a gift, really.

"Killian…" Siân followed him across the gangplank to the shore. "What the fuck are you doing? Get back on the boat."

He ignored her and got in his car. Not that it helped since he had no clue where Adie was.

Siân drummed her fist against the window. "You're a piece of work," she said, when he lowered it. "For someone who's just lectured me on shades of grey, you might want to explore them yourself, in place of the hot and cold routine. Let it be, Boss."

"Where is she?"

"I'm not telling you. Punish me for that if you like, it won't change a damn thing. I'm not going to let you ruin whatever good thing she has going."

She about turned and marched onto the boat. He followed her with his gaze as far as her cabin door. Then drummed his fist against the steering wheel when her door slammed.

Damn her. And damn him.

He should have bloody listened to Joe Levine and left Adie at home in the UK. It was only since her arrival that he'd started experiencing such seismic mood shifts.

"It's about safety and security, that's all," he growled at the non-present Siân.

They both knew that was a mere fraction of the truth.

~Ж~

Killian spent the night in the car huddled under a couple of travel rugs, alternating between seething, cursing, and worrying his goddamn nuts off. It didn't matter how often he told himself he should go to bed and that he wasn't responsible for the actions of a grown woman; he just couldn't make himself do it.

He believed in looking out for his team, both the members of it and their interests.

His worry wasn't anything to do with how much it prickled to think of some other fool jabbing his dick in her pussy... or filling her mouth... or kissing her... Damn the bastard for even looking at her. He'd like to poke the bugger's eyes out.

He'd also like to bugger her, which was a highly...highly inappropriate thought.

Also, if he was poking eyes out, he'd have to

start with himself, because he couldn't stop drinking his fill of her. One glimpse or whiff of her perfume, and he had to take an extended bathroom break. He was going to wind up with a repetitive strain injury at this rate. Four times, he'd jerked off today, and that was while doing his damnedest to keep his distance. If he was around her...? *Pfft!*

On the other hand, if he hadn't been so absent, maybe he wouldn't be sitting in his car fretting and inventing increasingly extreme means of torturing whichever fool currently had his hands on her.

God, where was his head at?

It was as if the perfect storm of Sadler lurking on the periphery, and Adie 'tomb raider' Hamilton wiggling her curvy arse about on his dig had rewired his nervous system.

She was too young.

Too eager.

Too bold.

Too everything...

They were completely wrong for each other.

Not that his libido agreed. It was all for some serious pogoing.

But he wasn't about to risk his career again.

Was he?

No.

Passion was just a synonym for danger, and he was far too sensible for all that these days. His shadow in the windscreen provided a very good reminder of why. That white hair wasn't anything to do with genetics.

In any case, it was foolish to imagine Adie was

even interested after the way he'd acted. In fact, she definitely wasn't, or she wouldn't be off shagging someone else.

Assuming that *was* reality, and not just a line Siân was feeding him.

They could just be having dinner.

She might not be with a man at all.

That possibility went out the window the later the hour got. One only stayed out this late for a handful of purposes; to get drunk, to nurse a friend, or because you were shagging someone senseless.

And the later the hour got, the more worried he got.

And the more worried he got, the more his anger crystallised and the less rational he felt about the whole damn thing.

Thus, when he woke from a doze to the bang of a car door, the purr of an engine, and the hazy glow of dawn, he burst out of the vehicle and charged straight towards her without a single sensible thought in his head, lizard brain chomping for a fight.

Adie shrieked on seeing him and clamped her legs together. "Oh, my, God!"

Killian came to a halt less than a foot away from her.

"What in hell are you wearing?" He'd meant to open with a line about the stress she'd caused, and where the hell she'd been all night. Make it clear that it was professional concern causing his gruffness, and not the fact that he was jealous as all hell and had been seething for the last eight hours, but the sight of her sporting an outfit that oughtn't to be seen outside of a Sultan's palace nixed that.

"Clothes," she meeped.

Barely.

He'd only ever seen her in sensible business attire and work clothes. Whereas this number was designed with temptation in mind. The sequined cups perfectly bound her breasts, while the chiffon-like material of the trousers emphasised the curves of her hips and the narrowness of her waist. Plus, she had kohl smudged around her eyes.

His heart rate accelerated to a gallop, and his cock bucked with glee.

Her midriff was bared, and there was a purplish stain around it. Happened that he noticed she also had the perfect amount of curve to her belly. Soft, feminine...flawless.

"Killian." Her nervousness showed in the way she swallowed. "I didn't realise you were planning such an early start, or I'd have made sure I got back sooner."

"You didn't mention you were leaving," he said, while dragging his gaze up to her face.

"Siân knew."

"You didn't mention *to me* that you were leaving."

A frown twisted both her lips and brow. Her jaw clenched. "Well, considering how well our last few conversations have gone, I didn't exactly fancy a chat."

"I expect to be kept abreast of everyone's whereabouts, Doctor Hamilton."

Adie folded her arms. Her gaze became stony. "Yeah, well I expect to be treated with some degree of dignity, so I guess we're both disappointed. I'll make sure I put details of any other excursions I plan into writing for you, or maybe you'd like to install a tracking app on my phone?"

"You're meeting him again."

"Excuse me?"

Killian kept his mouth shut. Best policy, since he was only saying the wrong things. In any case, he oughtn't to have asked in the first place, so he wasn't going to repeat himself.

She huffed and shook her head. Then she barged past him. "If it's okay with you, I'm going to take a shower. You might want to consider one, too. You look like shit."

She stomped over the gangplank. Killian followed her onto the deck, bristling at her bristliness.

"Probably because I haven't exactly slept due to worrying myself sick—"

She whipped around. "You stayed up waiting for me to get back?"

Killian dragged a hand through the front of his hair. "I didn't know where you were, or if you were safe."

"You stayed up? All night." She came a step closer.

Too close, so that she was right on a level with him, her chin tilted up to meet his gaze. "I'm a big girl. I can look after myself."

"I'm aware."

She was close enough now that the citrusy scent of her was all he could smell.

She held his gaze a moment, before giving a sniff, and backing up a step. "Cute. But you didn't need to fret."

"Adie." His hand shot out and grasped her upper arm. "We should talk."

"Talk?" She exaggerated the syllables. "What about? Do you require a minute-by-minute accounting of my night? A summary of how many times I came?"

He winced but didn't release her. "We should talk about what happened between us."

He refused to give headspace to the notion that some other man had been getting her off all night. Nah. Nah. It was just white noise.

He'd peel the bastard's skin from his limbs.

Adie shook her head. "It's forgotten. Didn't you catch the memo? I moved on. Met someone who understands the concept of reciprocation and who doesn't have a stick up his arse."

"Adie..."

"You need to let go of me."

Her every word was like a knife in the guts. "What happened was a mistake—"

"Yes, a fantastic display of lack of judgement on my part."

"That's not what I meant. I'm... I'm sorry."

He bowed his head, devastated by the derisive look in her eyes, only to realise why she'd been so horrified to see him. The inner seam of her trousers was split... No, it'd been cut. The edges were smooth where they parted revealing tantalising glimpses of her inner thighs, the skin there creamy smooth. Moreover, if he wasn't very much mistaken, she was entirely without panties.

He let go of her arm, fascinated, and instead traced the edge of the frayed seam.

"My God, are you for real? What are you... How dare you? You can't just touch me there."

"You're indecent, Doctor Hamilton."

The skin of her thigh was so soft. And, he could smell her too.

"And you're behaving like a—"

He dropped to his knees, bringing his head down level with the slit. "Did you let him put his mouth on you?"

"Oh, my God! You've no right."

The scent of her was in his nostrils now, making him even hornier. With each breath, the anxiety that had riddled him all night metamorphosed further into lust. "Isn't this exactly what you wanted from me the other night?"

"Yes, the other night. Not now. Not after I've met someone else. After you've been a fucking monster all week."

"I was trying to protect you."

"Fuck you. You were trying to protect yourself."

"Both. I was protecting both of us, but it's no good, I can't turn it off... this draw... the tug between us. I'm on my knees, Adie. I want you. Isn't that what you want to hear?"

Killian scented her with his tongue, stopping short of touching her by a matter of millimetres.

She shifted. Her thighs trembled. "Oh, my God! You're unbelievable. I've just... I've just spent the night with another man. What is this, some sort of one-upmanship? You didn't want me, but now someone else does, you do?"

It was exactly that. Or rather, he'd always wanted her. He'd just erected barriers before because he knew it wasn't sensible. His heart, on the other hand, didn't give a flying fuck about that. All it cared about was the fact that another man's scent was all over her. Ergo, he needed to stamp his mark all over her too, until he'd removed every trace of this other lover from her body. Until she forgot there'd ever been another man.

He wanted to be everywhere he'd been. Touch every part of her that had been touched. Coat her in his scent. Leave her pussy dripping with his seed.

Humans only masqueraded as civilised higher intelligent beings. Really, they were nothing but raging sacs of hormones.

Killian's mask slipped further the more he breathed her in. The plump ruby lips of her sex were right before him. Shiny with arousal. And certain to respond to his kiss.

"Killian. We are standing on the deck of your boat. Someone will see."

That was her worry? Being seen?

"Is that your only objection?"

She shivered as his breath hit her skin. "You know I'll taste of him."

Not by the time he was done, and he sincerely doubted she'd been so irresponsible as to go bareback with a man she'd known all of five minutes. Nor would it change anything even if she had. He'd consider it his personal mission to remove every trace.

"What happened to the icy professor who's been throwing me shade for days?"

"He's having a nap. Now, are you going to let me lick your pussy or not?"

She grabbed hold of him by the hair, which he interpreted as a yes.

Killian licked along the full length of her slit, which made her squeak, then groan and pull his hair harder. She was pure nectar on his tongue.

It had been too long since he'd allowed himself such pleasure.

Too long pretending he didn't want to worship her in this way.

Too long being the man with the stick up his arse.

Touch, taste, scent, the sight of those pretty pink folds. The scent of her. All five senses quickly became attuned to her and her pleasure. Her breath caught at the culmination of each lick. Music for his soul.

And here was another thing Siân would probably be shocked to learn about him. His control freak ways extended to the bedroom... Well, sometimes...

He gave Adie's clit some attention, teasing sucks before he moved to fucking her with the full length of his tongue. Followed by a combination of it and two fingers. The result was that her knees buckled, and he had to wrap his free arm around her to hold her up. It meant she was perched on his face. Killian encouraged that further by easing her legs over his shoulders and having her brace her shoulder blades against the nearby wall. Then he folded his right arm over the top of her thigh to secure her in place.

Pretty soon she was grinding against him, chasing pleasure that only his fingers and tongue could provide. In turn, he ravaged her. Worked his tongue hard enough it'd probably sustain a sprain, but he was so deep into what he was doing that he didn't care. So what if he spoke like Donald Duck for a week? All that mattered was the feast before him and ushering her towards an explosive release. This wasn't about being delicate. It was about need and desire combining into a heady whole.

"Fuck me," she commanded. "Get off your knees and give me some dick."

He surfaced for air, panting. "Rude."

"Are you saying it's not what you want to do?"

The very hard wedge beating for release behind his zip said otherwise.

"Do you have condoms secreted about your person?" Unlikely, given the outfit. "Because it's not something I carry around in my pockets."

"Fuck," she muttered, with a genuine ring of disappointment. "Do you have some in your cabin?"

Did he?

He wished he could say so with absolute certainty. Were there any in his bathroom cabinet? And if there were, what was the likelihood of them being in date? He'd never been the sort to carry one about in his wallet, even back in the past when he'd been ready and willing to bang at a moment's notice.

"Shit! You don't, do you?"

"I don't need my cock to make you come."

This wasn't about that though. It was about connection. The tremble of her limbs as he returned to tickling her g-spot made her frustration all too evident.

"Are you going to come for me, Adie? Are you going to squirt all over my tongue?"

"That's not a real thing."

"Oh, it's a thing," he purred against her clit, making her hips buck.

"Not a thing I do."

"Well, if not this time...." He winked. Which he realised might be taken as a promise of a future event.

Dammit, it *was* a promise.

"Now you're all swagger and charm." She tugged on his hair again, so that he'd look up at her. She was all loose-mouthed and starry-eyed, a woman on the brink of surrender.

"Up," she mouthed, and dug her teeth into her lip.

Killian slithered upwards, his body crowding her smaller frame. Their mouths met in a hungry clash. He invaded her mouth. She invaded his senses.

He lifted her and ground his erection hard against her bare pussy. It wasn't enough, but it was as far as this was going this time around.

Yes, he wanted to split her lips and drive himself

deep. Yes, he wanted the pistoning of his hips to yield more than the insane levels of frustration they currently equalled. At least he was hitting it right for her. He didn't even need to rub her clit; his cock was doing all the work.

"God, yes. Yes." Her words sparked off him, like flint striking steel.

He slid his hands around her arse. Pulled the plump cheeks apart as he continued to grind. She was all his... All his... "Mine," he declared, possibly aloud.

She responded with a cry. Her head tipped back, chin coming up so that her neck was stretched before him. "Say it again."

"Mine." Killian raked his teeth along its tenderest inches, and she exploded for him.

The sound of her bliss was enough to carry him over the line too, thus leaving him in dire need of a change of clothes.

Adie slithered her arms around his neck. Then leaned in, eager for kisses. After a dozen or so, she pressed their brows together. "I don't understand you. I've been right here all week, and barely got more than a growl out of you, and then when I find someone... someone I like, who is kind, and fun, and gave me a shit ton of orgasms, you're... you're like this, and I don't know what the hell I'm supposed to do or think. Tell you to fuck off, probably, if, you know, that wouldn't be inappropriate seeing as you're my boss."

Killian held his position, keeping her trapped between his body and the wall. "Drop him. Don't see him again."

She grinned, but it was a wary tension riddled form of a smile. "Seems harsh, you know, given the orgasms."

"I can make sure there's not a deficit of those."

"Yeah, well I think I need to consider whether I want to let you. Until now you've been all, 'We can't.' Why's that suddenly changed?"

"Adie." He stroked her face. "I was fretting over what other people would think. It's not so much the age difference"—a mere decade—"but I'm your boss, and Joe... Joe Levine's going to give me so much shit for this. Bad enough that I had the gall to employ you. If he learns that I'm... that we're—"

"Fucking," she supplied.

Yeah, that. "I'm going to be next level persona non grata."

She shook her head. "I love Josef to bits, but he doesn't get a say in this, just like it wasn't his call to make when he tried to stop you interviewing me. I don't even know why he did that. Or is it this he was worried about? Do you have a rep for seducing female colleagues?"

"No." He cleared his throat. He didn't have a rep for seducing anyone. His sex life was a barren wasteland. "It's because he doesn't like how I reinvented myself after all the shit that happened a decade ago."

"A decade ago, I was still midway through high school. What happened a decade ago?"

He didn't really want to get into the details. Not now. "Short version, I napalmed my street cred.

Look,"—he raised his hands, palms together as if in prayer—"we should both freshen up before everyone else surfaces."

"Alone, or together?"

Much as he relished the thought of her naked in his shower, "Alone might be best. Which is not me giving you a brush off, but maybe you need some space... to think, like you said."

As long as all her thinking resulted in her winding up in his bed.

"And will I see you at breakfast?"

He gave a nod. "At the daily briefing. It could be time for a switch around. It'll help provide us with some different perspectives." Every team benefited from a shake-up occasionally. It stopped things stagnating, and if he was being honest, they hadn't been making the progress on the tomb that he'd have liked.

Time to give the pop bottle a good old shake.

-28-

Adie

Killian walked her to her cabin door, though he resisted her attempts to coax him over the threshold. That was probably for the best. She did need to think. Although not that hard. Not really. Anton was a great diversion, but it wasn't anything serious. It was just dirty, flirty fun. Although, she would feel bad about ditching him given the lengths he'd gone to making sure she'd had a good time.

Once showered, she sat on her bed air drying, while her stomach gurgled. Whether that was through hunger or indecision wasn't certain. It was easy sitting here on Killian's houseboat to say she was choosing him, but not so easy to type a message and say thanks but no thanks to the man in whose arms she'd spent the night. She cast her phone aside in disgust, message unsent, unwilling to burn any bridges yet. After all, what was to say Killian wouldn't change his mind again? For someone everyone claimed was frosty, he was awfully volatile.

She was last to the breakfast table. Deliberately, as she knew Siân would be full of questions, and she wasn't ready to share or have another person's opinions offered.

Killian announced they were all switching work pitches. Killian and Siân would be joining Adie in the magazines, while Lucas and Mathew worked on the jigsaw puzzle of fragments from the mural room. Nothing much had come of the room they'd found at the end of the robber's tunnel, so they were putting it on second billing for a while until the other rooms were cleared.

They all rode over to Saqqara in the same vehicle that morning, which made for a further reprieve, and then there was no opportunity for gossip because Killian was working alongside her and Siân. Not that it stopped the other woman shooting her inquisitive looks.

Siân eventually cornered Adie after lunch. "Well, how was it?" she asked as they shuffled along the main passageway, heading back to their individual pitches.

"Fine."

"That's all you've got to say? Fine. You were gone for hours. I was expecting a call."

"I got a taxi."

"From where?"

"Turns out we weren't that far from civilisation, and he knew some people. I got back, that's what matters, and you got some sleep rather than being dragged out at all hours."

"Yeah," her friend said, giving her some curious side-eye, "but I was quite looking forward to hearing some of the deets on the drive back. Was it fabulous?

Did he fulfil your wildest dreams? Or was it all hype and total snore? I'm guessing not considering how long you were gone."

"I had a good time. There's not much else to say."

Siân pursed her lips. "You're holding out on me, Adina Hamilton."

"Using my full name won't unzip my lips, Ms Lawrence. I'm not a sharer. It was fun, okay. Can we leave it at that?"

"Sexy times happened though, right?"

Adie made a buttoning her lips motion.

"You're no fun." Siân turned right toward her pitch, while Adie turned left. "Wait, though. Has Killian spoken to you?"

"About?"

"About last night. He knows you went ashore. I'm sorry, he cornered me when I arrived back from dropping you off and was rather keen for us to go pick you up again immediately."

"Oh." She dug her teeth into her lip.

"It's okay. I told him not to be such a killjoy. I'm surprised that he hasn't challenged you over it, though. He was supremely narked about it at the time."

Adie shook her head, not daring to risk her voice, which would surely give her away. He challenged her all right.

"Really, he's not said a thing?" Siân wrinkled her nose, clearly perplexed.

Adie gave her head another shake before adding an 'uh-uh' sound. It seemed to satisfy Siân, who continued to her new pitch at the opposite end of the corridor.

~Ж~

As was often the case when lost in the flow of her work, Adie put aside thoughts of anything but the task at hand. Picking and scraping might not be the most exciting part of archaeology, but it was a necessity, and one could do it in a mindful way.

A couple of hours on, she was so deeply entrenched in that zone that she was startled to find Killian occupying the doorway.

"How long have you been there?" she asked, looking at him over her shoulder. He had on beige coloured cargos today, with a button-down shirt, the sleeves of which he'd rolled up so that the tan skin of his forearms was showing. In the crease of his arm sat a tattoo of a winged scarab.

"A while."

She turned her attention back to the wall carving she was working on. "Are you lurking for a reason?" She sincerely hoped he wasn't here to tell her he'd made a mistake earlier and was about to make a screeching U-turn.

"Just observing your technique."

Was that good or bad? "And does it pass muster?"

"Hm." He moved into the space, strolling until he was directly behind her, thus instantly putting her every cell on high alert. "It could benefit from a few refinements." His breath stirred the wisps of hair beside her ear.

"Then do instruct me, o' great one."

His lips traced the pulse point below her ear. "No need to be facetious."

"Please instruct me, professor," she amended.

Killian's pressed two fingers against her hip, where he began to trace concentric circles. The touch created goosebumps all across her skin.

"You're a too aggressive. A bit less grind and more tease is how it ought to be done."

Was he talking about archaeology or seduction?

"Perhaps if you demonstrated."

"That's a good idea."

She expected him to take the tools from her. Instead, he pressed in closer, so she felt the wedge of his erection lodged against the groove between her cheeks. "Keep at it, just more delicately."

"I thought I was being delicate."

His lips grazed the side of her throat, and he spoke directly into her ear. "Lift up your top, Adie."

"What?"

"You asked for instructions, are you now going to quibble over obeying them?"

"I don't see how what you said will help my technique."

"Who's the professor?"

He waited, leaving a silence for her to fill with her answer.

"You are."

"That's right, and good girls who want to work on special projects do as their professor asks them."

"What special projects? You've abandoned the

room I found, and you've barely scratched the surface in there to focus on us excavating magazines full of pots and ancient wheat grains."

"Less of that petulance, please. And it was not your find. It was a joint effort by all the members of this team. Besides some pretty tiles, we've not found anything down there that makes it a priority over anywhere else in this tomb. Now, do I need to repeat myself?"

His fingers crept under the hem of her T-shirt and made a circle around her navel.

Excitement fluttered in her chest. Did she dare? What if he was testing her? Was she supposed to swat him away in the name of professionalism, or obey? The jittery feeling in her chest said it was worth the risk. She took a chance and hitched her top up over her breasts.

There was no hiss of outrage. Instead, Killian released the catch on her bra. "Very good, Ms Hamilton. Eyes on the task, now. Remember, gentle sweeps." He cupped one breast in each hand and gently pinched her nipples between his fingers and thumbs.

Eyes on the task! She was dying here, suddenly excruciatingly aroused. How was anyone supposed to concentrate in such circumstances?

Still, seeing how she was a sucker for praise, she kept at it.

"It's nice to see that you can in fact obey instructions. I was beginning to wonder, considering how often you ignore them in favour of doing exactly as you please. That's it. Use your wrist."

He was the devil. He released one breast and slid his hand down to her trouser front, where he mimicked the sweeps she was making, before he slipped the top button and dragged down her zip.

"I wanted you that first time we met, and Joe knew it, even if he didn't say so. And then you turned up in Cairo all sleep softened and warm and wearing that ridiculous dressing gown. I wanted to take you right there on the kitchen counter. I should have done it. Given you a proper welcome to the team instead of the half-arsed hazing the rest of them made."

She swallowed. She'd no idea that the pull she'd felt toward him had been reciprocated.

His hand found its way into her knickers. She was already wet for him, a fact that made his cock jerk against her rear. Heaven knows how she kept working, but she did it. Despite the tremors of joy racing all over her body.

"Killian? Are you down here?"

The sound of Siân's voice made her jump.

"Lucas thinks he's found something."

Now? Really!

"Don't move." Killian said into her ear.

Siân would find them. She'd realise right away what they were doing. It was taking Adie all her willpower not to roll her hips in time with the rhythm of Killian's fingers on her clit, and Siân was no fool. What plausible reason could there be for them to be sandwiched so close?

"I'll be right there. I've just got to finish something off," Killian called.

Adie bit her lip until it hurt. A rough piece of skin on Killian's fingertip kept grazing her in a particularly sensitive spot, so she was forced to drop one of her tools to shove her fist into her mouth. It barely stifled her groans.

"Go tell Lucas that I'll be there in a sec," he called to Siân.

To Adie it seemed like a lifetime passed before she was certain Siân had gone. By then, she was bathed in sweat and the breath she'd been unconsciously holding in erupted like a cough. Killian knocked the remaining tool from her hands, then drew her T-shirt over her head and twisted it to capture her wrists. Subsequently, down came her trousers and panties.

Warm air caressed her bare bottom, before his cock nuzzled equally bare against it.

Yet again, he made her breath catch.

This was... Was this really the man who was buried beneath all that legendary ice, and scholarly seriousness? The same man who refused to speculate over what was depicted in a mural and who'd chastised her for her unprofessionalism because she'd offered commentary on two of colleagues adopting similar poses.

Not that she was complaining. Oh, no. She liked this Killian very much.

"Still no condoms, sadly," he said, curling a possessive hand over her mons. "Such a pity, because I really, really want to fuck this pussy. This pussy that's all wet for me and that's going to fit my cock just right. You'd like that too, wouldn't you, pet?

You'd take your professor's cock like a good girl, wouldn't you?"

"Yes."

"Yes, what?"

"Yes, professor. I'd like you to fuck my pussy. And I'd take it like a good girl."

There was something so wrong about saying those words that made them so right and split her face with a grin.

"Hm, such a dirty mouth, Ms Hamilton. I bet you'd like to suck my cock clean after I've fucked your tight pussy too, wouldn't you?"

"Yes, professor. I like sucking cock. I'd particularly like sucking yours for you."

He ringed one thumb around her lips, then pushed it into her mouth. Adie sucked. "And maybe, pretty girl, if you're good, and quiet, and don't make a fuss, I'll even let you. For now, I want you to close your legs. That's it, press them tightly together."

He adjusted his position, sagging at the knees a little, so his cock angled down towards her pussy, but instead of entering her, his cock slipped into the groove between her thighs.

"That's good, Adie. That's really good. Keep those legs tight together now." He caught her earlobe between his teeth and nipped.

While he might not have come by any condoms, he had seemingly found something to use as lube. His cock rode between her thighs, hard and slippery, while he held her in place with one hand splayed across the front of her upper thigh and the other kneading her clit.

"Need you," he said, slamming against her, and making them both increasingly slick with sweat. His hot breath scorched her neck. Adie jerked back against him.

"Need to make this quick, or Siân will be back here to see what the delay is, but I don't want it to be quick, or over after one climax. Want to fuck you until I'm goddamned dry."

"Yes," she whimpered, teetering on the verge of coming. Her heart fluttered like a caged bird. Then she was falling and crying out. Killian jammed a hand over her mouth, and she pressed two on top of it. She kept on making those muffled sounds as he jerked off against her. He came apart a handful of thrusts later, leaving her wet with his ejaculate.

A moment passed in silence.

"Professor? Killian?"

He touched her with two fingers where she'd received his ejaculate and rubbed it into her skin.

Oh, yes, he'd definitely been hiding all manner of kinky secrets behind that frosty veneer. He pulled up her panties and trousers and fastened them again.

Adie about turned to face him, and looped her hands over his head, capturing him, before he untwisted her T-shirt and released her wrists.

"Places to be," he said. "Work to do."

Adie planted a kiss on his nose. "It's waited three thousand years; it'll wait another two minutes."

"What's it waiting for?"

His white hair was damp with perspiration,

while his eyes were so dilated that only a tiny circle of grey bordered his pupils. "This." Adie locked her mouth over his, demanding a kiss. Damn him for having lips that were so soft, and a tongue that put butterflies in her chest.

"Thank you for the tips, professor," she said cheekily, before letting him go.

-29-
Killian

Killian strode along the dingy corridor, following the line of fluorescent yellow tape that marked the cables of the lighting rig. He hadn't hurried because he didn't expect Lucas to present him with anything especially noteworthy. His second in command might be a fabulous linguist, but he was also prone to inflating the worth of anything he found, and despite Adie enthusiastically chatting behind him about all the possibilities, it was more likely to be a piece of pharaonic dental floss than a golden sarcophagus.

Not that dental floss wouldn't be interesting on a domestic level, just not actually all that riveting really, and certainly nothing that was going to bring him the sort of joy Adie's body had provided.

He glanced back over his shoulder at her, and she beamed at him. Christ! He was crazy to get involved in a relationship right now.

Then again, which was more distracting, tearing his hair out over trying to maintain some distance, or indulging his urges? He knew which one made him feel more in control.

Adie smiled back at him. There was still a rosy blush to her cheeks that deepened when their gazes met. The entire team were going to realise they were shagging in short order, because there was no subterfuge about her. She wore her heart right on her sleeve alongside her ambitions.

In any case, while her hair was mostly hiding it, he'd just left a mark behind on her neck that someone's eagle eyes was sure to notice.

He hadn't done it deliberately—or maybe he had—but he sure as hell wasn't sorry about it. Seeing it there against her pale skin gave him the warm fuzzies inside. The sort of warm fuzzies he hadn't felt in a very long time.

Hell, he'd barely felt any sort of connection to anyone in a very long time outside of professional relationships, and they were just that – working connections he was obliged to nurture for the benefits they reaped.

He reached the mural chamber and found Siân, Lucas, and Matthew all gathered around a tray of pottery fragments, lit by a bright heavy-duty lamp. "What have you got, then?" he asked. "A pharaoh's dick?"

That got their attention. It made him want to howl the way they all blinked at him.

Lucas cleared his throat. "Um, no. Nothing to do with the mural. I found this among the potsherds we scooped up after Adie smashed that urn. It's a cartouche."

"Okay." A name had potential to be important, on the other hand, he could feel Adie's displeasure coming off her in waves. None of them had needed a reminder that her desire for adventure had led to destruction. Also, why was Lucas looking at potsherds and not the fragments from this room?

"And?"

"Take a look for yourself," Lucas said, making room for him to get closer. He may as well have said, "Here boss, look at what my awesomeness had found."

Killian leaned in. Frowned. Adjusted the lamp and looked again.

Well blow him! The bugger actually had a reason to be preening. The hieroglyphs in the oval cartouche were perfectly clear. "Huni."

"I know, right?" Lucas beamed.

"He could be here," Siân added, voice rising. "We could be standing in his bloody tomb!"

"Let's not get giddy, eh?"

"Of course, boss." Siân tempered her grin a fraction before turning to Adie and mouthing the name of the third dynasty king again. The pair of them clasped one another's arms and exchanged the sort of excited mutterings one usually associated with teenagers about to meet their favourite pop idols.

Killian allowed them their moment of excitement, while he fought to temper his own. There were a couple of other pyramids tentatively accredited to Huni, father of Sneferu—one at Abu Roash and another at Selia, but no one had found a body in either tomb. If he was here, somewhere in this tomb, that would seriously put the site on the map, and of course, coupled with the unusual mural...

He raised his head to look at the vibrant colours of the gods and courtiers depicted on the eastern wall. Were they about to make the most important discovery since the re-opening of KV5?

"Killian?" Siân's voice intruded on his thoughts.

He pressed his fingertips together and splayed his fingers. Okay, time for a reality check. The main descending passage was still blocked, and only a specialist mining team would get through that. Too expensive, plus it would generate far too much publicity, assuming the Egyptian authorities would even sanction it. But how else could they reach the burial chamber?

He thoughtfully tapped his index fingers to his lips. Of course, there was the robbers' tunnel and the chamber beyond. What if it wasn't merely a side chamber, but an alternative route into the pharaoh's final resting-place? Other tombs had them.

They were all gazing at him expectantly, awaiting instructions.

"Lucas, Matthew, see what else you can find amongst the pottery we've gathered from room three. Take it all back to the boat if you need better lighting. See if there are any other references to Huni." The reference to the elusive third dynasty pharaoh was significant in itself. "Siân, Adie, you're with me. There has to be a way past that blockage in the main corridor."

Adie whooped.

Killian stepped back when she looked as if she

might leap into his arms. The inevitability of the team cottoning on to their relationship was one thing, but that didn't mean he was ready for full on public displays of affection. She wound up hugging Siân and then Matthew instead, which he didn't much enjoy witnessing, but then he was a jealous guardian of his treasures these days, not the man who'd been happy to share all the joy in the world with anyone who was looking for it.

-30-
Adie

Seventy-two hours later, Adie winced as she stretched to ease the tension in her muscles. Her eyes were beginning to cross too. Based on the Huni pot, Killian had mounted a systematic search of room three from one corner to the next ensuring nothing was left unturned. The hours were long, the conditions cramped, and the lighting shit. With no safe way of running cables along the tunnels, they were relying on hurricane lanterns.

She flopped and rolled onto her back.

"Anything?" Siân enquired.

"Nada. Nothing. Completely zilch." No clues. No convenient this way to the treasure signage. Nothing to suggest Huni was here or had ever been here. She turned a bucket over and scrambled onto her knees before taking a perch.

"I'd kill for a cup of Samīh's coffee right now, or hell, even a lukewarm cup of instant."

"Go get one."

She shook her head, too pooped for a verbal reply. Exiting required wriggling her way through the robber's tunnel on her belly, and she was already scuffed and bruised enough, not to mention smeared with enough dirt for it to qualify as camouflage. She rubbed at a long stripe of muck on her forearm, but only succeeded in spreading it out.

God, to think she'd been so desperate to be allowed in here. And it was cool, like something straight off a movie set, with its painted borders and stelae. The tiles of the fake door had a pinkish tint in the dim light. It was a beautiful piece of craftsmanship, like many Egyptian works, and of course, buried underground where no one would ever see it. The image depicted the pharaoh – presumably Huni – performing the ceremonial Heb-Sed run while holding the deeds to upper and lower Egypt.

If only it were an actual door, and not just a facsimile intended for the ka of the deceased to pass through. In her childhood adventures, fake doors had always been a synonym for secret doors.

Honestly, the realities of archaeology weren't nearly as exciting as the adventures she'd concocted growing up, nor as vivid and crocodile filled as the tales Esther had spun. That, to be fair, was probably a good thing.

"Got anything to eat?" Siân asked.

Adie patted down her pockets, which yielded a couple of dried and not very appetising looking figs. She offered them to Siân, only to pull her hand back at the last moment.

"I'm too tired for games, mate."

"I just thought...What if we make him an offering? I mean, it's traditionally what stelae were for, right? Roll up in this direction if you're looking for some grub."

"If you're gonna try it, I suggest you do so before Killian gets back. He won't be impressed. You know what he's like about spurious mumbo-jumbo." She offered Adie her water canteen to do the honours. Adie tipped a little onto the ground before the depiction, then knelt and presented the fluffy figs.

No spectral entities emerged, nor did a hidden door suddenly creak open. "Reckon we're ever going to find the burial chamber?"

"Yeah."

Adie arched an eyebrow at her companion's chipper tone. "You sound super certain."

"Killian's not going to leave a stone unturned. It might not be a quick find, but we will get there, eventually. Come on, Adie. Look around you. No one goes to the effort for doing this much decorating, ahead of constructing the main accommodations." She patted Adie on the shoulder. "There's a burial chamber. It's probably closer than you think."

She bent down and claimed a fig.

"Hey, you can't steal sacred offerings."

"Says who?"

"We'll never find the way in now. Also, yuck. That's been in my pocket for at least three days."

"Waste not, want not. I'm starving, and I don't think he was about to eat them."

Adie swatted at her, to prevent her claiming the remaining figs. "That's not how offerings work."

"Offerings. Smofferings." She popped the fig into her mouth. "Heard anything from you know who?"

"No."

"Is that a lie?"

"Yes. What am I supposed to say to him, Siân? You were fab, but..."

"But what?"

Dammit! She gritted her teeth, before adding in a quiet voice, "I've hooked up with someone else, and..."

Siân bolted upright. "Excuse me, you've what? Adie?"

She kept her gaze studiously focused on the figs. They were starting to look rather appetising.

Siân snatched them from under her nose. "You've hooked up with who, exactly? Not...Oh my God, are you kidding me? When?"

She shook her head as Killian slid out of the tunnel and dusted himself off. It wasn't fair that even dust-streaked, he got to look yummy and stylish, whereas she looked like a down-and-out. He combed his hand through his hair and the silken white strands fell into salon perfection.

"What?" he asked in response to the pair of them staring at him.

"Nothing. What now?"

"We keep looking. We dig. We sift. It's what fieldwork is."

"It was definitely more fun playing in the dirt as a child."

"Hey, if you don't want to be here..."

She stuck her tongue out. "I never said that."

"If you want adventure stories, you're in the

wrong place."

"You know, sometimes people do find amazing things. That's how the Hollywood legends came about. If Lord Carnarvon hadn't found Tutankhamun's treasures, then—"

"Adie, this is an early dynasties tomb, probably third, possibly later. Tutankhamun was from the eighteenth dynasty."

"They still had gold."

"True," Siân added, earning herself a frosty sigh. "Although personally, I'd rather we found a body than a bunch of trinkets."

"Back to work," Killian barked. "Because that's the only way we're going to find anything."

Siân leaned in close to her ear. "I reckon you picked the wrong hottie. Oh, wait, you haven't actually picked. The other one's still on hold. Seems you're wiser than you look after all."

"Piss off."

"Love ya," Siân replied, barely holding back a laugh.

Pfft. Her phone began to vibrate in her top pocket. No need to look to know who was calling. Only one person outside of the team had her number.

If it had been clearer where she stood, then it would have been easier to make a definitive choice. The thing was, while Killian was happy enough to shag her, he still held her at a distance. Presently, while it was fun, there was a time limit on the relationship, defined by the length of the dig. Once it ended... well, he'd move on, and he probably wouldn't look back, and too many of the relationships in her life had melted away for her to take such things in her stride. If he turned his back, it'd hurt. Was Anton looking for more than that? The fact that he was still calling, despite her lack of response, certainly suggested it.

An easy forty minutes passed in silence before Adie noticed that Killian had stopped working. He still had a trowel in his hand, but it hadn't touched the ground for a while. "Something up?"

"I've been thinking."

Her ears perked. Siân swivelled on the spot, at what had to be the most un-Killian like thing he'd ever said. "What if the door isn't false?"

Siân wiped a dusty smear across her brow. "Woo, déjà vu,"

"I wondered that earlier." The confession earned her a stern look, all chin, and frown lines.

"Yeah, but did you check?"

"Yeah, we checked... I mean, I guess we didn't actually check. Not in any detail." Siân left her pitch and planted herself before the door. "I guess, we assumed."

"I fucking hate assumptions."

And didn't they all know it.

"Other tombs have similar features. It's reasonable to suppose the edges are decorative, and aren't actual edges," Siân said.

"Well, how do we figure it out?" Adie got to her feet too. The *ka* door didn't scream *I'm a portal* to her any more than it had earlier. Alas, nor did she spy a secret keyhole one could open with an ankh.

Honestly, it wasn't even that exciting a depiction either. The pharaoh—Huni, if that's who it was—wearing a particularly stupid milk churn hat, and someone had bandaged his beard so that it stuck out from his chin like a deformity.

Killian flung a pair of work gloves at her. "We see if it moves."

~Ж~

"Left a bit. A bit more. Steady, now." Killian guided them as they eased the stone slab out of the wall with a block and tackle. He'd been right about the door. The wooden splints they'd wedged into the widening gap creaked, then one splintered.

"Gently!"

Adie felt her muscles strain as Siân slotted in another wedge. The tension was near unbearable. The whole team was crowded into the underground chamber, making it even more cramped and sweaty than usual, but it had taken their combined strength and ingenuity to ease the stone from its seating.

Fat beads of perspiration were rolling down Killian's back. He was bare from the waist up and streaked with grime. Adie's vest was stuck to her, and equally filthy, dark patches of sweat making a camo pattern across the khaki.

The grating sigh of stone against stone made her clench her teeth. There was a gasp of cooler air, then the block slid onto the rollers they'd so carefully positioned.

"It's out," someone said.

Which meant they were going in.

Killian caught up a torch and shone it into the void. While the stone they'd removed was a good six feet high and her arm span in width, the hollow behind it was half that size.

"Siân, you're up," Killian drew back a little to give her space to manoeuvre.

Adie peered into the crawlspace as Siân pulled on a head torch. It didn't feel real. Howard Carter's response to Lord Carnarvon when they opened Tutankhamun's tomb in the Valley of the Kings kept playing in her head. "Wonderful things," he'd replied. All Adie could see were shadows, clinging like cobwebs beyond the range of the beam.

"Not too far. Don't take any risks, we don't know how stable any of this is."

"I know the drill, Killian." She ducked her head and wriggled in on her belly, her long blonde plait hanging behind her. It was the last thing Adie saw before the inky shadows completely swallowed her.

There was a dull hard thud followed by an "Ow!"

"Everything okay?" Killian spread himself flat in the tunnel entrance.

"Fine."

"Where are you? What do you see?"

Siân's torches flashed at the end of the tunnel. The dual pinpoints of light swept left, then right. "Some sort of gallery. There are statues ahead. I can't make out what they are from here. Hang on." The light vanished again to the left of the hole, leaving them all staring into the darkness, ears straining to pick up the soft scurry of her footsteps. "Oh! They're all missing their heads. And they're bound. Naked and bound."

"Slaves?" Matthew asked.

"Like the prisoner statues from the Pepi I's mortuary temple?" Killian asked. "Adie, pass me another lantern."

"Similar, I think. Except these are completely naked. There are four of them, I think. Two facing each other where I am now, and another pair further on, beyond what looks like a portcullis slab."

"Could you be looking at the other side of the main passageway?" Lucas yelled. He had a compass in his hand.

"Yeah. Yes, possibly. Makes sense. Which means behind me along here should be..."

"Should be what?" Adie asked.

"The burial chamber," Killian and Siân said simultaneously.

"I'm coming in." Killian scrambled forward. "The rest of you stay put."

"But...!" Adie protested. Goddammit! She didn't want to be left out of this.

"Until we're sure it's safe," he said, hand on her shoulder. Then he was gone.

"Bastard," she swore under her breath. That was the second time he'd left her behind when there was a discovery to be made. She slapped the block they'd removed with enough force to make her palm smart beneath the protective layer of her glove.

"Chill your knickers," Matthew bent forward to say into her ear. "We'll get our turns."

In fact, she only had to wait another ten minutes

for Siân to shimmy out of the opening, grimy sweat running down her beaming face.

"Go for it." She nodded at Adie, while she set to swapping over the batteries in her head torch.

"Really?"

"Yeah, really."

"Just last time..."

"Killian's instructions, not mine. Go on, girl. Get wriggling."

She slid carefully into the crawlspace. Siân made manoeuvring look easy, but it was tough on the limbs. She brought her knee down on a loose stone and cursed in pain.

"Yeah, watch out for the loose rubble," Siân called from the other room. "Some of them bite."

"I could have done with that warning a bit sooner."

A few more metres and she was through. Adie straightened to her full height. She'd emerged into a broad gallery. Many of the wall facings were chipped and fractured, but every surface was covered in painted images. One depicted the fertility god Min with an erect phallus the colour of oxblood. In another, hunters had cornered two hippopotamuses. She traced a section of hieroglyphics, picking out the pharaoh's name – Huni.

Suddenly, she found herself laughing. It didn't matter that she wasn't the first to witness this wonder. She was seeing what no one was meant to see, a tomb sealed for eternity. This was a private abode of an emperor. The liminal space between the world of the living and his afterlife among the gods.

This was what all the years of study had been for. It was what her father and Esther had both encouraged her to seek. They'd both dreamed the same dream as her, although neither had come close to fulfilling it. She... she on the other hand had done it. "We've done it," she said to them. They might not be here with her to see the fruits of love they'd inspired, but she carried them in her heart and in her memory always. They'd found the tomb of a pharaoh who'd been lain to rest here four and a half thousand years ago.

Adie found Killian in the centre of the burial chamber. Here the smooth walls were undecorated, although the ceiling was painted blue and embossed with stars to resemble the night sky. A huge sarcophagus was situated in the centre of the room. Adie hurried over to the granite sepulchre to run her palms over the stone. The sides were carved; the top stone etched with hieroglyphs. Adie pressed her cheek to the lid. It was icy cold.

"It's empty."

For a moment, Killian's words didn't register.

"What? How can you—"

"There's a crack in the bottom corner. You can see right through to the head. There's no mummy. He's not here. This isn't his final resting-place."

Adie stepped back. Excitement draining from her tired limbs and leaving her chest feeling tight. She'd never really expected gold or treasures, although she'd hoped, but for there to be no body... a body was a given. Without one, this was just a hollow vault.

"Thieves?" she asked.

He had his back to her, and he'd grazed his shoulder, so the skin there was smeared with blood. "We can check the casket for traces," he said. "But it was probably never used. We already know the earthworks above ground were never completed, so maybe it was only intended as a cenotaph, or a decoy. It seems the mystery of Huni's final resting-place will persist. The various writings might shed some light on his reign, though.

"Right." Adie rubbed her brow with the back of her hand. She was going to need a giant bar of chocolate and a bath to compensate for the lack of a body. "So, what now?"

Killian put his arm around her shoulder. "It's still a burial chamber and a major find. We photograph everything and then learn what we can. This is going to keep us busy for a long while."

"Of course. What do you need? I'll get—"

"We'll begin tomorrow. With fresh eyes and fresh enthusiasm. It's taken a lot out of us all to get this far, and there are people who need to be notified before we go any further. Some of whom might get extremely shirty if we do anything without their explicit say so, and I for one, would rather not be shut down and ejected from this site for lack of a signature on the right form."

-31-
Adie

Killian knocked on Adie's cabin door later that evening. The sun was waning, and the aphids were chittering among rushes. Adie was on her third gin martini. Ostensibly because they were all celebrating the find. Though honestly, it didn't feel like much of a discovery. She knew treasure hoards consisting of acreage of gold and trinkets were the stuff of Hollywood legends, but childhood dreams were a hard thing to let go of.

"Hey," Killian said, filling her door frame and perking up her mood with his presence. He'd showered and changed into a pair of wide-legged linen trousers and white shirt with a pale blue stripe that he'd yet to button. His white hair caught the light above the doorway, giving it a moon-like luminescence. She spotted another tattoo, a tiny ankh positioned under his left pec held in the mouth of a stork-like Bennu bird – yet more symbols of rejuvenation and rebirth.

"Have you eaten yet?"

"Not unless you count a few olives." She sucked the one off the cocktail stick in her drink.

"Good. I sent our sponsor the snapshots I took of the find, and I've just heard back. He demands I come to dinner, and that I bring you along. Get your glad rags on Adie, we're going out."

"Shit!" she swore, regretting her current drink along with the previous two. "You realise I don't have anything posh with me, just work clothes."

He roved an assessing eye over her. "I'm sure Siân will loan you something. And stop panicking. It's just dinner not an interrogation. He just wants to look you over and make sure you're not too suspect now that we have a genuine find on our hands."

"Suspect," she echoed, immediately feeling like she was a member of an illegal international antiquities trading ring. She wasn't. At least, she didn't think she was.

"He'll love you." Killian laughed.

He was certainly chirpy.

"Will he? Why will he?"

He stepped into her cabin proper and closed the door. Adie stood as he approached. Killian took the drink from her hand and put it aside on the trunk at the foot of her bed. "Because he trusts my judgement, and what's not to like?" He brushed her cheek with his curled fingers. "You're honest, hardworking, intelligent. I won't demean you by mentioning you're beautiful, too."

"You just did."

"Did I?" He gave an impish grin, and his tongue lashed his teeth. "You should pack an overnight bag, too."

"Overnight. You said dinner."

"Yes, but his place is a way downriver, and it makes more sense to make the return trip tomorrow morning than come back in the dark. There'll be a boat here to collect us in a little under an hour. Be ready for when it arrives. Masud doesn't like to be kept waiting."

He pressed a kiss to the centre of her brow, then about turned.

"Where are you going?"

He looked back at her over his shoulder, and there was that mischievous spark in his eyes that she'd hardly imagined could exist a handful of days ago.

"I've a couple of things I need to do before we leave. Errands to run. Don't worry, I'll be back in time." He paused, hand on the door handle. "And Adie, make it a sexy dress."

"Oh, is he that sort of sponsor?" Just what she needed; an evening being ogled by a misogynistic old dude.

Killian shook his head. "The dress is for me. Masud is happily married. I want to see at least one bare shoulder."

"A bared shoulder? You're a strange man."

He laughed and wriggled his eyebrows. "Shoulders are very sexy, don't you know."

"What if I mislay my knickers?"

That earned her the sort of glare that knitted his eyebrows together.

"Okay, Professor Stick-in-the-Mud." She rolled her eyes. "I'll put on my best pair, just so your sponsor knows I'm serious."

"Adie," he chastened. "He doesn't need to know a thing about your underwear."

Sometimes it was difficult to tell if he was absolutely serious, or plain old messing with her.

~Ж~

A motorboat collected them and sped them to their destination. Adie stepped off the gangplank and gazed at Masud Al-Saddiq's home in awe. Occupying an island within the Nile river, the house's opulent Mamluk design of banded red and white stone, with stalactite-like stone carvings, rivalled many of the mosques she'd seen dotted across the Cairene metropolitan skyline. Flame trees shielded the building from the shore, and bedded plants provided flashes of saturated colour. It made sense that whoever was sponsoring the team had money, but it was quite another to come face to face with it.

She smoothed her outfit with clammy palms. Killian had been distant on the journey here, barely speaking other than to approve her outfit. Siân's wardrobe had yet again provided, this time furnishing her with an ankle-length Nile-blue satin evening dress, which bared one shoulder and emphasised the curves of her waist and hips. There were matching shoes with kitten heels, and a clutch that she was hanging onto for dear life. Why Siân kept such an outfit on the houseboat eluded her. The most glamorous thing Adie had brought with her to Egypt was a glitzy black thong. Wishful thinking while she was packing, she supposed, although it had come in useful this evening.

"Sometimes I go out," she'd said, treating Adie to a wink, as she'd fussed over the fit. She'd then ordered her to remove her bra and employed a roll of medical tape to secure Adie's breasts where they ought to be to ensure the correct line. She'd winced through the ordeal, already anticipating the point where she'd have to peel it all off.

Yes, sometimes she was a wimp.

Also, she was going to have to leave her phone in her cabin.

"That him again?" Siân nodded at her vibrating bag. "Honey, you need to put your big girl knickers on."

"What if I'm not certain?"

Siân squeezed her shoulder. "Then you need to figure it out, and fast."

Killian offered her his arm as they strode along the white gravelled pathway towards the house. He'd opted for an all-black suit, worn with a crisp white shirt, and a pair of what she suspected were antique emerald cufflinks.

A member of staff showed them into an airy hallway. Adie was still removing her sunglasses when a slender Egyptian woman in a vibrant red dress shimmied down the stairs and straight into Killian's arms.

"Doctor Carmichael, such a pleasure to see you, as always."

"Safiyya." He acknowledged her in return. Killian didn't return her touch, but kept his hands positioned inches away from her body, and perhaps no wonder, given that her dress was little more than a handkerchief held together with ribbons. It shimmered against the black of Killian's suit. Modest, it was certainly not. It made her outfit seem decidedly prudish.

"And you must be Bill's replacement." She kissed Adie on the cheeks three times. "Adina, isn't it? We're very informal. I'm Safiyya."

Adie was only ever Adina when she was in disgrace but didn't correct her hostess.

"Come, let's go through. Masud is waiting, and you know how little he likes that."

She led them through to a vast dining room, overlooking a shaded courtyard and a well. Masud Al-Saddiq was at least twenty years Safiyya's senior, smooth skinned save for a score of deep grooves round his wise, friendly eyes, with dark hair perfectly silvered at the temples. Adie instantly warmed to him. He reminded her of Joe Levine. Nor did he look the slightest bit impatient over having been kept waiting.

~Ж~

"Killian, I know you despair over the repercussions," Masud said after dinner, when they'd retired to the veranda over-looking the gardens and the black of the river water. "But, with today's discovery we need to feed the official press channels. Giving them a story of our choosing is better than letting their imaginations run wild over what you're doing down there under that unassuming pile of rocks."

"Why do we need to say anything?"

"You know why. The EAO have all the power, and they leak like a burst water main. If we give a statement, then at least we control the narrative. I assume you've informed them, so it's just a matter of time. Let's get ahead of the game, eh?"

Killian shook his head, but it was a denial already weighed by resignation.

"Come now, there may even be some benefit that comes of such a spread. I'd like to see that mural complete, and you keep telling me you don't think you're going to find the central piece of that puzzle—"

"I like to manage your expectations."

"—A photograph might jog someone's memory. There are fragments all over the world, in display cases and dusty boxes. What if it's right now sitting on someone's mantelpiece?"

"Chances are, a press release will gain us even more unsavoury interest."

"More?" Masud levelled Killian with his gaze. "Oh, yes, your little spat the other day. A somewhat overzealous response, don't you think?"

Adie's ears perked. She still didn't have the full details of that display, but Masud seemed entirely unfazed to find his chief hire had thrown a fist at someone.

"No. Not really. I thought it was a quite a civilised response all things considered."

Masud shook his head, but there wasn't a hint

of irritation connected to it. "We're not looking at a piece in the nationals, Killian. Only a quiet release in the academic press."

"And we both know that will only delay things twenty-four hours, so let's not pretend otherwise. Then work will grind to a screeching halt, because I'll have a pack of hungry jackals camped outside, and once they're there, the tourists will follow, and we'll be managing constant security breaches."

"Why don't you let me worry about security? I've offered you guards before."

"Aye, and I've refused them, because I'm not interested in having my dig constantly disturbed. Sure, they'll be useful for keeping people out while we're working down there. It's what happens after hours that concerns me. A few backhanders and I'll turn up to find a few more bits of the mural missing and graffiti in its place."

"Would you rather the press be given free rein to speculate? Allow that and you'll have twice the number of people camped outside, all convinced there's a hoard big enough to pay off the national debt down there."

"Why is everyone so blinking obsessed with treasure?" He bowed his head to his hands and rubbed at his eyes. Adie felt a blush rising over her cheeks, knowing she fell firmly into that category.

"It's a fantasy," she said. "Plus, everyone can gaze on golden treasures and ooh and aah over. We all know that real insights into the past depend on much more than that, but it's hard for the layman to get excited over the more mundane items. They want

Hollywood Egypt. Scooby Doo Egypt. Sand, treasure, gold, mummies, and mysteries."

"Your colleague's right, Killian."

"I know she's bloody right. It doesn't mean I have to like it."

"So, we give the press details about the mural room, and give the public a mystery to dig into."

Killian simply rolled his eyes. "As if I have any genuine say in the matter."

"Then we're agreed. I'll get on with arranging it."

"Since we're talking about the mural," Adie said. "I've been wondering. Aren't there experts on erotic art we can consult? Museum catalogues that we could check for our missing piece?"

Killian and Masud both squinted at her. What? Had she said something dumb? She didn't think she had. "Samīh thinks it's in the Cairo Museum. It's where Jacob's journal ended up, and it did open around the time of his excavation."

Killian snorted. "What's far-fetched is that you imagine that permission for such a search would be granted, and secondly, that it'd yield anything within the next decade."

Meanwhile, Masud thoughtfully stroked his chin. "Dear Adina, I don't wish to disregard your idea entirely. It's a sound proposition. It is only that as Killian says, securing permission to scour their archives is unlikely to be granted. Also, it would be an extremely lengthy undertaking. As to experts on erotic art, they are few and far between, particularly those specialising in Egyptian eroticism. Greek,

Roman, Indian, Japanese, even Persian, certainly, but few dedicated to that aspect of Ancient Egyptian culture."

"But there are some?"

"Aye, perhaps one or two with any credentials. Possibly, even one whose email address I can provide you with."

Killian sat back in his chair. "She doesn't need to be wasting time on this."

"I'm happy to pursue it in my own time."

Masud slapped the arm of her chair. "Ah, I like this worker you've brought in from your homeland, Killian. She's definitely more dedicated to our goal than her predecessor. Now, the press release. Two photographs, a panoramic shot of the mural chamber, I think, and then a detail of the mural, featuring everyone's favourite missing part."

Killian said nothing. A moment or two later he strode to the far end of the veranda and stood with his back to them staring out into the dark. Masud traded a look with Adie, then lit a cigar and smoked a good portion of it before intruding on Killian's jasmine shrouded sanctuary.

"Don't imagine I don't know what you're afraid of?" Masud kept his voice low, but save for the gurgling of the river, their surroundings were silent, and so his words carried. "Thumping his minion was rash."

"It was hardly planned."

"Still, you let him bait you."

"What should I have done? Invited him in to take all the photographs he wanted, so he can make me look like a fucking fool again?"

"Now, now." He gave Killian a paternal pat on the shoulder. "There's no need for such language. We know Sadler's a leech better kept at a long arm's length, but losing your cool in no way aids the situation. If all we release are the two photographs I've suggested, then he can attempt to spin whatever drivel of a narrative he wishes. It'll amount to nothing, and certainly won't reflect on you or your team. It'll be obvious that he's fishing."

Sadler! Adie strained her ears. Dareth Sadler was the man who'd been signing books at the museum. What had he to do with Killian? What had Anton said about him? Something scathing. That he was an academic leech with a sad cult of middle-aged cat-loving followers and an unhealthy interest in nubile virgins. It'd certainly painted an unflattering picture.

"Yeah, and when he gets his wallet out to bribe the officials and gets himself a nice, guided tour?" Killian grumbled.

Masud gave his shoulder another pat. "He could do that at any time. Releasing a press statement has no bearing on that."

"Except it does. It proves there's something down there worth his interest."

"Oh, Killian." The older man gave a dry chuckle. "He already knows that. You're there. The leading expert on the early dynasties doesn't take a five-strong dig team of experts to Saqqara without a damn good reason for being there. I'm sure he has all the historical documentary evidence about what's down there already collected on a zip drive, the same as you did before you set foot in the place. He already knows about the mural, and of course he's interested. It's a story about a penis, and we both know cock and bull is his forte."

Adie pushed back her chair, meaning to join them, but Safiyya caught her arm. "Leave them to their talk. Everyone knows Killian never ceases to work, but you...you are allowed to take a break. Come, it grows chilly, we'll take coffee inside."

It would have been rude to refuse, so Adie reluctantly allowed herself to be dragged away. Safiyya welcomed her into a comfortable den, with squashy brown armchairs, and a low table already holding a waiting coffee pot. One entire wall formed a gallery of framed black and white photographs.

"Masud's parents," Safiyya elaborated, offering Adie a cup. She gestured to the tray, offering sugar and lemon. Adie declined and curled her fingers around the paper-thin china.

"When are these from?"

"The sixties. It was something of a golden age. There was a post-war boom. The place was full of bright young things, very cosmopolitan. Masud's mother was an English aristocrat. She arrived as a tourist, here for the cafe culture."

Adie shook her head at the reference.

"Turkish coffee, belly dancing, and bikinis on the beach. Then she met Masud's father." She pointed to a man on the extreme right. It was a portrait-style shot, taken outdoors on the terrace outside. "Handsome devil, isn't he? All the ladies fell for him, which was of benefit to his trade."

"His trade?"

"He was a gigolo, although he billed himself as an actor. Film was all the rage back then. There were several Egyptian actors of that era that went on to gain international acclaim, although, he wasn't one of them."

"These aren't all of that era though," Adie remarked, shifting her attention further along the wall. The right-hand side offered several more modern images. "This is you, yes?"

Safiyya kicked off her shoes and curled into an armchair. "Yes."

"A hobby?" In the image her hostess wore a similar outfit to the one Anton had gifted Adie and then subsequently ruined.

"I danced professionally. It's how Killian and I met. He came to see me perform at the Sheraton. Oh, a few years ago now. Not so long..."

Adie took a swallow of steaming coffee. It wasn't so hard to infer what the woman actually meant. He hadn't just gone to watch her dance.

"He was a very different man then, of course."

"Different, how?"

Safiyya waved away the question. "One night, he brought Masud along too, and the rest as they say is history."

Her chance to make further enquiries about Killian's past was sadly cut short by Masud's arrival. "Killian's decided to turn in. He asked that I communicate his desire to make an early start."

"Yes, of course." Adie drained her cup and set it

aside. "I'd best do the same."

"Let me show you the way. I'm afraid we've put you in the guest house, so that the rest of the household isn't disturbed by your early departure. There are two rooms, so you need not disturb the bear with his sore head."

"Is he very out of sorts?" she asked.

Masud shrugged. "He does so hate to be managed. But here, I have this for you." He pressed a business card into her hand. On the back he'd written a name and email address. "Franks is an old associate. Retired now, but if you wish to know about the eroticism of the ancients, then he is the man you consult."

"Thank you. But should not Killian—"

"Killian will not approach him. Have you not learned that much about him yet? He is not one to seek counsel outside of the core of personnel he directly employs. He will probably not thank you for doing so either, so keep that in mind, and remind him who gave you this address if he takes you to task over it."

"Thank you. I'll do that. And I'll get on with this."

He led her across the lawn along a pathway lined by solar lights to a squat white building near the water's edge. "*Tesbahi 'ala Kheir*, Doctor Hamilton."

"Good night and thank you again."

-32-
Adie

The guest house consisted of a central room with two adjacent bedrooms and a small kitchen area. There was no immediate sign of Killian, or indication of which room he'd claimed. She tried the first door and found the room empty, with her overnight set atop of the dresser. Adie kicked off her shoes, then about turned and knocked on the second door. "Killian? Can I come in?"

She tried the handle and found him standing on the far side of a vast bed, looking out of a lattice-screened window at the river.

"I suppose it didn't occur to you that the answer might be no."

He was nursing something that looked suspiciously like brandy. "Did I do something wrong?"

He turned while sliding the knot down his tie, then cast it over a vibrantly patterned stool.

"Killian?"

"No, you didn't do anything. You made the right noises. You sided with Masud. I'm sure he's delighted with you."

Unlike him, evidently. "He's given me the email address of someone to contact."

"Of course he has. That's what he does. He interferes."

She frowned. "Isn't he your boss? Isn't that his job? To steer you?"

"No, Adie. It isn't his job, and he's not my boss. The fact he backs the dig doesn't give him a say in how I run it. I involve him out of courtesy."

Okay, that was her told. "Am I to take it then that you don't wish me to use this?" She turned the business card between her fingers.

"What do you even intend to ask?"

"Oh, I don't know. I thought I'd open with something like, 'Hey, do you know where I can find some ancient cock?'"

That earned her a disbelieving smirk. "Be serious, Adie. If you can."

"Lighten up a little. If you can. Not everything has to be serious all the time. Sometimes,"—she sidled up a little closer and claimed the glass from his hand—"it's okay to relax and have a bit of fun. For example, we're not working, right at this minute, and while we might not have found the Ark of the Covenant earlier, or even Huni's mummified corpse inside a golden sarcophagus, we did still make a find worth celebrating. Right?"

"Right," he reluctantly conceded, watching her sip his liquor.

Adie set it aside on the dresser.

"Oh, come on. You're not telling me that you're such a big shot that you no longer get a thrill out of making discoveries." She shook her head. "I don't believe it. I think there are all sorts of celebratory fireworks going on inside here." She tapped the side of his head. "And here." Then lay her hand over his heart. "Also, did I mention how goddamned sexy you are in that suit?"

He made a dismissive snort and turned his head away.

"I can see I need to up my flirting game."

"Oh," he said, thawing a microscopic fraction. "Was that flirting?"

"More like a flat-out invitation." Her reply won her the response she'd been seeking.

A slight adjustment in his stance and the set of his shoulder. A sexy glint amidst the frosty glare.

"I know we've an early start, professor, but what do you say we both sacrifice some precious sleep in favour of..."

"Of?"

"Oh, I don't know." She crossed to where his overnight bag sat open at the foot of the bed. "I wonder. Did your little excursion earlier happen to involve a quick trip to a pharmacist?"

"Excuse me! What the hell do you think you're doing going through my things?"

Unthwarted, Adie held up the item she'd been hoping to find. It was sat right at the top of the bag, like it had been shoved in there last minute. "What's this, professor? Were you planning a little party?"

"Give me those." He reached out to snatch them from her, but Adie hid them behind her back, so that he wound up hunched over her, his body curved over hers in a way that would have been intimidating, if she wasn't quite so keen on him crowding her.

"You've got yourself a whole party pack here, you must imagine you're going to get incredibly lucky."

"Luck, has nothing to do with it."

"Oh?"

He stared at her a moment. Then his eyes narrowed, and he hooked his arms beneath her legs and lifted her off her feet.

"Hey! Put me down."

"With pleasure." He dropped her onto the carpet, which while soft, she still hit with a thump.

"Fucking bastard!" But then he was there, curled over her, his hands tight around her wrists while his hips pinned her legs open. Beneath his zip, his cock was already stiff.

They stared at one another. His nostrils flared with every ragged breath. Her heart was hammering against her ribcage.

"What's the matter, Ms Hamilton? Isn't this what you were angling for?"

She still had the box of condoms clasped in her right hand.

"Isn't the very reason that you're here in my room, that you're desperate for me to fuck you?"

"I'm not desperate," she said, her body already arching up to meet his. The heat of him was an aphrodisiac. The smell of him, intoxicating. "Only desirous. You see, my boss is a very sexy man. He has this whole gruff professor thing going, but really, I think it's a disguise, and underneath that stern glacial exterior is an unrepentant dirty boy just dying to get out."

One eyebrow quirked. "Careful what you wish for, Ms Hamilton." He leaned in so that his next words were spoken softly into her ear. "You might get more than you bargained for from this grumpy, unrepentant bad boy."

"What like a damn good pounding from your cock? In case you haven't worked it out, that's kind of what I'm here for – the bloke and the treasure."

He eased back a fraction onto his knees and grasped the bedsheet. "Whereas I'm here to torture the fuck out of you."

"I beg your pardon."

"Oh, come now, Adie. I'm sure you've heard me described as a sadistic fucker. It's not because I give A+ students Bs on their assignments. Although, your performance so far is more like a C."

"Is that a euphemism for I'm going to claim your cunt?"

Instead of denying it, he drawled, "Possibly."

"So, how does one get an A?"

To her complete astonishment, he started tearing strips from the cotton sheet. "Use that big brain of yours, I'm sure you'll work it out."

"Arse," she said through gritted teeth.

Was he serious or just teasing her?

Also, "Um, why are you tearing up the bed sheets? Isn't our host going to have something to say about it?"

"Oh!" he remarked as if he hadn't noticed he was doing something unusual. "He'll know exactly why I've done it. I mummify all my victims."

"You do what?"

He responded by tying one of the long strips around her ankles, then using it to bind her feet. Adie gaped at him, mouth and throat dry. "That's more than a little odd, you know?"

"Is it?" He said it so nonchalantly, she couldn't tell if he was being serious.

Killian kept winding strips up her legs, so they covered her up past her knees, and she, in her bewilderment, let him.

"What are you doing? Or rather, why are you doing it?"

He tsked. "Because I'm a kinky fucker, and bondage turns me on."

He said it in such a deadpan way she still wasn't sure if he was entirely serious or just messing with her.

"I'm afraid this dress is going to have to come off." He grabbed it by the hem and swept it up her body and over her head. When he saw the tape around her breasts, something feral lit in the depths of his pupils.

"Oh, Adie!" He teased the end of one strip off her skin with his fingernail, then ripped it off.

"Fuck!" she swore at the sting. Okay, so the sadistic fucker part did appear to be accurate. "That hurt."

"I know." He did the same with a second strip of tape, causing her to hiss through her teeth, but then his head bowed towards her breasts, and his mouth was nursing away the sting with tender kisses. The bandages were temporarily forgotten as his focus coalesced on mouthing her breasts. Her nipples, he sucked into two taut points. Then right when she was groaning over the pleasure of it, he relieved her of another piece of tape.

"You're fucking evil."

He didn't stop worshiping her breasts. "You have fantastic tits. More than enough to wrap around my cock and fuck."

"Is that how one earns a B?"

He knelt back grinning and loosened off his belt. The sight of that strip of leather in his hand caused a storm of butterflies in her stomach. "I thought you were a straight-A student."

"Are you seriously asking me if you can fuck me in the arse?"

"Well, your consent would certainly be preferable."

He lay the belt aside and leaned over her, capturing her wrists again, and binding them with another strip of sheeting. He hovered above her a moment, holding himself just shy of kissing her. "Don't get me wrong. It's not that I don't relish the thought of making use of this pretty cunt." His right hand pressed between her thighs. "I mean, I'm not ruling out dipping my wick in there. It's just... You're kind of twitchy about me exploring other places, and that makes me want to do them even more."

"I'm not twitchy."

"You're very twitchy." He proved it by flipping her over and pulling her onto all-fours, before shoving a pillow beneath her hips.

Okay, she was a little nervous. He'd rendered her essentially helpless by tying her wrists, and her legs were fastened together from her toes to her knees.

Killian pulled her glitzy thong down to her thighs. He was staring at her arse, so that she was burning with embarrassment over the scrutiny. She wasn't ashamed of her body, but she wasn't used to being ogled in quite such an obvious way.

"You know, you're still owed some chastisement for breaking that urn. An urn that is likely a very important indicator of the pyramid's intended resident. A pharaoh there is scant evidence about."

She swallowed uneasily, aware of him fingering his discarded leather belt. "Don't, please."

"You don't think I should stripe your arse as punishment for your behaviour?"

"No."

"You don't think it's justified?"

"I don't think I'll like it."

"Well, it wouldn't really be a punishment if you liked it, now, would it?"

"Isn't it enough that you're planning to fuck me back there?"

That prompted a chuckle. "All you have to do is say Osiris, and this stops. All of it. I'll untie you. You can go back to your room. Sleep in your own bed. And we never have to speak about this again."

That wasn't what she wanted either. "Please don't spank me," she said. Her breasts were still tingly from where he'd rid her of the tape.

"Maybe I'll bite you instead," he said and grazed

her with his teeth, a sensation that made her shiver. "Then again, maybe I like these pretty cheeks all smooth and unblemished. His lips alighted where his teeth had pressed, while his breath stirred a thousand tiny hairs making her skin come alive. Finally, his tongue poked rudely into the channel between her cheeks and tickled her puckered hidden entrance.

Adie wriggled in response. The sensation more exciting than she'd anticipated. It made her tremble and gasp, and her insides excitedly squirmy. It made no sense that touching her there should render her so loose-limbed and wet for him, but it did. Moreover, he knew it. He could see it. Was tasting it.

Her head bowed towards her bound wrists. Cheeks aflame.

"Watch the shadows, Adie. Don't you want to see what I've got for you?"

She turned her head. The low lighting from the lamp cast their entangled silhouettes upon the wall. His erection looked impossibly huge, certainly far too big to be going up her virgin arse. Still, there was something about the shadow-play that was strangely riveting. For certain, he was in no rush. He fisted the head of his cock, giving himself some encouraging tugs. Then he reached for his overnight bag, not to claim the condoms which lay beside them now on the floor, but something else.

Lube. Jeezus, he'd bought lube in addition to protection. He'd planned in advance for this.

Where his tongue had been, she now felt a more insistent pressure. Not his cock. Not yet, but a finger worming its way inside.

She tried to clench against it, but he only laughed and licked her from front to back so that her clit was tingling from the assault and her limbs were rendered all docile.

"It's such a shame there's nothing to fill this pretty pussy while I fuck your arse. Would you like that, do you think? Both holes filled at once? Each stretched around a thick hard dick. Do you think you could handle that?"

"I don't know," she gasped, honestly. The notion of it was doing strange things to her, though. She didn't think she'd ever felt so squirmy with anticipation in her life, and she'd been on a lot of exciting adventures. Admittedly, predominantly imaginary, but the brain was the main erogenous zone.

Killian slid his finger a little deeper, finding nerves she hadn't known existed, and fattening her clit as a result. When she groaned in frustration of a touch there, he swapped the finger in her arse for his thumb and used his mouth to anoint her nub.

His murmurings of contentment vibrated against her skin. "Hmm, you're so eager for this, aren't you, sweet thing? So ready to take your professor's cock and earn that A. Of course, you're going to have to let me get balls deep for that."

"Yes," she agreed, now stupidly aroused and eager.

"Always chasing those A grades, aren't you?"

"Fuck me, professor. Put that thick hard cock in me. Put it in my bum."

"Yeah," he drawled all languid and husky. "You know, I think I will. Watch the shadows, now, Adie."

Her attention was rivetted on them as he sheathed his cock and coated it with lube, before squeezing some into the crease between her cheeks.

Where his thumb had stretched her, she now felt the head of his cock. Like the tip of a firebrand, it scorched her. Light-headed with uncertainty, yet hopelessly desirous and intrigued, Adie held herself still, so very still for him. The inside of her head was buzzing, and every nerve in her body seemed to be alight. His cock slid against her, past her pucker toward her pussy, dipped ever so briefly just inside, and then he was back to her arse, prodding and pushing his way in, encouraging the muscles to relax.

"Oh!" His exclamation matched hers when it finally went in.

"Oh, you're quite big. I mean you feel big."

"Flatterer." He slid in another inch. "We're just going to take this nice and slow." He was moving as he spoke, but keeping the thrusts shallow, only deepening them as her body slowly relaxed. To Adie it was a strange tangle of blissful agony. She wanted him deeper—maybe. She wanted him in her cunt too. All the way in, to the hilt. Plus, his fingers on her clit and his mouth on hers... and on her breasts again. She wanted him everywhere all at once. Claiming her, filling her. Peeling pieces of tape from her breasts, even though that had stung.

Oh God!

The tape was no more than curls on the carpet,

but the filling her part... that he was definitely doing, and so creating an ache that could only possibly be eased by his repeated thrusts.

"Lord, touch me. Touch me please."

"Where should I touch you, hm?" His hand wrapped around her face, covering her mouth, then his fingers pressed inside. He fucked her like that, using his hold to pull her onto his digits. It was hideous and lovely. She cried when he relinquished that grip and paid attention to her needy clit instead. She was so aroused, his touch there rode very close to being intolerable.

Every tender membrane in her body was seemingly bursting with nerve endings, and each was now singing and screeching with need. All she wanted was to slake the lust building inside by meeting his thrusts and urging him deeper, but Killian steadfastly controlled their rhythm.

"Please." Her pussy ached to be filled.

He pushed his thumb into her, as he continued to pet her clit.

Adie's back arched in response. Senses heightened by the restriction of her freedom and the novel stimulation brought her orgasm on fast. It pounded through her, smashed against her like ocean waves. She thought she screamed. Killian made a low, restrained sound in comparison to her keening, but she felt every pulse of his bliss.

Exhausted by the ferocity of it, Adie's limbs became limp, and she sagged onto the pillow, her head making a cushion of her bound wrists.

She felt the loss of him when he withdrew. Was

aware of his absence for several minutes. On his return, he lifted her onto the bed, where he gently relieved her of the mummy wrappings. When she opened her eyes, he was sitting by her on the bed, wholly naked. He'd left two long streamers of cotton bound around each of her wrists.

"Are you okay?"

Her mouth was dry, but she gave a nod. He seemed to have predicted as much, for he was right there with a drink. After she'd swallowed, she asked, "What are these for?" while raising one wrist. Of course, she glimpsed the bed posts at that point and made the obvious connection. Apparently, they weren't done yet. "Encore," she croaked.

"Drink some more water first and consider how much sleep you want. It'll be a long day tomorrow."

"Do you want to sleep?"

"What do you think, Adie?"

"I think, professor—" she said reaching out to touch him.

Killian clasped his hand over the top of hers, but he shook his head over the name.

"What I think, Killian, is that we should make use of at least one more party hat."

"Is that so?" He rolled onto his back beside her, with his arms raised, hands behind his head.

Adie turned onto her side to look at him. Every inch of him was toned and beautiful. His was not a gym honed body, but one gained through genuine labour. His chest was bare, no hint of any hair, and none lower either. Waxed, she guessed. His cock wasn't entirely at rest, but not slumbering either. He was uncut, and she rather liked that about him. It rather betrayed his English roots.

"Who's Sadler?" she asked.

Killian instantly scowled. "Seriously? That's what's on your mind, now?"

"I'm curious. His name keeps cropping up. He was at the museum the other day, and Masud mentioned him in the context of the photographer you punched, and there's clearly history between the two of you that I'm unaware of."

"Then you must be the only damn person on the planet unaware of it. Go look it up, Adie. I'm not about to rehash it. And come to think of it, maybe you should sleep in your own bed, too. I'm shattered, and on considering, I think maybe I would like some sleep."

She lobbed a cry of, "Seriously?" in return. "You're going to kick me out of your bed over a simple question?"

"Well, maybe it's not so simple a question."

"If there's an issue, and it's related to the dig, shouldn't I know about it?"

"Ask Google. Ask Siân. Ask fucking anybody but me."

His chin was jutting out, his mouth stubborn, and his grey eyes turned the colour of granite. She bit her lip. "What did he do to you?"

Killian shook his head and rolled onto his side facing away from her. Whatever it was, he wasn't about to enlighten her. She stared at the knots in his broad shoulders a moment, then snuggled against them, resting her head against his uppermost shoulder blade. "I'm staying," she said. "I'm sorry I've upset you. If I'd realised it was such a touchy subject, I wouldn't have brought it up. I was just... curious. I've only heard of this Sadler guy since I arrived here."

He gave a quietly disbelieving huff.

"Killian, I'm being honest. I know nothing about your past, about you, beyond the fact that you're a brilliant Egyptologist. And this other guy? I've never even heard of him."

"No one worth your time, now please, stop."

"Okay." Adie buffed her lips against his skin. She didn't want to stop. She wanted answers, and while in other circumstances she'd have tenaciously pressed on, she didn't want him to order her from the room. "I won't say anything else about it. Okay."

"Hm!"

"Does that mean I can stay?"

He gave no response either way, so she interpreted that as a *yes, but don't expect me to say so because I'm still pissed off that you brought the topic up and I intend to stew over it for at least the foreseeable future.*

She'd certainly blown any chance of finally getting him in her pussy.

"I think I'm going to be hyperaware of my arse for the whole of tomorrow. Your dick's huge."

No response.

"I can't believe you went shopping for johnnies and then used them to fuck my bum before you've even shagged me normally."

It was like talking to a statue, except this statue

had warm skin, and a pulse, and sweat was pooling where their bodies touched.

"Okay, I'll be quiet and let you rest."

She rolled over, so that she lay back-to-back with him, her feet pressed against his legs, her bum touching his bum. It seemed unlikely that sleep would take her, but her eyelids soon drooped.

She was teetering on the very edge of sleep when she felt the mattress shift. Killian had left the bed and stood in that same spot by the window as when she'd arrived. Though slitted eyes she watched him stare out into the darkness.

What was on his mind?

"I want to understand you," she thought at him. "I need to know why this Sadler guy is such a burr."

She fell asleep, with Killian still standing naked by the Nile facing window.

-33-
Adie

The thing about making a discovery, however big or small, was that it left little time for anything outside of work. Members of the team began to guard their precious moments of downtime with unprecedented zeal. Matthew, no matter how late they got back of an evening, rushed off for a couple of hours to swim. At least that's what he said he was doing. Lucas, at least one night out of three, muttered something about Mark, and vanished, and Siân... Siân flopped into a deck chair of a night and poked her nose into novel after novel, each with an increasingly sinister sounding title and the sort of blurbs that made Adie shiver.

Adie had tried to engage her in conversation once or twice, but fast learned it wasn't wise. Not if she didn't want a reply likely to corrode their friendship.

Killian... Killian worked until he dropped. He didn't avoid her, but he didn't specifically seek her out either. She interpreted this as him brooding over the seemingly unforgivable mistake of mentioning Sadler. Her interest was now thoroughly piqued. Not that she was about to seek answers on the internet. While that would give her some insight into the situation, it would likely provide a very skewed version of events. Mostly though, it felt intrusive to run a search engine query about someone she was intimately acquainted with. And weird. Definitely weird.

She did email both Joe Levine and Doctor Franks. Joe's response was speedy but acerbic.

JL: Ask him about Petra.

That was it, not a damn thing about Sadler, and not even a hello. How are getting on? Is it what you dreamed of?

She screamed between her gritted teeth and slammed her phone down so hard it was a miracle she didn't smash the screen. Mind you, considering how often it vibrated at inopportune moments, rending it into smithereens might not be such a bad idea. She silenced the buzzing, then frowned over the new message.

AK: If you want me to stop calling, all you have to do is say so.

She only half wanted that. That was the problem. If Killian had been more communicative the answer would have been straightforward. But he wasn't, so more than once her fingers hovered over her phone pad.

Thus, the better part of a week sailed by without

Adie replying to Anton or learning a thing about who Dareth Sadler was, or how he was connected to Killian's past. A week over which Killian grew increasingly tetchy. The tourists had found them. Curiously, they were mostly women. They'd turn up in twos or threes and observe from afar. Then, after a while, they'd sidle up and ask questions or attempt to strike up a conversation. Most of the team found reasons to hurry underground fast, but Matthew inevitably had them laughing and hanging on his every word, even when he was describing very boring processes. Pretty soon, he had a regular entourage turning up, and he was meeting them for "drinks" afterwards.

On Thursday morning, Samīh, and Jason arrived at Saqqara, so while Killian was busy briefing them on what he wanted them to do, Adie managed to corner Siân in the mural room.

"Can we talk?"

Siân lifted both eyebrows. "Sounds serious."

"No. Yes. I mean... I want to know what the big secret is regarding Killian and this Dareth Sadler dude."

Siân straightened up and took off her hard hat. She eyed Adie thoughtfully. Then, lifted her boot on to a storage crate. "Have you asked Killian?"

Adie nodded. "He won't tell me a thing. Said I should consult the internet."

"Wow, and have you?"

"No, of course not. That would be weird, and probably not very accurate."

"Well." She looked about as if the walls had ears.

"What I can tell you is little more than hearsay. You know how private he is."

"I know. But give me something."

Siân tidied up the rest of her work pitch. "Let's get lunch. I'll feel better talking about it away from here."

They eventually found a table in a shady corner of a nearby cafe, out of sight of the large and loud group of American tourists who were bargaining furiously with the hustlers for camel rides to Giza, and away from the table occupied by Matthew's ankh-wearing fan-club.

"Don't they get to you?" Adie asked.

"Nah, other than they look a lot like Sadler groupies."

Adie looked down at the black syrupy liquid before her. Steam curled from the surface of the thimble-sized cup, and sugar granules clung to the rim.

"How about we start with what you know about Sadler? Then I tell you what I know."

"Next to nothing." Adie took a tiny sip of coffee and set it back down. "He's a writer, sensationalist stuff I guess, he has a cult following, and for some reason Killian hates him enough to punch the photographer he sent sniffing round here. Your turn."

"Okay," Siân said thoughtfully. "What he writes is pseudo-archaeological bullshit, which is offensive enough, but about a decade ago, he somehow managed to hoodwink Killian into thinking he was a legitimate scholar. Got involved with a project he was working on here at Saqqara and listed Killian as a major contributor to his book. Except, when the book came out, everything Killian had said had been twisted and used totally out of context. The fallout nearly destroyed Killian's career and earned Sadler a nice windfall and a coterie of ankh-wearing groupies."

"What book is this?" Adie asked, trying to reconcile the Killian she knew with this past version.

"Six Steps to Heaven. It's tripe. It was the book of the moment when I was at university. Let me spare you the brain cells. It claims that the Egyptian gods are—note the are—space travelling aliens who seed planets and set up pyramids as huge transmitters."

"And Killian had opinions on that besides, 'You what!'"

"Like I said. He was extensively misquoted. He was very opinionated in those days, and free with his thoughts. I mean, he's opinionated now, he just doesn't bother communicating said opinions unless he's done his due diligence to a degree that makes both his students and archangels cry. Anyway, Sadler's book, there are pages and pages of Killian's theories on Egyptian magic and ritual. And, while at no point does he mention space or aliens, within the broader context of the book, the implications are there."

It sickened her to think of being so misquoted.

"So, what exactly are the pyramids transmitting?"

"The pharaoh's *ba*."

"Right, because his majestic life force needs zapping into space to…"

"Join the space travelling gods on their journey to seed worlds, obviously." Siân rolled her eyes.

Adie frowned. She'd heard plenty of wacky theories before, but this left a bad taste in her mouth.

"It sounds just about plausible while you're reading it," Siân said. "It's certainly no wackier than the *Ani Papyrus*, and honestly, Sadler's an easier read."

The scary part here wasn't that Siân had clearly read this drivel, but that numerous people, based on the crowd Sadler had attracted to the museum, evidently bought into it wholesale.

"There's more to it though, right?" What Siân had said was awful, but it didn't adequately explain Killian's reaction, or the way he refused to even speak about the guy. A decade on with a very healthy career, she'd expect him to at least be able to look back and laugh over how grim it had been.

"I'm sure there is. But that's everything I know. If Lucas knows more than that, I doubt you'll get him to share. Also, is it me, or is he being really sketchy lately?"

Adie shrugged. Lucas seemed the same as he'd ever been, but she'd only known him a handful of weeks.

"Oh, come on. He is. He's forever hurrying off to see Mark Leyham."

"Perhaps they just get on well."

Siân huffed. "I think he's buttering him up just in case."

"In case?"

It was Siân's turn to shrug. "Killian has another nervous breakdown over all this Sadler shit."

Adie sighed into her coffee cup. "Wait! Another?"

"Babe, I don't think he's prematurely white due to genetics. His whole life got blown to pieces thanks to Sadler's stunt. And now he's back, threatening to derail it all over again. It's surely not a coincidence that he's appeared again right when Killian's digging at Saqqara. I bet someone's tipped him off about the mural. It's right up his alley. He's been leaning hard into the whole sex magic thing for the last five sequels, so of course he's going to be interested in an erotic mural barely a handful of people have seen. Bet he's already got the copy written. 'Learn how to attain immortality by reciting from the Book of the Dead while standing in a pyramid having your cock sucked'," Siân enunciated in her best voice-over impression.

Adie pushed her coffee aside, unease making her queasy. Siân's mimicry ought to have been funny, only, Killian was clearly stressed out, and she didn't want him going to pieces for well... spades of reasons. Plus, it didn't seem remotely fair that Sadler should wield so much influence over their lives. She pulled out her phone, determined to chase Josef again, and maybe send Killian a text. Only there was another string of messages in her inbox from Anton. The last of which read,

AK: I can see that you're reading them.

A shadow fell over their table, as someone scraped back a chair and joined them. "Did I overhear you guys talking about Sadler?" Samīh put a plate holding a flatbread dish down on the table. "That's brave of you. I thought he was a forbidden topic."

Jason's arrival necessitated them all shuffling round a bit to fit around the table. "What are you talking about?"

"Sadler," Samīh said, simultaneous with Siân and Adie denying it.

"You so were." Jason laughed. "So, what have you been saying? Come on, spill all the gossip. I mean, we've heard that he's back and sniffing about."

"You have?" Siân pushed up her penny shades to squint at them.

"Sure, we have." Jason tucked into his meal. "It's been in all the papers. They've stopped short of cycling back to Killian's past stint in Saqqara and all the juiciness that resulted, but give it time, and I'm sure they'll find a reason to regurgitate it. Next time there's a slow news day..."

"What juiciness?" Adie and Siân demanded simultaneously.

The two men exchanged looks. "You don't know about the past?" Jason's dark brows pulled super low over his deep-set eyes. "But you know about *Six Steps to Heaven*, yeah?"

"Siân was just telling me about how Killian was misquoted in it."

Jason waved away her remark. "Yeah, but that

pales into insignificance when you consider the bigger picture. I mean, obviously it was embarrassing, and it didn't do Killian's reputation any favours, but it's nothing beside what came next."

They were all leaning in, eager to hear the details. Adie's fingers whitened from clutching the table edge so hard.

"So, the book launched, right, and then within weeks, there'd been five mysterious deaths associated with the rituals in the book. Rituals our illustrious boss had pontificated on at length, though probably he was talking about translations of historical records, and not Dareth's twist on the original.

"The second it became obvious there was going to be an investigation, Mr Sadler skips town allegedly on a promotional tour of the Far East. So, without mister charisma around to take the flak, the press promptly turned their attentions on the archaeologist who contributed so much of the information, and who just happened to be working right here at Saqqara on Djoser's pyramid—the very six steps described."

Adie grimaced, as acid reflux crawled its way up her throat, leaving behind the taste of sour dolly mixtures. Poor Killian. No wonder he had beef with the man.

"What sort of ritual are we talking?" Siân asked.

"I'm not sure," Samīh gave his head a shake, and Jason followed suit. "I was barely in my teens at the time. All the stuff I've heard has been passed down by successive cohorts of students."

"The joys of the student gossip mill. At my uni, there was all this mad stuff about Aleister Crowley conducting weird magic in the woods," Siân said.

"Yeah, well this was along those lines, except it was something to do with mummy wrappings and auto-asphyxiation in the desert."

"It was? Damn." Jason gave his head a shake. "I thought it was to do with asps and meat-hooks."

"No. That's the apocryphal guy *stranded* in the desert tale."

"I think a version of that one is told the world over," Siân said, her attention flying to Adie, whom she nudged with the toe of her work boot.

Adie flashed her a reassuring smile, but truthfully, the mention of mummy wrappings had skyrocketed the number of butterflies currently resident in her stomach. Of course, their boss hadn't been involved in any sort of dodgy rituals. She couldn't even imagine him making a wish over some birthday candles. But it was just all so reminiscent of him winding her in bandages before fucking her senseless. What if they were wrong, and he'd been more involved than any of them imagined?

"What happened?" she asked.

"I think the final verdict on the deaths was misadventure, or something like that. Sadler wrote a few dozen sequels—"

"To Killian. What happened to Killian?"

The two locals continued to be shocked by how ill-informed she was about the man they were all working for. "His name was mud, and there was a stink hovering over him. He got fired from his excavation. Well, not fired, but they pulled the funding or something. And then his partner left him."

"Work partner? Life partner?"

Neither man had a ready answer. "Could be both. It's rumoured he was engaged in the past, right?"

"Right." She nodded. Killian had told her as much, but it hadn't seemed like the kind of thing he'd want sharing.

"It's kind of a miracle he recovered," Samīh added. "But he did. Within two or three years, he'd gained a permanent position lecturing at the university and then within another eighteen months he was working high profile digs again and being headhunted by places around the globe."

"He was freelance for a bit," Jason said.

"Yeah, but eventually he came home to Cairo, and he's been here ever since in one capacity or another, working his way up the ranks."

"He pulls in funding, which is always a guaranteed bonus in the eyes of any university."

That was true, but it was still a testament to Killian's strength, tenacity, and work ethic that he'd managed to claw himself back to any sort of position, let alone to the eminence in his field he currently occupied.

"Meanwhile all the shade has only added to Sadler's notoriety," Siân remarked.

Jason made a little drum roll on the tabletop. "Obviously. He turns up in Cairo at least once a year for some sort of gathering or other. Hobnobs with the high ups, slides them a few backhanders, and what do you know, he's got permission for a private gathering of him and a hundred or so of his favourites at Djoser's Pyramid Complex. Normally, that's when Killian leaves for anywhere else on Earth, but what with the excavation in full flow, that's not been an option this time around. Bet he wishes otherwise."

"Wait! That's not actually happening though, right?"

The look the boys exchanged sent a chill down Adie's spine, which is when she saw it. A relatively unobtrusive poster on the wall stating that Djoser's Pyramid Complex would be closed for a private function on an evening not too far away. Then, a foot further along the wall, there was Sadler's smug mug flashing his pearly whites, and a curiously worded invitation to join the author of *Six Steps to Heaven* in an exploration and celebration of Ancient Pharaonic practices. Matthew's fan club were sitting right under it. Dammit, they probably *were* Sadler groupies, hanging about to wheedle information about their dig out of unsuspecting idiots.

Oh, God! That was it. It was true. Sadler was coming here to Saqqara and would be right on top of them. The Stepped Pyramid was visible from their dig. And the stream of girlies flirting with Matthew were here fishing for titbits they could report back to their fucking leader.

Did Killian know? Did he realise?

Dammit, no wonder he was so irritable and antsy about making any sort of statement to the press. Any indication that he'd discovered something would bring Sadler straight to them, and then Killian's past would come back to bite him. Everything would be regurgitated right alongside Sadler making a new meal out of their discovery.

It didn't matter how amazing you were. How much expertise you possessed, no one bounced back for a second time after having their reputation shredded.

No one.

You got full on cancelled.

She made her excuses and left the table. She had just enough of a phone signal to check her messages. Still nothing from Franks, and nothing more from Josef. Honestly, how was he doing anyone favours by hiding information about Killian's past? And why couldn't he have given her a summary before she took the job? It wouldn't have changed her mind about coming here, but it would have prepared her and alerted her to the potential threat Sadler posed.

-34-
Adie

Killian wasn't on site when she got back, so it wasn't until evening that she had a chance to speak to him. The moment Siân pulled up on the riverbank, Adie shot over the gangplank onto the houseboat and headed straight for Killian's cabin.

"Give me a minute, I'm nearly done," he called in reply to her urgent rap on his door.

Adie, not in a mood to wait, let herself in and crossed the bedroom heading for his ensuite. "It's me. Can I come in?" Without waiting for an answer, she cracked open the interior door, releasing a surfeit of steam. Killian killed the water flow, then wiped the moisture from his eyes.

He did nothing to hide his nudity, merely gazed at her in that frosty, shutdown way of his. Only the glitter in the hearts of his eyes revealed that he was affected by her sudden appearance. She, meanwhile, was mesmerised by the glitter of water droplets across his broad shoulders and pecs. He had exactly the sort of body that appealed to her. Wide at the shoulders, trim at the waist, and nothing extra to him anywhere. Not a speck of hair on his body, either, neither on his chest or lower down at the juncture of his legs.

"Ahem," he cleared his throat, which brought her gaze up from the weight of his cock and balls to his face.

"Assuming you didn't just burst in to stare at my cock, where's the fire?"

He grabbed a towel, and dried off his face, before securing it around his waist.

"Sadler's having a party at the Stepped Pyramid this weekend."

"Is that so?"

Wait. What? He sounded completely disinterested, while she'd been able to think of nothing else all afternoon. She'd harangued Matthew about what he was doing/discussing with those girlies, but he'd just oozed charm at her and ultimately saw her off with a grin and remarks about jealousy. "I just... I just thought you should know. You already knew, didn't you?" She sighed into her clenched fist. "Can't you do something about it? Stop it? He's going to be right on top of us."

Killian stepped free of the shower enclosure. There wasn't much space in the compact ensuite, which left her pushed up against the sink. He was facing her with his back to the steamed up full-length mirror.

"You overestimate my influence, Adie. Besides, it'll have been cleared by the authorities. Correct forms filled; right palms greased." Ergo, there was nothing he could do.

"But what if it's just a cover for him to break into

our site?"

He goddamn rolled his eyes at her. "Let me tell you something about Mr Sadler, Adie. He's scum of a very particular persuasion, and, while I wouldn't put it past him to break in, he won't because it won't deliver the things he wants. That being photographs that he can build a narrative around. He needs sanctioned photographs. Ones he can clearly state the provenance of to the authorities. Also, he's not the sort of man to bow out of a party at which he's the number one attraction. The man thrives on adulation."

"But still..."

"Let me put it another way for you." He touched her then. A glancing trace across her hip, before he pushed a hand between her thighs and cupped her pussy in a presumptive and rather domineering way that she couldn't quite disapprove of given how it electrified her senses. "He's a sleazy pervert. He's going to be far too busy stuffing his cock into the various orifices of nubile, and very, very willing young women, to worry about photographs. Leastways, photographs of ancient wall art. I'm sure an abundance of them will be taken of him fucking women a fraction of his age and lording it over his subjects like he's an actual god. Now, shall we get you out of these cargo pants?"

"What?" She blinked at him confused. Days of ignoring her, and now he was straight in with the let's get sexy routine. Not that she was objecting. Her pussy would welcome a workout.

"Does the notion of a sleazy creep screwing

impressionable young women get you going?"

"No, Adie, but it'd be odd of me not to discipline you for disrupting my shower, which is the one time of day I get any genuine peace."

Oh! Oh, right. "Wait, does that mean you're going to spank me? I don't want to be... We already discussed this."

Those pale eyes of his glittered like rime on a window. "Oh, you sweet summer child, there's more than one way to dole out a punishment. Now, trousers down, and balance yourself on this here basin."

Intrigued, she hesitated only for a moment. "Shall I take my top off—"

His gaze burned her with its frosty intensity. Adie shed her clothing and made a rather unbalanced perch on the edge of the sink.

"Spread your legs. I want to see that cunt." His hands tapped against her thighs. "Wider. More. In fact, lift them up. Knees bent."

"Do you expect me to levitate?"

"I expect you to do as you're told, but we both know you have a real issue with that."

"I don't. That was one time," she protested. She always did as she was told... except for when it was obviously bollocks or hindered the spirit of adventure. But if it mattered and was sure to earn her a pat on the back, then...then she always did as she was asked.

Killian hoisted her legs off the floor, and positioned them as he wanted them, bent at the knees, and spread wide into an M shape. It was neither a comfortable nor dignified position. Her balance was precarious; her arms taking most of her weight, and her lower parts lewdly spread for his viewing. That she felt his scrutiny, and each whisper of movement against her exposed lips soon added to the shaking of her limbs.

Killian smoothed his hands along her inner thighs. His focus was intensely concentrated. His head dipped. Then, his breath whispered hot over her skin. When he peeped up at her, the tip of his tongue was touching his upper lip.

He didn't, however, use it to caress her pearl. That was his thumb. But his breath stayed hot against her ruby skin, while he teased her opening with two blunt fingertips. "Such a delicate little opening. It hardly seems big enough to take a single digit, let alone two. Yet, he slid both of them into her and proceeded to pump them in and out of her body in a way that soon set her squirming and panting with need.

"You'll have to spread a bit wider, I think, if you're ever going to be able to take my cock."

"Is it a very big cock that you have, professor?" She looked at him through her eyelashes, playing coy.

He laughed at her. "It is. Would you like to see it?" He reached for the simple tuck holding the towel in place around his waist.

"If it's a real monster, might I not be frightened by it?"

"Are you often frightened by monsters? I thought you were a fearless adventurer."

"Not entirely fearless."

"Mostly, we fear what we don't know." A trace of a smile pulled on his lips, as he continued fucking her with his digits, and his thumb kept up a delinquent patter against her clit. "How well do you really know yourself, Ms Hamiliton? I wonder, for example, if you realise how easily I can make you come right now? I could more or less make you do it on command."

That was only bollocks that appeared in spicy books, where the hero would growl, *"Come on my cock."* And the heroine would shatter as if a switch had been flicked.

"Is it not?"

"People don't orgasm because someone instructs them to."

"Incorrect. It depends on how on edge they are. I think you'd be surprised exactly how easily it can be achieved." He curled his fingers inside of her, so that they kneaded some surprising point of pleasure there. At once, she was both sopping wet for him and squirming with an urgent need to pee. She blew out her next few breaths as heat rose in her cheeks, until she was sure they were burning and her insides were clasping at his fingers, even as she grew more terrified of embarrassing herself.

"Which do you think is going to happen first, Adie? Are you going to come at my command, or are you going to disgrace yourself?"

"You're not playing fair."

"Fair?" He chuckled. "If you're going to play, then might as well play dirty." His eyebrows lifted in a flirty, suggestive way.

"That doesn't seem very..."

"What, professional? You don't get to the top of any hierarchy without a few tricks up your sleeves." His thumb swirled over her clit. Back and forth, back and forth, meaning she was being stimulated to the max in multiple places. It wasn't just about his fingers though, it was thoughts he kept planting, and how he'd mutter her name, or good girl under his breath. On top of that, there were the visuals. Lovely visuals, of him bending over her; of his fingers buried inside her; of his cock, stiff as a broom-handle, its outline perfectly apparent through the towel; and his reflection in steam hazed glass. The man had a spectacular arse.

"I'll come for you," she said.

"Will you?" He arched a brow. "You're quite sure about that?"

"If it pleases you."

"Oh, Adie." He briefly pressed their brows together. "Yes, it will please me. It'll please me very much. You like pleasing me, don't you, my little pet? Shall I show you what I've got to pleasure you with if you please me?"

The tuck in the towel loosened, so it disengaged from his hips, revealing the thrust of his full erection. If she was aroused, then he was equally so. He was already at full tilt; thick, ruby tipped, pearls spotting against his belly. Perfect in every way, and god, he was going to feel good. She really hoped he had those condoms to hand.

"I'm not sure that's going to fit," she said,

making her eyes round as if astonished.

"And yet you were made to take it." He pulled his fingers free of her and spread the liquid of her arousal all over his shaft. "I think you'll be surprised how easily you'll manage. Keep those legs nice and wide, now."

He rubbed himself against her lips, drawing himself back and forth along that slippery channel, before trying the head against her opening, as if it might not actually fit.

The almost, almost, nope, let's do some more of the slip and slide soon had Adie digging her teeth deep into her lower lip. The muscles in her arms were screaming. She shifted one, which unbalanced her and left her clinging to the tap.

"Careful, now." The wriggling caused the crown of him to notch just a little way inside her. Oh, God, and he was bare. Hot, firm, and very eager for her, and with not a thing in the way of all that sensation.

"Killian," she gasped, staring at how they were almost, but not quite joined. Her gaze riveted on his cock, long, thick, and all velvety heat, poised right at her opening, the tip lodged just a fraction inside. Not actually inside, just... It wouldn't take much. One quick jerk of his hips and he'd have his whole length inside of her. She'd be full of him right to his root. A scenario bursting too brightly across her mind's eye. And damned if that image didn't take her breath away.

"One little push." His words echoed her thoughts. "Do you think you'd like the feel of me inside you, claiming you like that? My bare cock filling up your pussy, no barriers, nothing to stop me flooding you with spurt after spurt of precious come."

"We shouldn't. You won't." If there was a hint of genuine panic behind her words, then that was only to be expected. She trusted him, but she wasn't sure she trusted herself, because the stretch and the heat of him did feel nice. If he said, maybe just a taste, or maybe if I only put it in for a moment, then she'd absolutely agree, and they'd both be done for, because once he was inside her, she wouldn't want him to pull out. She wouldn't want him to withdraw and put a barrier between them.

She never fucked without a condom. Never.

Who did?

It wasn't safe.

Couples in monogamous, longstanding relationships? People looking to conceive. Neither applied in this situation. It'd be a blindingly stupid thing to do, birth control notwithstanding.

The tension in his body matched her own as he held himself there, gaze still glued to the point of their connection. It showed in his jaw too, the lines of it made more pronounced, and the tendons in his neck plumped like cords.

"You're such an outstanding student, Adie. Always so amenable to my demands. Always rising to the occasion. You deserve to feel the whole length of me. Every goddamned inch. You deserve that pleasure, we both do."

"I'm not sure we should, professor."

"What's that?"

"I don't think it's a good idea."

"Do you believe I'd ever lead you astray? Don't you agree that I know best?"

"Yes, professor, but—"

"Then be a good girl, Adie, and stop arguing."

"Please put something on."

"Are you telling me what to do, Ms Hamiliton? I don't care for this insolent streak. I think we're fine, just like this. More than fine. In fact, I'm going to fuck you with my whole length, every naked inch of it."

Oh, God. Oh, God. Her arousal was like a cord wrapped around her senses, and growing ever tighter, while her head was rebelling against the insanity, and her pussy wept tears of desperation to feel the whole of him stretching her. The tip wasn't nearly enough. But they weren't going to do anything dumb. They weren't... Neither of them was that stupid. "Please, I..."

He leaned closer, so his head was level with her ear. "Osiris," he said. "You know how to make this stop."

It was torture, pure and simple, and he was getting off on her frustration, evident in the flush of his skin, the set of his ridiculously perfect chin. She wanted him so damn much, but he wouldn't do it. He wouldn't. Would he?

If she didn't say the word, how far would he take it?

It was too easy to imagine lifting her hips, bringing her arms forward to wrap around his neck. Sliding herself forward on his prick, until he was completely embedded, and she was thoroughly and completely full of him. Her imagination elaborated on the moment, the back and forth thrusts, the fire in her veins, the wet heat of him ejaculating inside of her, and it then running down her legs after he pulled out and gravity got its say in the matter.

Jeezus, she was on the verge of coming purely from the thought of it.

"Come for me, Adie." He pressed his thumb down hard on her clit right then and she did exactly that. Her muscles clamped tight and released, and she jerked to his tune, mouth open, screaming out her release. "That's a good girl. That's a very good girl." He coaxed her through it, his cock still notched at her entrance as her muscles and pulse each built their own rapid tattoo.

The moment she was wrung out, he pushed fully into her. One easy glide and she was wholly his. Adie's head sagged against his shoulder. "Please tell me..."

"I'm not a fool, Adie."

She saw the crumpled foil packaging there on the floor. In her moments of oblivion, he'd sheathed himself, and now, now he was pumping inside of her with steadfast determination. Hands tight around her hips, his cock in her to his balls. Adie wrapped her legs fast around his waist. "Give me your come, professor," she said into his ear. "Fill me with it. Stripe me with it. Fuck me like you'll never get enough. Fuck me like I'm the best student you'll ever have."

"You're telling me what to do again, Ms

Hamilton. I really can't tolerate this cheek."

"I'm not. I'm pleading with you."

"Is that so?"

He took her weight and turned them around, pressed her fast against the chill of the mirror for a dozen or so strokes, before he carried her through to the bedroom, where he eschewed the bed in favour of planting her arse on his desk. The moment her back hit the surface; he flipped her over. Then, he entered her again, from behind, and fucked her until she was seeing stars, and what do you know, she came again right when he told her to. This time, she orgasmed around his cock, which made her giddy as a goose, especially when he whispered good girl to her as she surrendered.

Killian stripped the condom off, right at the point of ejaculating. He came across the puffy flesh of her labia, and the reddened groove across her thighs left by the rim of the sink. Adie basked in that moment. He was hers, right then, as much as she was his. The Killian who made love to her, was no frosty faced stickler, he was ruthlessly passionate, and hot as sin.

In the aftermath, he fetched a cloth and cleaned her up, even offered her the use of his shower, which she was tempted by, but wasn't persuaded to jump into. Real contentment was lying here in his arms, his hot body pressed against her, and his arms tight around her in a possessive hold.

"Hungry?" he asked after a while.

"A bit, yeah."

"Can I make you dinner?"

Adie turned her head to peer at him. "You cook?"

He snorted. "Adie, I'm a single, thirty-six-year-old man who values his health and has never been married. Of course I can cook. I'm even not bad at it, providing you like the things I know how to make."

"Then yes, Gordon Ramsay, I'd like you to cook for me."

He got off the bed and offered her a hand up. "Fair warning, I'm a better Egyptologist than cook, so just keep that in mind."

She grinned. "I'll expect nothing less than perfection."

-35-
Killian

Cooking for Adie, rapidly turned into cooking for everybody. That was another downside of living on the *dahabiyya*. There was no privacy. Siân and Lucas were translating plaster seals on the deck as they headed towards the kitchen, and immediately hollered, "Hell, yes." And "Count me in." The boys were playing football on the riverbank.

Adie lingered by the doorway watching him as he got out pans and a chopping board. So, he gave her a show, ensuring the way his shirt pulled across his back was just so as he retrieved items from the fridge. He loosened a few buttons of said shirt too and rolled back his sleeves. He might have a reputation as a scholarly stick-in-the-mud, but he knew a thing or two about enticement. Also, something—possibly to do with having his shower interrupted—had put him in a surprisingly amiable mood. He juggled a couple of onions, before slamming them down on the chopping board and wielding a kitchen knife like a pro.

"Wow! Show off," she chided, but the delight in her face said that she was genuinely impressed.

"Don't get too excited just because I can cut an onion. I do three dishes with any kind of competency, and the rest are so-so, edible, functional but never going to earn me a Michelin star."

"Well, I hope I'm getting one of the good ones. The ones that are star worthy."

He scratched his jaw. "Hm, yeah... Would you like Chilli con Carne, Prawns with Piri Piri, or Tapioca pudding?"

"Chilli."

"Good choice." He placed a tin of kidney beans on the counter, followed by a selection of peppers.

"Gotta ask. Tapioca?"

"My nana taught me. She always served it, along with a dollop of homemade raspberry jam. Shame I never mastered her chicken soup or Yorkshire puddings. I can make both, but they don't taste the way she made them."

"Is she still about?"

Killian tipped the onions into the pan to brown. "Yeah. I see her when I can. We Zoom chat sometimes. She's in her nineties now, in a nursing home and a bit frail, but she likes to hear what I've been up to."

"Have you told her about the find?"

He smiled. "Not yet, but I will do."

Her mouth turned down. "Hey, what's up?"

She shrugged. "It's nothing. It just... my great aunt... I wish she was still around to call and tell about this. She'd have loved hearing it. She's the one who really encouraged my love of Egypt, especially after my parents were gone. Do you have..." She cleared her throat. "I mean, are yours still around?"

He nodded. "They don't get all this. Dad's a tax broker. My mum files and paints peoples' nails for a living. The only thing we have in common is blood. Josef told me you didn't have anybody."

She gave another of those quivery nods, then surreptitiously attempted to wipe her eyes.

"Are you okay?"

"Fine. Like I said, I miss Esther."

He didn't press for more information. He'd met orphans before, and hated how people pried about their losses, as if they had a right to the details because the person had obviously been careless enough to lose something of such significance, instead of being victims of circumstance.

His own family, apart from his Nan, were strangers, and there were plenty of folks out there with families that delighted in torturing one another. He'd take a wonderful one that was only around for a short time over a lifetime of mediocrity or the plain old bad variety.

"How's your wild goose chase going?"

Adie gave a girly huff. "What's up, are you frightened I'll actually find it?"

"No."

"Are you sure about that? Because it's almost like you want me to fail."

"Don't be ridiculous."

"Then don't call it a wild goose chase. If I find it,

it'll complete the mural, and we'll all benefit."

That was him told. Perhaps he was hard on her. "I just want you to realise that the odds aren't in your favour. We've no idea what Jacobs did after he vandalised that mural. He could as easily have crushed it beneath his boot as carried it to Cairo, or overseas."

"That doesn't mean I shouldn't try to trace it. And if the journal ever turns up, then perhaps I'll get lucky and find a clue."

"This isn't a movie, Adie. No one is going to hand you a convenient lead at the exact moment you desperately require it. Whatever leads you produce will probably lead nowhere, or you'll spend the next decade hunting through archives convinced it'll be in the very next box, and one day perhaps it will, but it's far more likely that it won't."

She sucked her lips into a pout in response, and silently watched him cook for several minutes, until he eventually put a lid on the pot and left it to simmer.

He was being unduly harsh, he knew that, but he didn't want her fantastical idealism getting her hurt.

He opened a bottle of wine and pushed a glass toward her with his fingertips. Adie stared at it, while she worried a groove into her lower lip. Eventually, she relented and took a sip, "Do you think you're possibly a little jaded?"

Ouch! "Adie, I've seasons and seasons of dig experience under my belt, not to mention years of practice chasing artefacts around the globe. I'm not jaded, I'm realistic. Things rarely turn up where you look for them. Leastways, if they're not lying around on the floor in the immediate vicinity..."

"But Jacob's journal might hold information about the location of the piece."

"Yes. Sure. But we don't have it as it's gone walkabout? Who knows if it'll ever surface again."

"What if Sadler has it, or finds it first?"

He finished off his glass and poured a second. "What if he does?"

"Why did nobody scan it?"

He made a dismissive clack with his tongue. "Funding, most likely."

Adie followed him when he wandered outside to the table on deck and started laying out the cutlery.

"Just so you know, I didn't look up your history," she said, hanging back within the doorway. "That's not how I want to get to know you. I'm not interested in what the internet has to say."

He rubbed a tear from the corner of his eye and mumbled something about sand in the air. "You're sure you don't want to know my exact time of birth, the auspices thus decreed by astrology, and details of every breakfast I ate during the stint I did in Dashur? Oh, and the scores of my primary school maths tests?"

"Are they out there?"

He hitched his shoulders. "I don't know. I don't google myself. But the shit that occurred...that involved Sadler is definitely out there, and that's what you really want to know, isn't it? It's why you keep bringing up his name."

She didn't deny it.

"Adie, he's the sort of history better left buried."

"Except he's about to be right on our doorstep, and those women who keep turning up are likely part of his posse, aren't they?"

She reached for him, and he allowed her to take hold of his hand and rub circles across the back of it with her thumb.

"It's part of my past I don't need to relive."

"Killian, please. I'm not asking for an event-by-event breakdown, just some understanding of the truth. Josef said I should ask you about Petra."

Of course, the damnable old git had. He wouldn't miss a chance to prod that wound. He'd been livid about it at the time, like he'd had a vetted interested in the relationship that died amidst those ruins, just because once upon a time he'd paired them up to work together on a project for some tutorial or other.

He sighed and swished a finger across the base of his glass.

"Was she your fiancée?"

Laughter crackled in his throat.

"That's amusing, why?"

"I see the gossip mill is as robust as ever. Adie, I've never had a fiancée. But then Joe isn't talking about a person." Well, he was, but not in the sense that she'd interpreted it.

It took her mere seconds to make a connection that ought to have been obvious. Whereupon, she clapped a hand to her brow and groaned. "Petra in Jordan. Okay, why is that significant? Did something happen there? I thought you were working on a dig here in Saqqara when Sadler published his shit."

Killian continued to paint circles in the condensation on the base of his wineglass. "Petra is where I wound up after Sadler's drivel tanked my career. I went to work for Professor Woicek of Harvard until the fuss about…about…"

"The deaths."

"Until it died down. You know for someone who claims they didn't go snooping, you know an awful lot."

"Well, you have a team here and I have ears."

"Great!" He headed back into the galley. "Nice to know you talk about me behind my back."

"Oh, come on." She followed him back to the hob. "You're the boss, of course we fucking talk about you. That's what underlings do."

"Fine." He held the spoon out for her to try.

Adie sucked a little off the end. "It's good."

"I'll talk." With any luck, she'd learn a valuable lesson from his experience. He turned the heat down and left the dish to simmer with the lid on while they returned to the window bay seats. "You need to understand who I was when I first came here. Not only was I young and idealistic, I believed in a very hands-on approach." He'd been supremely full of shit.

"You still do."

He shook his head. "Not remotely to the same degree. Then, if there was a sculpture or a pot, I wanted to understand everything about it. How it was made. Why it was made. I'd try my hand at constructing reproductions. Whatever it was, I'd recreated it. Pots, rituals, spells. If I'd had the funding, probably the pyramids themselves. I thought such antics gave me valuable insights about the past, but really, I was just young, ambitious, and so full of my own self-worth that I never suspected Sadler was anything but what he seemed — a genuinely interested academic.

"Turns out, he's a more than competent actor.

"The excavation of the western massifs of Djoser's pyramid complex wasn't my first big dig, but it was my first as team lead. Leastways, as joint lead. Me and a friend of mine from university alongside a bevy of archaeology students desperate for excavation experience. They were paying their own way. All we did was provide shitty accommodation and equipment. Everyone assumed Sadler was one of the vols. If you showed up, the assumption was that you'd got your visa and were here to dig."

"You didn't check?"

"There wasn't time to check, and the paper trail was shockingly bad. Besides, the important thing was the dig, and we were on a strict timetable. Twenty weeks, not a second more. Then we had to be out of there. They were long hot days. There was little rest. There was a lot of discord going on in the run up to the presidential elections and in response to the changes to the Egyptian constitution. It seemed like another group was targeted every day. And so many people lost their lives to bombings."

"I remember hearing about tourist buses being targeted."

He nodded. "Frankly, a head down immersive approach to archaeology was a blessing." He shrugged. "Until it wasn't. Sadler claimed he was writing a book about Djoser's complex. He wanted to really hone in on the step pyramid and why it's so special. It doesn't get the same recognition as the Giza pyramids, but it's still a major site. It should have been an obvious warning sign, when he started showing increasing interest in our reconstructions of the spells and rituals related to our work, but nope, I failed to smell the shit. Hence, I failed to realise he was targeting the sensationalist market, not the academic one.

"What you have to understand, is that we'd been hanging on a daily basis, having all these intense conversations, working together...

"After he'd made me a laughingstock, the backers pulled out one by one until the project collapsed. Josef and several others tried to calm things, but it was too big a shitstorm. And things were volatile enough as it was. Foreigners were being advised to go home."

"And with the deaths..."

He put his head in his hands. "Yeah. First I knew about any of that, was when the press descended. They were like vultures. I'm not even sure those deaths were connected to the book, but it made for a good story."

"So, you escaped to Petra."

"It seemed a better option than sticking around

and risking being arrested or deported. Plus, I needed work, and that's what was on offer.

"All the students had already left. There were only the two of us, so we flew to Jordon and got to work on the ancient burial chambers that are part of the stone city. I think it lasted about three months. I probably wasn't very good company." He paused. "I know I wasn't good company. We argued. A lot. Things came to an eventual head, and he left. That was it. My best friend and ally, the partner I thought I could rely on was gone. I had nothing left."

"Partner?" Her voice was barely a whisper.

Killian returned to the stove and furiously stirred the chilli. "I blamed him... for a long time. I blamed him for...for everything, really. He was there the whole time, you see, and it's easy to point fingers. It's not so easy to accept you were at fault. Everything changed when he walked away. It was like all the cracks that I'd been desperately trying to shore up crumbled at once."

Killian massaged his chest, transported back to that past moment, when he'd been nothing more than a hollowed-out shell of his former self.

"I guess the project in Jordon wrapped a couple of weeks later, but I wasn't around to see it. I went to Sudan. From there to Oman, then on to Madagascar, a couple of weeks in Kenya, South Sudan, followed by a stint in Greece. I finally arrived back in Egypt around March the following year. The same day a bus fell off a bridge over a canal near Giza killing around thirty people. It felt like I was some sort of harbinger of death.

"So, I went south to the Valley of the Kings. "

"And then?"

"I put my head down and worked. I did any archaeological dog work I could get. Everything, and anything. It didn't matter what it paid, or how shit the conditions were. I did it. Eventually, that led to me meeting Masud, but it still took me five years to claw my way back to the point I'd started from."

"Was he one of the sponsors of those shitty digs?"

He shook his head. "Actually, no. We met in a hotel bar in Luxor. He was trying to make a long-distance phone call and kept getting cut off. We exchanged a few sympathies, had a drink and it went from there. He's been my main sponsor ever since."

"You just happened to stumble across a guy looking to invest in archaeological digs?"

It was an assumption many had made.

"No. What he invests in is high-end tech. I'm the tax write-off."

"Oh! I thought we were his passion project."

"We can be his passion project and a tax write-off." Admittedly, that wasn't romantic.

Adie spent a couple of minutes seemingly chewing over that thought, until she eventually asked, "What happened to your partner? Is he still working? Did you never make contact again?"

"We both said some unforgiveable things." And he'd been too fucking proud to grovel.

Adie wrapped her arms around him from behind and pressed her head into the space between his shoulder blades. "I'm sorry you had to endure all that."

"Yeah, well, I guess it was a lesson in humility I needed to learn, and it worked out okay in the end." He was a leading authority in his field, and he had a team, ample funding, and a score of prestigious credits to his name in terms of papers and finds.

"But do you never think of looking for him?"

"What would be the point, Adie? What existed, the understanding we had, it's all long gone. We're not those people anymore. I have a team, and I imagine he has one of his own somewhere. I don't know that he's even in Egypt."

Siân barged into the kitchen at that moment, prompting him to put some distance between them rather than face any sort of remarks about the appropriateness of his behaviour.

"Delivery." She dropped a large crate of bottled water in the middle of the room and wandered over to the cooking pot, while shoving her sunglasses up onto her head. "Smells nice." She dipped a spoon into the pot and had a taste. "Needs something."

"No, it doesn't." Killian attempted to shoo her out of the kitchen, but Siân already had her nose in the cupboards. "Aha!" She brandished a bottle.

"Siân," he warned.

"Oh, shush. It's only a little juju to spice things up a bit."

She added a generous splash before he could stop her.

"You know Lucas likes it hot."

Lucas considered radishes too spicy.

Killian snatched the bottle from her and placed

it out of reach on top of the cupboard.

"Spoilsport."

"Adie, if you have any complaints about dinner, address them to Siân." He wagged a finger at her, which only served to make her rub her hands together in impish glee.

"Lucas'll benefit from having a fire lit under his arse. He's an even bigger killjoy than you are."

"Well, thank you."

She saluted him. "No probs. And handily, I took delivery of extra loo roll along with the water, so we're prepped for any ill effects. Although, I reckon his ring is already burning from how often it gets stretched by Mark Leyham. I swear if he tells me how *ah-maz-ing* that man is one more time, I'm going to do way worse than add a little tabasco to the evening meal."

"Like what?" Adie asked.

Siân lowered her penny shades over her eyes. "Not sure yet, but it'll be evil. What were you guys talking about?"

"Nothing much."

That earned them a penetrative look over the top of her glasses.

"It's ready," Killian announced, obliging them to grab plates, before that look metamorphosed into an interrogation.

-36-
Adie

While the juju didn't ruin the chilli, it did ensure it was hot enough to put a sweat on Adie's brow. She'd idealised a candlelit dinner for two, but the rest of the team settled alongside her and Killian under the striped sun canopy on the houseboat foredeck.

Matthew commenced making a tower out of his kidney beans, while Siân waved away the offer of soothing kefir.

"Killian, we're getting the same cartouche turning up again and again among the fragments Siân and I have been piecing together. I think we can safely conclude the tomb was intended to house Huni. Even without a body." Lucas said, having pushed the volcanic mass to one side of the plate and the rice to the other.

Killian inclined his head, so the evening sun caught in the white strands making them shine like spun silver. Adie loved watching him when his mind was working. The way his expressions would change so subtly as he worked over conundrums; she'd learned he wouldn't voice until he had an answer that he was certain of. Then his frosty eyes would gleam, and she'd find herself enchanted by the thaw. "Perhaps."

"Oh, come on. At minimum we have enough here to categorically state his existence as part of the third dynasty." Only a handful of other references to Huni had ever been found. Some still questioned his existence, and his inclusion in the lists of pharaohs.

"We've a few cartouches, great, but there are plenty of things about this tomb that don't fit with current theories. The level of tomb decoration, for example. It's not been seen anywhere else until the fifth dynasty. That's not a great indicator that Huni's part of the third."

"It doesn't rule him out either. Just because we haven't seen them, doesn't mean there aren't other examples out there. New sites are being discovered all the time, and relics we thought we knew all about re-examined and different conclusions being drawn."

"You don't need to tell me any of that, Lucas. I'm aware. All I think is that we should keep our minds open. It makes no sense to rule out anything at this stage. Let's keep our heads down and see what else we unearth."

"As long as we're not unearthing anything until Monday. You promised us a long weekend starting tomorrow," Matthew said. "This boy needs some chill time. I was planning to head into Cairo."

"Yeah, I've things... Well, I promised Mark..." Lucas added.

Killian shoved his chair back. "I'm perfectly

aware of what I promised. Have your three-day weekend. No one is obliged to do anything. Do whatever it is you insist on doing. I'll see you all fresh and early on Monday. He left in the direction of his cabin.

Adie sucked on her lip as she watched him go. Ought she to follow? He'd seemed so chilled, but his moods seemed to shift as rapidly as the desert sands.

"Grumpy sod," Matthew said.

"Want to hitch a lift?" Siân asked him. "I'm going to head to Gezira too. Adie?"

"Not sure." There didn't seem much point in heading into the city without a firm lead to follow, especially when the alternative was to stay here on the houseboat with Killian and his bumper pack of condoms. What if she suggested they headed downriver? Just the two of them on a cruise along the Nile, taking in some of Egypt's other monuments, or just the wildlife. Would he go for that? If she said she'd work Friday morning, would he agree to spend the rest of the weekend having fun. No doubt the remainder of the team would tell her he wasn't capable of that, but she knew otherwise.

Although possibly Killian was planning to get out of here too, given that Sadler was going to be partying on their doorstep. Hell, was that why he'd agreed to them all taking an extra day off, to make sure they were all well away from Saqqara and any chance encounters?

"Can I let you know in the morning?"

"We'll be leaving around half nine."

"Got it."

With that she left them reminiscing over uncovering an entire family of mummified cats and wandered along deck, not to her cabin, but to Killian's. There she found him reclined on the bed, his hands tucked behind his head of snowy-white hair.

"Okay if I come in?"

"Sure, as long as you're not planning something dramatic, or here to grill me some more about my best forgotten past."

She straddled his middle. "Hm. There are things I'd still like to know."

"Figures."

"Like, if you were ever wild as a student."

"Totally," he deadpanned. "I was very wild. Truly, the ultimate bad boy."

"Were you though?"

"What do you think?"

She wasn't sure. It was hard to imagine him as anything other than a workaholic authoritarian, but hints of things she'd gleaned from others suggested he might once have been, if not a bad boy, then at least, a maverick, and well, he hadn't learned how to make her come on command sitting in a lecture hall.

"Are you planning on working all weekend, Doctor Carmichael?"

"Most likely."

"You know all work and no play makes Killian a dull boy."

He pitched her to one side, so that she landed on the mattress. Killian turned onto his side. "Well, Killian is a very dull boy."

Not based on her experiences he wasn't. She splayed her hand across his chest, then began fiddling with his shirt buttons. "I like him better when he's a dirty boy." She cocked a brow, then leaned in so their mouths were mere millimetres apart. "My dirty professor."

"What are you after, Adie?"

"It isn't obvious?"

He brushed her hands away from his shirt. "I think that's a distraction. What are you really after?"

She pouted and pushed into a sitting position as Killian got off the bed. It wasn't that she wasn't interested in getting naked with him. She very much was. He was a very sexy and delicious man. Something of a deviant too, she was learning. After a second, she asked, "What'll happen if Sadler publishes something related to the site?"

"And there it is. I don't know, Adie. Nothing good."

"Could he get us shut down?"

"There are thousands of things that could get us shut down. Sadler hopefully isn't one of them. The fact he's here sniffing around means he's likely a way off publishing and still looking for an angle. With any luck he'll find one elsewhere. Maybe he'll go hassle Mark Leyham instead, since he's working on the Stepped Pyramid and that's where the party's happening."

She wished she could believe that. She knew Killian didn't.

"But when you were talking to Masud..."

He leaned against the dresser. "Maybe you

should spend less time eavesdropping. Sadler is my worry, not yours. It made sense to highlight the threat Sadler poses to Masud considering his desire to publish. Sadler is not worth your attention."

"But what if he finds the missing fragment before we do?"

"Taking you to meet Masud was a mistake."

"I was invested in finding the fragment way before that. Just like I was invested in you, way before you gave any indication that you might like me back."

"Who says I like you?"

"You like me," she insisted, crawling along his bed, then stalking him across the room on hands and knees. She stopped at his feet and rose onto her knees peering up at him. "Go on, say something sullen, I know you want to. It won't convince me otherwise."

"I like you against my better judgement," he said, making her laugh.

"Maybe your judgement sucks."

"Maybe it does." You're at just the right height to suck me, said the heated look in his eyes, but when she reached up to slide his zip, he slapped her hand away. Never had she known a man who blew so hot and cold. It'd been confusing enough before they were... whatever it was that they were... sexual partners? She wasn't going to make the mistake of claiming he was her boyfriend. Things were far too unsteady for that. An affair, perhaps, although she hoped it would last beyond the season and their work on the buried pyramid. She'd like for them to still be excavating ruins thirty years into the future.

Adie fell backwards onto her bottom and pouted up at him, her hands resting on her bent knees. "Want to tie me up again?"

"Not really."

"Sure?"

"I'm sure."

"I hope you haven't lost interest now you've had me."

He looked down at her, face all frowny. "Adie, I haven't lost interest in you. I just have a lot on my mind."

Shit! Any second he was going to ask her to leave.

"I don't mind you using me as a distraction."

"I do."

"What if I like being a distraction?"

"You like a lot of things that aren't good for you."

"What thing—" she asked, covering her lips with one finger "—that's bad for me would you like to do to me right now?"

He didn't answer.

"Gag me, right. I know that's crossed your thoughts. If you gagged me, then I wouldn't be able to ask you all these annoying questions. On the downside, my mouth wouldn't be free for other things. Although, I suppose that depends on what you gag me with."

She stuck her tongue into her cheek to give him a hint.

The annoying man didn't drop even a fraction

of his icy haute.

"Would you like to know what sort of knickers I have on?" That earned her an even sterner look. "They're cotton navy-blue. Terribly sensible."

"How very practical of you."

"They are. I save the itty-bitty ones for special occasions."

"As I recall, you didn't have any on when you went on your last hot date."

"I most definitely did. You saw my favourite thong. Our night at Masud's counts as a special occasion for me, even if you don't think it was. For all I know, you routinely take women to his house, and then cut up his sheets so you can practise your mummification techniques and do them in the arse. For all I know, it's a standing arrangement."

She'd got his attention now. He was listening, Smiling from his eyes, even if his mouth remained set.

"It's absolutely written into the contract between us."

"You make that sound altogether too believable."

"Your thong was pretty," he remarked. For some reason, his observation set her off balance. It felt like he'd turned the tables, and now he was baiting her, rather than her being the temptress. "Although, I'm not so sure my libido won't be permanently destroyed by your Enid Blyton-esque frumpy pair."

"They're not frumpy. They're practical. And blue is a very sensible colour."

"Take them off, Adie."

"Take my knickers off?" She fake gaped at him. "Why I'm positively shocked. Shocked, Doctor Carmichael. What possible reason could you have for wanting me to shimmy out of my knickers for the second time in one day?"

"It's professor, Ms Hamilton, and I want you out of them, because it occurred to me that I wound up with hair between my teeth the other day, and that needs dealing with before I lavish my attentions on your pussy again."

"I beg your pardon, Professor?"

What did he have in his hand?

"Off, Ms Hamilton. Don't make me say it again."

Fuck! It was a razor. He was holding a razor. Well now! Anton had stolen a curl, but did Killian mean to claim the entire lot? She'd never been one to wax, or do the whole bikini line thing, as she never wore a bikini. How would it feel to be completely smooth? Was she going to let him do this?

"I've never—"

"I like firsts."

Of course he did.

"I'm not sure…"

He held her gaze, steady as you please. It made it feel like both a question and a test. Do you, or do you not trust me? Are you as interested in playing games as you make out? How much autonomy are you prepared to hand over? And most importantly, are you a brat or a good girl who is obedient?

She dug her teeth into her lower lip. "Where do you want me?"

He patted the stool.

On coltish unsteady legs she rose and shimmied out of her knickers as gracefully as she could. Then awkwardly, she draped herself over the stool. If there was an elegant way in which one could splay your legs, she'd yet to discover it. She was certain she looked sleazy, not sexy. The fact that he grinned when he saw her didn't settle the matter either.

"I don't kn...maybe."

Killian positioned himself between her legs. He'd brought a shaving brush along with a bowl of warm water. "Let's see what's hiding beneath all this fur, shall we?"

He positioned a towel, then lathered her curls, and worked his fingers over her mound until the hairs clung together in soapy locks. It was strangely arousing, the attention making her lips plump, and her clit enliven. Many a time she'd share a shower or a bath with a lover, but never had she allowed anyone this level of intimacy. It was both luxurious, and weirdly subversive to have him sheer away her curls. She kept finding she was holding her breath, almost as if she was waiting for it to sting. It didn't. He didn't so much as give her a nick as he slid the trio of blades over all her delicate areas until she was entirely denuded. Not a tuft remained. Not a whisper. No landing strip. Just bare, smooth skin, the same as he was. He patted her dry with a towel.

Anton may have appreciated her body hair, but Killian was all about total epilation.

More intriguing than the sight of all that pink skin, was the possibility of heightened sensitivity in the area. If he fucked her now, while she was all bare and tender, what would it feel like? The air stirred with his movements. If he touched her, rubbed her clit... She gasped in confusion as he retrieved her knickers and slid them up her legs.

"I don't get it. Aren't we going to..."

"To?"

Damn him, and people accused women of being teases.

"Fuck," she said, trying to make it sound lady like, and not hopelessly crude.

Killian wrinkled his nose. "Ms Hamilton, I'm your professor, not a boy you picked up in a museum. We will not be fucking. There are more important things to attend to than your rampant libido, like the four and a half thousand-year-old ten-zillion-piece jigsaw puzzle waiting in the workroom. I think that takes priority over your aching cunt, doesn't it?"

"Git!"

"Is that any way to talk to me?"

"Sorry, professor." She splayed her legs to the extent her knicker would allow.

Killian tugged them up her legs and back into place covering her up.

"Bastard."

He grinned, then snagged his index finger inside one leg hole and lowered his mouth.

"You make too many assumptions, Ms Hamiliton. "One day you'll learn to consider all the evidence available to you, not just assume you know what's what based on a single facet. You also need to work on better reading people." He licked her then, through the cotton, probing her slit with his tongue until the soft barrier was entirely wet and moulded to her form.

"Yes, I intend to worship this pussy. Yes, I intent to fuck you. But the knickers are staying on throughout. You can call it a kink, if you like." He stroked both hands over the expanse of cotton then, both the dry parts, and those he'd wetted.

"How are you going to fuck me with them on?"

His index finger followed the edge of the leg hole, then beneath the fabric to press inside of her.

"So, you're going to slide aside the gusset. That's weird."

"It's not weird."

"It's a tiny bit weird."

"Also, never say gusset again. It's a horrible word."

"Gusset," she said all breathy, like a sex-line operator.

"Adie," he warned, pulling his perfect lips into a moue.

"Guss-set."

"You were warned." He flipped her over as easily as if she were a rag doll, leaving her draped sideways across the stool with her arse up and her head and arms hanging. Then he thwacked her across both cheeks in a way that made a percussive clap.

"Ow!" she protested, which incited him into delivering another two smacks. Then another five for back chatting when she protested, plus another five when she protested again. "You really aren't very quick on the uptake, are you?"

She thought better of responding, realising where it would likely lead, hence only squeaked the first syllable of her objection. They hadn't been gentle swats. He'd put some power behind them, so her skin was rendered hot and tender, and her newly shaved mons was now all puffy and itching for attention. She'd stopped him spanking her twice before, she guessed she could have wimped out, said the word, but truthfully, liked the attention too much, and the sting in her behind was kind of... interesting.

Killian wriggled a finger beneath the concealing cotton and pulled it out again wet with her arousal. This he proceeded to suck from his digit. "Eyes front, Ms Hamilton."

"What are you—" She stopped when he raised his hand and clamped her lips closed. She kept her gaze focused forward as he positioned himself behind her.

"What I'm doing as you're so eager to find out, will be perfectly apparent in a second or two."

It was apparent already. Also, she had a grand view of his reflection in the mirror, as he loosened off his belt and fly and shoved his trousers and underwear down just enough to free his cock.

Adie swallowed hard at the sight of his erection. There was something about the way he stood in command with his cock out, rubbered up, his shirt-buttoned, but his sleeves rolled up to the elbows that short-circuited something in her brain.

She made a whimper as he pulled her panties to one side and felt him position himself at her entrance.

One hand fastened in her hair. Then he both pushed and pulled her onto his cock and fucked her until she'd come twice over and was jelly-limbed and utterly sated.

"Such an accommodating pussy you have." He made her arch a little more, allowing him to get deeper. He made sounds of deep contentment as the rolling of his hips became jerky. Then, at the last moment, he pulled out, tore off the condom, and ripped the cotton off her cheeks. His load splattered her smack-reddened skin. That was the second time he' spent over her rather than inside her. Interesting.

"Beautiful," he crooned, and spread the mess over her skin. "Your arse is fire-engine red, and in a moment or two...." He didn't finish that sentence, already pulling another condom from the box. Evidently, it was going to wind up even redder.

-37-
Adie

Killian was gone when Adie woke in his bed the next morning. She used his shower before trekking along the deck in one of his shirts to her own cabin. He wasn't onboard, and his 4x4 was missing from the riverbank. Presumably, he'd gone to Saqqara. She was torn between following him and following her meagre leads.

Siân burst in on her a few moments later looking far too perky for the hour.

"Where were you? I looked in half an hour ago, and there was no sign of you." She extended a hand toward Adie, revealing her phone. "It's been bleating. Thought it might be something important."

Reluctantly, Adie took possession of the device. Had she been mislaying it about the boat and the excavation site? Yeah, because that meant she didn't have to contend with Anton's messages. Really, she ought to let the man down considering how things were progressing between her and Killian, but she just couldn't seem to make herself do it. Moreover, the longer she left it, the harder it was proving to convince herself to opt out.

He was sexy and fun, and there was an air of mystique about him that appealed to her sense of adventure. That was it, Anton was exactly the sort of man one imagined trekking across deserts to hidden wadis with, and unearthing tombs full of long-lost treasures. Whereas Killian was doggedly practical. Sexy, for sure, but in a very different, very boss-like way. He could be naughty though. She'd learned that. He wasn't all grump and discipline. He just hid all his best bits, but with time, maybe she could pry them into the light.

"I suppose you were shagging the boss."

Adie made a non-committal grunt as she scrolled through her messages.

"Are you...were you, Adie?"

Scrolling...scrolling...scrolling...

"Is that wise?"

"He has a wicked side, you know."

"Babe, I don't doubt it. I just wonder if you know what you're doing? He's a little older... A onetime scratching an itch thing, even a repeat performance, but ongoing, are you sure this is what you want to do?"

"Coming to Cairo with you." That's what she was doing. She didn't want to hear the rest. No lectures about the gap in their ages. Ten years wasn't that long, really. And she was perfectly aware that it could end messily, but so could any relationship.

She held up her phone, pointing the screen towards Siân. Doctor Franks had finally replied.

"And has he given you an actual clue?"

"Read it for yourself."

Franks was flattered by her email, and gracious in his response. While he was sadly no longer in a position to aid her directly, having long since retired, he recalled many fruitful hours cataloguing items of a more erotic nature in museums across the globe. The Egyptian Museum in Cairo, like many others, held a multitude of such treasures, including, in his words, boxes upon boxes of male genitalia, hacked off sculptures, or removed from artworks by censorious Victorian gentlemen and assorted other prudes.

"That's nothing we didn't already know," Samīh remarked when Adie related the contents of the message later that morning as five of them, Adie, Siân, Samīh, Jason, and Matthew headed north towards Cairo. "If that's all he said, you're no further forward than you were."

"I hadn't actually finished. What he went on to say, is that while he can't be sure he catalogued our missing fragment, his former assistant would be able to say so with more certainty, as he did most of the drudge work."

"Does this assistant have a name?" Matthew asked.

"I'm getting to that. He can't give me an address, because they lost touch after his guy was dismissed on suspicion of theft and illegal antiquities dealing. It was after Frank's time, but he seems to think it was a stitch up. Anyway, he says the man has a phenomenal memory, that he was able to recall the provenance of every piece they ever worked on. Plus, he thinks he's still in Cairo, so all we need to do is track him down."

"Dead end." Siân clacked her tongue.

"It's not. We've a name."

Approaching central Cairo now, Siân began her customary slaloming through the lanes of traffic.

"Which is?" Jason asked.

Adie opened her phone screen again to check. "Ihsãn Fuãd."

There were several chortles from her companions.

Siân bullied her way across two junctions. "Adie, do you have any concept of how many Ihsãns there are in Cairo? What's the current population, about twenty million?"

"Twenty-two and a half," Jason corrected her.

"Okay. Well, shit!"

"You need someone who knows him, who's been in recent contact," Matthew said, as if that wasn't obvious, just as it was equally obvious that none of them happened to have a convenient uncle who happened to be one of Ihsãn Fuãd's besties.

"I bet Sadler has contacts who know him," Jason said. "He's exactly the sort to be in with a bunch of grave robbing arseholes."

"Yeah, you're not helping." Adie slumped in her seat, but wriggled upright almost immediately, as the seatbelt dug in across her throat when Siân slammed on the brakes and proceeded to exchange an assortment of rude gestures with a carful of men, and a man on a donkey cart.

"Guys we need to find him. There must be a way."

"Gatecrash Sadler's shindig, and ask him if he knows him," Matthew suggested.

"You did not say that!" Siân growled.

"Pretty sure I did."

"He's not going to know," Jason piped up. He was clutching the two other men in a death grip as they were jostled about by the vehicles motion. "And even if he did, he wouldn't tell you."

Adie was inclined to agree, and sadly she didn't live in the era of convenient telephone directories that you could work your way through, Terminator style. "I'd settle for getting Jacob's journal off the bastard."

"Sneak in, Indy style and steal it from under his nostrils—"

"Matthew!" Siân chastised. "Yeah, pretending I didn't hear that too. None of us have any business being anywhere near Sadler's cult of sycophants."

"Do you think he'll have it there with him?" Adie asked.

Matthew leaned deeper into the seat divide. "Course he will. He's exactly the sort to show off his assets. He's all about the look of things and puffing himself up."

"I bet there's tons of useful stuff in that book."

Siân cast her a wary glance. "Dumb plan, Adie. Stop it. It won't matter that you're shagging him, if you go anywhere near Sadler, Killian will make mincemeat out of you."

"But the journal," she whined. And what do you know, she couldn't get that notion out of her head.

"You should ask your hot admirer about Ihsãn,"

Siân said, when Adie's phone began bleeping again.

"Why would he know?"

"I'm not saying he would. I'm spitting out ideas."

"She means she attempting to divert your attention from planning your infiltration. Also"—Matthew wrapped his arms around the head rest—"hot admirer? I thought you were bonking the boss. Um, correction, I know you're bonking the boss."

Jeez, did everyone know?

"We all heard you come like a dozen times. Killian. Oh, my God, Killian!" he aped her in a mock falsetto.

"Fuck off," she ineffectually batted at him. Matthew sat back to avoid the swipe, while Adie made another couple of attempts to reach him.

Siân shook her head at the pair. Jason yelled watch out, as they narrowly missed a donkey cart.

"It's fine. We're fine," their deranged driver declared. Except they were all shaking. "Yeah, anyway, before Adie was bonking the boss, she was shagging this other mega hot guy she met at the museum. I love Killian to bits, but I'm not sure you chose the right guy, girl. I'm just sayin'. I mean, you've been letting him hang, and he still hasn't given up. Also, did I mention, he's fucking hot."

"You've never even met him."

"I saw the pictures on your phone."

"Well, lady—" Matthew put his hand on his heart and bowed his head to her. "I didn't think you had it in you. I thought you were an innocent. But here you are, sexing your way up the career ladder."

"Oh, fuck off. It's not like that."

"Seriously, though, A. When did you even have time to meet anyone? You've barely left the boat other than to dig. I'm just saying, you work quick, girl."

"Shut up. Really, shut up."

"He keeps calling, because they had a hot desert date, and then she ghosted him because she started shagging Killian," Siân elaborated, setting them all off chattering again, and making the sort of remarks she'd mostly avoided being the subject of during her undergraduate and college days. She'd been far too much of a girly swot to attract that sort of speculation.

"I haven't ghosted him," Adie huffed, and crossed her arms. "I just haven't replied yet."

"Too busy shagging the boss," Siân said, which prompted a dozen more questions she declined to answer about whether Killian even had a libido, whether his hair was only white on his head or elsewhere too, and whether he was a decent lay because a man that tight, had to either be a two pump chump, or a secret sexual ninja.

"This poor dude got a name?" Matthew asked, circling the conversation back to the guy she professed not to have ghosted, but had totally ghosted.

"Anton," she mumbled. "Doctor Anton Kelley, if you must know. He's another Egyptologist, okay."

Silence. Complete instantaneous silence, at least from the cackling monkeys on the back seat. Then, "Kelley?" Jason spluttered, and he and Samīh made several incredulous coughs. "For real? You were screwing Anton Kelley. No way, you're fucking with us." He and Samīh exchanged a convoluted fist bump across Matthew's lap. "This is gold. You're screwing...correction, were screwing, Anton Kelley, but you dropped him for our boss instead? You couldn't make this stuff up."

"What the heck are you talking about. Just shut up about it." Her cheeks were burning.

"Not bloody likely," Samīh crowed. "You do realise they know one another?"

"Hardly surprising, it's a relatively small field, and everyone knows who Killian is. It's hardly surprising that one Egyptologist in Cairo is acquainted with another."

"Adie." Samīh swapped seats with Matthew so he could lean into the divide between the seats. "They don't just know each other. They *know* each other. He's the partner that walked out on Killian when Sadler published his shitty book all those years ago. They were besties. Went to uni, and then came out to Egypt together. And that's before we get into the rumours, of which there are a shit ton."

"Like what?" Matthew asked, prompting Adie to maintain her focus, in spite of the urge to curl into a ball and shut her ears to everything she was hearing. This could not be reality. Of all the twenty-two and a half million citizens in the greater Cairo area, how could she possibly have ended up in entanglements with two men who happened to share an explosive past? Unless... unless Anton had known the whole time who she was and had orchestrated their meeting deliberately. But for what purpose?

"What rumours?" Siân asked in lieu of her.

"Well, he got arrested last year, and accused of black-market trading."

"No way!"

The pair nodded like bobble headed Funko Pop! Vinyls.

"It was last year, wasn't it?" Samīh asked, turning to confer with Jason.

"Possibly the year before. It didn't stick, but that doesn't mean shit. Everyone knows how corrupt most of the officials are. Plus, there are the rumours about him and Killian having been more than just work partners." He raised his hand to make inverted commas.

"Bollocks," Matthew said. "He's not gay. I'd know. My gaydar is finely tuned."

They were on the outskirts of Gezira now, not far from the apartment. Siân slowed the battered Land Rover to a more moderate pace. "He might not be gay, but he's not straight either, and that's straight from the horse's mouth."

That was evidently news to most of the vehicle.

"Well, Adie. You wanted a contact. Seems you have one."

"Wait! You can't seriously mean me to contact Killian's former partner and ask him if he knows a black-market antiquities dealer—that's nuts!"

Siân honked the horn. "Serendipitous, is what I'd call it." She pulled over to the kerb. "Text him back right now."

"I can't. What'll I say?"

"Right now!"

-38-
Adie

It took the best part of an hour for Adie to catch the metro downtown from the Gezira apartment. She'd arranged to meet Anton at Fishwari's, hoping the public location would help keep things civil. She hadn't made an apology for the tardiness of her response or said anything about why she wanted to see him. But then, Anton had been rather curt in his response. She could hardly blame him for being peeved. The last time they'd seen one another, he'd covered her in fruit syrup and opened her clothing with a knife, before shagging her senseless. Then she'd ignored him. Let him send message after message without even attempting to clue him in to what was going on.

He arrived and slipped into the seat across the table from her, without voicing a greeting. There he sat in stony silence, his dark hair shrouding his handsome face, while his eyes formed two fathomless inky pools.

"I should have called," she began, hating the mistrustful wall between them. She paused, took a sip of her iced *limoon*. It did nothing to soothe the heat in her cheeks.

"Yeah. Let's not pretend you dragged me here to apologise. What do you want, Adie?"

"Why didn't you tell me you and… That you and Killian were former partners?"

He sighed, and then catching the eye of the waiter, ordered a drink. "Because it was a decade ago and hardly seemed relevant. I didn't hide that we knew one another. Seriously, that's why you've been ignoring me?"

Her shoulders lifted and stayed there awkwardly hiked. "It might have been a while, but you were involved in the whole Dareth Sadler fiasco. I think that makes it important."

"I didn't hide that either. Was my aversion to Sadler not blatant enough? Why's it even important? What's Killian said about me?"

"Nothing. He hasn't said anything about you. He doesn't know that I know you." Heaven knows how he'd react when he did find out. His jealousy that night she'd met Anton was the reason she was now regularly occupying his bed, but things were hardly relaxed, or stable between them. There was no predicting if revealing the acquaintance would result in explosive fury or glacial calm. "I know you abandoned him in Petra."

That earned her a scornful laugh. "I abandoned him! That's a good one." His arms remained folded across his chest. Adie clutched her glass and allowed the click of dominoes from the adjacent table to fill the uncomfortable rift between them. The waiter delivered Anton's drink, along with a bowl of olives.

"Do you know an antiquities dealer by the name of Ihsãn Fuãd?"

"Jesus! Are you for real?"

"What does that mean? Do you? Know him?"

His deep brown eyes turned hostile. "I'm aware of his reputation."

"But you're not..."

"I'm not what? His pal? His lackey? No, Adie. I'm not. No more than I'm in league with Sadler. I approached you that day at the museum because I was interested in you. There's no hidden agenda, at least not on my part."

She even believed him. Mostly. "Yeah, but that's also what you'd say even if there was. This just all feels very coincidental. I mean, if you hate Sadler so much, why would you be hanging around in the location where he was giving a speech?"

"My reasons have nothing to do with you or whatever it is you're doing out at Saqqara. I don't care what you're doing at Saqqara. What Killian's doing at Saqqara. Or, at least, I care no more about it than I do any other excavation presently occurring in Egypt. We stopped being involved in one another's business a long time ago. Moreover, I'm offended that you think I'm pals with a notorious antiquities racketeer, and that's before we even get started on us."

Yes, them.

"I thought we had a good time, Adie. What did I do wrong?"

"Nothing." He'd done everything right, but then she'd gone back to the boat and Killian had been waiting.

"I didn't mean to leave you hanging. I did enjoy that night. Things just...they got complicated."

"So complicated you couldn't manage to send a five-word text? Thanks, but no thanks, Anton."

She deserved his ire, but that didn't make it easier to face. Head bowed, she watched the snake of dominoes on the next table lengthen while hoping the right words would pop into her head. "I'm sorry. I started seeing someone else." She was not going to tell him that it was Killian.

Anton stabbed an olive with a cocktail stick. He didn't lift it to his sensual mouth. "Of course you are. I bet he's all over you. You're exactly his type. Reckless, fucking naïve, and so determined to have an adventure and win the day that you can't see what effect your actions have on anyone else."

"Now hold on." She jerked her chair backwards. "I'm not... That's not a fair description, and you're making big assumptions about who I'm seeing."

"Am I?"

"I never said it was—"

"It's Killian. I know it's Killian. I mean, of course it is. So, I get it. I can't possibly compete with your golden boy boss."

"He's not..." Killian was too frosty to be anyone's golden boy, but that didn't mean a damn thing in terms of his reputation. People spoke his name the world over. He was a leading authority in their field, and honestly, she'd never heard of Doctor Anton Kelley before she'd met him. "I'm sorry."

"Don't be." He pushed himself to his feet. "It

was nice knowing you, Adie. I hope he gives you everything you're looking for."

"Wait!" She caught hold of his sleeve. "I really need to find this man, Ihsãn Fuãd."

He shook her off. "I can't help you." She dug into her money belt and pulled out several Egyptian notes.

"Keep your damned money. *Baksheesh* might drive the economy, but you can't buy me. We were lovers, Adie. I thought we understood one another." He turned his back and began to move away. Adie frantically stuffed the banknotes back into her pocket, after throwing some on the table. Anton was already out of the cafe by the time she was done.

She waded into the crowded street, but he'd vanished into the confusing sprawl of the Khan al-Khalili. Goddammit! That had gone even worse than she'd anticipated. Now she was back to square one.

She wandered into the great bazaar, mind awhirl with futile plans. At least the labyrinthine alleyways of the market were everything she'd expected of the middle east. It was all overloaded market stalls, boxes of lamps and brass kettles, mixed in with cheap phones, incense sticks, spices, snakes, spell-books, fruit, and gold.

Soon enough she was lost and disorientated. Hot sticky bodies surrounded her, and the air became increasingly muggy with competing perfumes. In the heart of the market, even the sun provided a feeble directional marker, its rays filtered through multiple heavily patterned shades. She'd blown her one lead. Realistically, her only option now was to head back to Gezira and start trawling through the local phone directory, terminator style.

"Hey lady, look for free."

A small boy of about eight grabbed her hand and pulled her past a trough of snakeskins, into the dim confines of a fuchsia-coloured stand. Adie managed to extract her hand from the boy's clammy palm, whereupon she rubbed it irritably against her trousers. She was standing outside a stall filled with stuffed camels, plastic 'magic razor pyramids' and 'real genuine mummified hands'.

"Buy gifts." The urchin announced, a jovial grin cemented on his grubby face. He began thrusting items at her. "You like. Good prices. Very cheap," he said emphasising the 'ver' in very. He showed her his wealth of teeth. "Many relatives?"

"No thank you." She replaced the sphinx money-boxes on the tablecloth.

"Tell Nagubi what you like. Nagubi has lots of friends. He can get you what you want." The boy determinedly plied her with more goods.

"I'm fine, really," Adie insisted, trying to shake him off. "I don't need any gifts."

The boy chuckled. "Why come to bazaar if you don't need anything?"

"I was meeting someone." Adie paused. The light was a murky pink under the canvas, giving everything a peculiar rosy glow, but there was something familiar about the collection of figurines in the old Sprite crate. She lifted one of the plastic figures. "Sadler!" She'd only seen his posters, but his mug seemed to be indelibly imprinted on her brain.

She lifted the keyring and let the tiny replica spin.

"300 *irsh*," said the boy holding out his hand.

Adie sighed. "What? No. I don't want this." She returned the miniature to the crate.

"200. Very reasonable. You like pretty man. I can tell."

"Nagubi! *Imshi*!" A raspy male voice sent the lad scurrying beneath the lurid raspberry coloured tablecloth. The figure appeared out of a portal behind the stall. Slender and weathered, dressed in shabby white robes and a ragged head covering. A semi-circular scar graced one cheek, giving his mouth a crooked tilt. He smiled, revealing numerous missing teeth. "Don't mind the boy."

"I won't. It's fine."

"Step inside. More wares within." He raised an arm and brushed back a beaded curtain.

"No, actually, I'm good, thank you."

"Very interesting things within."

"No." She raised her hand, intending to back away, but he grabbed her wrist, and twisted it painfully into the small of her back. "Hey, let go."

"Don't be so foolish as to cause a scene, Doctor Hamilton." He pressed so close now that the foul tobacco on his breath made her gag. "There's someone who'd like a word with you."

Adie recoiled, but the instinctive urge to scream died in her throat when she felt him poke something solid into her back.

"This way."

He nudged her around the stall to the beaded doorway, and through into a room stacked high with boxes of many things.

"Who are you? What do you want? If it's money, you can take my money." Her pulse took on a flighty pace, lending a red haze to her vision. Nor did the bite of the fake wedding band on her finger provide any comfort.

"No one wants your money, Doctor Hamilton."

"Who is it that wants to see me?"

Could word have somehow already spread that she was seeking Ihsãn? This was the sort of operation she imagined he'd be part of.

The man continued to coax her forward, through the back room and out onto another canvas-covered alleyway. Here clothing and banners hung from every available surface, and the chemical-signatures of numerous dyes and spray paints made the air burn as it passed over the membranes of her nose and throat. Shadowy figures turned away from them as they passed by. Adie pleaded for help, but no one would even look at her.

Finally, a few yards, and several turns later, her captor pushed her though a set of double doors into the cool foyer of a one-star hotel.

"*Alghurfat alraabieat wal'arbaeun,*" he barked at the man on reception, who gave a nod and summoned the lift.

Adie took advantage of his momentary lack of attention and kicked at his shins. Her heavy boots connected with the bone, making him stumble and curse. She got all of two paces before another man caught her by the hair and dragged her into the lift.

"Let me go! Help. *Yusaeid.*"

This new thug laughed and slammed her head into the wall of the rickety cage. Pain jabbed through her skull, and a trickle of blood fell into her eye. Adie pressed the heel of her hand to the cut. This new assailant was broader than the last, and wore a short, cropped beard. Various scars were interwoven with tattoos on his bare forearms.

Two floors up, he dragged her along a corridor, then pushed her through a doorway into a dismal little room. Adie stumbled, crashing to her knees on the tiled floor.

"Good afternoon, Dr Hamilton. A pleasure to meet you. I hope Jamãl has treated you with some courtesy. I'm afraid he's not always as civilised as one may wish."

"The bitch kicked me in the shin."

Adie lifted her head. The man wore an expensive tailored suit, cream, and a patterned cravat, like aristocratic dilettante from the 1920s. She recognised his visage immediately, having so recently seen it rendered into a plastic charm. "Dareth Sadler, I presume."

He was seated half in the shadows, but he leaned forward a little in response to her identifying him.

"What do you want with me?" she said around a lump in her throat.

"A chat, no more. I believe we're hunting the same thing."

"I doubt it."

He overlooked her hostility and nodded towards a vacant chair. Adie hesitated, then took it.

It beat the bite of the tiles on her knees.

"It's a fragment of a third dynasty mural, does that ring any bells?"

"No."

Dareth gave her a thin smile. He was polished and suavely presented; his hair expertly cut into a style that would've melted hearts back in the 70s and wouldn't have looked out of place on a child member of any of the various European monarchies. His eyes were neither brown nor green, but a speckled mismash of the two.

"You are a poor liar, I think, Doctor Hamilton. May I call you Adina?

"No."

He gave a delighted huff.

"Tea, Jamãl." He snapped his fingers. "And perhaps a dressing for the cut our esteemed guest appears to have sustained." He cocked an eyebrow at the thug as if questioning its necessity, but Jamãl didn't offer an explanation or any sign of remorse. He looked as if he'd happily do the same again, and worse. Much worse.

It raised the hairs on the back of her neck, how he looked at her, but eventually, after locking gazes with Sadler, he left the room. It meant there was now an exit available to her, for otherwise there were no doors, and only a tiny skylight set high in the crumbling walls.

"Now, as I was saying, we have a shared interest, and you cannot deny that it would benefit your research to find this missing fragment. It is the key piece of the whole mural, the true and only treasure of that disappointing pile of rocks."

He didn't know everything then. He didn't know about the possible connection with Ḥuni. Would that even interest him? It wasn't something you could spin much of a story around. Whereas, a picture of unknown providence, depicting a ritual... a pornographic ritual was very much what she understood him to be about.

"I'm simply seeking an exchange of information, Ms Hamilton. I have... Let us say that certain materials have recently come into my possession, that I'm willing to pass over, in return for an item I believe you possess and something to compensate me for the inconvenience you've caused—"

Jacob's journal. Was he offering her the journal? "What item?"

"I need photographs, Ms Hamilton. Multiple photographs. Wide angle, and close-up. Official photographs, from an official source."

"So that you can sell books off my back and ruin another career?" How had Killian ever fallen for this ploy? It was blatantly apparent that Sadler was the sort of weasel who used people and discarded them just as readily. "I'm not going to give you anything."

"You know, I had a feeling you might be difficult."

Jamāl returned with the tea. Sadler laced his with sugar and lemon and cocked an eye at her. She had no intention of drinking his tea. None. Every hair on her body was standing on end.

"I'm disappointed, Doctor Hamilton. Very

disappointed. One last chance to make this a civil affair."

"No! You're insane. There's no way on earth—"

Sadler shook his head sadly. "Jamãl, she's yours. We'll talk again when you're feeling more amenable."

Out of the corner of her eye, she saw Jamãl draw a long-handled knife from his pocket. She had no intention of sticking around to find out how he intended to use it. She snatched up the teacup, and hurled it and its contents in Sadler's face, no doubt spoiling his expensive suit and hopefully giving him a headache to match the one his thug had given her. The moment the cup parted with her hand, she fled towards the exit.

Jamãl lurched towards her, but Adie dived. She'd never been much of a gymnast, but she had gone on a multitude of adventures as a child that involved escaping from thieves and ruffians, and those memories propelled her forward. She rolled under his arm and through the doorway. Somehow, she landed upright and managed to lurch toward the lift.

She jabbed the button, but barrelled onto the stairway beside it instead and took them three at a time. The man behind the desk called out to her as she ran across the foyer, but she didn't stop. Outside, in the alleyway, she headed toward the honks of the traffic, all too conscious of the heavy footfalls of pursuit dogging her.

Adie didn't stop, and she didn't look back. Her breath burned in her lungs, and a stitch laced through her middle, but she kept going, past row upon row of mediaeval facades, until the sweet aromas of turmeric and cumin mixed with the odour of petrol, and she darted out into the middle of a busy road.

"Adie!"

A strong arm hauled her out of the flow of traffic, as various hollers and beeps sounded around her. A bus sped past just inches from her face, leaving her choking on a lungful of benzene exhaust. "Christ, woman! Do you have a death wish?"

"Anton!" *Oh, God! Anton.* She turned in his embrace, as relief drained the vigour from her limbs. There was no sign of Jamãl or Sadler. They were standing facing an elaborate mosque, where people were lining up ready to enter and pray. Several of them were staring at her and pointing. She turned her face away from them and let her head rest on Anton's shoulder. "How are you here?" Thank God, he was here. "Did you follow me?"

"Adie." He put a little space between them, making her realise that their closeness wasn't considered appropriate. "Following, no. I thought better of my exit, or rather I found I had other things I wished to say, but I lost you inside the bazaar."

"I got dragged... taken to meet Sadler. They were chasing... He wanted me to provide photographs...was going to give me to his thug." Although she'd stopped running, her head hadn't caught up with events, so her heart continued to race, and panic roared in her veins.

Anton's deep gaze fastened on the contusion on

her head, and he passed a finger over it, causing dried blood to flake away. "Sadler did this?"

She shook her head. "Not him, his thug." She began walking in no particular direction, needing both to escape the attention they'd drawn, and to satisfy her flight response. Anton fell into step with her.

"Jamãl?"

She nodded.

"That bastard." Anton turned her away from the main road, into a side-street. They stepped into the shrouded doorway of a tiny incense shop, where he insisted on taking a good look at her.

"I should report it, I guess," she offered. "Have him dealt with?"

She expected him to nod, to advise her where the nearest police station was, but his mouth took on a sour tilt. "It's wrong of me to ask, but please don't."

Adie's attention snapped to him. "Why not, Anton? He just dragged me off the street and did this. He threatened me with a knife, and I only got out of there through sheer dumb luck."

"I know. I realise I'm asking the unreasonable, but if you could at least put it off until tomorrow..."

She caught hold of his wrist. "Would you like to tell me what the fuck is going on?"

He shook his head, then looked around with wary eyes. "There's something in motion..." He forced a smile onto his face. "The less you know the better."

"Fuck that! What are you involved in?"

"Adie." Again, with the wary look. "A shit ton of

stuff you don't need to worry about and that I'm not about to spill on the street."

"Yeah, I heard you were arrested before..."

It was his turn to blaspheme.

"So, it's true?"

He considered; head inclined. Then, his fingers traced over his lips. "It's not what you think."

"Yeah, what is it you think I think?"

"Fuck. Dammit. Not here, okay. We're not discussing this here." He gave a weary sigh and pinched the corners of his eyes. "I think...we need to have this conversation in a less open location. Somewhere we're less likely to be overheard or attract attention."

Agreed, the shopkeeper of whose doorway they were occupying was scowling at them and throwing them shade through the front window.

"My place isn't far."

His place.

"Coming? Or I can escort you back to the metro station."

-39-
Adie

She'd expected him to take her to an upmarket apartment in the heart of the city. Instead, Anton led her via an underpass to the southeast of the city, to where electricity cables hung like giant cobwebs between the crypts of the City of the Dead. Washing lines and signs of human detritus mingled with fresh and decaying tributes to the deceased.

"You should see the place on festival days. People come here for picnics."

"What I don't understand is why we're here." Unless the dead were going to provide them answers, it struck her as an odd place to head for a conversation. Anton quickened his long-legged pace, forcing her to hurry to keep up with him. Not five minutes later, she got her answer, when he unlocked a crypt door and led her inside one of the boxy sepulchres.

"I appreciate you said you wanted to go somewhere we wouldn't be overheard but—"

He struck a match, and lit a candle, revealing a small wash basin alongside a camping hob. Further in, stone shelves clearly meant to hold the accoutrements of the dead instead housed his clothing and miscellaneous artefacts of life. "You live here!"

She'd heard that the eerie Northern Cemetery was home to many of Cairo's expanding number of residents, but she hadn't expected Anton to be among them. She'd expected a more typical residence, perhaps in one of the leafier areas.

"Have a seat," he said, pointing to the only piece of furniture, a bed formed from a mattress placed on a base made from two wooden pallets.

"Are there any bodies in here?" She wasn't squeamish about mummies, but she recalled his tolerance for them hanging about was rather higher than hers.

"They moved out before I arrived. The previous resident sold them to tourists to fund his degree."

"You are joking?"

Anton shrugged and Adie decided not to pursue it. Instead, she gingerly took the offered seat on his mattress, while he lit an oil lantern. As buttery light spilled over the walls of the tiny building, and painted deep shadows in areas it didn't quite reach, he took a seat beside her. Not touching, but close enough that she was hyperaware of his every move, his every breath, just how attractive she still found him.

"Where do you keep the tent?"

"That was borrowed."

"Okay, right." She nodded. "Well, we're here, so dish the dirt, I guess."

He didn't seem to find much humour in her words. There was a soul deep sadness clinging to him when she raised her head to meet his gaze. Their flirtation had only lasted a short while, was he genuinely saddened by her calling it off? They'd just been having fun, hadn't they?

"Adie, are you sure you want to pursue this?"

She held up a hand. "I'm sure. I promise I wouldn't be pursuing it if there was any other way, but now I know that Sadler is after the same thing, then I really can't let this go. It's imperative that I find it before him. If I don't, it won't just mean trouble for the dig, it'll likely destroy Killian's credibility, and... well, I don't want that. I'm sorry, I know you don't care either way—"

"I care."

She took a hard look at him then but couldn't read beyond the obvious conflictedness that she'd already observed. "What happened between you and him?"

A wall snapped into place between them. "That hardly matters."

"Except, suddenly it feels enormously like it does." She wasn't imagining the ramrod straight set of his spine, nor the hollowing of his cheekbones. "So, tell me. I know he won't, so please, at least unravel that particular mystery for me."

"What's to tell?"

"A lot, evidently." Whereas if she'd been having this conversation with Killian his obfuscation might have been construed as teasing, Anton said it entirely straight faced.

"I know you were close. Best friends. A team."

"Well maybe I don't want to open that particular can of worms."

She wasn't prepared to let it sit on the shelf any longer proudly displaying a decade old best before date.

"I feel like it's something I should know, given the circumstances."

"You mean because you've been shagging us both?"

Heat bloomed in her cheeks. Adie fastened her attention on a lone beetle scuttling along a gash in the wall. The way he put it made it sound premeditated, whereas, she'd had no idea what the two men were to one another. Moreover, the fact a decade had passed since they'd spoken made it seem like whatever their history, it ought to be long done and dusted.

"Once upon a time that wouldn't have been an issue."

Up popped her head like a burn blister, so she could frown at him, communicating silent askance.

"We shared pretty much everything back then."

"Back when?"

"BBS."

"Back Before Sadler," she intuited, receiving a nod in response.

"Adie, we were once as close as any two people could possibly be. We did everything together. We were partners in every sense of the word."

He sighed, then shuffled over the mattress to rest his back against the wall.

Adie followed him to do the same. "Go on," she prompted.

Anton uncomfortably chewed his lip. Then he sighed and reached over to a rusted biscuit box on a shelf. Curiosity roused, Adie leaned in, straining her vision, as he sifted through what looked like scores of luggage labels and old receipts, until he pulled out a dog-eared photograph of three men. He passed it to her, and she recognised it at once. The middle figure especially was desperately familiar. Indeed, it was in her old professor's office that she'd seen this image a thousand times before without ever paying it any heed. It was a graduation day photograph, the figures resplendent in gowns and mortar boards. Josef was much the same as she knew him, bushy of brow, and kindly faced. Perhaps a fraction less wrinkled, and a little more upright.

The two men flanking him were the ones who had metamorphosed.

Anton stood on the left. Hair cropped short, his skin several shades lighter. He never gave the impression of weariness, but the comparison with his younger self made that sense of lassitude stick out.

On the right, Killian was virtually unrecognisable, save for something in his eyes, a fervour, a hunger she'd caught the odd sight of now and again. The rest of him, though... The transformation was stark. His hair was an unruly dark brown tangle in the picture, but white as snow, now. The grin on his face too. She'd never seen him smile in remotely the same way. It was grossly self-indulgent in its breadth, but painted such a light in his eyes, that it was impossible not to see it and return it.

She traced her finger across his form. "He's so different."

"Keep in mind we'd been drinking free champagne all day."

"Even so... You know he's gone fully white these days."

Anton shook his head. "I've not seen him to know that, although it's not exactly a surprise to learn. His father went prematurely white, and the stress had already begun to paint its marks on him before we parted ways."

"Why did you, Anton?"

He huffed, took the photograph from her and stowed it back in the box. "Sadler."

"I gathered that, but why?"

He rested his head in his hand, so he was looking at her with his head tilted "Because what he did changed Killian fundamentally. He'd always been so open to everything. Free with his thoughts. He'd argue concepts with you all day long, and he was always questioning, and digging for answers, trying to root out the meaning of things. He absolutely believed in free expression and exchange of ideas. What Sadler did ripped that right out of him.

"It was agony to watch, Adie. He shut down. Battened the hatches. Quashed most of the characteristics that made him him. I tried to be there, be the support he needed, but he was like a stranger.

"We'd been incredibly close, and then a chasm opened at our feet, and we wound up on different sides of it."

He seemed perplexed by the turn of events even now.

"So, you left."

"No. I stuck around. We soldiered on for eight months after the Sadler shitstorm hit. I tried. God, I tried. I kept thinking he just needed time. That when the storm eventually died down, the man I knew would emerge again. Only, it never happened, and it seemed likely that it never would. That's when I left, Adie, and I likely wouldn't have done it even then if he hadn't categorically told me to piss off. The final argument we had was rather heated and personal. You'll forgive me if I don't repeat any of it."

"And that happened in Petra?"

He nodded. "I left. He stayed on a while, I think. From there, our careers took us along different trajectories."

"You must want to kick yourself sometimes... Shit! I didn't mean that how it came out. Sorry!"

His eyes smouldered, but in the end he just laughed. "I've never been interested in accolades or having my peers fawn over me."

"Money?"

"I get by. There's freedom to be found in doing without and not being obsessively materialistic, unlike most of the world population."

"You're happy living in a crypt?"

"I have a villa in the south of France," he said

straight-faced. "No, not really. I did have an apartment in Alexandria for a while, but what's the point, when I'm always on the move?"

"Killian has a houseboat," she said.

"He was enamoured of those from the first time we both saw the Nile. I think he imagined cruising up and down like aristocratic dilettantes from a century ago. And he did always look good in a cream linen suit."

"He looks good in most things." She'd yet to see him look anything less than scrumptious in any outfit, from formal evening wear to the scruffy shirt and cargoes combination he wore while working.

"How did you end up working for him, Adie? You must make his blood boil. You're everything he despises these days, intuitive, impulsive..."

"Perhaps he doesn't really hate those things. They're just lines he feeds to us and to himself to convince himself that he has everything under control. What if at his core, he hasn't changed so fundamentally as you think, and all that youthful passion you knew is still there, it's just nailed inside a box waiting for someone to crowbar it open?"

"Do you imagine you're that person?"

"No. Not necessarily." She sounded super defensive even to herself. "Let's move on from talking about Killian. He isn't why I'm here. I need to find that fragment, and you certainly implied that—"

"I'll help. I'll help because you're just stubborn enough to pursue this regardless of any sort of warning to do otherwise, and I don't want to see you getting into any more trouble than you've already found for yourself."

"I haven't found—"

"Sadler," he reminded her. "You said he had you snatched off the street."

She wetted her lips. Yes, that was true. Point taken. Also, of course she wasn't going to give up attempting to find the fragment. If there'd been other leads, sure she'd have followed them too, or even before attempting to contact a notorious criminal, but there weren't so it was irrelevant.

"Tell me about this thing that you're looking for."

"Okay." She resettled herself against the wall. "It's a section of plaster, chiselled out of a mural. It probably doesn't look like much on its own, but in context... It's kind of a keystone. The piece has a pharaoh's cock on it, and without it, it's impossible to say with any certainty what the image depicts. Clearly, it's some form of ceremony, but what manner of ceremony can only be speculated on."

"Something your boss abhors."

"Something my boss abhors," she repeated. "Also, not having it leaves room for the Dareth Sadlers of the world to interpret it in the manner of their choosing. Which will potentially throw shade on the entire team and make Killian a laughingstock again."

He nodded. "And why do you think Ihsãn Fuãd knows how to find it, or is that just a wild stab in the dark?"

"No, it's... I've been in contact with his former

employer. That's who pointed me towards him. Said if anyone knew, then it was sure to be him. Apparently, he has a photographic memory, and they catalogued a lot of ancient cocks together."

"I trust he didn't phrase it quite like that?" He pushed his tongue into his cheek.

Adie grinned. "No, thankfully. Can you imagine if they used that in advertising for archaeology degrees?"

"Careful, Doctor Hamilton, that could be construed as ageist."

She snort laughed and poked him, setting him off grinning too, which landed them in an awkward moment of connection. She, gazing into the depths of his eyes, his mouth ever so slightly parted and mere inches from hers. The warmth of his breath on her skin.

Adie's heart started performing flips.

Hot damn!

She backed up and coughed into her hand. "So, Ihsãn Fuãd. Do you really not know him, or was that just..."

"Adie." He combed his fingers through her hair. "I'm going to tell you something, and the chances are, you're not going to like it. Firstly, no, I don't know Ihsãn Fuãd, nor am I sure I wish to. However, I do have certain contacts."

"Yeah, I heard you were arrested for—"

"I was stitched up. I'm no thief, but I have cultivated friendships among certain families here in Cairo, who've been in the grave robbing business for centuries."

"Why?"

"Why?" He gave his head a shake. "A multitude of reasons. To help stamp out antiquities trafficking. To re-educate. Many of them know things modern archaeologists could spend hundreds of years failing to learn. I'm trying to offer them alternate uses for their knowledge and talents, but it's not easy. Many of them live in poverty. Think about it. If you couldn't feed your children, and you knew where a dead man was laid to rest surrounded by gold, wouldn't you dig it up?"

This didn't seem the right moment for an in-depth debate about Egyptian social history.

"There's a real movement at the moment to repatriate thousands of items stolen from Egypt, which is all well and good, but pointless if you don't simultaneously clamp down on the black-market trade of those items."

"I get it. So that's what you do? Where you focus?"

"Yeah. It's what I do. It's fascinating, a unique opportunity to learn history from the descendants of the people who created those monuments in the desert. But not everybody is onboard with the scheme."

"Some of them like being career criminals."

"Yeah. Some of them make silly money from it. I'm trying to cut off their supply channels. Adie, Ihsãn Fuãd is rumoured to be one of the big guys in the industry. He's not somebody you should be associating with, or even thinking of associating with."

"But if he's the only source of the knowledge I need, then you can see the logic, right?"

"You realise he's not going to assist you for free? There'll be a price. It might be more than you're willing to pay."

"Are you talking money?"

He bowed his head, so that the shadows masked his expression. "I'd say he's more likely to demand a favour, something he can hold over you."

"I'm not going to steal for him."

"Nor would he likely expect you to, but he may ask you to turn a blind eye or to pick your brain over a certain site or set of items."

"I'm not going to agree to that."

He lifted his shoulders as if to say, precisely, which is why this whole thing is a pointless endeavour from the get-go.

"But I also can't not try. Not if it nets us a complete mural."

Anton huffed and bowed his head. "Does your boss have any idea what you're up to?"

"He knows I'm looking."

"Meaning you haven't spilled the details." He raised a hand to his brow and shook his head. "I might not have seen him in years, but I can safely say he'll tear you a new one if he gets wind of any of this."

"Then I guess he'd better not find out. Are you going to tell him?"

There came a rap on the tomb door, which startled them apart and jerked Anton onto his feet. At first, she interpreted his glare as a warning that he just might. Then, he pressed two fingers fast to his lips.

The knock came again. More urgent this time.

He made a wafting motion, ahead of reaching for the door. Adie pressed herself deeper into the shadows. Not that she was at risk of being seen, since he barely cracked the door open an inch. Alarmingly, he slid a knife off a shelf, which he held clasped, thumb up and point down behind his back. God! What the hell?

She had no visibility from this position, and the exchange was conducted in low voices. Her Arabic hadn't greatly improved, but she caught a time—ten thirty, and a location, Northern Saqqara. Also, a name—Jamãl. Not a coincidence surely, that Sadler's thug had that exact moniker.

"Good luck." The unseen figure departed. Anton closed the door and returned the jambiya to the shelf. "It's time you left. I'll see what I can do, Adie, but I'm making no promises. If he agrees to a meeting, it'll be because he's intrigued to learn what you're offering. So, you'd better figure out what that is. Gather your stuff. I'll walk you to the road so you can get a cab home."

He offered her a hand onto her feet, which she accepted, but made no move to collect her stuff. "What was that about?"

"Nothing of any concern to you."

Untrue. "My Arabic might be utter crap, but you were talking about Jamãl. You know, the man responsible for this?" She traced two fingers over the contusion on her brow. "So, I'd like to know why the fuck you've just received details of a clandestine meeting with him. Is this all part of some sort of sting, or are you in fucking league with Sadler?"

"I'm not meeting him, and I'm not in fucking league with Sadler. The only thing I'd like to do to that son of a bitch is punch the smarmy grin from his face. Adie—" He quietened, obviously formulating his words. "Look, this has nothing to do with you. It's not about your excavation, or a plaster fragment with a willy on it. It's not even anything to do with Sadler."

"Then what is it about?"

His lips remained stubbornly closed.

"Jamãl kidnapped me this afternoon and gave me a fucking great bruise. He threatened me with a knife. I don't think it's unreasonable for me to ask what's going on, because from where I'm standing, you meeting him seems highly fucking suspicious."

"Adie, seriously. This is not something you need to poke your nose into. Go back to your trowels and blowing your boss."

How dare he! She pinched the bridge of her nose, to ease the well of tension pounding there.

"Ten thirty, Northern Saqqara. That's not anywhere you should be, or anywhere you can stop me from being."

"Adie." There was an edge in his voice she hadn't heard before. "Don't. Do not fuck this up for me. Christ, it's nothing you even need to poke your nose into."

"Yeah, well, that seems to apply to a lot of things of late. All I hear is hang back and let others do the leg work. It's not why I'm here."

"This meeting is not why you're here either."

"True, but I'm involved now. So how about you tell me what the hell is going on, and why you answered the door with a knife in your hand." She snatched the sheathed *jambiya* from the shelf in emphasis.

Anton immediately took it from her. "That's not a toy to be played with."

"Why are you meeting Jamãl?" Even though he'd claimed otherwise, she couldn't shake the suspicion of betrayal. It filled her mouth with a sour tang and made her eyes cloud with angry tears.

"I'm not fucking meeting him." He shoved his hand backwards through his hair then wrenched it into a knot. "I'm baiting a trap. And I need you to leave, as I've things to prepare."

She sat right down.

"Adie!"

She crossed both her legs and her arms. "I'm not going anywhere. Not until you tell me the full story." And probably not even then.

He thew his arms up in despair. "I don't have time for this shit. I really don't have time."

As standoffs went, this was an easy one to hold out over. Comfortable seat on his mattress, no place she had to be.

"There's no goddamned reason why I need to tell you anything."

"Is telling me worse than me showing up later?"

"God damn you." He snarled through his teeth, then pitched a pot at the wall. It shattered, spraying shards in every direction.

Adie calmly plucked a few splinters from her clothing.

"If you trail me, then everything's going to go tits up."

"So, tell me." She patted a relatively splinter free spot beside her.

Anton did a few back and forths, muttering under his breath, before he finally caved and sank back onto the mattress. "It's not anything sanctioned. It's a personal vendetta, and I've put months of effort into setting it up to ensure he takes the bait. I know you're angry, about what he did earlier, but please,"—he put his hands together in prayer—"don't muck this up for me."

"What sort of set-up? And why?"

The tension through his back and shoulders right now was making him rigid as a beanpole.

"Like I said, it's personal. It's not of any relevance to your dig, or Sadler."

He had said that. What he hadn't provided was the why, and Adie, with her background in history was all about asking why. Perhaps more importantly, it was also turning her thoughts to how it might benefit it. Jamãl worked with Sadler, and Sadler remained the biggest threat to their dig at present. If he found the fragment before she did... Oh, it hardly bore thinking about. Too many things would go tits up. Moreover, it would hurt Killian, and while he might be grumpy and a pain in her behind when he was being all serious, she hated the idea of him being hurt.

He was hurting already. She'd figured that

much. The whole Mr Frosty thing was such an obvious shield, especially now she'd caught glimpses of his playfulness.

"I want in."

"Adie don't be a fucking fool. This isn't something involving radios and backup and friendly law enforcement."

All the better.

"If it goes tits up, I won't be able to protect you, and you could get seriously hurt. You had a lucky escape earlier. Others who've crossed him haven't fared nearly so well."

That sounded like even more reason to pursue it. Also, why it was madness for him to go it alone. "Do you have *any* backup?"

The fact he didn't jump right in provided her with the answer.

"I'm coming."

He tsked. "Did anybody ever tell you that you possess a fundamental lack of common sense? This isn't an adventure story. There's no treasure to win."

Not everything in life was about treasure or winning. Sometimes it was about justice. "I think you'd better fill me in on the exact particulars. You're not going to dissuade me, so let's get that straight right now."

"And how are you going to explain it to your boss? I guarantee, this isn't going to net his stamp of approval."

"I'm not at work. This is my own time." Killian didn't need to be privy to every single thing she did. "You know, you're acting just like him right now, talking to me like I'm an imbecile, and like only you know what's best for me. I don't need anyone to make my choices for me, Anton. I'm good with making my own mistakes and accepting the repercussions of them. Also, it's interesting that it's never over sex that you start making quibbling noises."

"That is unfair."

She shrugged.

Interestingly, that seemed to settle it. "Fine." He grimaced. "You're the boss of you. But if you do anything to fuck this up—"

"I won't. I'll do exactly as you say."

He made a low rumbly sound of exasperation.

"What was that?"

"I said that assurance doesn't fill me with faith."

-40-
Adie

Adie messaged Siân to let her know she wouldn't be back until late, or possibly until tomorrow. It earned her a barrage of messages in return, none of which she replied to. Siân didn't need to know the details, and if that meant she drew some erroneous conclusions about what she was doing with Anton that was probably better than her learning the truth. Any suppositions could always be corrected after the fact.

Night had descended by the time they left the City of the Dead. Anton had dressed in black Bedouin robes and insisted on her wearing a similarly swaddling disguise. Worryingly, he strapped the jambiya in its ornate silver scabbard to his waist, where now and then Adie caught a glint of it in the moonlight.

They took a taxi south out of the city as far as Abu Gorab, then walked into the heart of the Abu Sir pyramid field. The pockmarked cemetery was closed for the night, and anything that remained knew how to get around without making a sound. They too became slinking shadows, moving between one broken shell and another while the dying khamseen blew fitfully around them.

"This is the one." Anton stopped before a first dynasty mastaba. The entryway was a black slash in the stonework, partially covered by a stone portcullis slab, which was tilted at an angle with wooden splints. Nothing obvious differentiated it from any of the other early dynasty tombs surrounding them. They had seen no signs of any other people, but that was to be expected. It was after dark, and they'd slipped over a wall to get in.

Anton ushered her down the sand dusted steps toward the entrance, then felt around the doorway and found a small hurricane lantern. The bright orange glow instantly infused Adie with a primitive sense of security after navigating the desert thus far by moonlight.

"What's down here?"

"Stuff. Nothing of genuine interest. That's the whole point."

"Okay," she said, not understanding at all.

"Careful," Anton advised. "There's only a narrow lip, and then a drop."

She squeezed through the entryway behind him and found herself on a narrow platform that might once had been the top of a flight of stairs, but now hung over a void. Even when Anton raised the lantern, it was impossible to make out more than flashes of barren stonework in the chamber below. Above them, the roof rose in steps like Djoser's pyramid.

Anton swung onto a hereto unseen ladder and

began to descend. Adie followed, hitching her robes to make it easier. "You have a permit to be here, right?"

"No."

Okay, so she'd kind of known that. Really, she oughtn't to have asked. By the time her feet found the floor she was trembling, and telling herself it was the place, that it had a weird vibe, not that her unease over them trespassing, or meeting Jamãl again that was causing it. And she categorically wasn't thinking about what would happen if they were caught. It wouldn't be Killian's wrath she'd be facing. They'd be arrested. She'd probably get deported, or worse. Seemed, a tiny voice in her head said, Anton had had a point when he'd told her to keep her nose out of this, but she hadn't been able to keep her curiosity in check. After all, this was the sort of adventure her career in Egyptology was built upon.

"Why are you all set up as if you are working here, if you know the place is bare?"

"To make it look like it isn't, obviously."

Anton offered her his hand as she stepped off the ladder and held up the lantern. The floor was pitted and cracked, the walls an uneven patchwork of bricks and rubble that reminded her of castle ruins ravaged by time and war. There was no sign of a casket, but two darker archways led into further rooms.

"Storage areas," Anton said, following her gaze. "The right one has a small granary. The left side I've been using for storage. It's mostly full of rubble from a cave-in. This is the burial chamber, but the body went long ago."

"Okay."

"I've been trying to catch Jamãl's attention by regularly sneaking in here for weeks, but I guess that Sadler's been keeping him busy. Normally, he's more inquisitive than that."

"But..."

"But tonight, it so happens, I've had a tip-off that he'll be in this part of the desert with acquisition in mind."

"And you think he's coming here?" It crossed her mind that there was another excavation site that might be more appealing just a fraction further south.

"He's not that dumb, Adie." Anton had evidently read her worry right off her face. "Killian's site is way too high profile, whereas this mastaba is of no real significance. No one is keeping an eye on the place, or even half an eye on it."

She nodded. That made logical sense. "I'm sensing there's a personal element to why you want to catch him out."

"That should probably be a story for when we get out of here. I don't mean to linger."

"Tell me while you do whatever it is you came here to do."

He produced a small bag from the voluminous folds of his robes. This he upended, disgorging an array of small items, among them gold earrings, combs, small ushabtis statues, and a piece of inscribed alabaster.

Adie gazed at them in wonder, reaching out to pick them up, but Anton pushed her hands away. "They're fakes, and you don't want your DNA all over them. A friend of mine makes them. Usually, she specialises in mummified pets, but I smiled nicely." He winked at her, then moved a couple of items to the shelf just inside the door. The guardian figurines he placed inside a crate of straw, as if they'd been packaged ready to transport. They were dull brown, difficult to see the details of in the dark, but carved as to appear bandaged.

"The al-Aziz clan, they're well know petty criminals. The sort of criminals who happily stitch up others if it wins them a better pay day. I wasn't aware of that when I first encountered them."

"In your role as part of the trafficking rehabilitation program."

"Right. It's not easy earning the trust of people who've been in the business of graverobbing for centuries. Rehabilitation takes time, and not everyone is down with the program."

"Go on."

"About eighteen months back, I was working on a mastaba a little north-west of here. I'd been turning up some promising material. Nothing major. Nothing that was going to bring the news agencies along, but some nice bits and pieces, nonetheless. It was thanks to a tip-off from certain quarters that I'd found what I'd found, and I had an agreement in place that worked for us both. They got compensated for their knowledge, and anything of archaeological significance got passed on to the authorities, rather than disappearing abroad."

"I'm guessing that's not what happened."

"What happened is that I uncovered a series of reed mats rendered in blue faience tiles, and a casket of jewellery. All rather more significant, I think we can agree, than a few bits of pottery. The thing is, the whole compensation thing doesn't scale because the find is bigger than expected. It's basically buying tip-offs. Naturally, certain quarters weren't happy. And when people aren't happy, they start muttering, and that's how rumours spread, and someone leaps in and takes advantage."

He pressed his curled knuckles to his lips. "Jamãl and his brothers got wind of the find, and decided they deserved the whole of the pie. They turned up, left me with concussion and a couple of broken ribs, and stripped the place bare while I was out cold. By the time I came round, there was nothing left. What might have been an important site was just another hole in the ground."

"You got arrested over it," she said recalling Samīh's story from earlier that day.

"Yeah. Luckily, I have friends in the Egyptian Antiquities Authority, who helped get the charges dropped. They'd never have stuck, because they couldn't prove there'd ever been anything down there in the first place, but that does mean I didn't endure a whole world of pain. I had my passport and all my visas taken from me."

He bowed his head and shook it slowly. "I don't know if you're acquainted with the Mogamma building on Midan Tahrir? It's a fourteen-storey monument to the gods of bureaucracy. I spent fifty odd days in there trying to recover my passport, my work permit, and my identity, being shuttled from one person to the next, so that they could sign and countersign and approve all my documents. I lost days of my life to that nightmare, waiting for the only person who could sign each fucking document, outside locked offices where 'back soon' signs could mean anything from five minutes to five days."

"So, this is about revenge."

He flashed her a bitter smile. "I guess you could call it that, but believe me, he deserves his comeuppance."

She had no arguments to offer on that point.

"Now, let's get out of here."

She started forward, only to shriek as something scuttled past her foot.

Anton clamped a hand over her mouth. "Quiet."

"Sorry, there was a rat."

"It's not a rat. It's a gerbil. There's a whole horde of them living here."

"Is that what you call a family of them? A horde?" The scare had left her heart pounding in her ears.

"Yeah, rather conveniently. It's been useful when I've been shit talking about the place around town. It's much easier to lie convincingly, when you're actually telling the truth."

She chuckled over the play of words, only to have Anton instantly shush her. "Quiet, I think I hear something."

She listened too but didn't hear anything. Even

the gerbils were walking on silent feet.

"Goddammit, he's here."

"What!" She made her exclamation into his hand, as he covered her mouth. Adie felt the blood drain from her face. She'd figured out enough of Anton's plan to know they were supposed to be long gone by the time Jamãl arrived, not huddled down here with him blocking the exit.

"What do we do?" she said into his hand.

"Stay here. And not a sound." He dowsed the lantern, leaving her straining to see what was directly in front of her nose. She heard the whisper of cloth and sensed Anton's loss as he moved into the burial vault.

"Good evening, Doctor Kelley. You're out late. Are the authorities aware of this excavation?" The voice was horribly familiar, as that of the man who'd dragged her from the bazaar to meet Sadler.

She couldn't hear Anton's reply, nor see either of the two men. Just then, a lighter flame flared, bringing a small plume of visibility, which was set to a hissing gas lantern. The illumination made Jamãl's mirthless face visible. Clinging shadows emphasised the cruel smirk on his lips. The two men were only a few paces apart. Jamãl blocking the exit, with Anton opposite him. Jamãl was holding a knife, not an ornate and traditional jambiya like the one Anton had on his belt, but a long straight-handled weapon that he clasped in a backhanded grip with the blade protruding from the bottom of his fist. The sight of it made her already racing heart quicken so that it pounded in her temples and her nose.

A fight seemed inevitable, given there was no way for them to escape the tomb without first getting past Jamãl. She kept expecting Anton to draw his blade, as they exchanged Arabic phrases that she couldn't make sense of. Insults? Anton instead unwound a sash from around his waist and held it loosely in both hands.

Seeing them poised like two vicious panthers painted her body in a cold sweat. One horror scenario after another played out within her mind. Anton falling. Jamãl coming for her next. There wasn't a weapon or anything at hand for her to use. She'd bleed out here. Sadler and the news agencies would spin their deaths out into some kind of ritualistic suicide pact. She'd never get to uncover any gold, or run from enormous rolling boulders, or translate ancient scrolls chockful of wisdom.

Jamãl hissed as he lunged forward. His blade streaked twice through the air in front of Anton's face, forcing him backwards. Then it swept upwards towards his throat.

Adie's mouth opened in horror, but the scream never came. At the last moment, Anton dodged. He caught Jamãl's arm in the loop of the sash, twisted it, and jerked Jamãl forward off balance. It sent them both careening into the back wall where the blade skittered off the stonework creating sparks.

Balance righted, Jamãl stabbed downward toward the top of Anton's head. Again, Anton parried, this time with the scarf pulled taut between both hands. It stopped the attack, but as Jamãl drew back, the knife sliced the cloth in two.

Instantly, the Egyptian's vicious grin widened. He spat out an insult, then began to weave the knife back and forth in what she surmised was a taunt. Only to then swoop in low. There was a cry. The sound of ripping cloth.

Adie snatched one of the ushabtis from the crate and launched herself out of the granary. She brought the statuette down as hard as possible on the back of Jamãl's head. It was enough to buy them a moment. He dropped to his knees in a daze.

"Run!" Anton yelled. She dropped the shattered figurine and leaped onto the ladder, causing it to wobble alarmingly. Anton steadied its swing as she scrambled up the first few rungs, then followed her up.

Adie burst into the cool night air.

Behind her, there came a clatter; Anton having kicked the ladder free of its mooring. He squeezed through the entryway, one hand clutched to his side. "Help me with these." He began kicking at the splints supporting the portcullis slab. Adie grabbed the largest and pulled with all her might. She toppled onto her arse as it shot loose. The stone rocked unsteadily, several of the smaller supports snapped. Anton threw his weight against the stone, and it fell, crashing into place, sealing Jamãl inside.

On her knees, Adie stared at the portcullis slab. They were safe. She was safe. No, Anton was bleeding. Blood spread like a black stain between his fingers and into his sleeve.

"How bad?" she asked.

"It'll be fine."

But the terror in his expression proved he wasn't certain of that. She knew how adrenaline worked. How once the danger was gone, the pain and reality of a situation would seep in. "We need to get you to a hospital."

"We need to get out of here and call the authorities. I don't trust that weasel not to wriggle his way out of the trap." He began walking back the way they'd come across the desert, his pace unsteady.

"Anton, stop. You need to let me look at that. And yes, I'm going to be stubborn about it." There was a long slash in the side of his *galabeyya*. She got him to lift his hand, but that only caused a fresh deluge of blood to escape. "It's not deep, but it's clean. That's why it won't stop. Have you another scarf we can wrap around it?"

He loosened a long black streamer of silk from around his neck and handed it to her. Adie tied it around his body as a temporary dressing. The moment made her think of Killian binding the wound she'd caused herself.

Why hadn't she stayed on the houseboat this weekend, instead of running off to Cairo? They could have spent this evening drinking wine and getting creative in the bedroom.

"Will you make it over the wall?" she asked. The barrier hadn't proved much trouble on the way in, but now it loomed before them far too high for her to scramble over without a boost. "Can you?"

He cupped his hands, but there was already a sheen of sweat on his brow, and another forming over his lip.

"Anton?" Even if he helped her up, he'd never manage to pull himself over.

Adie reached for her phone.

"Don't you dare call an ambulance."

"We need help."

He looked set to argue, only to slump against the wall.

Her first choice was Siân. But Siân, was on Gezira, assuming she was home and hadn't gone clubbing with Matthew, as had been suggested on the drive into Cairo that morning. That was at best a forty-five-minute drive. Her head turned south across the sand. The Saqqara necropolis wasn't nearly so distant, and the houseboat on the Nile not so very far away from that.

"Don't hate me," she mouthed as she dialled Killian's number. What else was she supposed to do?

-41-
Killian

"I'm not going to ask," were the only words Killian said to her. He was studiously sticking to that promise as he drove his two passengers back to the houseboat. Yes, he knew precisely who was on his backseat. A headful of long dark hair hadn't proved much of a disguise. His former partner currently had that head resting on Adie's lap, and Killian was struggling to keep his gaze off them and on the road.

How they'd met or come to be hanging in the desert after dark, he didn't know, and honestly, he didn't want to. Plausible deniability was a very powerful tool. At least that's what he was telling himself. Sadly, that didn't mean his head wasn't full of questions. Nor did it stop his gaze sliding sidewards to the rearview mirror or change the fact that his knuckles were white upon the steering wheel.

It'd been a decade.

Time had changed them both.

A web of fine laughter lines lay etched around Anton's eyes, and that framing tumble of hair changed the shape of his face. The rest was every inch the man he knew. His physical reaction—sweaty palms, the quickening of his pulse—remained visceral.

Then... then there were the memories bursting in an unstoppable tide from the locked chest he'd buried them in: memories of dreams so big, one mind couldn't contain them; of nights when it seemed no boundaries separated them; and days when it felt as if the whole of human history was biding its time waiting for them to uncover it.

His life had been beautiful, one of colour, passion, and adventure, until Sadler arrived and destroyed everything with his bullshit.

Attention co-opted by the weight of the storm cloud Sadler's book flattened him with, he shot a red light without realising it until he was halfway across the junction. Thankfully it was late, and the traffic sparse.

Would he ever stop being weighed down by that baggage? Every step, every breath he'd taken since that day had been infinitely harder, and time hadn't really lessened the load, he'd simply become accustomed to carrying it.

Adie wasn't weighed down by any such baggage. Her world was still one of opportunities and possibilities. One in which errors of judgements didn't cost you everything of value in your life. No wonder she drew him like a magnet. She was the physical embodiment of everything he'd lost, and now, to top it all off, here she was with his former partner, and it was goddamned obvious they were more than friends.

He wasn't sure what about that fact hurt most. That she was hooking up with someone other than him—they'd never made noises about exclusivity—or that it was his former partner that she was shagging?

Had Anton known, or was this all a surprise to him too?

In the past, he'd have been appalled by any such smirch to his reputation. The man was loyal to the goddamned core. Back when the shit had hit the fan and every other bugger of his acquaintance had made themselves scarce, Anton had stuck by him; stoic, undaunted, unjudgemental...

Killian figured he had two major regrets in his life, the first was that he hadn't pitched Sadler headlong into a ravine on first acquaintance. The second... that was severing the lifeline between himself and the man currently bleeding over his backseat.

That didn't mean he welcomed this surprise reunion. The last time they'd seen one another... Well, the parting had been acrimonious. Things had been said on both sides that ought never to have been voiced. Words he'd take back if he could, but they were a decade old.

After Sadler had published, they'd gone to Petra out of necessity. Funds were low, Killian's name trash, but neither of them wanted to give up. In retrospect, he'd ought to have slinked away and hid under a rock for a bit, returned when he was no longer a hollowed-out shell of a man. His joy had left him. The wonder that had motivated him all his life was gone. He'd craved it like a starving vampire seeks the vein, and Anton had still possessed it, so of course he couldn't let him go. To Anton, the feel of sunlight on his face and of sand running through his fingers remained the heralds of adventure, when to him they'd become the harbingers of doom.

In the end, he'd let his jealousy, his temper, get the better of him.

He could have salvaged things with an apology, but he'd been so fucked up at the time and devoured by grief that he'd convinced himself they were better off apart.

Stupid bugger!

He no longer bought into that notion, though presently it would've been convenient to do so.

Head bowed Adie whispered a soft reassurance as she brushed a strand of hair back off Anton's face.

"How long?" she asked. The question targeted at him, even though her attention remained elsewhere.

"Five minutes."

She lifted her gaze a little to throw him some thanks.

Killian put his foot down. They reached the berth on the riverbank in three.

Adie got out first. He followed.

"I promise you; I can explain."

He stared at her over the top of the car door. "Oh, I'll bet."

She twitched, and looked set to argue, but Anton took a sucking breath that sent her scurrying around the vehicle instead, ready to help.

What he ought to have done was driven them both to the nearest hospital. The fact he hadn't, with zero quibbling meant he was now fully embroiled in whatever mess they'd created.

The thing was hospitals asked questions. Lots of questions, especially when you were a foreign national. They did things like informing the British Consulate of your injuries, who then got in your face about how it'd all happened.

On top of that, there was the matter of expense, and hygiene standards that didn't meet those of facilities back home, especially in the public system. His workroom here on the boat was probably more sterile than most of the local medical facilities.

They crossed the gangplank, Anton leaning heavily on Adie for support. Since the closest cabin was his, he went ahead and opened the door. Whatever the story, the man was hurt, and Killian had loved him with every ounce of his being in the brightness of his youth.

"Fetch the first aid kit from the workroom."

Adie ran for it, while he lingered on the threshold, watching Anton gingerly lower himself onto the bed. To save them having to find words to speak to one another, he turned to the mini fridge that sat in the corner and pulled out a bottle of water. The wound would need cleaning before it was dressed, and he didn't trust what came out of the taps. Next, he raided his bathroom cabinet and came up with some leftover Naproxen. He offered both up to the patient.

"Thanks. I appreciate it."

Shit! They were going to have to communicate. He ought to have gone for the kit. "It's fine."

It wasn't, but hearing Anton's voice felt like waking from a dream to find the person you'd long ago lost and grieved was miraculously alive and well again. Sitting smiling at you as if death had never happened, only you recalled its bitter agony in all too excruciating detail.

"We both know it isn't."

He opted for ignoring the remark. That seemed easiest. "To dress this, you'll have to take your..." He was already picturing the contours and lines of a body he knew so well. "You need to get undressed."

Anton made a small huff, perhaps recalling a time when a request for him to take his clothes off had been a prelude to some spicy fun.

This was goddamned agony.

Killian rubbed his clammy hands against his sides as Anton struggled free of his *galabeyya*. He had a simple pair of linen trousers on underneath, and nothing more. Even in his late teens he'd been well-portioned, with the sort of genetics that skewed towards leanness. By his mid-twenties, he'd grown into his physique, a decade on, he was sculpted in ways Killian didn't remember, but definitely approved of.

To stop himself staring, he concentrated on finding a towel to press against the wound. Removing the improvised dressing had opened it again, spilling a fresh trickle of thankfully sluggish blood.

"How does it look?" Anton asked.

"Like it'd benefit from stitches."

"It's not deep. That is, it's a slash wound not a puncture."

"Yeah, but it's still not going to knit together very easily without help." He folded the towel into a square for Anton to press down on.

"I notice that you're not asking how it came about. In fact, you're not asking much."

"It's none of my business, and I imagine I don't want to know, right?"

Not knowing meant he could imagine Adie had just stumbled on Anton and his injury. Then he didn't need to think about why they'd met up, how they knew one another, and what they'd been doing.

Shagging, his brain supplied. Definitely shagging. And bollocksing Indiana Jones stuff that neither of them had any business engaging in.

Odds were on that Anton was the guy Adie had hooked up with that night she'd sneaked off the boat.

"It's been a while. It's good to see you, Killian."

Heat rose up the back of his neck, creating prickles.

Where the hell had Adie got to? It shouldn't have taken her this long to find the kit, which was more of a first aid plus box than the standard issue sort, since it contained handy items like suturing implements and iodine, although, it did stop short of an actual medical stapler.

Something to contemplate.

"Got it." She burst in and threw it open on the bed.

Killian pulled on gloves, contemplated the

suture kit, but opted for a series of steri strips instead. Once they were applied, he layered a couple of adhesive dressings on top. It wasn't perfect, but it did the job. "You might want to invest in some antibiotics over the next few days."

Anton nodded, while Adie unnecessarily wound a bandage around his middle.

"I'll call a taxi, get out of your hair."

Adie lasered him with her gaze the second Anton's words were out. "There's no need for him to rush, is there? Killian, we can't…"

What the hell was he supposed to say? No, piss off. It's too uncomfortable having you here. He grunted, "It's fine," again, then tossed the gloves and left the cabin.

He might as well accept he was going to have his former lover in his bed tonight. Not that he had any intention of being there too.

At the back of the boat, he leaned against the railings and did nothing but stare at the black water.

What had existed between him and Anton might be ancient history, but Adie had wittingly, or unwittingly excavated it, and she certainly wasn't about to put such an interesting relic back in the ground.

One could almost laugh at the absurdity of this situation. It was funny, right? The three of them trapped on a boat, their lives having overlapped…

What was the point in being angry about it?

Of course he was angry.

He was always fucking angry. The gas was always on. Anger was what fuelled his ambition these days.

He pictured returning to his cabin, wrenching the door almost off its hinges and finding them canoodling in his fucking bed.

Except, who the hell did that while injured?

You, once upon a time, the voice in his head supplied. Remember that time you broke your arm, and you were dosed up on so many painkillers that you... that you let him fuck you for the first time... You'd been coasting along, never letting it get that far, even though the both of you were desperate for one another, but you'd liked pretending otherwise, liked the taste on your tongue and the rush of staying on that precipice. You'd been frightened too, convinced it'd hurt and that you'd hate it. Afraid you'd fucking love it.

Had it ever been as good as that first night? His fingers smeared with Vaseline kneading your prostate, the friction of the natty old rag rug he'd owned against your cock. Then, the blunt crown of his cock burrowing deep, spearing you open, pinning you down. The rigidity of him inside you. The velvet heat. Words of love and anger and agony repeated right into your ear. Commands of 'push back,' and 'I've got to get deeper' and finally, 'Hold still. Oh, fuck, hold still.' And not holding still but driving him over the goddamned edge so you felt every pulse of his ejaculation into your arse, because it was always a competition, and you always had to come first except in bed, when it was always about seeing who could hold out the longest.

His cock was like a brand behind his zip now.

The teeth of it were surely leaving goddamned imprints. A little adjustment was therefore necessary, only touching himself there was a mistake. Heat rushed from his balls to the crown, and through his neck and into his cheeks.

The creak of the decking behind him alerted him to the encroaching presence.

How much time had passed?

The figure's shadow reached him first; too tall and broad in the shoulder to be Adie. Shit! He wasn't ready for this.

"I wanted to say thank you before I left."

It'd be weird not to turn about in response, not to say something. "Not staying the night?"

"Adie's asleep. It seemed a good point to make my exit. I don't imagine we'll see one another again any time soon, so..."

He did turn then. He couldn't help himself. Anton stood in a shaft of moonlight, long hair lifting around his shoulders. He'd borrowed a shirt. An old one. The type he slept in some times. Worn thin with age and mostly held together with memories.

"I'll see it's returned," the other man said following his line of sight.

"I believe it actually belongs to you."

Anton dragged a hand over the front of its wash softened surface. "I always liked how you looked in it."

Bam! Another memory reared, this one of them clutched together, hip to hip, facing a mirror in a nightclub bathroom somewhere. Him in that shirt. Anton in drag. RAG week, perhaps? He didn't recall the details of why or where, only the juicy recollection of skin and sweat, and the salty exhaustion that followed.

"I feel it too."

Killian's gaze snapped to his former lover's face. "What?"

"The draw. The ghostly fragments of our past reaching out."

"I don't know what you're—"

"K." Anton stepped closer, leading with a hand that fastened straight around the back of Killian's neck.

"Don't!" He spat out the word, just as Anton's lips whispered against his own. "Fuck, no! This is—" His head wasn't on board with this, even if his body sure was, and as for his heart... Nope! He was not consulting that motherfucker.

Anton breathed him in, then retreated on a sigh. "Okay." He raised his hands. "My bad." He retreated half a pace. "I'll just get on with fucking off, then."

Yes. That's what he meant to say. Only what came out was, "No."

"No?" Anton's dark brow quirked.

It'd been a millisecond of contact. That's all, but now the ignition was lit, there was no way Killian was letting him walk off this boat. He fisted the front of the memory-trap shirt and reeled Anton in.

Sparks flew as their mouths clashed. His dick of a dick got mashed up against Anton's hip, which made the pair of them moan. He didn't think Anton had been hard when this started, but the familiar weight and shape of him was sharp butting up against him in return.

It was so wrong. Everything about this. The fact no apologies had been made; that Adie was asleep in his cabin; that his relationship with her was distraction enough without adding a bigger and more vastly complicated distraction who was kneading his arse, and whose kisses were tearing groan upon groan from his throat.

This couldn't go anywhere. It couldn't be more than this moment.

He wanted it to be every moment, from now until the end of time. Wanted to face judgement before Anubis standing hand in hand as their hearts were weighed against Ma'at's feather.

Their lives had moved on. They were different men from who they'd been back then. Still, their bodies remembered exactly how perfectly they fit together. Meanwhile, the racing thunder of his pulse drowned out the voice of reason in his head.

Can't... Shouldn't... Utter madness... He needed the inevitable shitstorm that would result about as much as he needed a subdural haematoma. Still, his fist didn't unfasten from that damn shirt, nor did his tongue extract itself from Anton's mouth.

"Holy fuck!"

Evidently Adie had woken.

Of course she'd woken, because nothing in life was ever simple. He couldn't be hopelessly attracted to any young woman a decade his junior, it had to be the one currently in his employ. And he couldn't have just been caught by her playing tongue hockey with a random man. No, it had to be the man she'd also been shagging, and whom she'd brought to him when she hadn't known where else to turn.

None of them had any fucking business snogging each other. He and Anton, because dammit, it'd been a decade, and it was all water under a fucking bridge, and either of them with Adie, but particularly him, because she was too bloody young for either of them, and in his case, he was her boss.

He knew better, and he still kept shagging her. All it took for his resolve to crumble was her blinking at him and sighing, yes, professor, and he was putty.

Putty was precisely what he was in Anton's hands too.

His body remembered.

His heart craved.

And still, they didn't part. Nope, they went right on the kiss fest.

"It's true, then. You weren't just work partners."

"Nope." Their cheeks remained approximately five millimetres apart as they turned to face her. Zero hands relinquished any grips on anything.

"This is who you were engaged to?" That question was directed squarely at him.

"You told her about that?" An overblown grin stretched Anton's mouth wide. "You never even officially answered me."

"I answered."

"He didn't actually tell me it was you," Adie interjected. "In fact, he was very non-specific about it." She levelled her gaze at Anton then, taking in the hand he still had clamped on Killian's butt. "What happened to we've not seen one another in a decade? Our lives went in different directions, and I doubt either of us want to rekindle the past?"

Anton sucked his ridiculously kissable lips into a pucker. "I didn't know that..." He looked at Killian and swallowed. "I didn't know that everything would come rushing back. That the chemistry would still exist."

"You didn't know that you still loved him?"

Love was a stretch, perhaps. The need they'd given into had been of a physical nature. Was there an emotional layer beneath that? Given the way his heart was paining him in this moment. Yes. Disquietedly, yes.

"Obviously, we're all going to have to discuss this," Anton said, very reasonably.

"Sure, I'll just pop the kettle on, shall I?" Adie slapped the railing, making it hum. She turned away from them, biting her lip, and stared out over the water. "I can't believe the pair of you... Shit! This is mucked up."

She was still so young and ready to make a bigger drama of everything than it needed to be.

Killian crossed to her. Gently, brushed the hair off her shoulder, then leaned into the side of her neck. Her back remained rigid, and she folded her arms a little tighter. "Adie, I'm sure that we can all find reasons to be pissed off with one another. I could ask you what you've been doing tonight. Can you honestly say that I'd like the answer? I could ask how long ago you met him, if he's the guy you went ashore that night to meet..."

She nodded.

"Whether you've continued to hook up with him while we've been—"

"No!" She about turned. "Killian, I haven't." Outrage blazed in both her eyes and her cheeks. "I'm not a cheater." Unlike him in this instance being the implication.

"She's telling the truth." Anton drew closer to their huddle. "I got unceremoniously ditched. Us meeting today wasn't anything to do with sex."

"I was looking for... I've been following a lead I got from that contact of Masud's about the possible whereabouts of our missing fragment."

"Who pointed you at my former partner?" His scepticism was still alive and kicking.

Adie chewed her lip. "No, I just—"

"She had a notion that I might know the man she's looking for."

"And do you?"

"Not personally, no."

"How does this relate to why I had to pick the pair of you up from the necropolis post-midnight?"

"It doesn—"

"I thought you didn't want to know anything."

He had said that to her.

Then, "Sadler had me abducted."

It felt like being kicked in the balls. "He did what?"

"He had his henchman bring me to him. I was in the bazaar, and he grabbed me."

"Adie, this needs reporting." Unconsciously, he was already reaching for his phone.

"It's dealt with," Anton, shook his head at her, when she opened her mouth to elaborate. "Jamãl Al-Aziz is currently in custody, and Sadler's way too slippery for any sort of accusation you make against him to stick. Killian, you and I both know that."

Unfortunately, all too well. Still, this was information that filled him with dread. He'd always known that his team were at risk from the moment he'd learned that swine was lurking about, but to be so bold as to snatch one of them off the streets? The man was deranged. Or rather, he corrected himself, he had a fucking God complex.

"What did he want with you?"

"I didn't tell him anything."

"Adie," he soothed, drawing a hand down her hair to her shoulder, "I never implied that you did."

She nodded. "He offered me Jacobs's journal in exchange for photographs of the dig site and specifically the mural. I told him no, and I ran. I managed to get out, and then I bumped back into Anton, who helped me deal with Jamãl."

Anton's expression remained curiously neutral, when he tossed a glance in his direction. Okay, he wasn't going to ask for elaboration. The pictures his imagination was painting were quite disturbing enough and given the outcome had apparently been Jamãl's arrest and Anton sporting a knife wound, they likely weren't far-fetched.

His former partner had always been a risk taker.

He'd always admired that about him.

He'd been one too, once upon a time.

The Killian who'd departed Petra hadn't been

able to take risks anymore. Another reason he and Anton had parted ways, and why their lives had no business meshing again now. So, why did he suddenly feel so stymied by that fact?

"I need a drink," he announced, not because alcohol would provide any answers, but to give himself space to screw his head back on. His reaction to Anton remained visceral. He desperately wanted to pin him against the railings and screw him senseless. It'd be wild, and deeply, deeply satisfying. He didn't even mind if Adie watched. Hell, the three of them could have some fun together. It wouldn't be a first for either him or Anton. It would, he was certain, be one for her, and he liked supervising her firsts.

Oh, the games that three of them could play.

On the other hand, he had to consider whether the payoff would be worth the inevitable fallout. Josef would string him up. The inevitable lecture he'd receive was already ringing in his ears. *I let you take her out there against my better judgement... You swore to me you'd look after her, keep her safe... Instead, you used her like a sex toy, introduced her to a bunch of seedy games and polyamory.*

It was just a bit of roleplay, Joe.

Come to think of it, they'd had that conversation before. He and Anton had always enjoyed an open relationship when it came to women. And yeah, sometimes they'd shared the same one. There'd been a particularly curvy post-doc back when they'd both been undergrads, Joe had almost popped a few blood vessels when he'd found out. Not that it'd been any of his business who any of them were screwing. The same as it wasn't any of his business now.

He headed towards his cabin in search of that drink.

Okay. Time out for a reality check.

He poured. Knocked it back. Sloshed another into the glass.

Relationships were complicated things, and the more people, the knottier they became. Also, he and Anton—that was an open sore that neither of them ought to be poking.

None of which was the source of the pressure building in his head.

No, that was entirely down to the knowledge that despite logic and his better judgement, he was going to follow his guts and screw the pair of them in any manner they let him.

-42-

Killian

Killian never left his bed unmade. The covers were rumpled now, and at least one head shaped indent marred his pillow. He stared at the bed as he nursed a snifter of brandy. Fantasy figures occupied the space in his mind. Three of them, contorting their bodies into multiple arrangements.

He was still hard.

He wet his lips with another sip, before dragging a hand through the weight of his white hair. He'd figured one or both would have followed him by now. He'd left the door open – like he could make the invitation any clearer.

Were they discussing him? Working out a plan of attack, or furiously debating whether one of them should bow out. Maybe they'd do him a favour and run off together.

He squeezed his eyes closed, not wanting that, and feeling a crack opening in his heart over the possibility.

The boards creaked. Adie came in. She looked sheepish. "I never cheated on you," she said.

Had he accused her of doing so? Possibly in a roundabout, unspoken sort of way.

"I ended it with him when we—"

"Yeah, I got that bit."

She inched closer, claimed the glass from his hands and took a drink before setting it aside on the table. "If one of us ought to feel guilty, it ought to be you. You're the one who was making out with someone else."

"Do you want me to feel guilty about it?" The way her eyes shone suggested that she expected at least a little remorse. He wished he could find some.

"I want to know where I stand, Killian. You were engaged to him once. I assumed your relationship died a decade ago—"

"I believed that too."

"But it didn't though, did it?"

He'd never forgotten Anton, he'd... he'd just buried the memories of him. Suppressed them along with all the other things he'd set aside as being of no value anymore.

"If I hadn't interrupted, it would've progressed way beyond first base, right?"

"Maybe," he offered up. "Probably."

"It was like you were trying to meld yourselves into one another."

Hadn't he demonstrated that he wanted her with a similar ferocity? When his libido took hold... well, that was one area in which the former version of himself still got a look in.

"So, I'll ask you again, where do I stand?"

God, he wished he had a sensible response to

offer her.

"Killian?" She rolled her hands up his shoulders, like she needed the contact to convince herself he hadn't already put her aside.

"What do you want me to say, Adie?" His mind was awash with emotions he didn't know what the fuck to do with. "I can't give you a sensible answer any more than I could give Anton one." Any more than he could give himself one.

She pursed her lips, while tilting her head up to look at him. "I'll take the nonsensical one. Just give me something."

His stomach hitched. His cock got all twitchy.

"That'd be very off brand of me."

"Yeah, I'm not so certain about that. Sure, you put on a good show of being a dispassionate frosty grump, but that's not the true you. The real you is volatile, creative, adventurous, intuitive..."

"No." That's who he'd once been, not who he was now, and not the person he could be with Sadler posing such a threat.

"She's right, Killian." Anton filled the doorway. "Just because you chose to suppress those things, doesn't change the fact that that's who you are underneath, and for the record, none of those were responsible for the shitstorm you endured. That was wholly Sadler."

"The real you," Adie said, her hands falling to his elbows, then skating over his forearms to clasp his hands, "Is considering having a white-hot threesome. Tell me I'm wrong." She lifted his knuckles to her lips and kissed them. There was a twinkle in her eyes that said she was speaking with absolute certainty. And she wasn't wrong, except over the contemplation part. His mind was already made up.

His attention flashed to Anton. "You realise he's injured."

Christ, he might as well have just signed an affidavit saying he was a horny arsed maniac with no self-control.

Alas, true, true, and true.

"He isn't that injured," Anton remarked, and copped a feel of his junk.

God, they were going to undo him. His cock was already battering his zip.

Adie turned his palm over and kissed the centre of it, then she opened her mouth around his middle finger and sucked it deep.

Yeah, he was done for.

"Why don't you tell me what to do, professor?"

Oh, he wanted to show this flighty girl what it was like to have two men possessing her at once.

She was going to love that. Them both filling her cunt at once... or one doing her in the arse and the other in her pussy. A myriad of possibilities existed. Perhaps he'd spread her over his desk and invite Anton to fuck her, while he sat and watched, stroking his dick, taunting them with the promise of it, while remaining out of reach.

Shit! His pulse was now galloping.

Adie's slim hand slid down the front of his shirt and slipped in between two of the buttons. Her fingertips tickled the tops of his abs. She was peeping up at him through her eyelashes, all coy. He lowered a hand between them and undid his fly.

Immediately, her tongue swept her lips.

Behind her, Anton's coal-dark eyes gleamed.

Killian put a hand on her shoulder. He gave no instructions beyond the exertion of a little downward pressure. She understood. *I need you on your knees. Your mouth around me.*

That was the thing about Adie, she was ever ready for adventure, but at her core, she was a good girl. One who was always desperate to please and prove her worth.

She kissed him through his briefs. Nuzzled her face right up against the hot cotton like she couldn't get enough of the texture. Was she also teasing him? Yeah, a little, but not enough that he wanted to chastise her for it. He liked the way she was building anticipation by planting open-mouthed kisses along his shaft, while her fingers curled over the waist elastic ready to release him. He stroked a hand through her hair to let her know she was doing a good job, then his gaze locked with Anton's. His former lover's gaze sat heavy on him, perhaps a fraction bemused.

"You always did like that game."

So, he'd caught Adie's murmur of professor.

"I don't recall you ever complaining about it."

"It's nice to see that some things haven't changed."

Adie bared him at that moment and took the crown of him in her mouth.

Killian breathed out a soft, *fuck!*

"Do you want me to stop, professor?"

Naughty imp knew perfectly well that he didn't.

"No, Ms Hamilton. Please, carry on."

She took him almost to the root, startling a second somewhat embarrassing gasp from him. Anton leaned over her right on that exhale and clasped both hands around Killian's head. Then their mouths were colliding again, and it was all he could do to stop himself groaning like a man about to blow his first load.

Not long after, he shed his shirt, and helped Anton out of that tatty rag. His skin was so smooth and firm. Not a millimetre extra on him anywhere. Killian pushed a hand inside his trousers and cupped his cock. "You never did learn to shave."

"And you're still plucked naked."

Two different men. Two different preferences. But he was cool with getting hairs stuck in his teeth.

Jesus! He was grinning like a bloody lunatic. The muscles in his face aching even as he and Anton duelled with their tongues. He kept working Anton's cock, painting the pre-come he was leaking along the length of his shaft. Damn, he wanted a taste of him. Wanted the taste of him, so hot and thick in his mouth, his nose pressed into the wiry bush that held the essential scent of him.

"Yeah," Anton crooned, as if he'd spoken all those thoughts aloud.

It wasn't easy to manoeuvre with Adie on her knees between them. "On the bed," he ordered them both in the end.

The bed! God, how civilised.

"Lie back," he instructed Anton. "Don't want you opening that wound." Also, he intended to get that taste of him he was so needy for. "Adie, clothes off, and then why don't you straddle his head?"

"Like, sit on his face?"

"Like, sit on his face," he mimicked. "That way he can stick his tongue in your pussy."

Amusingly, she blushed up through her neck, and into her cheeks. It was there across the top of her breasts too as she stripped.

"Every stitch," he prompted, when she hesitated over her bra and panties.

"But that's not fair, you're..."

His look shut her up. She clamped her mouth closed and bowed her head. "As you say, professor."

"I'm good with getting naked too," Anton said, reminding them of his presence. Like either of them had forgotten. He was spread out like a banquet. His dark hair fanned over Killian's pillows, and that long sexy body ate up most of the mattress. Killian tugged his trousers down to around his knees, but left them there, forming a hobble around Anton's legs.

He meant to wait until Adie was in position, but the temptation was too great. With his pulse racing in his ears, and his cock beating against his lower abs to the same rhythm, the dick standing before him wasn't to be resisted. He bent to it. Tilted his head considering its beauty. The shape. The veins running beneath the skin. The lack of the same collar of skin that he possessed. How the crown was so shiny and ripened like a plum, not to mention the pearly fluid he was leaking.

He hadn't sucked another man in eternity.

There'd been a couple of one-night stands with guys over the last decade, but none that he'd describe as anything more effusive than satisfactory.

The explosion of taste. Followed by the assault on the back of his throat caused by his own eagerness.

Damn, but that felt good! The taste, the smell, the sensation, all of it addictive.

Adie jostled him as she climbed into position. He'd thought she'd be faced away, hands on the headboard, to steady her position, but she'd put her back to the wall instead. Her eyes were all shiny and wide. Her mouth, hanging open.

"Fuck, that's hot!"

Anton was guiding her into position over him, but her attention was on him.

"I've never seen a guy go down on another guy before. I mean, not in real life. What you see on the internet doesn't count, right?"

"I hope that naughty viewing hasn't been happening while resident on my boat?"

An immediate guilty expression contorted her pretty features. Thus, he almost choked on the combination of his mirth and Anton's cock.

"Shit! Is it illegal?"

Sweet. So, fucking sweet.

"That'd be a yes, Ms Hamilton. Has in fact been so since 2009."

"Shit!" Her hiss turned into a croon as Anton started doing his thing. She lightened, a moment later. "No, it's okay. I thought—but I haven't. That was before I got here... I need to shut up, right."

"No, no, why don't you keep telling us all about how much you enjoy watching porn."

"Gay porn." Anton's correction was muffled but perfectly distinct.

"Well, I like men," she said, all bolshie. "Why wouldn't I watch them? Also, it's hot, and I bet both of you have watched it too. So, stop trying to shame me."

"No shame. I'm just filing away the knowledge that visuals do it for you."

"Watched a few threesomes, too?" Anton asked.

"A live one right at the minute."

He cracked a smile at that.

"I may have seen a few others, yeah."

"Good," Killian flashed her a wicked grin. "Then you're not clueless about how this is going to work."

"How is it going to work? Professor?" She added all smiles and curiosity.

"Well, my devoted little student," he began, making her preen, while simultaneously reminding her that she wasn't a brat, "once Anton here has your pussy thoroughly sopping, I'm going to invite him to put his very, very nice cock into it. Then, I'm going to watch him slide in and out of you, while I wank myself, and then, maybe if I'm pleased with how you're taking him, I'm going to stroke your pearl while he fucks you."

Another wave of heat coloured her cheeks. "And then?"

"And then, why Ms Hamiliton, isn't it obvious? I'm going to put my cock right alongside his and we'll fill you together. You're going to feel completely stuffed with both of us inside you at once, but because I know you're a good girl, you're going to take it even if it makes you cry."

"Oh, shit!" she said her voice shaky with excitement, while her eyes shone sparklingly bright. "You're really going to spread my legs and have me take you both?"

"It's a promise."

"Fuck me!" Anton contributed from beneath her.

"You'll have to wait your turn." It wasn't what the other man had meant, but he couldn't resist the quip.

Killian gave Anton's cock a final lash across the slit, then rose onto his knees. He claimed Adie's wetted lips. Stroked his tongue into her willing mouth as Anton made her sigh and pant with the tickle of his tongue on her sensitive flesh.

"Will you like that, do you think? Having the both of us inside of you? I mean, you've had us both apart, it's the logical next step."

Well, logical if you were a filthy beast like him.

Lord God, this was wrong, but he was loving every second of it.

His whole relationship with her had been wrong since the moment of their meeting, but he didn't give a fuck about that at present. Likewise, reigniting things with Anton. Truth: he'd recognised this man as his soul mate the first time he'd flashed that wicked smile of his in Killian's direction. Time evidently hadn't eroded that.

Adie began twisting and struggling a little in his arms. "Oh!" she gulped, and he understood. All this excitement was bringing her close. He reached down and helped her along with the rub of his thumb, while Anton continued to tongue fuck her until she came apart in his arms.

He'd seen a lot of beautiful things in his life. The sparsity of the desert. The night sky studded with the diamond-light of stars billions of miles away. Sunrise over the pyramids. Water flooding over a parched landscape...

But was there another more intimate and beautiful sight in the world than watching another human being find bliss at your hands? During his moment of introspection, both Adie, and Anton had moved positions. Anton had propped himself, so he was seated upright, his back to the padded headboard. Adie was still straddling him, but they were now facing.

"Can I kiss him, professor?"

So polite. "You may."

She proceeded, not to kiss Anton at first, but with delicate licks to remove the shine left on his mouth and chin by her climaxing over him.

Killian took the moment's breather, to shed the rest of his clothes, relieve Anton of his hobble, and fish both condoms and lube out of the dresser drawer.

One day, he'd like to do this bare, but for now, he got a kick out of rolling the condom onto Anton's cock, then torturing him with some agile strokes under the pretence of lubing him up.

What really gave him a kick, though, was lining the pair of them up, rubbing Anton's cock against her blood flushed pussy lips making her mewl with longing, then connecting them.

There was no twang of jealousy as he watched them fuck, only excitement gripping him. He played with himself, making sure he was also well lubed. Then, ringed his fingers around Anton's cock as he thrust so he absolutely felt he was part of it, before teasing Adie's winking arse hole with his thumb and the tickle of his tongue too.

She'd learned to take him in her arse so beautifully, but that wasn't the pleasure he'd claim tonight.

Slowly, he encroached, letting them both get acquainted with his presence. Soon enough, they stilled. That was the thing with this position, it put him in control. They just had to hold tight while he dictated.

He ran his cock right up tight against Anton's. That was a thrill in itself, then he went knocking against the top of her entrance, demanding his place inside her too. It was a little uncertain at first. She was relaxed from her orgasm. They were all slippery. People said you could never have enough lube, but while slippery was good, it was... well, it was slippery.

The first couple of inches were the most exacting, but once he was in...

Killian held absolutely still, letting the sensations of Anton beside him, and Adie surrounding them both crawl through his muscles and tendons, veins, and viscera. Every part of him felt alive, and he submerged himself wholly in that sensation.

Then, smile teasing his lips, he thrust. He rocked them. He drove them all wild...positively demented.

It was hot and tight. Fricative? Was that the word? No, that was something to do with sound. Such sounds surrounded him. They came from Anton, from Adie sandwiched between them, as well as straight from his own throat.

He wanted so badly to ejaculate. Also, to keep floating in this moment of twisted bliss. It was all so damn tight, so fucking intimate.

Anton put a hand on his thigh.

That shouldn't have been a trigger for anything, but it was, because he was still in love with the man, and he'd missed him on a soul deep level. It seemed unreal that he was here now, that they were doing this. That he was doing this with Adie and Anton, and they were all so very into it.

"I'm going to come. Fuck!" He tried fruitlessly to get a hold of himself, but the tide was already tossing him. His ballocks squeezed themselves dry, as he stiffened and arched backwards so he was braying at the ceiling. Adie peaked too. The squeeze of her contracting muscles driving him to an even higher level of bliss.

He pulled out, thoroughly spent. Adie rolled over onto her back and lay panting, eyes wide, and thoroughly blissed out. Killian crawled over Anton, who was still stiff and wanting. He melded their mouths in sloppy, delirious kisses, then he wrapped him in a firm grip and gave him the release he absolutely deserved.

They were all quiet in the aftermath.

All a little unsure of themselves, now the moment of true connectedness was gone.

Weirdly, he found he didn't want to pull his familiar armour back on.

They all needed to talk, but for that he needed at least a few defences in place.

Besides, the hour was late. Ra would begin his daily passage across the sky in his solar barque before long. So, he tidied them up, disposed of the condoms, then snuggled them both to his sides. And they slept.

-43-

Adie

Adie awoke in Killian's bed. It wasn't the first time she'd done so. It was the first time she'd woken in the crook of his shoulder, facing another man across the landscape of his chest. She watched the two of them sleeping for a while. On the surface, they were so different. Anton, a free-spirited adventurer, who consorted with criminals. A bad boy romantic, with his long hair and flowing outfits, his jewelled jambiya, and abject lack of respect for rules. Killian, the white-haired grumpy professor, with his air of scholarly gravitas, discipline, and impartiality. Together, though, they told a different story. She'd caught glimpses of the one reflected in the other, saw only too clearly how they'd dominated one another's lives.

She ought to have felt like a spare part. There was no such soul deep bond between her or either of these men. Yet, they'd made her central to their reconnection.

Very, very central.

She grinned broadly at the memories of them both inside her and smiled at the twinge of tender muscles this morning. Nothing was so sore that she'd cry off from participating in another round though.

What would happen when they woke?

It was Sunday. The rest of the team likely wouldn't return until evening. That gave them the whole day to potentially share one another's company. To talk, to touch, to fuck... She wanted to believe in that future. Simultaneously, her mind kept throwing up images of the two men waking. Of all the barriers that had existed between them falling straight back into place. Killian would fix on his mask. Anton would stalk off.

Was there anything she could do to stop that being their line of travel? Make things easy?

She sat up, dislodging the covers and provoking groans. "Who wants breakfast in bed?"

"We are not eating in my bed," Killian said, without so much as cracking an eyelid. "Also, since it's way past a time when breakfast can reasonably be eaten—"

"It's quarter past ten."

"—lunch would be more appropriate."

"Fine, lunch. Who wants some?"

"I'll take some painkillers, please." Anton had blinked his eyes open, but the surrounding skin wrinkled into a grimace.

Killian was fully alert immediately. "Your side? You said it didn't hurt that much last night."

"Last night, I was dosed up, and had a metric ton of happy hormones whizzing around my body. This morning—"

"You've realised who the fuck you're in bed with."

"That, I never forgot. The drugs just wore off."

Killian leaned over and planted a kiss in the centre of his brow. "Pills are on the table right behind you, and if you need me to take another look at—"

Anton roped his arms around Killian's back, pulling him down on top of him. "Can you give us a few, Adie? And yes, breakfast...lunch, would be lovely."

Shit! "Sure." Was this good? Bad? Were they going to talk? Fuck? Take a shower together? She didn't want to miss out on any of those. On the other hand, she guessed they hadn't really done a lot of talking last night, and after a decade apart, they probably had a fair amount of stuff they needed to get straight. She just wished she could listen in and be sure it was all going to be fine between them.

Except, she understood the need for privacy too. In similar circumstances, she'd want some. "Don't be long, eh? It won't take me a moment to whip something up."

In fact, having walked out of Killian's cabin without a stitch on, she blinked at the mid-morning sun, came to a screeching halt at the sight of another boat in the middle of the river, and made a mad dash to her cabin for clean clothing.

Only, there she glimpsed her reflection, so a shower happened, and at least half an hour passed before she even made it to the kitchen, where she discovered they were out of orange juice, so made a mad attempt to squeeze some.

The truth was that her nerves were in shreds this morning. Her relationships with both men had been largely non-serious before now. Anton had been a passing fling, and Killian... He'd never let her in, not really. He'd fucked her, and she'd liked that, but beyond him getting his rocks off with her, the rest of their interactions hadn't mellowed much. Most of the conversations they had were still about the dig, and they mostly consisted of him giving her orders and warning her not to break things or theorise without concrete facts to back up her suppositions. Still, it'd be really fucking heartbreaking if the two men decided to reignite their passion, and thus she got left by the wayside.

It was great fucking you, but we've decided to get re-engaged. Cue hand holding, sickly besotted looks, congratulations, and wedding invites. Dammit, she was the reason they were even speaking to one another, and last night had been too much fun not to want to do it again.

After collecting some breakfast-ish lunch items, all cold, because who wanted hot food in this heat, Adie set them aside plated up in the refrigerator. Then took a stroll back along the deck.

Outside Killian's door, she shuffled from foot to foot. All she had to do was turn the handle, announce brunch was ready, and she'd know what they were doing, so why was her stomach in knots over the prospect?

Killian opened the door as she was reaching for the handle. He was freshly showered, water droplets clinging to his towel-dried hair, sporting a fluffy white bath towel around his waist. Her gaze instantly dropped from his face to his torso, and the very lovely display of masculine beauty.

"You're not dressed."

"I saw you coming through the blinds."

"Right." So, he knew she'd been standing out here prevaricating for umpteen minutes.

"Is it ready?"

She offered up a nod.

"I'll be there in two minutes. Just need to pull some trousers on."

"Where's Anton?" The rumpled bed sat empty. Had they not done any talking?

Killian, already reaching for his clothing tipped his head towards the ensuite, "Getting cleaned up."

Annoyingly, the tension tightening up her shoulders wasn't relieved any by learning he hadn't made a swift exit. Killian clapped his hands on her back and dug his thumbs into the knots of tension she was sporting. "Having regrets? You seem really tense this morning."

"No. No regrets." She lingered as he finished dressing, unable to tear her gaze away from him. In an unprecedented show of affection, he held her hand as they left the room and walked along the deck.

"Are you?" she asked.

"Honestly,"—he turned her, so they were facing—"I've hit pause on analysing it too hard, though I imagine that'll only work for so long."

"I thought you were a realist."

He nodded. Took a seat at the dining table that sat under the sun canopy of the main deck.

"Did you talk?"

"A little." He rearranged the cutlery to his liking.

"And everything is good again between you? You're friends again."

He blinked. A shadow crossed his pale eyes.

"Friends?" The word hung in the air like an unexploded firework. "I've said sorry. He's said sorry... Beyond that, I'm not prying into his business and whatever you've embroiled yourself in at his side, and he's not getting into mine."

"He will still help me, though?"

Killian shrugged. "I wish you'd drop this."

"But you know I'm not going to. It's important, and I have a lead..." She left him glowering at the salt cellar while she fetched the plates. By the time she'd piled everything onto a tray and carried it out, Anton had joined them at the table. He was dressed in a pair of Killian's cargo trousers and a still unbuttoned shirt.

"We all cool?" he asked.

Killian gave a nod, and Adie followed suit, even though her head was knotted with tension. It felt as if they were all balanced on the edge of a precipice and if one of them so much as breathed the wrong way, disaster would result.

The best thing, therefore, seemed not to say anything that wasn't related to the food as they all tucked in.

"Do you still see Joe Levine?" Anton asked a

short while later.

"He's how I found Adie. Not that he wanted to let her go."

"That's not quite how it was," Adie insisted, and proceeded to relate it all from her point of view, which in retrospect, perhaps wasn't such a good thing, since it involved highlighting what Joe had against her working with Killian. "Sorry," she kept repeating to him, but he kept brushing her apologies aside, as if they didn't matter.

"I know what Joe thinks of me, Adie."

"Yes, but you're not nearly as fierce as he made out, and you've not ruined me. You've been a bit high handed and grumpy, but—"

"Yet," Anton remarked, making himself the target of a glare. "I mean that in the nicest way possible."

"No, you don't," Killian retorted, simultaneously with her. "Don't be an arse."

"Don't ruin her. I was just pointing out that there's still time. Adie keep your mind wide open to possibilities. Never stop asking questions and ignore him when he tells you not to speculate."

"Excuse me." Killian rose to his feet. "I've never suggested anyone should stop asking questions. I just like it if the members of my team think before they open their mouths. It saves us all the loss of sanity and makes sure no one—" He clammed up. "It does matter. It's my opinion that's all. Adie is perfectly capable of making rational decisions for herself."

Adie's teeth were currently clenched so hard she

was sure they'd fracture. She struggled to stand as Killian marched off along the deck.

Anton caught her wrist. "Let him go. If you scurry after him now, you're going to get your head bitten off."

Staying with Anton made her feel like a traitor, but she remained in her seat. Why had he said that stuff? Sure, it was an accurate reflection of how Killian could be but pointing it out like that had been deliberately antagonistic.

After a while, she shuffled along the bench seat, and hooked her legs up over Anton's lap. "This isn't going to resolve itself into anything lasting, is it?"

"Don't you think it's a little early to make that call, and do you even want it to? I mean, I know it was fun, but enjoying a single night of hot dirty sex is a different beast to managing a threeway relationship routinely." Moreover, unlikely, given the two men couldn't seem to exist in one another's company outside of the bedroom for more than a handful of minutes without being irritable.

She lifted her legs from across his lap. "What I'm hearing is that you're not interested, even if I am."

He made a grab for her calves, pulling her legs back into place. "That's not what I said, Adie."

"It's sure as hell what you implied."

A sigh oozed from his lips, like this was an old argument he'd grown tired of having, not one freshly arisen. "I just think a little realism ought to be applied. Adie, you can't possibly understand how much history Killian and I share. We can't just pretend—"

"No one is asking you to pretend anything, and I get it. You were close. Engaged. And it's been a decade. And you said a lot of shit to one another before you parted ways, but it's not like there are no feelings left between you, else last night would never have happened."

"There are too many feelings, that's the point."

"So, because you know it'll be difficult, you're not going to try?"

"I didn't say that either, Adie. All I'm trying to point out is that one good fuck doesn't wind back time and make everything whole again."

"Two or three might."

"Do you really think he's going to be on board with my way of working? He's not asked a damn thing about last night and how I ended up with a knife in my side, and we both know why. He can't be seen to condone that sort of behaviour. If he knew the details, he'd be obliged to give me immediate marching orders, and you'd... you'd be lucky not to get the same."

"He'd understand if we explained. He would."

Anton's hair swished against her shoulder as he shook his head. "Look, I get it. You've had a good time, and you want it to continue. I do too, but wanting something doesn't topple the barriers, and in case you haven't noticed, he's stalked off, probably hoping I'll have disappeared by the time he comes out of hiding again."

"He's into you, he cares. Why would he think that?"

Anton failed to mask the twitchy smile that crossed his lips.

"Can't you just go and say sorry again a few times? Or offer him a blowjob?"

"If I thought that was all it would take, I'd happily drop to my knees for him, but really what you're asking is for a fundamental shift in his mindset, and that's not going to happen. You know, I hoped time might have mellowed him a little. Sadly, it hasn't."

His phone beeped, drawing his attention to the lit screen.

"What is it?"

"Jamāl's been charged with theft and antiquities trafficking."

"Yes!" She hissed through her teeth. "I'm glad. I hope they lock him up and don't let him out for a very long time." Both for his thefts and what he'd done to Anton, but equally, for what he'd threatened to do to her, and if he was in the hands of the authorities, she no longer had to worry herself over what would become of him entombed in that mastaba. "That means Sadler's down a goon too."

"If you want to see it like that."

"I do see it like that." She kicked her feet in pleasure.

"Adie, I ought to make a move."

And there was her brief moment of joy toppled. The rest of the team weren't due back until the following evening. "I don't want you to go." She didn't look at him as she said it. That was too difficult. She didn't want to see goodbye written across his face, so she dropped her gaze to his forearm and the dusting of dark hairs over his tanned skin.

The muscles beneath that fuzz were tensed, betraying his obvious unease, despite the relatively laid-back pose.

"We've been over this. I don't know what else you expect me to say."

"That you love him."

His laughter whistled through his teeth. The forced mirth of it contributing to the pensiveness building in her chest. "I did once, not so sure now." When she began voicing a protest, he fanned her rumblings away.

She met his gaze briefly. It was too hard to do more than that.

"He'll say the same, Adie."

That was probably true. In her mind, she thought of the two men as being nothing alike. Anton was the wild man adventurer, to Killian's frosty scholar, but in some things, they were stubbornly alike. Like the insistence on realism when some romanticism wouldn't have been amiss.

"And where does that leave me?" Was she supposed to pick one over the other? She'd had her hand forced over that issue once before and hadn't cared for it. Being honest, she'd downright avoided it. She'd left Anton hanging, rather than break it off officially. Goddammit, this wasn't fair. Last night had been epic. She refused to let go of a future that didn't involve the three of them getting intimately entwined that way again. Couldn't they at least make an effort to see if it would work?

Anton gently brushed the hair from her face and then let his fingertips linger on her chin. Adie nuzzled into the caress, closing her eyes to hold back the tears welling.

"I'm sorry. I know you want a different outcome, but this way, it'll save a whole lot of heartache."

"Will it though?"

If you were wise, you accepted love, welcomed it, even if it was only there to warm you for a short while.

"We're fundamentally different people."

"Are you?" And even if they were, did it matter? The ties between them hadn't survived a decade of drought for no reason, and they'd been completely attuned to one another the previous night. She should know. They'd both been inside her at the same time.

"You know most adventures are better in retrospect."

Nope, she couldn't agree with that. Sure, there was comfort to be had in knowing how things ended, but endings were also brutally final. She'd rather be in the thick of things, collecting bruises, thank you very much.

His breath ghosted across her face, ahead of his gently kissing her eyelids.

"I'm going to go round up my stuff."

"Please, don't." She grasped his hand as he rose to leave and held on. "I bet if we both tried together, we could coax Killian out of his mood."

His gaze danced softly over her, full of sadness. "You haven't listened to a damn word, have you?"

She had. She'd just rejected them.

Belief was powerful. You could get a long way on it. It'd got her to Egypt. Onto Killian's team. And it would win her the missing mural fragment, she was confident of that. She wasn't sure how, or when, but it would happen. "I'm not giving up on the idea of us working things out."

"Your optimism's cute." He bussed the tip of her nose with his thumb.

"Your negativity isn't."

"Realism, Adie. It's realism."

Fuck realism.

Anton extracted his hand from hers. "I'll contact you if anything comes of the feelers I put out about Ihsãn."

"Yeah, yeah." She could don a mask of nonchalance too.

He gave her a brief head bob, then he was off along the deck towards Killian's cabin.

-44-
Killian

Usually, Killian could becalm himself with work. After he'd left Anton and Adie at the table, he'd marched himself into the workroom and started on one of the multitude of tasks that inevitably stacked up, but though he turned multiple shards between his fingers, and fanned out photographs, and checked numerous measurements, it was all for nothing. His mind refused to see more than blotches of background colours while his memory played disparate moments in an endless reel. Adie between him and Anton last night. The changes time had wrought in his lover's face. The sandpapery scratch of stubble this morning. Anton's scent. His weight above him. Tidying up his wounds. Cleaning a different scrape long, long ago. Where had that been? Somewhere with water. He recalled the reflection of light playing on the whitewashed wall of their room. Good times. Arguments in the rain. Arguments in muddy ditches. Rose hued sandstone. Dust in his lungs. Pain in his chest so heavy that he couldn't speak. He'd literally been unable to speak for three days following their final argument in Petra.

The accusations of minutes ago...

Shrug it off. Just shrug it off.

He did the whole shoulder lift and lower thing, but the tension remained across his shoulder blades as if someone had knotted them together with a resistance band. It was the fact the remarks came from those he loved... that they echoed sentiments Anton had levelled at him all those years ago, that made them cut. They implied that time had passed, but nothing had changed, when everything had changed.

Hadn't it?

He'd dug himself out of the pit he'd been in. And while he'd admit the emotional scars remained, they didn't rule anymore. At least he didn't think they did. He'd just changed to accommodate them.

That was the thing with emotional scars. They didn't heal in the way broken bones did, rather the repercussions got entangled with your personality. Moreover, memories weren't facts. They metamorphosed over time, changing as your perspective on life changed.

They'd apologised to one another, he and Anton. Ostensibly made things good. Anton had made the first step, asking Adie to give them a moment, but he'd been the one chagrined and full of remorse.

It'd felt like something lifting when eager lips had captured his and whispered words of apology back to him. But it was just one moment. Time hadn't unwound, and the pangs across his chest, they were aggressively screaming, "Hey, the emotional shizz, it's still a thing. You might think life's all jolly but get real." A bit of superglue might hold things together, but weak points would always remain. Dream on if you think you've turned your life into a kintsugi masterpiece.

They'd had a night, but it couldn't be more than that.

Even if he wanted it, and he wasn't sure if he did, it would be impossible.

Same-sex unions weren't recognised here where laws were mostly based on traditional religious based concepts of morality. Most of the country's citizens abhorred the very notion of relationships that didn't involve one man and one woman locked in a traditional form of matrimony.

Head bowed over the desk; Killian covered his eyes and used the pressure of his fingertips digging into the bridge of his nose to ground himself.

He'd never been interested in getting married, and yes, his lack of a wife had been commented on many a time. He hadn't done relationships for a decade, so where would he find a wife? Besides, in his heart he was still bound. It'd been grey and rainy; the day Anton offered him that ring. He hadn't coveted it, but god...what it had meant in terms of emotional significance, words couldn't adequately portray. I love you barely scratched the surface. When you'd experienced the soul deep stuff, that three-word phrase always felt like wading in the shallows.

He still had the ring Anton had offered him while down on one knee in a puddle. It was a naff bronze replica of an Anglo-Saxon ring with a futhorc inscription. Nothing he could wear for more than a few days without turning his finger green. The inscription read as something inane, like 'I am ring,' and it'd barely fit even on his littlest finger, but it was one of the few treasures he'd clung to when he was content to let most of his possessions come and go without undue sentiment.

Crazy to think that if things had followed the trajectory he'd mapped for himself at eighteen, the pair of them would have been wed, and would have spent the last umpteen years underplaying that fact.

Would they have quit Egypt altogether? Based themselves in more tolerant climes?

He loved Egypt and her history, but he'd loved Anton more. Living as if they were each other's dirty secret would have grown old fast.

He didn't want him to be a dirty secret now.

Better they were nothing to one another than something sordid. It was bad enough that he was dating an underling. Was that what he was doing with Adie? Was that better or worse than just shagging her? Did it matter? It'd still earn him frowns of disapproval from the departmental heads at the university.

Not that it ought to matter what he did in his personal life. It ought to be all about his results. Except it wasn't, and it did. There wouldn't have been the accolades, the position, the funding if he'd been one half of a gay couple all this time.

Those things would dry up for certain if he became part of a polyamorous triad... Forget it.

Couldn't have an amoral lecturer influencing the minds of the nation's youths.

Fuck!

His jaw ached, prompting him to massage the joint.

Chill your nads, Killian.

It wasn't an issue. None of those things were going to come to pass.

Why are you thinking so hard about them, then?

Because tragedy rehearsing was a good way of ensuring that he didn't do anything so fucking foolish as believe something so ridiculous could work.

Like it was an actual prospect.

Ha! Face it, mate. You're terrified of the sheer possibility. Afraid that one of them will suggest it. Afraid that you want it so much you won't say no. Afraid that he'd mock the very notion and shoot himself in the foot as a result. That Anton would leave, and Adie would follow.

Was he genuinely afraid of that? Of losing the little ray of light that'd seeped into his grey world.

Yes. Yes, he was.

His phone burst into life, bleating a siren he never wanted to hear. Killian stared vacantly at it vibrating against the tabletop.

Someone had penetrated the door of the excavation site. That's what that meant.

They were being burgled...

Shit!

He shook himself free of the self-indulgent

trance.

Adie was still at the table when he rushed along the deck; head bowed to her knees in what was only ever a defensive pose. "Is something up?" She unfolded herself, straightening her neck to better see him.

"Someone's broken in. I need to get over there," he said while still moving.

"What? Oh, God!" Horror bled across her face and formed her lips into an O-shape. She unfolded from her repose, finding her feet, and scurrying after him. "I'll come with."

Of course, Anton was in his fucking cabin, attempting to exit right as Killian entered intent on picking up his keys. They collided in a head thumping way and rebounded with cries of "Ouch!" and "Sorry."

Anton's hand locked around his arm, serving to steady them both, while simultaneously injecting a shot of unwarranted heat into Killian's loins. A touch in a profoundly un-romantic moment shouldn't have had his senses screaming red alert, but it wasn't his urgency to save his dig site causing his heart to pound. It was his memory doing its fucking thing again.

Another time-lapse went skittering through his brain. Salty sweet lips, a pat on the shoulder, the trace of a single broad digit down the length of his spine that culminated in a place only Anton had ever touched.

"I was just getting my—"

"Yeah. Whatever." He shook off Anton's hold.

His keys sat on the dresser. Through the window Adie was visible on the deck, standing in a puddle of light, bowed from the waist lacing her boots. The river breeze stirred her hair, made her look young. Dammit, she was young. The short shorts that showed off her coltish legs proved that. Likewise, the flattering but inappropriate vest top.

"Has something happened?" Anton asked, from beside the bed, where he was now re-rolling his possessions into a bundle.

Adie swung into the doorway, fingers curling around the frame. "Sadler." She shot him a glance. "Or somebody else. Someone's broken in."

The chances of them getting there before whatever thief it was had been and gone were slim. Killian didn't need anyone to tell him that. That was assuming it was an opportunist, and not just a couple of rogue tourists. He kind of hoped it was tourists that he could steer out without too much hassle.

If it was Sadler, as Adie proposed... No, he really didn't want to contemplate that. The man was a rat, and like most rats, annoying difficult to eradicate, unless you resorted to poison, and hello, he didn't want to end up with his head in a noose.

If it was Sadler, he wouldn't be alone. There'd be an entourage, and probably an official escort, courtesy of a bribe.

"Adie, do you have a shirt or something?"

"In my room. Is that what we're worrying about right now?"

He faced Anton. "We can drop you somewhere

on the way."

Adie still hadn't move.

"Shirt," he spat. "Now, if you're coming." He pushed past her, arm outstretched towards his car sitting on the riverside, thumb on the key fob.

"We need to lock up first, right?"

Shit!

Yes. Yes, they did.

He backtracked to seal his cabin door, Adie and Anton both getting in his way. Oh, and he'd left the workroom unlocked, and probably a dozen other doors. "Adie, stay. I can handle things. It's going to take too long otherwise."

His phone was still vibrating at two-minute intervals in his back pocket. He needed to swipe the function off, but again, it was precious seconds he didn't want to lose.

"I don't think it's a good idea for you to face an army of burglars on your own."

An army was such an Adie exaggeration. At tops he was anticipating three or four people. "Nevertheless."

"I can come with you."

Why the offer came as such a surprise, he didn't know. Anton had always been the sort to offer himself up if a posse was needed for something or other. It stilled Killian's dash; one foot on the gangplank. It went against all his rules to invite someone not associated with the excavation onto the site. People always joked he guarded his sites like a dragon did its hoard, but he did it with good reason. Nothing got lost from his digs. He'd never once misplaced so much as a splinter.

He could ask Anton to stay behind and keep the boat secure. Make sure it didn't end up being hijacked and taken on a pleasure cruise to Luxor. However, he didn't know when Lucas was due back, and if he arrived and found Anton and no one else, mayhem would inevitably ensue. Lucas would phone the police first and ask questions after.

That'd result in a time suck none of them needed.

Better to accept. "Yes. Let's do that. The car's open, and I can drop you somewhere—Badrshein—on the way back."

He expected Adie to pipe up with a protest, but her usual chirp of disgruntlement when he sidelined her in favour of someone else didn't materialise. She did have a curiously wistful expression on her face as she followed them over the gangplank and stood on the dockside as he and Anton pulled away.

"Don't do anything that'll open those stitches," she shouted after them.

Killian shot Anton a glance out of the corner of his eyes. "No heroics, eh?"

"With any luck it's an animal, or a faulty circuit."

"Right." That was a scenario he could get behind. Except it wouldn't be. The universe liked to have its little jokes. Besides, if there was one thing he'd learned in life, it was that if you already had a metric ton of shit on your plate, life always found a way of adding another scoop.

~Ж~

The drive between the Nile mooring and the Saqqara Pyramid was only ten kilometres, but it would take at least twenty to thirty minutes to traverse it. Killian observed traffic signals, and unlike Siân, didn't routinely drift around corners, or use his horn in place of mirrors, indicators, and common sense. All things he moaned incessantly about whenever he had the misfortune of riding with her. Today, he found his hand straying in the direction of the horn every hundred metres. What was with people? Where the hell had they learned to drive?

Oh, yeah. Here.

And why, oh why was there a whole herd of goats occupying part of the road? What should he expect around the next bend? A hippo?

He didn't voice the possibility for fear of manifesting it.

By the time they rolled into the desert necropolis, he had a stress headache lancing through his left orbital socket. Just what one wanted when you needed to make a quick dash across a section of the Sahara. Usually, he didn't mind that parking was at a distance to the site. It made for fewer visitors. Today, not so much.

Anton followed him from the car park by Djoser's pyramid. Sure, he could have taken the Land Rover off-road, but driving on sand required a level head and he was self-aware enough to know his was currently anything but.

"Do you think you're going to find Sadler down there?"

Killian kneaded the top of his skull. "Dunno." Was it madness that part of him *wanted* to find the bastard down there? It'd give him a legitimate reason to break his fucking nose. Of course, he wasn't so sure that if he started thumping the bugger he'd ever stop.

"I can't believe he's still fucking with you. I mean I can—"

"Who says he is?"

"Adie, and his actions. He's not rocked up in town for nothing. And this party he's holding on your doorstep... We both know Dareth Sadler doesn't do anything without an ulterior motive."

"There are thousands of sites of archaeological significance in the Cairo area alone. He could be writing about any one of them. He's probably writing about Djoser's pyramid again. It'd make sense of the party."

"Yeah, but why would he, when he can write about the mysterious site Doctor Killian Carmichael is excavating? Come on, it's a no brainer. His sequels haven't sold in nearly the same quantity as his first offering—"

"Can't say I've paid attention."

"—when he had your expertise there to back up all his whacky theories. Of course he's going to attempt to milk that cash cow again."

"Well, if he's hoping for an interview, he's going to be sadly disappointed."

"Unless he's looking to conduct it with your fist,

eh?"

His fingers had automatically curled into his palms. He was not by nature a violent man, or one prone to fits of unreasonable temper. Although Adie probably thought otherwise. Sadler counted as a special case. He was the nuclear option. Just hearing his name turned Killian's brain into a mushroom cloud.

"If I kill him, are you going to help me bury the body?"

"I'm here, aren't I? And for the record, I'd have helped a decade ago. Bet we could've got away with it too. I mean, we're archaeologists. No one questions us about digging pits in random bits of the landscape."

Killian snorted. It lessened the ache in his head to joke about it, but really, Sadler was no joking matter, merely a world class dick. "With any luck, he's far too busy being pandered to by his groupies to be worrying about research materials. Did you bring that knife of yours?"

"So, I can stab him?"

"So, you can look menacing and scare off whoever is busy ruining my Saturday." He shot a glance at Anton, who had always managed to strike a more intimidating figure. The only people Killian scared were students.

"I thought that was me."

Hm. He made a non-committal grunt in response.

His head was doing the whole *thump, thump, thumpity thump* disco baseline thing again by the time they reached the mound of rubble that constituted his patch. The scruff the team used to conceal the entrance had been pulled aside. At least three sets of footprints were evident in the sand. Fresh, because the *khamseen* inevitably shifted the sands each night.

"Buried Pyramid?" Anton asked, as they descended the initial few steps to where the metal door sat soaking up the sun. His gaze roved left and right, taking in the details in an all too familiar way. "Fifth dynasty?"

"Possibly third."

"Intriguing."

The locks were unclasped, the largest padlock hanging loose on the hasp. Good sign? Bad sign? Depended on your point of view. In his experience, professional thieves used bolt cutters, and opportunists saw more opportunities pick-pocketing foreign tourists.

"I'm surprised Adie hasn't filled you in on everything."

Anton clucked his tongue, then landed his hand on Killian's shoulder. "She's way too loyal to you for that. All I know is that there's a mural, and it's missing a bit. I've intuited that said missing bit depicts a phallus, but she's not told me anything directly, or shared any details that weren't directly relevant to me assisting her find the man your sponsor put her onto."

"Masud put her in touch with some retired professor, who's told her to look for some other retired somebody or other. It's a wild goose chase, and almost definitely about to amount to nothing."

"Such confidence in your team's abilities."

Killian stiffened at the shade cast in his direction. He did believe in Adie—in every member of his handpicked team. He just recognised the odds of one email leading to a success as being so miniscule that what she was doing was essentially a waste of time and effort. Then again, the whole excavation might wind up amounting to that, at least for him, if Sadler started stamping all over it.

He blew out a sigh. He'd known it was a risk coming here, taking charge of this project and took it when he ought to have stayed further afield.

"You're right, it does show a phallus. At least, allegedly. We've only William Jacob's word for it. He hacked it out to preserve his daughter's innocence."

"Are you talking about something in the journal Adie's been so desperate to see?"

"Yeah."

"So, you've read it."

"A while back." The journal was what had lead to the initial GPR scans of the area that had helped them pinpoint the tomb entrance.

A blast of cooler air welcomed him as Killian stepped inside that entrance now. Even from the topmost step beyond the door, he could tell that someone was within. He was invariably first down here every day they worked. The sounds, the mien of the place was utterly familiar. "There's a light on down there." Several of them, in fact. Moreover, he could hear the faint chug of the generator. That suggested one of the team, or at least someone not in a hurry.

Familiarity meant he traversed the first antechamber in seconds, leaving Anton to follow more cautiously. He went straight to the mural room. All three tripod mounted lights were turned to form a single spotlight. Nothing was missing. Something had been left behind.

He gawped for half a second at the naked, hogtied figure, letting the familiarity of the face that turned towards him sink in. Matthew's face was streaked with dirt. Tear tracks formed dry riverbeds between the smears. Both eyes were swollen. His back was a sea of welts. A red rag stoppered his mouth, which he frantically tried to speak around.

None of his doom scenarios he'd entertained on the drive over had predicted this.

Anton entered behind him. The sharp puff of his breath stirred the hairs above Killian's ear. "He's one of yours?"

"Matthew."

How strange it must seem that he hadn't rushed to help him.

"Can you—"

Anton was already on it. While he untied the bonds around Matthew's arms and legs—someone knew their rope work—Killian fished around for a water canteen and the first aid kit. "What happened?" He pulled the rag from Matthew's mouth, which revealed the gag as being a pair of women's skimpy lace panties. He dropped them like they were hot. It seemed his rope work observations weren't far-fetched.

"Give him a moment and let him have a drink, eh? Before you start with the whole third degree."

Anton took the canteen and handed to it Matthew. "Sip. Try not to gulp it too fast."

"What are you doing here?"

Anton raised his arm, turning his palm to counter Killian's crowding stance. "Hold a moment."

"He's supposed to be in central Cairo." He'd gone for the weekend. "I'd like to know how he ended up back here all trussed up like a chicken ready for basting."

A smile flashed across Anton's face, which was gone the moment he took in Matthew's sorry figure again.

Matthew lowered the water canteen, but little more than a croak emerged from his throat, which forced Killian to lean closer.

"I didn't lead them here, I promise. I'm sorry. I don't know what their game is."

But he did. He could taste it. The utter spite of it like it was thick black ichor sitting on his tongue and clogging up his throat.

He needed a moment before he was apprised of the details. "I'm going to nip back to the car. I've some spare clothes in there." Leastways, he probably had. If not, there was a rug they could improvise with.

He was dry heaving in anticipation by the time he reached the car. He stuck his head inside and screamed.

It was Sadler behind this. He knew it. He just knew it.

It wasn't a robbery, or a prank. It was an opening salvo.

He found a semi-clean shirt. No trousers, but the blanket would double as a kilt with a bit of ingenuity and a few safety pins.

When he got back, Matthew was more comfortably situated, with marks where the rope had been, but his eyes were open, revealing bloodshot sclera. Killian buttoned him into the shirt and threw the blanket over his lap.

"Are you up to telling us what happened? Do you want to do that here? Should I take you somewhere else? Do you need to see a doctor?"

Matthew's shoulders edged up in response to the barrage of questions. His Adam's apple bobbed.

"Take your time." Anton rested a reassuring hand on Matthew's shoulder. He was managing this far better than Killian was doing.

"I'm sorry," he said, knowing he was being monstrous. That the guy probably needed a moment to process and convince his brain things were okay now.

"I'm not injured, Killian. I'm okay. Just a bit woozy, is all."

"That's probably down to dehydration," Anton said.

"The welts, they're not... I was fully consenting..."

"We've all had those sorts of nights," Anton said, easing the tension while Killian tried to figure out if he needed to moderate the level of sympathy he was feeling. He'd learned to be cautious thanks to his experience with Sadler, he only wished others would learn from his mistake, instead of making their own.

He didn't bleat on about caution and keeping things close to your chest for no reason.

"I went clubbing."

Inadvisable at the best of times.

"Met some people. Some women, who I've been seeing on and off for a while. We wound up back at their place—their hotel, and things got…" He turned his head to glance over his shoulder. "It was all cool. We were having a good time."

The stepping stones of this story were just so obvious, it was hard not to spit out something disparaging. Two girls just happen to both be into you, and suggesting you all enjoy a bit of restraint play… If you couldn't see that was a likely prelude to being robbed blind, then you were clearly thinking with your dick.

"I don't need to know the details of your make out session. I want to know how you ended up here, and what the fuck they've taken, or they want."

Matthew tilted his head to look up at him. "I'm not sure. I woke up in the back of a car and got dragged in here. I never saw them take anything. They didn't go any further than this room, and all they did in here was take some pictures."

"What about the lock?"

"I didn't feel like I had many options. I told them the combination, but not about the alarm system."

Killian nodded. That at least had been smart.

"You said they took photographs."

"Yes. Of me. Of the mural. And then they left, like it was a joke or something. I was terrified I'd still be lying here on Monday morning."

"In what universe would I not check up on a security breach?" He gave a frustrated groan and made to slap the wall. Though he stopped short of doing it. Delicate surfaces, and all that.

Sadler was behind this. It would only be a matter of time before his demands materialised. Although, if he worked quickly, perhaps he could mitigate the disaster before it happened.

"You're sure nothing else was taken?"

Matthew wearily shook his head. "Just my personal stuff, clothes etcetera."

"Okay." Killian rubbed his jaw as he thought. "Are you okay to hang tight here long enough for Siân to collect you if I call her now?"

"Yeah."

Killian trotted outside again, this time in search of a phone signal. Siân didn't pick up, but he left her a voicemail message, and then tried the Gezira apartment. Jason answered. He didn't waste time asking for Siân to be put on, choosing to believe his message would be relayed with the necessary expedience. He was succinct. "Make sure she gets her butt here pronto."

Following that, he called Masud, and left another message, then arranged a meeting with the head of department at the University.

After that he went inside again, and found the two men chatting amiably, as if disaster wasn't about to level multiple careers. "I'm heading to Cairo. You're welcome to hitch a lift. I'm planning to head off now, if that's all right? Matthew? Siân will be here within the hour."

Matthew nodded. "Go. I've water. She's on the way. I'm set. I doubt they're going to come back."

-45-
Killian

"**W**here can I drop you?"

"The University is fine. No need to make unnecessary stops. I can make my own way from there, no problem."

Likely, Anton's intent was to minimise any additional stress that would arise from negotiating Cairo's traffic systems, but all Killian's mind fixated on was the fact he wouldn't know where the other man lived, and therefore wouldn't be able to find him again.

Stupid, as arranging another meet had no business being on his agenda.

His usual parking spot was waiting for him near his office. Killian pulled into the bay but didn't immediately kill the engine. He'd arranged this meeting. That didn't mean he wanted to attend it. He'd reached this position in his career by keeping his head down and through damned hard work. And avoiding discord, whether it was political, departmental, or infighting over translation variances and hence interpretation of the Pyramid Texts or whatever other inscription was flavour of the month.

"Need some backup?"

Killian shot his passenger a look out of the corner of his eye. Anton's gaze was fixed on the steering wheel that Killian still held clasped at ten to two in a knuckle-whitening death grip.

"It's fine. It'll be fine."

It wouldn't be fine. At minimum, Matthew was facing a suspension. It shouldn't work like that, but religious conservatism didn't allow for leniency or even empathy when it came to screwing up in a way that drew attention to matters of a sexual nature.

"I've got this." He gave the wheel a pat, then cut the engine.

"I'll let you get to it, then." Anton got out of the car, and Killian's heart started a panicked flutter. If Anton walked away, what would anchor him?

Unable to tear his face from Anton's back, he watched his hair being ruffled by the wind. Then, him produce a scarf and wind it around his head to combat the inevitable splatter of airborne sand and grime.

Anton turned, but instead of closing the car door, he stuck his head back inside the vehicle. "Thanks again for the help last night." He pressed a hand to his abdomen where Killian had patched him up. "I lucked out."

It'd hardly been first class treatment. "Keep a close eye on that, eh?"

"I will."

Another pause.

"Have you got some—"

"Give me your number."

"—paper."

He reached for his phone and opened the contacts app. Tapped when Anton rattled off a set of digits.

"Just in case."

"Yeah." He sent a text, so Anton would have his number too, then grinned, hearing the other man's ringtone. It was a song by a Lebanese artist, they'd both enjoyed. *Deny*. Yeah, that kind of felt way too pertinent, even though it'd been less than eighteen hours since they were entwined, and only a gear stick stood between them now.

"I'll see you around."

Anton flashed him an enigmatic smile.

Maybe they would and maybe they wouldn't. It wasn't as if anyone was going to be racing to be his friend if shit blew up again with Sadler.

Who was he fooling? It already had.

~Ж~

Killian had arranged to see his direct superior, but on admittance to her office, multiple stony faces greeted him. Unease curled like a cobra in his gut. Flashbacks to being given his marching orders sliding over reality like a grainy filter.

"Come in, Killian. Sit down. We're glad you called."

"It's good to have a handle on things." A moustachioed gentleman, a recent vice-principle appointee remarked, and flashed him a toothy, highly insincere grin. "Oseye assures me you like to run a tight ship. Unfortunate that this has happened. Very unfortunate."

He hadn't gone into the details on the phone, just the summary, explaining how he'd found Matthew and the demands he expected to follow.

"It would be good if we could handle this with sensitivity. He made a foolish mistake. All things considered, it's a relief the outcome wasn't more serious." For example, they weren't having to explain why a member of his team had been hospitalised for dehydration.

Several of the room's occupants shifted in their chairs.

"Obviously, we can't give in to this sort of blackmail. To do so would set a precedent and put others at risk of this sort of exploitation. For Matthew, of course it's a major embarrassment. He fully admits his naivety in—"

"And for Doctor Lawrence."

"Excuse me?" He lasered his attention at the vice-principle again.

"This is surely a major embarrassment for her too. She is the other person depicted in this photograph, correct, and I believe, your second in command."

"No, actually, that's Lucas—Doctor Visser. I'm sorry, what? What photograph? The incident I reported to you earlier only involved one member of my team. I found him disrobed and bound after responding to an intruder alert."

Someone huffed, as if he was feeding them a

yarn.

"Matthew believes they took photographs—"

"I'm not one for obfuscation." The gentleman on the end leaned forward. It wasn't a face Killian recognised. Was he from human resources? "Also, I've another meeting scheduled in half an hour. So, I'd appreciate getting to the point. Doctor Carmichael. I feel either you're being deliberately misled, or your intention is to mislead. We received a photograph shortly after your call from an anonymous source who intends to make it public if they are not pandered to. That picture is of... Do you know... Can we not just show it?"

Various rumblings and ruminations circulated, then Oseye turned a laptop screen in his direction. "Sorry, Killian," she mouthed. Instead of Matthew naked and bound before the mural, the image showed an entirely unrestrained Matthew mimicking the art on the wall behind him, and Siân on her knees simulating fellatio. The fact the photographer had caught Matthew cock in hand made it hard to interpret the image as anything other than what it was.

Namely, highly unprofessional behaviour.

The weight in Killian's chest plummeted to his knees. It made him appreciate the fact he'd been offered a chair.

"This is not what you were expecting, Doctor Carmichael," the vice-principle observed.

"No." Killian cleared his throat. "No."

How the fuck?

"Were you aware of this photographs

existence?"

"Were you aware that the handpicked members of your team abuse their positions to create pornography?" That addition came from the HR guy.

"That's not—" He clamped his mouth closed ahead of saying anything revelatory.

Had he not told them to delete it? How the fuck had Sadler... whoever, got hold of it?

He needed to think, but with five pairs of expectant eyes on him, his brain was instead stuck in a repetitive groove. *How-huh-huh-how-how-how?* He'd been braced for images of Matthew trussed up like a Sunday roast going live. They'd have been bad enough, but this... this was next level. It was fucking disastrous.

Sadler wouldn't need to fucking visit the site. He could just publish this and then refer to it. *See here, Doctor Carmichael's team enacting the ritual of the pharaoh to harness his power. Yes, yes, it does look exactly like fellatio, but the thing is, the Egyptian's were all about the seed. One only has to look at the myths of Osiris, and those of Horus his son. Planted in the wrong place, the seed had the power to poison. But in the right place, used in the right way, it can birth new gods.* Cue some nonsense about drinking come and reciting poorly translated bits of the *Ani Papyrus* in order to be reborn or renewed or whatever.

His fists clenched against his thighs. This wouldn't just end his career. Siân, and Matthew were for certain finished too. Adie, too, if it got out that she was the photographer. Actually, it'd wash badly for the whole team. It wouldn't matter that whatever Sadler wrote was bullshit, the fact that there was evidence enough to support the idea they were fornicating at will on a heritage site would appear to be enough all on its own.

And no wonder this hastily assembled jury weren't interested in what he'd come to report. That didn't matter. This photograph eclipsed all that.

They were all sitting looking at him in anticipation. Waiting for what, he didn't know. A perfectly reasonable explanation for why two of his team members were engaged in sexual acts at work? There wasn't an alternative spin he could put on it. It was as it appeared. They shouldn't have done it, but they had. So, what now? Was he supposed to fall on his sword? Make a plea for mercy on their behalf?

Oseye took pity on him. "It's clearly a shock. Hard to comprehend how exactly how badly you've been duped, and undermined, I imagine."

She meant by his team, but he didn't blame them. This was Sadler. That manipulative arsehole. He'd never given a damn about whose lives he'd wrecked on his way to superstardom.

"Is there more? There's more, isn't there?" Obviously, there was. This was a warning shot, not the full arsenal. Where was the accompanying ask? As Anton had said, the prick banked on expert endorsement. This photo could do plenty on its own, but... "What does he want?" And were they really intending on giving it?

Given the five stubborn faces staring at him... Yes. Yes, they were. The matter had always been debated and discussed before he'd even got here. A consensus reached.

Whatever Sadler wanted he'd be given, so that this incident could be quietly brushed under the rug.

But what did he want? "I agree we should cut the bullshit." He addressed the remark to the room at large, though he pinpointed the HR man with his gaze.

"You have to understand," Oseye began. She rubbed her greying close-shorn hair. "It'd be a horrible embarrassment for the university. It could put the whole department in jeopardy. All those years spent bringing Egyptology home to Egypt, making this a world centre for our culture and history, would be wasted if this image were to be published."

"Horribly embarrassing for the Egyptian government..."

"Whereas," the vice principal took up the chain. "If we comply, then we can move on without anyone outside of this room being any the wiser. And it's a minor ask. It really is a minor ask."

That, he suspected, was a matter of opinion.

"Of course, we might ask for a few personnel changes down the line," HR man said. "But staff turnover isn't unusual. People move on. They relocate."

They did expect him to fall on his sword.

"This photograph didn't come from an anonymous source, so can we please stop pretending it did? Sadler sent it, no doubt along with a lovely letter beseeching you to provide him with an alternative. Me. Answering his bullshit questions to lend legitimacy to the wholesale bollocks that he sells to the gullible."

"Killian!" Oseye's chastening cry, barely registered over the grumbles from every other quarter about his language.

"The gullible contribute to the economy," one of the until now silent jurors said.

"You all know that if I speak to him, that's it. Game over. I'll not be taken seriously ever again."

"You're an asset, Killian, you truly are, but there's no good outcome, whichever way this goes."

He got it. It was him or the whole department.

"We'll announce your resignation from your teaching post, say something about dedicating your time to your fieldwork."

Christ, they were skipping the long sabbatical stage and progressing straight to firing him. Why the hell did they think he'd agree to any of these terms?

"We can talk about suitable remuneration—"

He didn't give a shit about money. They paid him a fraction of his actual worth, anyway.

"Put things into place to make sure your post-grads can complete their studies and that your team are paid through to the end of the summer. Of course, as all records of this matter will be expunged, there'll be no worries over them finding future positions."

Except for the fact that they'd have worked for him, and his name would be dirt again.

"All we need is a nod, and everything can be set up for tomorrow. He's in the area, so..."

Christ!

~Ж~

Once the meeting concluded, Killian went down to his office, and haphazardly shoved a few personal items into a box that had miraculously appeared on his desk. He stuck a note to it, so they could ship it to him along with his collection of books. It was just a room. Just an office. He didn't even like teaching much. Marking undergraduate essays sucked. But it had been home for a while. He'd at least felt as if he were part of something. He hadn't felt quite such a pariah.

That was about to change again.

He needed to speak to Masud.

He needed to speak to the team and apprise them of the shit storm that was about to hit and ruin their lives.

But couldn't quite... The words wouldn't come out. In the end he sent an email. One explanation, six recipients...seven, as he forwarded a variant of it to Masud. Then he followed it with a text to Siân, Matthew, and Adie.

KC:Don't leave the damn boat until I get back, unless it's on fucking fire.

He meant to head back at once, but he'd rather fallen out of love with Saqqara. If he went there, he'd be tempted to hunt Sadler down and do what he and Anton had joked over.

Nor could he stomach the thought of the team fluttering around him. All of them clutching at straws, making suggestions, imagining that their careers were anything other than over.

Taking the gamble to return to the desert necropolis had been a mistake. They'd lost.

They'd lost...

He could already feel everything slipping away from him, just as it had before.

-46-

Adie

When both Siân and Adie's phones beeped simultaneously, only Siân reached for her device. She and Matthew had arrived at the houseboat a little over twenty minutes ago. Matthew wearing one of Killian's shirts. They'd brushed off Adie's questions and headed straight for the shower. "Make some brews. We'll explain once we're out," Siân had said.

Now Matthew was sat on deck, dark hair glistening in the sunlight as he dried off, dressed in fresh clothes, his two fat eyes concealed behind a pair of sunglasses.

Siân glanced at her phone screen.

"Oh, you fucking idiot! Matty, what have you done?"

Matthew winced as he turned to Siân and rubbed his lower back. "I told you," he said.

"You told me they'd taken pictures of you tied up, not that they'd hacked your fucking phone!"

"Huh?"

"You never mentioned that they were Sadler's stooges either."

"I did. I'm sure I did. Actually, that's an assumption. I'm not completely sure."

"They were. Are... Oh, God! We are so doomed."

Adie reached for her own smart device. Killian's name flashed across the lock screen, alongside a message about staying on the boat. "What's the big deal?"

"Check your email. He's,"—she nodded at Matthew—"only gone and stuffed the whole project up."

Adie did just that, with Matthew reading Killian's missive over her shoulder. By the end, nausea roiled in her gullet. He hadn't said much, but what he had said was enough. The fact he'd informed them via email wasn't a good sign either.

"Why the hell did you keep that photo on your phone? Of all the imbecile things..."

"It's on mine too," Adie confessed. She opened her gallery to delete it, but it was already too late, right? Instead, she hit dial to reach Killian. She stood and moved away from her squabbling colleagues, as she waited for Killian to pick up, but the call went straight to voicemail. "Come on, come on..."

"I wasn't exactly anticipating having my phone nicked, Siân."

"That's because you're an idiot." Siân levelled her glare at Adie. "You too, if you've just got it basking in an unencrypted folder. Sure, we all should've known better than to fool around like that, but..."

"Like you don't have a score of risqué images on yours."

"Not taken at work of me mimicking the content of a bronze age mural or of anything that Dareth fucking Sadler is going to glom on and build a career-wrecking book around." Her long plait whipped from side to side as she shook. Fury turning her sharp features mean. "Fuck!" She pounded the table making all their glasses jump.

"What do we do?" Adie asked, as she listened to the dial tone purr, and then *click* dump her into Killian's 'I'm not available right now,' message loop.

"Sit tight until he gets here."

"No, I mean what do we do?" She let the dialling cycle perform another repeat. "It's our fault. There must be something we can do to fix things... Has to be." Looking around at the bleak faces of her companions, it was clear they weren't overflowing with ideas. "We can't let Sadler win. Guys, we can't."

"I don't see there's anything we can do. We can't un-take a photograph. And we're not about to invent time travel in the next forty minutes." Matthew hung his head and sighed. "There's nothing we can do to make this right, Adie. Nothing. We're long past the days when you could destroy all the copies and burn the negatives. Look, I'm sorry I screwed up. I'm sorry I was so busy thinking with my dick that I've ruined a good thing for us all."

Adie nodded. Remorse was all well and good, but ultimately useless. "It's not right that he should take the fall for us."

Siân patted her on the back, then pulled her into an awkward hug. "Sadler's not interested in us; it was always about Killian. We just played into his hands."

They had, resoundingly so.

"At least now you can stop spending all your time looking for a missing willy," Siân said making an attempt at a smile.

"Suppose," Adie huffed. Then again, It'd be something if she found it. A legitimate achievement she could wave around when looking for whatever came next. While they all currently had jobs, how long would that last. Killian might be on his way back to the boat now, ready to fire them all.

"You can ask your hottie for a job," Siân said. "Put in a good word for me too. I don't mind relocating to Bahariya."

The sadness in Siân's voice made a lump form in Adie's throat. This was the end for the three of them. There'd be no more digs, at least not in Egypt. If they were lucky, they might pick up work somewhere else. If they changed their names. If only they'd actually found Huni and not just an empty box, that might have been enough to save them.

"What happened with him, anyway? You went off to meet him yesterday, I was expecting you to be a couple of hours max, but then you never came back."

"I messaged you."

"Girl. What gives? You were all antsy about meeting him after pretty much ghosting him, but then you don't come home. Did he help you with that lead? Or were you too busy playing a different version of hunt the willy to get into that?"

In other circumstances, perhaps drinking

contraband amongst the clutter and disorder of her cabin she might have spilled a few details. In the here and now, Siân's inquiry felt decidedly accusatory.

"Come on, explain how you wound up back here? Did you feel bad and nip back to have a guilt-fuelled shagathon with Killian after doing something naughty with his ex?"

On second thoughts, this wasn't a discussion she'd ever have been comfortable having. The details of how things had panned out was her business. Hers, and Anton's, and Killian's. The latter especially, wouldn't thank her for gossiping about how the two men had wound up face to face after a decade, and rather than clashing like rhinos, had given her the time of her life. Frankly, there'd been enough talk of fornication. If everyone, including the damn pharaoh whose tomb they were excavating had kept it in their pants, then none of them would be in the shitty position they currently found themselves in.

Sadler wouldn't have been interested if it'd just been a typical mural of a pharaoh going about his usual pharaoh-like business of mooching around with the gods, crushing his enemies, and weighing his grains.

Her phone rang. Adie clamped it to her ear. "Killian."

"It's Anton."

"Oh, Anton. Hi."

"You needn't sound so disappointed."

"I'm not. I just... Is Killian with you? Is he okay?" She excused herself from her workmates company and strolled along the deck towards the rear of the houseboat.

"We parted ways at the university. He wasn't exactly eager to go into that meeting, but who would have been. Otherwise, he was in one piece. Did Matthew get back to the boat okay?"

"Yeah. He's here. And fine. He'll live."

This end of the boat didn't have nearly so appealing a view.

"Are you...fine?"

"Sure. Why wouldn't I be."

"I just didn't expect you to call so soon."

He made a throaty *hmm*. "I didn't expect to *need* to call so soon."

"Oh, God! You've heard something—"

"I thought it would take days to hear so much as a whisper from Ihsãn, but apparently word has got round about Jamãl's arrest." He cleared his throat. "It seems I'm not the only one who was none too fond of him. Which is the roundabout way of saying that Mr Fuãd is willing to talk to you."

"Shit! Really?" Her grin spread so wide and so fast it made her cheeks ache. This was something, maybe the something that would save them all.

"There's a catch, Adie. Before you get too swept up in that triumph."

Of course there was. Nothing was ever straightforward. "Payment? Is he asking something out of the question?"

Anton seemed to be considering his words. "There was no mention of that. It's more to do with logistics. He's given you a very narrow window in which he'll speak to you."

"Okay."

"Tonight."

Of course it was. "I can't…" She was supposed to stay on the boat. If she left and Killian got back and she wasn't here, there'd be hell to pay on top of what was already due. Oh, but… "Go on. Where, tonight? Central Cairo somewhere, right?" Somewhere out of the way, where she had no hope of making it to.

For a moment the line fell silent save for his quiet breathing. Why was he being so cagey? "Not central Cairo, no. He's going to be out at Saqqara tonight—attending Sadler's party. The bastard's extended him a personal invitation."

Oh, God! Oh, God!

Going there would be utter folly. Worse though, if Sadler had personally invited Ihsãn, that meant he probably wanted to speak to him for the same reason Adie did. Which meant Sadler was going to learn where the missing fragment was ahead of her.

If that happened, things were going to become infinitely worse than they already were. He wouldn't just ruin Killian's reputation; he'd utterly humiliate him too.

Amateur archaeologist beats the professionals to the prize and triumphantly restores a three-thousand-year-old mural to its former glory.

She could already picture the article.

No one would care about the empty burial chamber or the hours and hours of labour the team had put into the excavation. The narrative would be all about how Sadler had saved the day. Sadler triumphing where trained archaeologists...where the leading expert on the era had failed. Look at Sadler, the man who uncovered the secrets and treasures of the mysterious third dynasty pharaoh, Huni.

It'd net him another instant best seller. There'd be documentaries, possibly even a film deal—audiences liked an underdog—and they'd be the team who failed. Reduced to a footnote. Forgotten. Perhaps even villainised for holding him back.

Her Egyptian adventure would be over. Esther's dream for her obliterated. If she was lucky, she'd get a museum job, talking about exhibits to tourists and school groups. More likely, she'd be retraining as a barista.

"He's definitely attending. You're sure? This isn't just a set-up, and they're going to truss me up like they did Matthew?"

"It's legitimate, Adie. I think it's highly unlikely that Ihsān has mentioned to Sadler that he intends to sell his information to multiple parties. I imagine he thinks that makes for fatter profits and better sport. As for how you spot him, all the members of his gang have uraeus tattoos. I imagine you'll find him at the centre of them in whatever VIP pavilion Sadler has set-up for the purpose of wooing him."

So, it wasn't simply a matter of gatecrashing an event she wasn't invited to. She'd have to wheedle her way into the very heart of it. Dammit, she'd never been good at fast talk.

"I have nothing to bargain with. I'm not trading information with him or passing him artefacts."

"Good to hear."

"What is this conversation you're having?" Siân had sneaked up on her. Adie turned to face her, attempting to keep her guilt off her face and judging by Siân's expression, utterly failing.

"More grim news? How bad? It's bad, right? Because you look fucking ghastly."

"We have to go to Sadler's party. Ihsãn's going to be there. Franks' contact. I have to talk to him. We have to. If we don't, Sadler's going to find the fragment before we do."

As her words sank in, Siân's expression transformed from 'You've got to be fucking joking' to stoic acceptance. "If Killian comes back and we're gone—"

"I know."

"We have nothing to barter with."

"I know."

"Then what's the plan, Adie? How are we even getting into the event?"

Good question. Wait. She handed Siân her phone and scampered around the boat to her cabin. She could hear Siân exchanging flirtatious pleasantries with Anton. Her teammate followed her over the threshold and surveyed the room with a critical eye. There were clothes everywhere.

"I can never find anything on a morning."

She moved a pair of baggy shorts and several scrunched vests from the bed to the dresser and rustled some papers onto a chair. They spotted the leather strap poking out from behind the chair in the opposite corner.

"Got it." Adie wrestled the satchel she'd taken

with her to the museum onto the bed. The leaflet that woman had pressed on her was still tucked into its depths. "This is how." She brandished the leaflet at Siân. "We phone a friend."

"Did you hear that?" Siân said to Anton. "We're apparently phoning a friend." Then to Adie, she added, "I didn't think you had any friends in Egypt outside of this guy,"—she waggled the phone—"and us."

"I don't, but I have a prospective one. And she's probably just about batshit crazy enough not to question why we suddenly want to attend this party given that she thinks the sun shines out of Sadler's arse."

"Well, that's half a solution. It still doesn't give you anything to barter with, and you've got to realise that Sadler's not going to turn up empty-handed. Also, we're not stealing anything from the workroom before you even consider that."

While there was plenty in the workroom of value, none of it was the sort of stuff that was likely to open doors, and even if there was, she wouldn't take it.

"We'll have to work on that." She took the phone from Siân. "Anton, do you have any ideas?"

"Yeah, don't do this, and definitely don't do anything dumb."

"Says the man who got himself knifed."

"That's precisely why I'm advising against rash actions."

"Don't you have a fake we could barter?"

"Adie, no! That's a fucking stupid idea. What do

you think will happen when they realise they've been duped?"

"I can't do nothing," she spat. "I'm sorry." She hung up.

Siân blinked incredulously at her. "You treat them mean, girl."

Adie shook her head. She needed to think and didn't need Anton or anyone else pointing out how stupid this plan likely was. She had to at least try to salvage Killian's reputation. It's what you did for those you loved. You fought for them as best you could. Sitting here on this boat waiting for doomsday wasn't going to help anyone. Not Killian, and definitely not herself.

"We make our own luck," she said to Siân. It was something her father used to say. "Can you find us some suitable party clothes? I'm going to call that friend."

-47-
Adie

The sky had turned a vivid shade of magenta as Siân and Adie parked up by Djoser's pyramid complex, having first established that Killian's 4x4 was nowhere in sight. They'd opted for New Age hippy outfits, all bangles, and a motley of colours, with ridiculous false eyelashes and more eye-make up than Adie had worn in her entire life. Coming here to negotiate with Ihsãn had seemed like a good idea, but now they were here, doubts were emerging in Adie's mind. What if Killian had a plan and them coming here would undermine it?

He still hadn't responded to any of her texts or calls.

Then again, no one ever achieved anything sitting on their backsides. Esther had always encouraged her to be bold.

Still, Esther had never doubted that Adie would find a way to get to Egypt. *If it's meant to be, it'll be, Adie,* she used to say, "But making opportunities for yourself never hurts." And here she was with an opportunity to make her name for herself and save the team from humiliation all in one. A completed mural might not be the same as unearthing boundless treasures, but it would still be significant, and maybe help mitigate some of the damage done by that photograph she was responsible for.

She ought to have said no when Matthew told her to take it.

"You ready?" Siân snapped her compact shut and chucked it in the glove compartment, before sliding her penny shades up her nose.

They joined a steady stream of arrivals at the colonnade entrance to the pyramid complex. Thumping Egyptian dance music blared around them, amplified by the towering steps of Djoser's tomb.

"This way." Adie grabbed Siân's arm and dragged her over to a group of three women dressed surprisingly similarly to themselves, only done up with Cleopatra style eyes and thick brows that made hers and Siân's attempts look underplayed. "Hey. Hi there," Adie waved at the one on the end. "We met at the museum. The signing. I'm sorry I didn't manage to catch up with you again that day... You know how it is."

"It's fine. I'm just thrilled you've seen sense. I told you, didn't I? What did you read? You started with Six Steps, uh-huh?"

"Um—"

"She totally glommed the lot. Hey, I'm Layla," Siân extended a jingling armful of bangles. "And you're...?"

"Nadine."

"Sorry, this is my friend," Adie explained, while

Siân exchanged air kisses with Nadine and her two companions. "I'm so grateful to you for letting us tag along. We'd have totally missed out otherwise—"

"And what a total bummer that would have been," Siân said.

Nadine introduced her friends. "Dalia, and Mert. She's really Michelle, but we heard he's really into Arabic names and everyone wants to get into the inner circle. I guess you both heard the same thing."

"Oh, no, it's my actual name," Siân lied, ensuring everyone felt awkward.

"Um, it's quite a crowd," Adie said. "Looks like half of Cairo turned up."

Said crowd was predominantly female, with the odd weedy male mixed in.

It was alarmingly busy, which put Sadler's popularity into a hideous perspective. More importantly, it was going to make finding Ihsãn difficult. What were they supposed to do? Ask everyone if they happened to have a uraeus tattoo?

"Afraid you won't make it to the inner sanctum?" Mert, Michelle remarked, taking a drag on her clove cigarette.

"Don't mind her," Nadine gathered them close, as they moved along with the rest of the line towards the entrance. "She thinks she's shoo-in, because her mum allegedly used to hang with Sadler back before he released Six Steps."

"She did."

"Yeah, sure. What was she, a cradle-snatcher? He's not that old."

Mert dropped her cigarette butt and stubbed it

out with the pointy toe of her boot. "Girl, he's pushing fifty. For all I know, he's my dad."

"He is not. He's not even forty yet."

"Says who?"

"Says his Wikipedia page."

"Yeah, that's a totally reliable source."

Adie quickly determined that this was a long-running squabble, one that soon devolved into sneers and pouts on both sides.

"Let's go in." Nadine hooked arms with both her and Siân and dragged them forward through the crowd. Once inside, they made their way between the towering stone columns into the South Court. Here, Adie let her hand graze the ribbed stones as they passed. The structure had been the first of its kind, so far as was known, and had been a model for future generations of builders to grow their ideas from. She really did need to make more time to explore the landscape. All this impressive history stood within a kilometre of their excavation, but she'd only seen it from a distance.

Would Killian show her around a few of the sites? He was no doubt familiar with all of them, the Stepped Pyramid of Djoser that they were facing, Unas and Userkaf pyramids, both close by alongside the Tomb of Horemheb and countless others, large and small. The landscape was literally littered with history.

Too late, said another part of her brain. He's probably going to want to leave Egypt after this and never come back.

"What's the deal with the flowers?" Siân asked,

proving that her mind was firmly on their game, and not wandering along ancient avenues like Adie's. A woman in a floaty, white, organza dress carrying a basket of white flowers was circulating amongst the crowd in the Heb-Seb court. Now and then, she would offer a bloom to someone.

"That's Dareth's PA," Nadine confirmed. "His right-hand woman, Lana D'Rosa. The flowers are the tickets to the inner sanctum. Without one, you're barred entry. It's a huge honour. Everyone wants to be picked, but they only choose those enlightened enough to participate in the main ritual."

Clang, clang, clang.

Yeah, that right there was a warning bell going off inside Adie's skull, letting her know it was a stupendously bad idea to get oneself selected, also, obviously what they were going to have to do, if they were going to get what they'd come for.

If Ihsãn was truly here, he'd be in the VIP area. Also, that claxon appeared to be some sort of summons. Those with the white lotus blooms were slowly peeling off, and one by one heading towards a pavilion pitched at the far end of the plaza by the base of the pyramid.

"We need flowers," she mouthed to Siân.

"Yeah, already on it." Siân pulled her behind a ruined half column. "I'll create a distraction. You snatch and run?"

"What?"

Too late. Siân had already removed her shades and launched herself like a jaguar at a woman approaching carrying a flower. "Bitch! You stole my boyfriend." She knocked the woman right off her feet, causing her few possessions to fly. Adie hesitated, while the pair tussled, and then she heard Siân mutter, "Oh, sorry. Wrong person."

"Crap!"

She grabbed the bent bloom and scurried towards the pavilion, astonished that no one called after her. She slowed after ten metres or so. The path wasn't crowded, and it'd look odd that she was running. See here, she had nothing to do with the commotion going on back there. She did not look back at Siân or pay the commotion any regard. None of her business, right. Nothing at all to do with her.

The music wasn't so bass heavy here in the shadow of the pyramid. The canvas wall did little to deaden the clinking of glasses and chatter coming from within the pavilion.

She peeped around the edge of one panel. So, this was where the male invitees were. Being pandered to by waitresses while they lozzucked on comfortable curved sofas.

Surely, she would find Ihsãn here.

A man walked past her on the other side of the tent wall. The top of a uraeus tattoo extended from his raiment up the back of his neck. Well, what do you know... She dogged his progress around the pavilion. Not easy from the outside. Eventually, he joined a table near the back, where a middle-aged man with grey striped hair was manspread at the centre of one of the sofa booths. He had a quad of muscle around him.

Ihsãn? She'd anticipated a much older man.

One wizened by years, but Franks had never claimed his assistant was of his own generation. Thinking on it, it made sense that he'd be younger.

Now she just needed to go in and introduce herself.

Adie unfastened a couple of toggles holding panels of the pavilion together and made herself an entrance through the wall, but she'd barely wriggled through when a familiar figure joined Ihsãn's table.

Sadler.

The mere sight of the man made her itch for a blade such as Anton possessed, so she might hurl it at Sadler's head. Right now, it made sense why so many people chose to solve their issues with violence. So many ills would be eliminated by removing Sadler from the equation.

Sadly, this wasn't a movie, and she wasn't Indiana Jones, nor was Sadler an evil Nazi.

Were they bargaining right now? Was she already too late?

Ihsãn seemed restless.

Sadler irritatingly cocky.

The blonde woman she'd seen roving the courtyard came over and tapped him on the shoulder. "It's time."

Her voice carried where others hadn't.

"I'm sorry, I'm going to have to steal him away, gentlemen, but please, enjoy the hospitality." Two waitresses instantly arrived, ready to provide.

"Gentlemen. Mr Fuãd. So good to make your acquaintance. I'll be happy to make the exchange as suggested."

Adie held back until he'd left the tent, then she strode right up to Ihsãn Fuãd's table and presented herself. "Mr Fuãd, my name is Adie Hamilton. You sent word you were prepared to speak with me via my associate, Doctor Kelley."

While his compatriots hustled to place themselves between her and their boss, the man himself leant forward and patted the foremost of them out of the way. "She's invited. Let her be."

"Thank you."

Ihsãn gave her a swept head to foot look over.

"I'm looking for the missing fragment of a third dynasty mural. It was removed from a largely unexcavated tomb here at Saqqara by—"

"I know what you're looking for, Doctor Hamilton. I believe in thorough research. Franks sent you my way, did he not?"

"He did. He said... He said, you were the man to ask."

Ihsãn nodded. He picked up his drink and turned the glass slowly in his hand but didn't take a sip. "You're uneasy," he observed. "Is it me or my men making you so?"

"This isn't somewhere I belong, but I think you know that."

He laughed.

"I'd rather not linger. I've no desire to create unnecessary discord."

He nodded. "I believe Mr Sadler will be engaged with other business for some time now. We need not be unduly hasty."

"Have you already sold the information to

him?" She meant to sound firm, but her voice cracked. One of Ihsãn's companions poured her a drink.

"Thank you." She sipped what turned out to be *limoon*. "Have you?"

He made vaguely affirmative noises. "Mr Sadler has offered me seven hundred and fifty thousand pounds. What is your offer?"

Adie's heart very nearly stopped. Okay, wait. He meant Egyptian pounds. Still, that sum was astronomical. What was the conversion? About sixty something Egyptian pounds to one pound sterling. "I don't have that sort of money!" And even if she had...

Ihsãn finally took a sip of his drink. "I didn't imagine that you did. Shall we talk alternatives, then?"

"I'm not sure I have anything you want." Perhaps what she ought to have said, was that there was nothing of value to him she was willing to barter.

"No, but Sadler does."

That served to deepen her frown. "I'm sorry, I don't understand. Are you saying that's it? He's won?"

Ihsãn rested against the sofa back, re-adopting his spread-eagled pose. "Have you enjoyed the pleasure of Mr Sadler's acquaintance, Doctor Hamilton?"

Unfortunately, yes.

"I can see by your expression that you have. You were not warmed by his charm. Neither do I find him an agreeable man, but I will take his money even though I'd rather someone else beat him to the prize."

"Does that mean, you will tell me—"

"It means that a certain item exists. A journal, which is soon to become an extremely saleable item. I desire it, this journal."

He meant William Jacob's journal.

"I don't have it."

"No, Mr Sadler does. Take it from him. Bring it to me."

"Steal it for you, you mean."

"Can it be considered theft when the item you are acquiring doesn't belong to the person whose possession it currently resides?"

Yes, because she knew where it belonged.

"The alternative is eight hundred thousand pounds."

"That's another fifty grand more than you quoted a moment ago."

Ihsãn offered her a blinding smile. "That was Sadler's offer. You'd need to outbid him." He leaned forward, folding one hand over the other and resting his mouth against them. "What's it to be? Money, stealth, or total humiliation?"

-48-
Adie

Adie left the pavilion by the main exit. That journal was probably with Sadler. There was no sign of Siân. Had her antics got her kicked out of the party? Damn and blast, what was she supposed to do?

"What are you doing here?"

Adie turned in response to the sharp command to her rear and found herself facing Sadler's PA. Her pulse started pounding in her ears again.

"You're supposed to be getting ready for the ceremony. Karima collected everyone at least ten minutes ago. God, there's always one who can't manage simple instructions."

"Um, sorry, which way is it again?"

The slicked smooth woman with her boppity ponytail rolled her eyes, then pointed. "That way. Towards the pyramid. Inside, just follow the tunnel down. It's pretty straightforward. Did you not listen to any of the instructions?"

"Sorry," Adie offered, faintly bemused, though keen to be away from the woman's presence. The way she glared, practically convinced Adie she had a beacon on her head announcing her as an imposter.

Lana D'Rosa gave the heavens a second eye roll. "Well, go on then." She made a shooing motion.

In fact, it wasn't at all apparent where Adie was supposed to go once she reached the entrance chamber. At least it had handily been signposted. Down one supposed. If she was going to find Sadler anywhere, it would surely be at the heart of this 62-metre-tall mausoleum. Is that what she was going to do? Venture within, attempt to steal the journal?

Well, it was a direction of travel, while she scrabbled for an alternative.

The initial passageway gave way to a flight of steps, then a longer downwards sloping passageway. For once it was a benefit not to be tall, for the ceiling was often low, and only dim pockets of amber light lit the way. Soon a broader, columned passageway opened out to her left. Gentle susurrations reached her from the farther end. Adie tip-toed closer and found a gaggle of women standing around clutching wilting blooms. Her new friend Nadine among them.

Said friend greeted her with a scowl, when Adie sidled up to her. "I saw what your friend did. It was totally out of order."

"Sorry." Adie put her hands together in prayer. "Don't tell on me."

"The rest of us had to earn our inclusion."

"S-Layla can get a little overzealous, and she knows how much I wanted this."

Nadine clamped her hands on her hips. "Well, I just hope you're prepared, and don't muck things up for the rest of us. This is serious stuff. It's the most important ritual of the year. It's a greater renewal."

Whatever that was. "Cool!" From what she'd seen, Sadler's devotees were nothing but sheep, so she'd have no trouble following along.

"I don't know if you fully appreciate what an honour it is to be chosen to take part."

She'd have gladly passed on that honour, but she had a journal to find and a team to save.

"Where've you come from?" Another woman, with dark curly hair hustled up to them. She looked down her nose at Adie. "Why aren't you changed?"

This was the Karima, Lana had mentioned, Adie supposed.

"I got turned about."

That earned her a disbelieving tut. "Well, you're here now, I guess. Here, put these on, and be quick about it. Enough with the delays. The aim is renewal, not pissing him off by making him stand about." She handed Adie a semi-transparent robe and an elaborate gold eye-mask, like those the other women had on. "Clothes off first dimwit," she huffed when Adie made to slip the robe over her own outfit. "Are you sure you're meant to be down here? You don't seem very informed."

"Sorry, it's just nervousness. I'm totally committed." Adie shot a look at Nadine, then offered Karima a wary grin. "I get really fluttery when I'm excited."

"Right. Well, that's great. Just hurry it up, please. The rest of you, if you're ready, follow me."

Nadine bumped Adie's elbow, "Do you actually have a clue what you're doing?"

"Course," Adie bluffed. She stripped and let the light robe fall over her head. It floated down over her body and sat barely skimming naked skin. It hid almost nothing. Nadine pressed her feline mask to her eyes and turned so Adie could fasten the ties, then did the same for her. Adie's mask was of a plainer design, but with a large horned solar disc jutting from the top, meaning she'd have to keep ducking not to catch it on the ceiling. Someone hadn't thought the logistics through.

Suitably attired, they hurried to catch up with the rest of the line.

Would she find the journal down here? That seemed more unlikely with every step. Unless William Jacob had included a recipe for godhood in amongst his travelogue entries. Hell, maybe he had. That or a handy map of the internal structure of this ancient mausoleum. Crazy to think how long it had stood. All the generations that had passed since it's building. What was it Josef had once said. That today was closer in date to the reign of Cleopatra than Cleopatra's reign was to the building of the Stepped Pyramid. And here she was right in the belly of that structure. Touching the stone columns supporting all that weight piled above and tracing the rough rock walls that had been cut for a god-king.

The group halted on reaching the central shaft above the burial vault and there was Sadler again. At least, Adie assumed it was Sadler. He was also robed, and masked, but in sheer black ensemble in comparison to the women's white.

"Horus," she mouthed, on recognising the

stylised falcon mask. *Pretentious git.*

Also, just what was going on?

A background drum began a slow, rhythmic beat. Smoky incense permeated the air as the women arranged themselves around the compass points.

Sadler, taking a central position, slowly appraised each supplicant. Few met his gaze, most dropped to their knees before him. Adie awkwardly kept her feet.

Seemed she hadn't given the fact she was a participant in a ritual adequate thought.

Next, a goblet of sacramental wine was passed around. Adie faked a swallow. There was something peculiar about the smell of it, though no one else seemed bothered. *It's probably drugged with something, you know,* she itched to tell them.

Chances were they knew and would laugh at her outrage.

The cup having traversed the circle, it was returned to Sadler, who consumed the rest.

Okay, perhaps it wasn't drugged. Or it was a high he was into.

The drummer picked up the pace, building to a crescendo, the women joining in with their voices. At the crest, Sadler swept open the front of his robe. *Behold!*

The son a bitch was stark bollock naked beneath.

Really ought to have predicted that, Adie love.

There were only three reasons people aspired to the role of cult leader. Power, money, and sex. She guessed the latter two came with the first.

He'd completely depilated his body, to better display the huge ankh design that covered his chest and upper arms. It wasn't that causing his acolytes to gasp though. Oh, no! That was the mighty staff he was wielding.

This was no crook or flail.

Adie bit her lip. The man was fully hard, but not only that, the whole of his cock—tip to base—was Nile blue and cuffed with a series of gold cock rings.

Beside her, Nadine gave a squee of delight. "He is God."

No, he was a man with a not bad bod, and a possible Viagra prescription.

Time to bail, Adie! Time. To. Bail.

She sure the hell didn't want that appendage coming anywhere near her.

Beside her, Nadine fell to her knees as if overcome with awe.

The woman who'd given them their robes advanced bearing a decorative faience cup from which the aromatic scent was pouring. Then Lana stepped forth with a small white urn. The significance of the vessels escaped Adie, though everyone else seemed to understand what was going on.

"Rise, oh Horus. Come into your inheritance as possessor of wisdom, vanquisher of fools," they pronounced. The assembled women echoed them. "Receive the blessings of your sister goddesses, to magnify your potency as you make your way among the stars to the table of Osiris."

Osiris. Osiris. Adie screamed inside her head.

Stop. Stop. Stop. But she wasn't here with Killian. There was no kill switch for this ritual.

"Mut, consort of Amun, receive the offering of Horus, and bestow with your kiss the gift of your wisdom."

A woman, masked with Mut's symbol, obligingly shuffled forward and opened her mouth to receive Sadler's cock.

Nope. Just no, she was not sucking Sadler's cock.

"Maat, daughter of Ra," the ritual continued its echoing repetition. "Bestow with your kiss the gift of truth." Another woman shuffled forward.

Things were moving too fast. Nut, Sekhmet, Hathor, all mouthed Sadler's cock. Then Nephthys. Nadine gave her hand an excited squeeze, as her name, Bastet was called.

"Isis—"

No. Absolutely not. The surrounding chanting grew louder, creating a buzzing sensation in her brain.

"—consort of Osiris, bestow with a kiss the power of your magic."

Her heart was thundering so loud, it was making her headache. She took a wary step back, but someone shoved her forward again. "Kneel."

No!

The lights faltered.

A breath of relief whistled through Adie's lips. A low hum of confusion rippled through the assembled women, but no one else moved.

Adie tore off the mask and shuffled sideways

until she hit one of the stone columns. Without the wall lights, it was pitch black, leaving her nothing to depend on but touch.

They'd come in this way, hadn't they? Unless she'd got turned around.

Someone seized the back of her gown and dragged her along. She banged both her knee and shoulder against the rock wall, then lanterns flared to her rear.

Adie looked back, for a moment, and Sadler stood spotlighted, as if the descent into darkness had been anticipated.

"Adie," someone hissed, causing her to turn. Siân had a torch tucked between her boobs down her vest top, and one hand fisted in Adie's garments. In the other she held a pair of wire cutters. "You might want to shift your arse."

She took off at a run. Adie attempted to follow, only to clang her headdress against a beam. She bowed forward and scurried to keep up.

They slowed a little way on, once out of sight of the ritual.

"I don't want to know where you got those but thank the gods..." Adie nodded at the wire cutters.

"You can thank me once we're out of here. Take that dumb hat off. Here," Siân cut through the ribbon. "I take it you've had no luck finding Ihsãn."

"Found him. Couldn't meet his first demand, I'm currently failing to make headway on his alternate offer. He wants either a ludicrous sum of cash or Jacob's journal, but we don't have it, Sadler does, and I can't find it, and even if I could, I'm not sure I'd want to hand it over. But if I don't get it to him before the arse crack of dawn tomorrow, then he's going to sell Sadler the information."

"Sadler has the journal?"

"Yeah." How did she not know that?

"You know that for sure?"

"Yes. He has it. It's what he offered me in exchange for... That is, I saw it when..." She slapped a hand to her brow. "God, I should have grabbed it then."

Siân goggled at her. "Huh?"

Of course, she didn't know. That nightmare sequence had all happened yesterday. It only felt as if it'd been weeks ago. "I'll explain once we're out of here. Yesterday was eventful. Let's hurry. They're going to realise I'm gone, and I'd rather they didn't catch up with us."

They stumbled into the area where she'd been forced to change. "My clothes."

"Leave them. There's nothing there that can't be replaced. Unless you have name tags in your underwear or something." Siân tugged her onwards. "I'm pretty sure the only reason we haven't been rugby tackled yet, is that they're all way too busy getting busy. That ritual is straight out of *Six Steps to Heaven*. All the goddesses suck him off, then he comes in a jar, which they all seal with lip prints, then they smash it, and fuck like monsters."

"Shit!" Adie hissed, relieved to be out of it, and not currently on her knees being pounded by his mighty blue todge.

They reached the stairs and began climbing.

"What were you going to do?"

Adie shook her head. Their ascent slowing as they climbed. Her knees ached, but not half as much as her head. "Not sure, but I certainly wasn't going to suck it. It's bad enough that I have the image of it scarred onto my retinas."

They emerged into the oceanic like night sky.

"And why the fuck did it need to be blue?"

"Blue?"

Adie nodded.

"Painted?"

"Not sure. I've never looked at him and thought, you're the type to go for a full cock tattoo, but what the hell do I know? It's not like I ever looked at Killian before I knew and thought, you're a seriously kinky fucker."

"Weird," Siân offered her moue. "I've always totally suspected that."

Adie let out an exhausted breath. "Is it even possible to tattoo a cock? And if it is, why would you?"

"Never mind that," Siân linked arms with her, and hurried her into motion again. "The pertinent thing here is who chooses that as a career? I'm definite that cock tattooist wasn't on the list of career options when I spoke to the advisor at school. If it had been, I might have considered it. Then again, a lot of dudes have very stinky cocks."

"I reckon he's just soaked it in blue food colouring or something. All this is just spectacle, anyway, right? He doesn't actually believe in the stuff he spouts, it's just a way of making him cash."

"And getting all the girlies. Don't forget that bit. And you know, we women are easily fascinated by a bit of novelty." She winked.

Adie gave a hysterical sob. "God, I fucking hate him. Maybe I should have just stayed down there, and fucking bitten him."

That startled a laugh from Siân. "How revolting." She made heaving noises. "Not sure you'd have wanted to explain it to the boss afterwards."

No, but she wasn't sure she fancied explaining any of her antics this evening to him. He'd told them to stay on the boat, yet here they were.

The party was still going on in the Heb-Sed court. Tempted as Adie was to nip back to the VIP pavilion to renegotiate with Ihsãn, she knew it would achieve nothing.

"This way." Siân got them out of the party without having to wade through the crowd.

Most of the vehicles in the car park were crammed into one end, but a single car stood slightly apart in a wider bay.

"Reckon that's his?" Siân nodded towards the sand-coloured Mercedes. The plate was Egyptian, but a figurine of Sadler dangled from the rearview mirror and sheafs of promotional bookmarks covered both the dash and the parcel shelf. The driver—local, by the look of him—was asleep over the wheel.

"You don't think he might have left it in the boot, or on the backseat?"

"Get real." Adie attempted to tug Siân away, but Siân gently but firmly uncurled Adie's grip from her clothing. "I think it's worth a peep."

Adie raised her arms in surrender. "It's not going to be in his car."

"It's in his car," Siân said pointing through the window.

"No way. What do we do, smash a window and grab it?" She started looking around for a rock and found nothing but sand. In films guys used their elbows, but hers were currently bare except for a thin layer of voile, not leather covered. Moreover, she'd probably just break her elbow and wake the driver without even putting a crack in the windowpane.

Siân had crouched. She waved at Adie to do the same. Then gently, gently, she tried the rear door.

"Oh my God. Oh my God!" Adie mouthed. "No way."

Siân inched the door wider, just enough to get her arm inside, and after a few nail-biting seconds she pulled the journal through the gap.

The driver continued to snore.

That way, Siân pointed, indicating Adie should lead.

She left the door just open a sliver, so it didn't make a noise as the latch engaged.

They stayed low and scuttled over the empty ground to the nearest car, then moved between the rows until they were back at the Land Rover.

Once they were inside, with the doors locked. Adie squealed. "Oh, my, God! You have not just lifted Jacob's journal from that car! No way! It's going to turn out to be his accounts book or something like that." She snatched the book from Siân, who started the engine. The front cover was embossed with Jacob's name and the dates it covered. "How is this possible?"

"Dunno. He wanted it on hand ready to make the exchange but didn't want to have it on his person? I didn't see much pocket space in what he was wearing."

True. Adie hugged the journal to her chest and breathed in the musty scent of old paper and fountain pen ink.

"So, early morning trip to Cairo?" Siân remarked, as they pulled out of the car park.

"Yes. No. I don't know."

"I thought you said—"

She'd only said that it was what Ihsãn wanted, not that she was ready to hand it over. "Siân, it belongs to the museum. I can't use it to..."

"Not even to save our skins... Killian's skin. You know, the man you're so hot for you're willing to sneak into pyramids to confront men with blue dongs for."

"Killian wouldn't agree to me trading it for that purpose."

"Alas, true." Siân took them out of the necropolis and onto the suburban streets.

"I want to help him, Siân. But I don't want to piss him off so much that he hates me afterwards." Theirs might not be the most stable or defined of relationships, but she'd invested her heart in it, nevertheless.

Siân nodded. "I know."

"I don't know what else to do though."

Sadler had littered the inside of the journal with thousands of coloured indexing tabs and transparent sticky notes.

"What if we copied it? Made a fake that we could trade?"

"Are you serious?" Belatedly, Siân remembered to turn on her headlights. "I doubt your man Fuãd is going to be fooled by some tea-stained pages we cobbled together overnight. Now if we had an expert forger on our team...."

Anton knew one, but... She stroked the leather cover. There wasn't time.

"Do you know if Killian's back yet?" He'd know what to do. She messaged Matthew, who responded that Killian hadn't yet returned. Nor was he at the Gezira apartment according to Jason, who he'd spoken to a little while ago.

"Where do you think he's gone? It's a bit concerning, don't you think, his being absent right now?"

Siân thoughtfully sucked her lips. "Nah, not really. If I were him, after today, I'd be in a bar drinking myself insensible."

Was that where he was? Alone somewhere, balanced on a bar stool surrounded by a sea of empty glassware. She clawed her fingers as a groan wriggled its way up her throat. "Dammit! Dammit, dammit, dammit! I can't believe everything has gone to shit like this and there's no solution."

Siân reached an arm across and patted her on the back. "Life sucks, sometimes. It's not always roses. In fact, it's hardly ever roses. Mostly it's just spade after spade full of shitty fertiliser that you pray is eventually going to produce some blooms instead of weeds."

"Very poetic. Also, watch out." She reached for the steering wheel, but Siân reacted, managing to swerve them around the camel standing in the middle road. They bumped over the surrounding verge, the left front wheel narrowly avoiding an irrigation channel. Back on the tarmac, Siân whooped and burst into crazed laughter. "Oopsie!"

Adie uncurled her arms from around her head and retrieved the journal from the footwell. She thought she'd grown accustomed to Siân's driving. "Your driving is bloody atrocious. How have you not killed anybody?"

"Sheer blind luck," her friend said. "If we're all forced to find new jobs, I'm going to have to check out the driving requirements for wherever it's based."

Adie yawned and rubbed her tired eyes. At least Siân was managing to keep a sense of humour about the situation. She was pretty sure she'd just left hers in the base of that pyramid.

"What did happen yesterday, Ades? You've given me dribs and drabs of it, but nothing concrete. It sounds like it was eventful."

"I'm frazzled, Siân. I don't really want to get into it."

"Yeah, but give me the highlights, anyway."

Highlights. Uh, yeah, no. A summary, maybe, as those two things were not alike. "Fine. I met up with Anton, who wasn't best pleased. I insulted him. We parted ways. I got hauled off the street and escorted to a Sadler meet and greet. He offered me the journal for photographs of the site. I told him where to shove that. Legged it. Ran into Anton again. Consequently, learned some shit, and did some shit. Had to call Killian to bail us out—"

"Wait. Hold up? You're going too fast. You called Killian to come rescue you from some situation you'd got yourself into with Doctor Hottie?"

"Please pay attention to the road, Siân."

"Please stop diverting attention from the story, Adie." Maddeningly, she swung the car left and right in a slaloming motion.

"Okay, stop it. Yes. That's the gist of it."

"Right. Glad we have that straight. So, tell me about the reunion of the exes."

"They didn't kill each other."

"Uh-huh. And? Come on, Ades, cough it up. Give this girl some deets. They used to be lovers, right? So, there was tension... Right?"

"Right." Somehow, she ended up saying rather more than she intended to and couldn't find it in herself to regret it. It helped to have a friend weigh in with an opinion. It helped too, to have said friend pat her on the knee once they were home, and promise they'd be there if things didn't work out. Not that Adie had got into all the details. In fact, she'd skimmed the juicy parts.

"I was just starting to feel at home here," she said to Siân as they sat transcribing page after page of Victorian travel narrative onto tea-stained paper.

"I'm not ready for it to end."

-49-

Killian

Killian wasn't one for drinking to excess or daydreams, but both seemed fine things just now.

Better than heading home.

Better than confronting the inevitable.

Which is how he ended up at the concierge desk of the Nile Ritz-Carlton, and thence the hotel bar. Also, how after an hour of drinking alone, he ended up leaving a completely ridiculous voicemail message for a person he had no business leaving a message for.

Anton turned up twelve minutes later, took one look at him and bought another round. Ten minutes after that, they were upstairs. Killian got a whole two paces into the suite, hadn't even manged to flick the lights on before Anton had him pinned against the wall and was roughing up his clothes and mauling his mouth like he meant to eat him alive.

Fuck! He'd missed this.

The roughness. The intensity. The sense that something more than his current project mattered in his life.

Had this possibility been in the back of his mind when he'd said, "Hey, I'm downtown," after the tone? Yes, maybe.

He hadn't been sure the other man would come.

Why would he?

Last night hadn't fixed things.

He'd known he'd come.

Leastways, deep down he'd believed in the possibility.

And thinking of coming, his mind was conjuring a whole range of visuals of how that might be accomplished, assuming Anton gave him a say in the matter, and considering how hands-on he was being, that wasn't a given. It was like he was determined to sweep Killian off his feet and make him forget anything beyond his touch. His hands and lips, and they were all that mattered.

Perhaps that was the truth.

Seemed miraculous in this moment that he'd managed to stumble through so many years without this man, this intense presence, in his life, right by his side.

"I should never have let you go," he said to himself as much as Anton. The other man caught him by the chin and looked him dead in the eyes.

"Yeah, well you're a stubborn jerk, but we're not doing regrets right now. Never mind the should'ves. I want you right here in the now."

He could vibe with that. It was surprisingly easy given the touches dialling up his libido. No deep thinking. Just lips and teeth, and the energy lighting him from within and crackling between them. The rub of the iron hard brand in his pants against the similarly hard rod in Anton's. Clawing and biting. Messed up hair and peeled off shirts. Stumbling into furniture and groaning when his knee hit the corner of a table and upset his balance.

And here was a thing, the only place he fell was right into Anton's arms, because his lover caught him. Anton caught him. Hauled him upright against his broad chest in the exact same way he'd done countless times before and would have kept doing if only Killian had let him. If he hadn't shut him out.

Sadler hadn't ruined what they'd had. He'd done it.

"Get out of your head you inscrutably self-obsessed arsehole."

He spat out a laugh, the novelty of being called out hitting him right in the vitals and leaving an indescribable warmth behind.

"I don't want you in the past. I want you now. Tell me you want me now, too."

So much that he just grinned instead of saying it, although he was bellowing it in his head. Good thing Anton had always read him like a book, dogears and all.

Anton got to work stripping him of his shirt, then possessively shoved a hand inside the front of his trousers. He didn't sweetly ask permission or hedge his bets with a, "Is this, okay?" Nope, he handled Killian's cock as if it were his right to do so. Like it was his favourite toy, and he'd bare his teeth and snarl if anyone tried to take it from him.

If any bugger else had tried that he'd have told

them where to get off. He didn't tolerate being pushed around. Didn't play nicely with those who didn't respect his authority. A therapist would no doubt tell him that was a reaction to all the shit with Sadler. They likely weren't wrong. Damn, shitting, bastard was out to fuck him up again. Anton manhandling him though... Anton showing his 'touch what's mine and I'll rip your throat out' side... His heart was thumping so damn hard, and he was ready to soothe his parched soul by drinking deeply from that well.

"Fuck me," he said into Anton's mouth as his legs collided with the edge of the bed. They knocked the table. He managed to steady the lamp.

"That really where you want this to go?"

Like Anton didn't.

And, yes, it was. He didn't want to be in control. For once, he wanted to devolve responsibility. Have someone else dictate, hold his hand, take the pressure.

He reached for the fly of Anton's trousers, only to have his hands slapped away.

"Answer me, K. Is this really what we're doing?"

"Stop asking fucking stupid questions."

A grin split Anton's painfully familiar face. "Well, then..."

Killian breathed him in. He sucked his tongue, traced multiple pathways down his neck, with both fingers and lips. The clothes came off, the remains of his and all of Anton's though for a few moments in the middle he was left clutching the bundled cotton of their shirts, while Anton swallowed the full length of his cock. He'd felt the pull of those sucks right down to his toes. Had made a lot of nonsensical vocalisations full of vowels and almost lost it completely.

Anton put a sharp stop to that. "You're not flashing out on me. I've waited too long for this. Get on the bed."

That was easy. All he had to do was fall backwards, but Anton spun him around, so instead of on his back, he wound up on all-fours, butt out, head down, and springy hairs brushing the backs of his thighs, and feeling not a shred of embarrassment about it.

Anton rough-handled his cock and balls. Sucked him from behind in a way that was both excruciating, and wildly exciting. Blood congregated in that place, and his face, if the heat tingling in his cheeks was anything to go by. Meanwhile, his skin came alive with an itch, that goddammit, he was going to scratch until he drew blood.

"You'll be happy to know I came prepared."

Behind him, a rustle from the piles of discarded clothing. Then a shoe arched across the edge of his field of vision and landed with a thud against the nightstand. A packet of lube hit the eiderdown beside his hand. Killian turned his head. Anton grinned at him, the corner of the square foil between his teeth. "Why yes, I did in fact realise this was a booty call."

Chalk that as a win.

Anton plucked the foil from his mouth with two long fingers. "I'd ask you to do the honours, my dear drunken fool, but I'm enjoying the angle too much."

He wasn't drowning in any sort of alcohol haze. He knew exactly who he was with and what he was doing. Would he regret it in the morning? *Pfft*, it wasn't going to get a look in when lined up beside all the other shit he'd have to face. Besides, Anton had downed more than a few shots too. Catch up time, he'd called it.

"Kiss my arse. I'm in no way pissed."

The warm hum of Anton's chuckle vibrated right though his body and straight into Killian's. It was like receiving a hug and feeling a purr all at once or leaning against a washing machine on the spin-cycle. They'd done that a few times in the old days. Fucked against the washer, home from a day of grimy digging, stripped to their socks and nothing else. It was a godawful visual—naked in socks—and utterly painfully perfect.

"I said, kiss me."

"Yeah, I heard your bossy arse. But we're not playing yes professor, no professor, I'll do everything you say, professor. We're doing this on my terms."

Damn. And yes please. "I wouldn't expect any less."

"Good. So, now that I know we're on the same page."

Anton's hands settled on his arse; his strong fingers dug into the muscle with enough pressure to bruise. Weird thing was, it turned his limbs to jelly.

Then, swish, swish, his thumbs traced the seam of his cleft, and the glide of his tongue followed.

He'd been sweating. Probably needed a shower.

"You taste hot."

The way the words rumbled in Anton's throat, saw off any worries in that department.

His face pressed more firmly into the cleft. Sparklers lit where his tongue probed. Killian's nerves sang notes his vocal chords attempted to mimic.

"It's been awhile, huh?"

"That obvious?" He coughed around another croon. His cock punched his abs, leaving behind sticky dots.

"I'd better go easy on you."

"You'd better not."

That earned him a couple of broad fingers worth of preparation, the tickle of which had him humming exaltations again. He started to tremble.

"Man, I've got to get in you."

Anton's hands left his arse and got busy with something. He claimed the packet of lube he'd dropped at Killian's side, greased them both up. "How's Adie going to feel about this, do you think?" He rose to his feet behind Killian and got a grip on his cheeks again. The thick bar of his erection slid against Killian's groove.

God, Adie! His heart did a weirdly painful skip. Would she understand? Actually, it was strange to lift his head and realise she wasn't here, watching them. She'd have liked this, he reckoned. She'd been all eyes for the two of them getting it on last night. "I reckon she'd be into it."

"You don't think she'll be expecting things the other way around?"

He hadn't considered it until now. She'd only really seen his bossy side. "I can be versatile..." The *can you?* he left implied. They'd done the whole switcheroo things a lot in the early days, less so as the years progressed, and they settled into what they both knew the other liked best.

Anton's grip tightened. He pushed, just a little. "I might be tempted in specific circumstances. Say, if I got to be inside of her while you were banging me."

There was a thought. One his cock got seriously happy over. While it was doing a jerky little dance and weeping happy tears, Anton kissed him mid-spine.

"Sucks that this is what it's taken to get us together again."

"A woman?"

"Your arch-nemesis."

A snake stirred in his guts. "I suppose the bastard has to be good for something." There was a circularity to it. Sadler bringing them together having been the thing that'd broken them apart.

Only it wasn't the whole picture.

Most of the blame ought to lie firmly at his door. He hadn't been able to handle the fact that Anton still had all the things he wanted but had lost, so in his frustration he'd torched the few things he still had.

"Ahh—you're seriously tight, K."

He untensed. "It's good. I like the sting." His muscles might not be used to this kind of workout anymore, but he was prepped, and Anton was teasing him with just the right combination of thrill and fire to keep him perky as they settled together.

"Feels so good." Anton's voice took on a sing-song tone, punctuated by mewls of pleasure as he began to stroke in and out. Not rushing but dragging the pleasure out of the pair of them in maddening waves that lapped at his body and made everything tight and tingling. A hum rose inside him, wrapped around his senses, causing them to vibrate in time. He felt the hairs rise across his body, the tickle of sweat where their bodies met.

"God, yes, take it. Take me."

"Yes. Deeper, please. Goddamned give me it."

"You want more of me?"

He groaned. Eating up the hope in Anton's voice nestled alongside the arousal.

Killian stretched back his head as his jaw moved. He scraped the next demand off his teeth. "I want all of you."

"Like this, professor?" Anton grabbed his hair and embedded himself to the root. Killian cursed like he'd been stabbed right through.

"Oh, that's interesting." Anton churned his hips again. "Professor." He chuckled at the jolt Killian made. "That really, really does it for you, eh? Professor..."

It really, really did. It was nonsensical. Illogical, especially when delivered in that bemused, slightly contemptuous way. That oughtn't to be remotely arousing.

"Stop it."

"Stop what, oh professor, professor."

"Shit, don't make me laugh." Too late. His chuckle stretched his cheeks into an ache the equivalent of the one he was feeling in his arse and completely at odds with the singing in his heart.

"Will you fail me if I do?"

"We both know there are only two grades. F if you fail to get me off—"

"And a shiny A+ if I do. That's a pretty low benchmark of achievement, K. Since we both know that all I need to do is keep doing this... Professor."

Shitbag! Also, true.

He'd only ever let Anton fuck him.

Had only ever wanted Anton to fuck him.

Anton bowed over his back and wet licked the side of his throat as he settled them into a taxing groove, hips gyrating, bodies moulded together, Killian's cock beating out their rhythm against his abs.

He closed his eyes and basked in the sensations of the sweet slippery fiction binding them. He'd have liked to have been able to look Anton in the eyes, but there'd be time for that. There wasn't an expiration date on the bond that tied them. It'd endured through all these years. He'd only thought he'd lost his soul mate, really, he'd just encased himself in ice.

Well, now he was officially blowtorching that permafrost.

It wasn't like it'd gained him anything.

Hadn't provided the protection he imagined it would.

The heat riding through him, had him panting for breath. Anton clung on, refusing to peel them apart, no matter how lathered they both were.

"I want to feel you come, K."

Anton raked a hand across Killian's belly. Then gripped his cock. He started milking him in tempo with the groan of the bed springs. Killian's arms gave out, pitching him forward, face to the mattress. Anton didn't let up.

It was hard to say who was making the most noise. Anton or him, as each thrust nailed him in the prostate.

Faster, harder, faster, harder. Static filled his ears, muffled those external distractions. Faster, harder, faster, harder. The effort of all that motion leaving him panting and his vocal chords dry.

He was losing it. Helpless in the face of such a sustained assault on his senses. A handful of thrusts later, his balls seized up and called time. He shattered, spilling what was surely buckets of come over Anton's fist and the formerly crisp white eiderdown.

"Fuck," he moaned. "Shit and holy fuck!" The pleasure kept on wringing joy out of him. Pulling it from he wasn't sure where, the hairs on his head, the soles of his feet. The rest of his body caved, joining his face in cushiony heaven while still riding the high of release.

His hand still fisted around Killian's hair, Anton wrenched his head to one side, and bit down on the soft juncture of neck and collarbone as he unloaded deep inside of him.

Neither of them moved for a score of... it felt like minutes, was probably only seconds.

He'd sweat a bucket. They both had, although not all the damp beneath him was down to that. "Are you going to let me roll over?"

Anton released his hold on Killian's person, and rolled in the wrong direction, landing with a thump on the carpet. Killian peered over the mattress edge. "Are you all right?" he asked, unable to stifle a laugh.

Anton huffed. "Never better." He peeped up at Killian, wearing the same daft grin Killian saw on his own face reflected in the man's inky pupils. "Wouldn't mind a hand up though."

Killian extended one. Not that the way he was currently sprawled provided for much in the way of leverage. After a failed first attempt, Killian backed off the bed, and helped Anton gain his feet from a standing position.

Upright and facing, the jolts of electricity that had connected them continued to arc between them. Anton gave a chuckle, and leading with his thumb, planted a kiss on Killian's lips.

"You're fucking something else, K."

If he hadn't still been so cabbaged by round one, that might have started round two.

"You too."

"I fucking love you, you know."

His heart gave another hiccup. "You barely know me anymore."

"I loved you before. I love you now. It's probably dumb of me, but there you go. Truth is nothing's changed. Not for me. I fell hard the day you parked your stinky sports bag in the space next to me in that lecture hall and I'm still yours now."

I'm yours too. He didn't get to say it, because Anton excused himself to perform some clean up.

It was still on his mind when they settled on the bed together a couple of minutes later, and Anton rested his head against Killian's shoulder.

"It shows that we're not two twenty-something's anymore. Time was, me landing on my back on the floor wouldn't have slowed anything."

"We're not old."

"Older. And I like to think a fraction wiser."

Was it wiser to hold his cards close or admit the truth? What would holding back gain him? Not protection. Not a shoulder to lean on when he damn well needed one.

"Anton, I never wanted you to leave."

His soul mate met his gaze. "I never wanted to."

"It's on me. I know it is. I pushed you away. I was a failure, and I craved everything you still had. If you stuck around, I figured I'd destroy you too. I told myself it was better if you went."

Anton sighed. "You know, I've never really been all that far away. I figured if you ever changed your mind."

"I changed my mind five minutes after you left. I was just too fucking stubborn to say so. I loved you so much."

"Loved?"

"Love," Killian admitted, planting a kiss on the top of his lover's head. "I love you, and I think you ought to know that I kept the ring."

Not satisfied with the head kiss, Anton tipped his chin up for a lip smooch.

"At least you haven't been wearing it all this time. It might have given you gangrene."

They stayed that way, dozing, breathing one another in, holding one another fast and being held, until Anton's phone beeped. He fished it off the floor and turned it off. When he turned back to Killian, his eyes were swimming with questions.

"Do you want to tell me what prompted this? I mean, I know you were angling for a means of hooking up earlier when you dropped me off, but I wasn't expecting you to actually call. Something happened, right? More than the shit already going down."

He didn't really want to talk and dredge all those spiky feelings out into the open. Living in the bliss of Anton's embrace was far more appealing. There was no containing the way his lips peeled back off his teeth though when he thought of Sadler.

"I'll take that as a yes."

Killian bunched down the bed so he could rest his head against the pillow and stare up at the white expanse above him. Many the late night conversation he'd had with such vistas. Cracked ones, stained ones, 80s artistic Artex throwbacks, even the too often bug harbouring one of his cabin on the houseboat. The good thing he'd found about ceilings is that they weren't big on advice giving. They just stoically heard you out, didn't get antsy about how long he spent ruminating, and didn't demand follow-ups like therapists did.

In the end, it was probably the fact that Anton didn't press him that convinced him to share the joys of Sadler's blackmail and the university's master plan of a solution.

"And you agreed?"

Anton hadn't been able to stay lying down and listen. He was upright, still on the bed, but looking like he might bounce onto his feet at any moment and run off to do battle on Killian's behalf.

It gave him the warm fuzzies.

"I didn't feel like I'd got a whole lot of choice. It's better that he sinks one career over dozens. And you know he'll not have any qualms about doing it. Wipe out an entire department,"—Killian shook his head—"no skin off his nose."

"He really is a total shit head."

No arguments there. A minute or two of brooding resentment passed. "You always maintained he was. I should've listened. I think it was the only thing you called him for the entire first week he was around."

Anton nodded in approval of his own apparent wisdom. "Must a had a premonition about the bugger."

"Nah, he just pissed in your water bottle. Do you not remember?"

He blinked, confused. "You obviously do."

"Curse of a fucked-up mind."

"Are you sure the water bottle incident wasn't Eddie Owens?"

Killian puffed a strand of hair out of his face. "I'm sure. Although, you had a name for him too."

Anton pitched onto his side, head propped on his hand, and began idly tracing the tattoo inked onto Killian's ribs. "Eddie who was forever chasing after Cassia Wang?"

"That's him."

Anton made another circuit of his ankh. "I think you're right. Eddie was..."

"Eeyore," they both blurted together.

"That's it. And Cassia was Pooh, because she found that dinosaur turd on that dig in France. What happened to her?"

Killian heaved a breath through his nose. "Last I saw mention of her, she was excavating a site along the East African Rift in Kenya."

"I think I quite fancied her."

"Everybody did."

"Not you. You were into Leila... Leila Sims, remember her?"

"We slept with her."

"That's right. We did. Naughty us." He rolled onto his front and slithered down the bed a way, a mischievous smile on his face. "More than once, as I recall. In fact, wasn't she the first woman who let us double—"

"Do not say that word. I hate that expression."

"Dick?"

"Especially in that context."

"Prefer to save it for Dicky McDickface?"

"I think I preferred shithead. It's easier to say with sufficient emphasis." Not that he wanted to spend his time thinking about that particularly persistent wart.

"What are you going to do, K?" Anton splayed his hand flat over Killian's abs.

Killian stared at that palm. The familiar blunt tips of Anton's fingers, the missing nail on his little finger, a casualty of a mole that had grown in the nail bed when he was a kid.

"I'm going to show up like I'm supposed to and let him have his factoids and take his pictures." Because every other scenario would result in more people being hurt, more lives being upended. If he took the fall, then the rest of them would survive. He'd be the poster child for rotten decisions, so that they could carry on doing what they loved.

"I should head back to the boat."

"Why?" Anton kept his hand on Killian's abs. "What'll it achieve? You'll all sit around chewing things over and nothing will change. An answer isn't suddenly going to rise from the Nile. Now if you'd said, I need to go and make sure Adie's okay—"

"Josef said I'd ruin her."

"—I'd understand where you were coming from. And you're not ruining her. You're doing the exact opposite. You're doing everything you can to protect her."

Not quite everything, or he wouldn't have started an ill-advised relationship with her.

"What's the plan there, K?"

Apparently, years apart hadn't dampened Anton's ability to see right into his head.

"What do you mean?" he bluffed.

Anton's expression settled into one of stony stoicism. Still, amid the stillness, flames burned in the dark hearts of his eyes. "She's into you, and you're into her. I don't think it's unreasonable to ask how you're intending to juggle things, given where we are now. How about I make it easier? She's totally up for dating us both."

"Shut up." He wasn't in the mood for joking around, and there was a world of difference between having a threesome with two guys and committing to a polyamorous relationship with them.

"She begged me to give you a blow job to convince you to get on board with the idea."

"She did not."

Anton lifted both eyebrows.

"Guess her mind was addled."

"Or she really knows what she wants and believes in going after it."

That was a startlingly accurate description of Adie. The minute she had her sights set on something she was all in, leading with both feet, consequences and details be damned.

"Is that what you want?"

Anton, on all-fours, stalked him up the length of the bed, until he'd slithered over the top of Killian body, and was looking him in the eyes from a distance of an inch. "I like her. And I'm massively into you. Can't think of a damn good reason not to board a solar barque with the pair of you and sail across the heavens. What's the worst that could happen?"

"We wind up in the underworld." Killian pushed against his shoulders, but Anton refused to budge.

"Don't be such a stubborn mule. I'm handing you a chance of a lifetime. It'll be amazing, and it's what you want. Think on it, you'll have two of us you can attempt to boss around and call you professor."

"You always sound so fucking insincere when you say that."

"Professor," he purred, making Killian's toes curl with the way his voice vibrated, even though he was still being glib. "Besides, you're going to need something to do with your time."

That was painfully true. He sighed and closed his eyes. Barely a second later, Anton bumped their brows together, and then their noses. "What say we revisit this after I've tried out the cock sucking part. Adie was quite insistent about me using that as a sweetener." He shifted a hand between Killian's legs, which caused him to sink deeper into the pillows.

A little persuasion wouldn't hurt.

Anton winced and put a hand to his side.

Goddammit, he was still healing a knife wound, and here they were engaging in vigorous sexual gymnastics. "Anton—" He reached out.

His lover slapped his hand away. "I'm fine. It's just a twinge. And I have the perfect thing in mind to stop me focusing on it." He bobbed his head lower.

Killian arched, already anticipating the hot breath on his skin. The slow pulls. Heat.

His hand fastened on Anton's hair.

Adie had floored him when she'd gone down on him in the workshop that night. She'd sure figured him out. It couldn't be a coincidence that she'd suggested this method of persuading him.

Damn.

Anton worked him slow. There wasn't the urgency of earlier, so he was taking his time and making the exploration thorough. Licking, nuzzling against the shaft, tracing his fingers across tender places. I'm going to blow your mind with bliss, his actions said, and I'm gonna do it at a pace that's going to have you begging for mercy.

Yeah, his stamina wasn't that good. Not when Anton kept hitting his crown with this feathery sort of tickle at the culmination of every suck, and definitely not when he started swallowing around him.

Killian's head came up as he blissed out, shoulders following as he spat a string of exaltations. When he was done, he flopped back down against the overstuffed pillows, and huffed a breath from the base of his lungs. For a moment, he stayed perfectly still, eyes closed, focused on the quiet inside himself. Then, he attempted words and managed only a feeble croak until he cleared his throat. "Okay."

He looked along the length of his body, and found Anton looking back at him, a cat-like grin on his lips.

"So says the well-laid man."

"So says the well-laid man," he echoed. A yawn stretched his mouth. "I should probably sleep." He'd have to rise early tomorrow to make sure he was at Saqqara at the appointed hour. "Although if you want me to return the—"

"Sleep," Anton insisted. "I'm not going anywhere."

Taking comfort in that thought he drifted off with surprising ease.

-50-

Adie

Adie lyingly told herself that if Killian had returned by morning, she'd have consulted him before heading into Cairo. But he didn't, and therefore she couldn't.

Siân dropped her at the train station shortly after six. From Al-Badrashein, she caught a slow train into Cairo. Siân had offered to make the trip with her, but in the end, they both agreed that someone ought to be around when Killian did turn up, and that it probably shouldn't be Matthew.

In any case, Killian would need support while dealing with Sadler and the officials, and Matthew with his two black eyes wasn't fit for the task.

Once in downtown Cairo, Adie headed towards the black-and-white striped Al-Ghoriyya complex, and from there south, following Google maps walking instructions through the city to the location on the card Ihsãn had given her.

Turned out the cafeteria where she was to meet Ihsãn sat nestled between one of Cairo's last remaining tarboosh-makers and a bizarre curio shop, with dried hedgehogs hung in the window.

Adie eyed the saloon-style doors apprehensively. Even out here on the street she caught the reek of tobacco smoke and sweat. Siân had repeatedly warned her to stay clear of the *baladi* bars, where the only women were prostitutes. But she had no choice. If she turned away now, the tide of publicity generated by Sadler's book would sink the project and Killian's career, along with every member on the team. With virtually no experience, she was unlikely to find anything else. "Be brave," she told herself. "Your future depends on it."

Not that this was really about that. Not anymore.

And it was likely going to come to nothing.

Her eyes adjusted slowly to the dimly lit interior. Six stone steps led down into a small square room, cluttered with tables, where coiling tobacco smoke hung like a cloud at shoulder level, obscuring both the customers and the bar. There were few patrons; a group of three old men positioned around a backgammon board and two loners, one at the bar, the other drawing heavily on an apple-scented sheesha.

The clack of gaming pieces and the low burbling of the water pipe ceased as she crossed the bare floor. Adie clenched her fists tight and took comfort in the bite of her fake wedding band. She couldn't see Ihsãn, so she guessed she'd have to ask at the bar.

"I'm here to meet Ihsãn Fuãd. Is he here?" she asked the gaudily dressed bartender, whose washed out *galabeyya* seemed to be made of tie-dyed polyester. To her relief, he nodded and pointed towards a beaded curtain, behind the man with the water pipe.

Adie scurried between the tables, then paused before the tacky curtain and parted it warily. In the centre of the small room beyond was a pitted table, surrounded by chairs. There was no occupant. Fearing a trap, Adie took a hurried step back, only to feel the terrifying sensation of warm breath tickling the back of her neck.

"Doctor Hamilton," said a voice. The third member of the backgammon trio stepped around her and held open the beaded curtain. "I am Ihsãn Fuãd. Will you join me?"

Adie glanced suspiciously at the wizened man. "I'm sorry, you're not—"

"I see you are cautious. You're wise, but I assure you I am Ihsãn Fuãd. The man you spoke with yesterday evening was my nephew. I send him out sometimes. It keeps him sweet, and as you see, Doctor Hamilton, I'm an old man. I prefer a gentler pace of entertainment these days, and less noise. Please, join me where we may speak freely. Some refreshment?"

"No... Thank you." She accepted the offered chair, facing the beaded curtain.

After a moment observing her, Ihsãn settled opposite. "Do you have what was asked for?"

Adie unfastened her satchel and took out the journal.

An avaricious twinkle shone in Ihsãn's dark eyes as he looked it over. She did not offer it to him.

"You hesitate..."

"I can't give you this... It's a fake."

"I see." He nodded. "Where's the original? I know you have it. My men watched you and your companion take it."

They had?

"It belongs to the museum."

Ihsãn steepled his fingers before his mouth. He seemed more bemused than angry. "Yes. Yes, it does. I'm not surprised that you're unable to hand it over." Adie put the fake back in her satchel. If there was any bonus from its creation, it was that she was now familiar with the journal's extremely tiresome entries. William Jacob had been an opinionated git, and few of those opinions had aged well. She was surprised his daughter, Eugenia, hadn't had an affair with a busboy just to spite him.

"I guess this means I should leave you to your day."

Ihsãn gave her another wrinkled smile. "That depends, Doctor Hamilton. My nephew demanded a rather ludicrous amount, I believe."

"I have no money, and I won't trade information."

"I was thinking more of a service."

Her heart sank.

He reached out to her but stopped shy of touching her. "Hear me out, please. It is, I will admit, an unusual and rather unorthodox request, but... Well, we will see. Najĩb, bring me that parcel, please."

One of his compatriots brought him a package. It was roughly twelve inches long. For a wild moment Adie thought the battered jiffy bag contained the missing section of mural, but the item he withdrew was cylindrical. Ihsãn unrolled it from the protective swaddling of bubble wrap, revealing the item to be the severed pride of some ancient sculpture.

Adie frowned. What did he want her to do – identify it?

"Greek, I believe," he said, dispelling that possibility. "Probably 5th century BC. I had it shipped from Alexandria last week. I have a buyer ready, but he has rather specialised tastes. Which is where you can help me."

Adie's frown deepened. Her gaze shifted uneasily between the marble cock and Ihsãn's wizened face. "What exactly are you asking of me?"

"You don't have the means of paying me for my information. You've denied me the sale of what will be a very valuable book come tomorrow. What I'm presenting you with is your final option. I'll give you the information you need to find your precious missing cock, and in return you'll give mine a polish."

If she hadn't already been on her feet, she'd have got up fast now. "You expect me to have sex with you?"

"Gracious, no. I'm a happily married man, and you are not my type, Doctor Hamilton. This is not about me, rather my client." He offered the severed phallus to her. "He collects..." He seemed to be searching for the right word.

"Dildos," one of the pair of guards who'd

materialised at the door supplied.

"Yes. That's it. Thank you, Najīb. He collects such things, stolen from statues. This is the same client that wished to purchase the journal. It's a curious fascination, do you not think? But of course, the world is full of curious men."

"I'm still unclear what you're asking of me."

He placed the stone cock in her hands. "Have you heard, I wonder, Doctor Hamilton—you strike me as a worldly woman—of a thing they have in Japan? Vending machines, where one may purchase the worn undergarments of young women. It is the fact that they are worn that gives the little scraps of cotton their value. They come with pictures attached and some minor details about their former owners."

Oh, God! He expected her to masturbate with it!

"We can, of course, provide you with a private space, and we will need photographic proof. Neck down, your face isn't necessary. In fact, he prefers it that way." The man from the previous night, Ihsān junior, as she now thought of him, entered carrying a Polaroid camera and set it on the table.

"Am I expected to come?"

Ihsān looked briefly confused, then flashed her a grin that displayed his discoloured teeth. "It just needs to be wet. To have been inside of you."

This was bullshit.

He raised his hands. "I promise you, in exchange I will give you the exact location of the item you seek."

"How are you so certain of its whereabouts?"

"It's a unique item, Doctor Hamilton. One that

has stuck in my mind all these many long years, and for many a reason. The one that is of relevance to you being the fact that I hid it, with the intention of stealing it. It is of course possible that it is no longer in that place, many years have passed, but... I'm inclined to think otherwise."

One of the two backgammon players stuck their head through the beaded curtain. "Sadler's on the way."

Adie's heart leapt into her throat.

Ihsãn, nodded to the fellow, who went back to his game. "I'll offer him the same arrangement. It'll take him twenty-ish minutes to arrive here from his hotel. He will no doubt have a lady or two in tow or will summon one with all haste who is ready to do his bidding. Or he may provide me the cash. His choice."

Adie sighed. This was bollocks, but she couldn't let Sadler win. "You said I could have some privacy.

"Of course."

Privacy consisted of a square stone room with nothing but a chair in it. The wooden frame of which wobbled on the uneven floor as she sat.

Oh, God! This was not the sort of adventure she'd hoped for when she'd flown here. Still, there was nothing for it. And, hey, it wasn't really an adventure, was it, if something unexpected didn't crop up and test your mettle.

The smooth cock sat heavy in her hand. Heavy and cold.

Nothing ventured, girl!

With her back pressed against the door to

ensure there were no sudden entrances, Adie shucked down her trousers and panties.

I'm doing this for you, Killian.

He'd never appreciate it, as she had no intention of ever telling him about it, but that didn't stop her envisaging him watching her. Making the odd corrective comment.

Whenever you feel ready, Ms Hamilton.

Heat flooded her cheeks as she pressed the cold tip of the dildo against her split.

She pictured Killian in the chair. The sculpted lines of his jaw as he maintained that frosty expression. Only in his gaze could she find any softness—a brush of lavender around the rims of his irises.

You're stalling.

Well, I was awaiting your instruction. I know you like things done in very particular ways.

Use your intuition, Adie.

She shook her head. *That isn't something you'd say.*

I'm saying it now. In this context.

So, I'm supposed to intuit what will best turn you on?

He's a guy, Adie. Anton had joined their little play party. *And you're flashing him your muff. It won't much matter what you do. Go ahead, rub that cock against your lips, tease your clit with it. Ride it like you rode the pair of us. Any of those things are going to turn him on.*

And will they turn you on too?

The mere thought of you turns me on.

This was for them. For a future where the scenario in her head had even half a hope of existing.

Adie dropped the dildo onto the table at which Ihsãn Fuãd sat, creating a new dent in its pitted surface. She put the camera and photograph—face down—beside it.

Ihsãn carefully retrieved the stone cock, touching only the very base of it and rolled it in its original bubble wrap.

"Now tell me," Adie demanded, all too conscious of the minutes ticking away and Sadler's imminent arrival.

"You're very hasty for an academic," he remarked. "Do you have some paper? You may wish to take notes.

Adie produced her phone. "I have a dictation app. Go ahead."

-51-

Adie

"Anton, I'm outside the Cairo Museum. Can you meet me here?" The day was already threatening to become meltingly hot, hence the battery on her phone was already drained down to half. Adie frowned at it in frustration. She hadn't thought to tuck her power bank into her bag when she'd left the boat.

"For a particular reason?" he asked.

"Yeah, I need to get into the bowels of the archives." He'd made it seem the easiest thing in the world to do when they'd slipped down there together and shagged one another senseless. She needed a similarly smooth entrance and exit this time around.

Of course, the museum had been packed with Sadler groupies that day, so security had been busy.

"You've located it?"

"Possibly," she hedged. "Leastways, I have a lead."

"Okay, I'll be with you in two minutes. I'm just across the street."

"You are? How come?"

"Look, where are you? I'm just crossing the

road."

Perplexed by his nearness, Adie looked around. She was nestled in a corner of the entrance garden next to a bunch of busts. "I'm by the August Mariette memorial."

"Spotted you."

Sure enough, there he was, strolling across the paving that crisscrossed the grass, dressed in western clothes—black, in this weather!—and smelling like he'd got out of a shower five minutes ago. The still damp ends of his hair as he gave her a swift hug seemed to confirm that.

"Where've you come from?" she asked, fearing it was a hot date in a hotel suite. The Ritz-Carlton hotel stood just across the street.

"I'm just up and about early. You look as if you're about to burst with excitement. I take it your meeting last night paid off."

Heat washed up her neck and through her cheeks thinking of all that had happened the previous night, but more especially what she'd done this morning.

"It's kind of a long story. One that'll have to wait. We need to do this quickly before Sadler arrives and beats us to the prize."

Anton glanced at his wristwatch.

"Sadler will be on his way to Saqqara, Adie. After the lengths to which he's gone to access your dig, he's not going to show up late."

Interesting. She hadn't told him anything about what was going on with Sadler. He'd known about the Matthew stuff, but not that Sadler had demanded access to the dig. Who'd told him? Killian, or one of his faceless contacts.

Had he in fact spent the night with Killian in a hotel suite?

She realised her brows were rising, when Anton squinted at her.

Adie wiped the expression from her face. It was their business if they hooked up, and she couldn't be angry about it. She'd even pressed Anton to smooth things out.

So the three of them could be together. Not so they could get back together and make a new lifelong commitment only to each other.

"Adie? Do you have a storage unit number, or something?"

She nodded at him. "Or something. Like I said, I need to get into the basement."

"Ah. It's like that, is it?"

Adie began walking towards the main entrance, leaving him behind a moment until he put those long legs to use and caught up. Yes, it was like that.

He clasped her hand, turning her to him. "Are you sure you want to do this?"

"It's not stealing it, Anton. I'm just borrowing it." As Ihsãn had pointed out, the item wasn't catalogued, so the museum wasn't even aware of its existence. Besides, she was only taking it to complete the mural. At which point, it would be part of a state-owned historical landmark. "If I wait around to complete all the paperwork, it'll be too late. And Sadler's certainly not going to." He had numerous acolytes all tripping over themselves to do his bidding. He'd send them to fetch it, and while most of them wouldn't get past the cordons, eventually one of them would slip through. "As soon as we've confirmed it's our missing fragment, then..." Well, she'd let the relevant antiquities bodies figure things out over where it belonged. And honestly, "How will anyone even know I found it here, if I don't tell them? I can say I found it on location, amongst all the other plaster fragments."

"He'll know."

She knew exactly who he meant.

She resumed her trek towards the door.

"Don't try to pull the wool over his eyes, Adie. It'll only backfire. You need to be honest with him, at least."

They reached the museums grand arched entrance. There was no queue yet. Only the early birds were currently about, all sunhats and fans, and smelling of coconut sun cream. They paid their money and went in.

"Have you seen him since we spoke last night?" Adie asked, marching them away from the other visitors. "He never came back last night."

"I've seen him," he confessed. So, what she suspected was true.

"And?"

"And he's hurting as you'd expect. He's trying to cling onto something he knows is slipping away from him, and he's determinedly playing the martyr, so that the rest of you suffer the least disruption to your lives as possible."

She turned to face him. "What does that mean?"

"It means, he didn't have to agree to this shit with Sadler. He could have told the bods at the university to swivel. He chose not to throw them, you, his team under a bus."

That was not how he'd presented things in the email... Although, she guessed reading between the lines... "Fuck!" The exclamation earned her a tut from a passerby. "He shouldn't have done that. It's lovely of him, obviously, putting us all first, but—"

"Adie, it's a no-win situation. At least this way, he's the only one to look like a fool. The rest of you will still have careers, and I know you get that, because otherwise we wouldn't be here hunting for a bit of rock."

"Ahem, it's a bit of rock with a stupendously important willy on it. Now let's stop gassing, find it, and get it to Killian before that smarmy git ruins everything."

"I think you'll find it doesn't show quite what everyone imagines it does, Doctor Hamilton." Those had been Ihsãn's parting words to her. She really wished he'd been less cryptic.

Anton lifted those big shoulders of his, then settled them. "All right, let's do this."

There was no sneaking past the roped barrier this time. Anton just walked up and took them through it like he had a right to do so, and no one questioned it. "The trick is to believe you belong. Then everyone else is happy to believe it too."

Down among the utilitarian shelving, the lights popped into brightness and winked out like car headlights flicking between dipped and full beam.

The deeper they travelled; the more dust tickled her nose. Labels became increasingly hard to decipher. They crunched over several curled like dead bugs on the floor, others lay in little drifts mid-shelf. At least the shelves themselves were numbered at the ends of each row, even if she had to rub the markers with her cuff to remove the grime to decipher some of them.

"I'm not sure I've ever been in this deep," Anton remarked. "Are we still on the right trail according to your instructions?"

Adie waved at him to hush. She had one air pod in, playing Ihsān's instructions directly into her ear. "Anubis." They needed to find the statue, next. "He's missing an ear. Might be difficult to spot."

At the end of the next row, she turned right, Anton went left. "Adie." His hand landed on her shoulder, turned her about. The damn statue was massive, and only difficult to spot because it was lying on its side, with its broken ear against the floor.

"Turn left," she instructed.

"That'll take us back on ourselves."

"Only half a shelf. There should be an urn. Bottom shelf."

Anton with his long legs strode ahead of her. "Got it." He waited, squatted for her to catch up. The huge stone urn lay on its side, pushed onto the deep shelf with its base pointed outwards. Faint blue tracery of chalked Arabic covered the base. Auction house notation? But this had to be it. It was in precisely the location Ihsān described, and there were no other urns about. Around it, the shelves held nailed shut wooden boxes. The one next to it had been partially pried open in the past. Within, a mummified croc was basking in a bed of straw.

"It should be tucked inside. Help me get it out."

Sweat beaded across Adie's forehead and her wrists protested as they eased the Grecian urn from its resting-place and set it on its base. The top opening bore a flat lead lid that curved over the rim but had been bent back on itself at one end as if crimped with pliers.

"It looks like some sort of Hydria," Anton remarked.

Adie tried shining the torch on her phone inside, but it failed to penetrate more than an inch of the gloom.

"Smells of mouse."

Anton chuckled. "Stick your hand in there and I think there's a fair chance you'll find the desiccated corpse of one or two."

As long as all she found was dead stuff, and not anything that would scuttle up her arm. Her toes still curled as she wriggled her hand through the gap and into the urn's belly.

Something dry dusted against her fingers. Paper. She tugged, and a piece came away. Adie withdrew her hand. She held a scrap of aged newsprint that she dropped into Anton's open palm.

"It's dated twenty years ago," he said, squinting at the torn corner.

"That plays with the narrative." She pushed her hand in deeper this time, kneeling to extend her reach. "There's definitely something in here. It's hard to get a firm grip. I think it's wrapped in the paper." Another piece tore away as she tugged, provoking a growl and a grimace. "I don't want to have to smash this thing." Her middle fingertip grazed something fibrous. Instantly, her pulse spiked. It didn't wriggle. No teeth found her flesh. Adie released her breath. Twine. It was twine, knotted around a box. She manged to wriggle her fingers beneath it and use that as a means of lifting the box. It was like playing one of those claw games at the arcade. Gritting her teeth, hoping, praying it wouldn't drop too soon. A tuft of cotton packing poked through the hole allowing her to grab it with her other hand and keep it secure while she twisted the box to fit through the narrow gap.

The butterflies in her stomach did a loop the loop as she finally wriggled it free. Anton released a breath that whooshed against her bowed brow.

Ancient tape secured the box in addition to the fibrous twine, forming a cross. The tape, made brittle with age, flaked on contact. Anton produced a pocketknife and cut through the twine. Then it was simply a matter of lifting the lid.

Part of her didn't want to. What if it wasn't what she was looking for after all?

"Is there a way out of here that doesn't involve us walking out of the front door?" Even if Sadler had gone to Saqqara, he'd have sent someone here to retrieve the relic. "I don't want to walk into a posse of—"

"Adie. Just open it."

The lid made a prophetic sigh as she lifted it.

The skewed diamond shaped fragment was smaller than the gap in the mural, with rough edges from having clearly done battle with a chisel. The palette of colours was stirringly familiar though. Likewise, the stylised form of the painting, though even squinting at it, it wasn't clear what was depicted.

Carefully, she replaced the packaging and stowed it inside her clothing.

"Why no *galabeyya* today? The one time it would've been useful, you roll up dressed like a rock star."

Anton flicked his glossy hair over his shoulder. "You think I look like a rock star."

"You're head to foot in black. Long hair. Add a pair of shades..."

"How are you planning on getting that past the security checkpoint?"

Adie turned to the crocodile and started stealing his bedding. She stuffed it under her top, making herself a mid-term baby belly.

Anton smooched his lips together and grudgingly nodded. "Nice." He helped massage her bump into a more convincing shape. "And rather disturbingly, it suits you."

"Well let's hope it works, because my only other plan is to distract them with my recent arts and crafts project, otherwise known as a semi-accurate facsimile of William Jacobs journal."

He goggled at her, as if she'd said something astonishingly strange. "Okay." He backed away a pace.

Adie smacked him in the side, causing him to

inhale sharply between his teeth.

"Shit," she said. "I didn't mean to hit you where you're hurt. Siân and I made a replica, because we thought we might need it to negotiate with Ihsãn, but we didn't because in the end... You know what, it doesn't matter."

They came up from the basement chatting away like they were deep into some meaningful conversation about recent developments in the Valley of the Golden Mummies. Anton maintaining the bulk of the dialogue and Adie nodding and smiling along. The security guard even removed the rope for them to let them out.

Adie's back was bathed in sweat by the time they reached the exit. She kept expecting that same guard to run up to them and say there's obviously been a mistake and please step in here for a private word.

Anton put his arm around her shoulders as they left the building. "Pet your baby bump," he advised, as they passed unchallenged into the garden. "We go out of here. We should easily find a taxi." Tourists were coming and going all the time, and of course, the glittering glass wall of the hotel stood directly opposite.

A likely vehicle pulled up just as they reached the street. "You grab it," Adie said, sending Anton ahead a few paces to secure the ride, while she made a more ungainly waddle, thanks to the weight of her plaster baby.

"There's the bitch!"

Startled, Adie froze.

Nadine. "Shit!"

Anton must have heard her swear, for he about turned. Another three women emerged from a vehicle: Lana, Karima, and Nadine's friend Mert. Adie started moving backwards. Not the brightest of plans on a busy street. She jostled a couple of tourists, who loudly warned her to look out.

Anton caught up with her, turned her about, and grabbed her hand. He pulled her along, propelling her into an ungainly run along the busy pavement and round the corner onto the Corniche el-Nil, where they squeezed between a donkey cart and a microbus to weave across the honking lanes of stop-start traffic.

Christ, what they needed was Siân to show up in her battered Land Rover. For her to throw open a door without stopping, so they could jump in, and then speed away in a Fast and Furious high-octane style. Alas, there was no such helpful screech of tyres, only an increasingly wobbly baby bump.

"Slow down, or I'm going to spontaneously birth this thing."

"Not yet. There's a felucca landing up ahead. If we can get there, we can lose them."

She didn't waste time looking back to see if the women were pursuing, but jogged on as best she could, cradling her ungainly unborn child.

A small crowd stood gathered on the quayside. Anton pushed his way to the front, dragging her along behind.

"Full." The attendant waved them back. "Next boat on the hour."

"Please," Anton pointedly presented her.

Shoving her in front of him. He began an urgent exchange with the man in too quick Arabic.

Adie put her hands on her stomach, as much to hold her plaster and hay baby in place as to draw attention to her fake condition. She was lathered and probably red in the face. Her back hurt too.

Anton got out his wallet, and a bunch of Egyptian notes were exchanged. The attendant lifted the little chain link barrier and ushered her onboard.

"Get off at the stop for the Pharaonic Village. I'll meet you there."

The chain barricade went straight back into place behind her. Adie about turned.

Wait. No. They needed to stay together.

"Keep your head down. I'll draw them off." Anton stole the hat off the riverside attendant and tossed it to her. "Here, money for a new one." He pressed the cash on the man before he'd had a chance to protest. Then he took off at a run toward the bridge, as the felucca moved out into the river.

"Sit, sit." The pilot waved her towards a chair.

Adie wobbled her way into a seat near the rear between a child in holiday shorts, and a lovey-dovey young couple she suspected were newlyweds.

A cry reached her from the street. She threw a cautious glance towards the shore from beneath her newly acquired and vastly too large tarboosh. Four women were pounding along the pavement in pursuit of Anton.

"Mom, why are people chasing that long-haired man?" The child beside her demanded in accented English.

"Not sure, dear."

"He's a rock star," Adie said, offering him a grin and a shrug. "They probably want his autograph."

"No fucking way!" the male part of the couple exclaimed. "I didn't think we were known here."

His blond wife, leaned in tight to his side and planted a kiss on his stubbly beard. "Chill, Danger Mouse. They're not talking about you. We're good. Nothing is disturbing our honeymoon. Nothing. This is a zero-drama trip."

"Aw, congratulations," Adie offered.

"Thanks."

"Tanner. Look, look," the kid kicked the teenaged girl sitting opposite him. "That man's a rock star, like from the bands you like."

She plucked one earbud out and scowled. "Yeah, from some douchey Egyptian band. Not a proper one."

"Egyptian's have proper bands," he retaliated. "Don't they?" he asked the passengers at large.

"Definitely do," said the guy half of the couple. "They have some cool instruments too. Are you into metal? You should check out the likes of Cresent and Lycopolis."

"I like Dua Lipa," the kid said. "Tanner likes Black Halo, but only because she has a massive crush on that dorky dude that just joined them."

"Have not."

Mom and Dad gave their kids an irritable glance.

"Jackson, don't talk to strangers."

"'kay, Mom." He held his tongue for a fraction

of a second. "Did you know you have hay sticking out of your top?"

Several tufty bits of dried crocodile bedding were poking between Adie's top and her waistband. "Thanks," she said, and covered them up.

The boatman began pointing out various riverside landmarks, silencing the general mutter. Adie gave him her attention. Her phone battery was now all but dead.

You'd better be there, Anton Kelley, when I get off this boat. If he wasn't, she wasn't sure how she was getting to Saqqara.

Also, the Pharaonic Village, yet another place she hadn't yet made time to visit. Esther would have wondered if she was the same girl.

-52-

Adie

Anton stood waiting for her on the quayside when she disembarked. He ushered her straight into the back of a waiting Uber. Adie then spent most of the forty-minute journey to Saqqara alternating between picking bits of hay out of her clothing and staring at the plaster fragment she'd retrieved. Would her efforts count for anything?

The driver dropped them by Djoser's pyramid, saving them the body melting walk across the desert from the ticket office. Their usually nondescript excavation site was surrounded by a collection of vehicles and nosy onlookers. The largest of the vans bore a BBC world service logo and had a variety of communications discs mounted on the roof. There were similarly vans from a TV network and Al-Jazeera.

Adie muscled her way through the crowd of onlookers to the entrance way. Voices echoed from below. Another hollered at her from under a tarp that hadn't been there before today. Siân streaked towards her, stopping herself by catching hold of

Adie around the shoulders. Her momentum nearly sending the two of them tumbling down the steps.

"Did you get it? Please tell me you pulled off this miracle." She cast a wary look at Anton, then an expectant one at Adie.

Adie patted her satchel, into which she'd moved the precious fragment after birthing onto the back seat of the cab. "Who's down there exactly?" She trotted down the first couple of steps.

"Some Antiquities bods, the departmental head from the university, Sadler, and a couple of ne'er-do-wells masquerading his assistants. A lot of people with cameras." Siân tentatively followed her a couple of paces, while Anton remained at the top.

"Is Lucas with Killian?" Someone ought to be down there supporting him.

Siân made a particularly rude noise. "No. Nobody. Dr Vasser resigned this morning, or last night, but we found out this morning. He finally made the jump to Mark Leyham's team. Bastard."

"You can hardly blame him for saving his skin." Especially when he'd been paving the way to make that jump for so long. This Sadler nightmare was clearly just the incentive he'd needed to make the call and finally be on his way. "So how come you're not down there?"

Siân sighed into her sleeve as she wiped the sweat off her nose. "I got my arse handed to me this morning. My help is not required."

Adie paused, her mouth falling open. "He didn't fire you, did he?"

Siân gave her head a vigorous shake.

"Miraculously, no, but he looked as if he was considering it. His face when I had to explain your absence." She shook her head "Grim. Hence, I've been making myself scarce. He's made it absolutely plain I'm surplus to requirements. Adie, unless you have a magic charm, I don't know that you want to go down there. He's like the winter king this morning. I swear the air temperature drops at least ten degrees cooler in his immediate vicinity. "

"Did you tell him where I was?"

Siân gave a strained laugh and raised her hands. "I told him only what we'd agreed. That you went to see a man about a stone."

"Well then, he won't be surprised when I walk in with a plaster rock."

"Company. Incoming," Anton called from above. "Adie, you might want to get out of sight— the fan club have just arrived in the company of the tourist police."

"Keep them out here, please."

Her friend patted her on the back as she headed back up the steps. "I'll do what I can."

Adie scampered down the rest of the steps and entered the tomb proper. She was out of time.

There was only a single dude in the antechamber. He glanced at her, before returning to thumb scrolling his phone. In contrast, the wet fragrant heat of multiple sweaty bodies reached her before she set foot in the crowded second chamber. Competitor stations were standing elbow to elbow, juggling boom mics and hand-held cameras pointing at Killian and Sadler standing before the expansive mural. Whatever discourse was going on had clearly been running for some time, and Sadler was evidently building to the core of his theory.

Pharoah as god. Pharoah granting the gift of his seed. The importance of ritual in ensuring one's advance into both the afterlife and ensuring your place amongst the gods. It was all horribly convincing as presented, and there was Killian beside him. A world leading expert on the early dynasties, ready to back up all that gospel with scientific facts.

Except, she wasn't going to let Killian do that. "Um, professor," Adie stepped in front of the nearest camera, creating a barrage of complaints, and calls to cut, and people trying to shuffle her out of the way.

She ducked away from their grasps and marched straight up to Killian. "So sorry that I'm late professor."

He gave his head a subtle shake.

"I've got it," she held the fragment out to him. He didn't take it. "I'm sorry I'm late in bringing it across, it took a little longer to get it cleaned up properly."

"Adie, what are you doing?" He shifted so that he was largely blocking the view of her from the cameras and the scores of people irritably moaning about getting on with it. Sadler being the most vocal.

"Trust me enough to follow my lead on this."

It'd taken her most of the car ride here, turning the fragment this way and that to figure out what she was looking at. It wouldn't take anything approaching that much brain power once she set it in place and all the lines joined up. "Trust me, you want this recorded, especially after everything he's just said about following the path of the Pharaohs to enlightenment."

Killian's frosty gaze continued to bore into her. "Please," she tried. He still hadn't taken the fragment. "Forget everything. What are your instincts telling you?"

He opened his mouth.

"Not your brain, your instincts."

Lilac licked across his irises. He turned to the assembled audience. "My assistant has the missing fragment."

"I thought it was lost," said someone.

Killian smiled for the now rolling cameras. "It was recently rediscovered. We've been holding onto that fact until we were in a position to reassemble the mural. None of us have seen it in situ yet. I hope you'll join me in celebrating this moment of unification. Adie…"

He moved aside to allow her to slot the piece into place. Of course, the fit wasn't perfect. A century of erosion had enlarged the cracks that Jacob's chisel had made, and some large splinters remained missing, but the focus of the picture was restored. It was awkward to hold, but she did her best to keep it positioned securely, while not obscuring anything.

"Oh," said the man from the Antiquities authority. "That's—"

"Goodness!" That was the lady, Adie assumed was the Cairo University Departmental head. She grimaced, showing a lot of teeth.

"Not sure I much fancy this ascension to godhood malarkey, mate." The guy behind the foremost camera remarked, before panning right for a close-up of Sadler's face.

Both Killian and Sadler stood gaping at the mural.

Adie locked her elbows and studiously concentrated on keeping the fragment in place despite her aching arms.

Sadler's nostrils twitched, and his lips puckered, giving him a mean appearance.

Killian cleared his throat. Then he spoke. He gave his opinions in crisp and concise tones. He explained with a smile precisely what they were seeing. "In this uniquely preserved mural, in what was intended to be the Pharaoh Huni's eternal resting place and means of resurrection, we see him preparing for that final voyage to the stars, undergoing ritual castration at the hands of the high priest under the watchful eye of Horus. Only by suffering as Osiris had suffered before him; by having his body mutilated and rebuilt, could he ensure his worthiness to reside among the true gods and not just the living god kings that walked the earth.

"It is just across the desert here at Saqqara that the myth of Osiris was first recorded among the many pyramid texts depicted in Unas's pyramid tomb. Osiris, only came to full godhood after his death and mutilation at the hands of his brother Set, and his restoration to life after the goddess Isis retrieved his missing phallus and was able to breathe life into his body once more.

"And here behind us, we see the kneeling Isis along with her sister goddess Nephthys doing just that." He pointed to a section of the mural a little further along. A part Adie had never paid much attention to. All any of them had ever focused on was what was missing, rather than what was depicted all along. Well, all of them, it seemed, besides Killian.

"Just to clarify, Doctor Carmichael," the man from the antiquities authority said. "Why would an all-powerful pharaoh choose to undergo ritual emasculation?"

Sadler, who had been slowly sliding himself further and further off to the side, winced.

Killian deliberately moved so that Sadler was centre frame again.

"Osiris, while often talked about as being the god of the afterlife, is also majorly associated with divinity. One can only assume that by emulating his fate, the pharaoh hoped to attain a similarly divine status. Also, again recalling our myth, while Osiris is physically castrated, it is only after his restoration that he comes into his full magic and divinity, and fathers Horus. Meanwhile, he renders Set unable to produce children, thus diminishing him. To the Egyptians, the seed was both a source of great power and poison.

"Wouldn't you agree to that being the case, Dareth?"

All eyes turned to Sadler's now bleached face.

"I don't think..." He swallowed hard enough that his Adam's apple visibly bobbed. "I think there's been some mistake here... Not what I was led to believe... Not a discussion..." He raised his hand to block the view of his face. "Get me out of here," he barked at his two assistants, who, seeming to remember their purpose, sprang to life to hustle him out of the room.

Killian turned again to the cameras, all sophistication, and smiles. "If you'd be so good as to give me a moment, I think we might try another take after we've given Doctor Hamilton a break. Rest your arms now, Adie." He left her and jogged after Sadler and his entourage.

The university departmental head kindly relieved Adie of her burden, allowing her to slip out after Killian. She arrived to see him block Sadler's exit to the outside world.

"A word before you fly off, Dareth."

"What?" Sadler snapped. He'd run his hand through his hair one too many times so that instead of lying in its artfully sculpted drapes, it now appeared as if he'd just crawled from bed following a three-day binge.

Killian stuck out his hand, surprising the man into accepting a shake. "I just wanted to thank you for your time. Also, to say goodbye."

Sadler scowled. He attempted to withdraw his hand, but Killian held him fast. "Also, that if so much as a whisper about any of those photographs you have gets out in the wild, then I will personally make sure that the footage we've just shot goes out on every news channel, is sent to every news forum and fan site and conspiracist in existence. Hell, I'll hire a whole team of TikTokers to make memes about it and how dedicated to the pursuit of godhood you are. I'm sure you'll have a whole host of volunteers raring to help with your ascension."

~Ж~

Eventually the crews and the officials departed, leaving only Adie and Killian below ground. They'd found a case and foam packaging for the fragment, where it would remain safe until work began to reinstate it properly. That wouldn't happen until they were done excavating, so it would likely be months if not years down the line.

"Do I want to know where you found it?" Killian asked. They hadn't really spoken yet, not since that initial exchange before the cameras.

Adie apprehensively sucked her lower lip. Be honest, Anton had advised her. She wished he was down here with them now, not still above ground. Was he above ground, still waiting to determine the lay of the land?

"I'm going to assume not, given your silence."

"Can we not just pretend I found it here, and all that bollocks you said about us cleaning it up was true?"

He nodded. "We can pretend. It can be the truth as far as anyone else is concerned, but I want you to look at me and tell me you didn't steal it."

She kept her gaze on the fragment.

"It's more like borrowing."

"You stole it."

"I mean, not technically. It belonged to the state, and it still belongs to the state, so no change of ownership." She offered him a wary grin.

Killian's eyes were narrowed, but that lovely lick of lilac was there around the centre of his irises that gave him an air of mischief.

"You're not going to get me to regret it. I'm looking forward to watching the replay of Sadler's face when he realised."

"Adie." The dimple that kept flashing in his cheek, betrayed his amusement as he fought to keep his expression sober.

"Admit you're looking forward to watching it too."

"Neither of us will be watching it. I had them record multiple takes of the restoration for a reason. Unless Sadler gives me cause, the footage of him will remain on the cutting room floor."

"You mean that."

"I was very serious in my promise to him. As long as he holds up his side of the bargain, then I'll hold up mine."

"But you're obviously going to keep a copy, and how are you going to stop those reporters releasing stuff?"

"This is Egypt, Adie. It's easy to censor things. Oseye will make sure the university sees all the footage and approves what is and isn't released."

"And what does that mean for you, and us... The team, I mean. Not you and me, though I have some questions about that too."

Killian looked around at their surroundings,

taking in the stone walls, the mural, the fluorescent tape, and tripods. "Our work will carry on. I'll be dedicating my time to the project from now on. I've agreed with Oseye that teaching isn't the right fit for me anymore."

She couldn't have heard him right. "You're taking a sabbatical?" That had to be what he meant.

"No, Adie. I quit. I hate lecturing. Essay marking and teaching seriously piss me off. I've done it all these years because it felt like it was expected of me. That if I wanted to be at the top of my field, then I needed to attach myself to a university, but that's just not actually true. I don't need to lecture. Ninety per cent of my funding comes from external sources."

"But, surely—"

"What, I should cling to that safety net and the expectations of others? Teaching isn't what I came here to do. I came here to dig. To play in the dirt and root out things that had been lost. To find things like that fragment, like—"

"Ahem!"

He stared down at her, noting her folded arms and stubbornly up-tilted chin.

"Sorry, who rooted the fragment out?"

A smirk tugged his lips. He wet them. "You did," he said, begrudgingly. "But if you're expecting a pat on the back for it—."

"I mean, that would be quite nice. A bit of what a good worker you are, Adie. How clever of you to pursue all those leads and utilise your intuition. If it wasn't for you, Sadler would have made a right dog's dinner out of the project."

That made him laugh, and God, if that wasn't a sound she wanted to keep on hearing. The chime of mirth gave her butterflies.

"At the very least, I deserve a raise."

"How about a permanent contract?"

"Ooh!" She considered. "That does have a nice sound to it. You're serious?" *Please be serious.*

"I'm always serious."

She nodded, but she knew perfectly well that wasn't entirely true.

"I have one criterion though... or possibly two."

"Go on?"

"You need to agree not to go over my head again and take tips from Masud, and—"

"You realise it was a very good tip."

"—And, you have to write to Josef and tell him he was wrong, and that I didn't in fact ruin you."

"Oh," she said. "Uhnn! That would kind of be a lie. You have very definitely ruined me, at least in one very specific way. Then again, I'm not sure I want to be writing to Josef about that." Her old professor didn't need to know that she'd been having spectacular sex with her boss and his very sexy, very present right here former fiancé.

"Are you all done down here?" Anton emerged from the shadowy doorway. "I thought now all the fuss has died down we might... I thought the three of us might talk."

"We should talk," Killian said.

Adie dragged her gaze from one to the other. Anton with his masses of dark hair and his sensuality. Killian, his eyes now licked with lilac and absent of their former ice. "Must we? Would it not be easier for us to just try out the fucking part another time or three and see how it all pans out?"

-Epilogue-

Killian

From the kitchen on the *dahabiyya* Killian could hear them laughing—his team: Siân, Matthew... Adie. He'd heard the tale of how she'd robbed the museum three times over, or rather he'd overheard it, for she was being true to her promise, and not directly poisoning his thoughts with her misdeeds.

If he *knew* he'd have to punish her, and he didn't want that. She'd saved him. Not by means he'd ever officially approve of, but they'd achieved the necessary outcome. He was still here in Egypt. Still heading an excavation. Still doing what he loved.

And hopefully doing who he loved.

Better still, Sadler had scampered off, tail between his legs, and with any luck wouldn't be back to trouble him again.

Anton came in from outside. He stopped on the threshold a moment, head tilted, long hair trailing over his broad shoulders and a silly smile plastered across his face. "Am I allowed to come in?"

"Of course."

"I just thought I'd check, seeing as you're hiding

in here."

He wasn't quite so drunk on the day's outcome as the others. "I'm not hiding. I'm just not getting in the way of a good yarn." He cocked a brow.

"Aah, so that's what you're doing. Well as it happens, I think it's way past time you got in the way of that."

"Why's that?"

Anton approached and wrapped him in an embrace from behind. "Because those three could talk the ears off a fish, and I for one am listened out. I think its high time they all went to bed."

He chuckled as he nuzzled against the pressure of Anton's chin against his shoulder, enjoying the warmth of the embrace. "I'm not their dad, Anton. I don't get to dictate their bedtimes. Besides, is this really about them heading bedwards, or are you angling for something?"

Anton squeezed him tighter. "I'm angling," he admitted, planting a kiss on the side of Killian's neck just below his ear. "For a sleepover. Not because I want to bang you senseless or anything like that, just because your bed is way more comfortable than mine."

He laughed, and basked in that moment of contentment that followed, feeling both wanted and connected. "I did wonder why you suddenly decided you loved me again. I thought it might be to do with my amazing medical skills, but no, it's down to my expensive Airsprung mattress?"

"Well, it is nice and firm, and suitably large."

"Hmm."

Anton's lips slid upwards to Killian's ear. "You know we could just slip away."

"We could," he agreed, and yet they didn't because doing so would mean abandoning the person who'd brought them together, and neither of them wanted that.

Hot breath tickled his earlobe. "The mattress isn't why I love you, Killian."

He'd never for a moment believed it was.

"I love you for the same reasons I always have. I'm a romantic fucking fool."

He turned in Anton's arms so that they were standing lip to lip, knee to knee, arms draped comfortably around one another. "You're no fool."

"Am I not? I want something... unconventional, risky one might even say, when I could just content myself with the very good thing that's right in front of me and be entirely happy like that."

"It's not foolish to go after what you want. It's being true to yourself. Plus, we already had one go at it, and it didn't work out so well, remember. What if we need another stabilising force—"

"Some glue to hold us together."

"Precisely."

"So, we're agreed, but what about Adie?"

"I think we already both know what Adie wants. She's been clear about it." She really wasn't good at obfuscation.

"And you're sure about this?"

Was he? "As sure as I am about anything." As sure as he was about holding fast onto Anton, and letting his world fill up with colour and warmth again. No more frosty professor, no more bottling ideas up in his brain and only sharing them after they'd been triple baked.

Or at least, less of it.

"So, ninety-nine point nine nine per cent surety, not that you'll ever admit it." His lover's dark eyes twinkled beneath the kitchen light right before he captured Killian's jaw in his hands and kissed him hard.

Killian returned his kiss with equal fervour. Was this not admitting it? He'd always adhered to the belief that actions spoke louder than words. Anyone could open their mouth and make noises, but to show someone how you felt, through touch, through actions... that required effort. Anton made him complete. His heart turned over every time he looked at him, and a little bubble of joy started exploding in his mind.

"What is it he won't admit?"

And here was the other person who made him fizz despite his better judgement.

They broke apart at the sound of her voice, so that their chests no longer touched, and their fingers were no longer clasping one another's clothing. She smiled when they turned their heads to face her, but not before he'd seen her rake her teeth over her lower lip. If she'd been closer, he'd have pulled her into their embrace, and nipped any worries in the bud, but she'd stopped just over the threshold, leaving an irritatingly large distance between them.

"Have the others gone to bed?"

"Yeah." She ruffled her hands through her hair.

"It's been a long day. I just came to tell you that I'm going to turn in too. So,"—again her gaze raked over the two of them still standing in comfortable proximity, then she hitched a shoulder— "goodnight." She turned as if to head back out again.

"Adie."

"It's early yet," Anton said. "It's all of... ooh, quarter past nine. You're sure you don't want to stick around and hang out with *us* for a while?"

She paused, one foot on the deck, one still in the galley. "I did rise before dawn, but—"

"So did I."

The way she twitched prompted him to close the gap between them.

"You were together last night." She blinked as he took hold of her hand, her gaze watery.

"We were, yes, but please don't read into that more than you should. It wasn't planned. After the meeting I had at the university, I wound up in a bar—"

"So naturally you called your ex once you'd had a few."

"Naturally." He stumped up a self-deprecating grin.

"So, you're... what now? Together again? Boyfriends? Re-engaged? I think you might have mentioned it."

That had spiralled fast. The hurt in her voice made him reach for her, but she was prickly as hell. "Adie, I don't know." He didn't precisely know what he and Anton were. They hadn't defined it. What he was certain of was that any drama was too much drama after the last forty-eight hours. Additionally, there was no sense in them all stewing over something they were all so obviously on the same page about or would be if they...*he* managed to spit the words out.

"Adie, what you said earlier at the dig—"

"We might want to take this to your cabin, K?"

Possibly. Wouldn't hurt.

"What did I say?" she asked.

"That we should try things and see how it goes. I think we should."

"Huh?"

"We all want the same thing, so, why not try it."

On that note, he gave them both meaningful looks, then headed out onto the deck towards his cabin. Hopefully, she'd have wits enough to follow.

"Was that seriously an invitation to... Was it an invitation invitation?" he heard Adie ask. "Or just a—"

"I'm pretty sure it was an invitation to the pair of us to fuck his brains out."

"Was it?"

"I think you know that we want you, Adie."

"But yesterday—"

"A lot has happened since then."

It had. He'd crawled out from under the rock he'd been hiding under, and the world hadn't fallen on his head. Adie had proved that her intuition was something worth listening to, and Anton had helped them both stand tall.

"Did you give him a blowjob, like I suggested? Is that what swung it?"

That made him snort, and Anton full on laugh. "Not sure."

"Pretty sure I fell asleep," Killian hollered.

"Did you not do a very good job?"

"I did an epic job, hence noodle-brain."

They appeared in the doorway of his cabin a few seconds later, hand in hand, which put a smile on his lips, even though he did his best to smother it and play it cool. Like it was no big deal that the pair of them had just wandered in, whispering together and exchanging meaningful glances and elbow nudges. Nothing out of the ordinary about that at all.

"Did I miss a joke?"

Anton broke into a grin. He wrapped an arm around Adie's shoulder and leaning in, kissed the side of her neck. "Adie was just being very nosy about our former sex life."

"I was not." She swatted at him, which Anton neatly avoided by moving behind her. His attention though remained focused on her neck. "Killian, I wasn't. I wasn't."

"Yeah?" He raised his brows. Of the two of them, he knew who he believed. "What do you want to know?"

She goggled at him. "Nothing, it's not any of my business... Do you fuck each other?"

Anton's eyebrows curved. The pair of them exchanged a glance. He wasn't the least bit surprised she'd asked, not after the confessions she'd made the night before last when they'd been right here messing up his bed.

"What do you think?"

The muscles in his cheeks ached as his urge to smirk warred with his attempted composure.

Adie squinted at him, as if he were a fragment of some pottery jar, she'd just unearthed. Her cheeks gradually pinking, and her smile growing. "I think..." She mewled in response to Anton's exploration of her throat and gave a sensual shudder. "That current evidence suggests, yes, but I'd like to find out for definite through intensive study of the subject. Conduct a thorough and proper investigation into the matter."

"We could just tell you," Anton said into her ear.

She fanned him away. Of course she didn't want to be told. She was Adie. His protégé. Always up for exploration, adventure, and discovery.

"So, this study," he prompted her. "Go on."

"I think I'll make it a largely observational study. You know, watch and record."

"Record, eh?" Anton remarked. "Haven't you caused chaos enough with your photographic skills?"

"I meant on paper."

"So, sketches? Or perhaps a nice tally chart of who blows who, and who fucks who and how often and in what position."

"Are there lots of positions?" she said in deadly seriousness.

Anton exchanged a look with him. "A fair few. Although not as many as with three participants. Would that not be a more interesting study, do you not think?"

"Possibly. What do you think, Killian?"

She came to him then. His Adie. Hands clasped together before her like a downward facing prayer. The hope in her gaze planted a red-hot ember in his chest, for he knew with all certainty what she was truly asking. It was there in her eyes, in the raking of her teeth over her abused lower lip and the way she rocked forward onto the balls of her feet.

"Killian?"

He shrugged. "I suppose..."

"You suppose..."

He turned his back on her and undid the buttons of his shirt. In the mirror he saw her throw Anton some funky side-eye. Was she still uncertain about the reality of this? She didn't need to doubt. He was all in. Hadn't he just said as much?

He shed the shirt. His trousers followed.

"Damn," she whistled beneath her breath.

"The man has a fine arse."

"But wait, what's your answer? When you say suppose, what does that mean?"

Killian turned and rolled his eyes at the sight of them both still clothed. "I mean, sure, we can give this here triangular arrangement a go."

"You mean that?"

He didn't say things he didn't mean. And he didn't share half-cocked thoughts or jump blindly into things he had doubts about.

"You're agreeing to me dating you both? While you're dating each other. For us to be exclusive with each other?"

That did rather seem to be the gist of it.

"I am."

She wrapped herself around him in a full body hug that sent them both crashing down onto the bed. Then smooched kisses across his face. "Oh, God! I didn't think you'd agree. I know Anton said, and you were acting like you did, but I couldn't be sure. I needed to hear it. You won't regret it, sharing your fiancé with me. I promise."

"Adie, we're not..." He guessed they'd never officially broken it off, but then he'd also never officially said yes. "Ah, but am I sharing him with you, or are we sharing you... or maybe you're sharing me."

Anton joined them on the bed. "It could be all those things. I hope it's going to be all those things." He clasped each of their hands in his. "We're going to figure it out together."

"I thought you were only here for the mattress."

"I'm here for you, Killian. And for you, Adie." He kissed them both in turn. "Now, what do you say we all stop gassing so much and indulge in some saucy depraved acts that'd probably get us kicked out of the country if anyone found out about them?"

"Sounds good," he agreed. "Got anything in particular in mind?"

"Adie?"

"I'm not sure I want to get kicked out of the country."

"Then keep your lips zipped." Anton mimed the action. "Now, what depraved fantasy would you like to indulge?"

Oh, God! Choices. Too many choices. "I could start my study. Watch you two. Then again,"—she had her hands all over them both already—"I'm more of a doer than an observer."

No kidding.

Anton relieved her of her top, leaving Killian staring at her plain and very practical underwear. "We could both of us fuck you together again?"

"I did like that." A pink flush washed across her breasts and into her cheeks. "And I guess there's more than one way... one position to do that in."

"Several positions," he confirmed.

"And I don't even mean just the two of you filling my pussy. There are other options too. Like me sucking one of you while the other fucked me, or—"

"One in each door."

"Oh my God!" She gulped. "I'm not sure I'd hold it together if you did that."

"Not sure holding it together is really the purpose." Anton delved a hand inside her panties. "I see the notion of it certainly turns you on."

She blushed a pretty shade of cerise. God, he loved those blushes. Loved how easy it was to make her squirm, but also, that she never shied away from pursuing what she wanted, what turned her on... or the things that made her happy.

He needed more of that in his life.

He let Anton finger her for a while without interrupting, indulging a voyeurism streak he barely remembered having.

"She's pretty wet," Anton said to him after a while.

"Yeah?"

"Yeah. Wanna feel?"

She made a soft whimper as he slid his fingers between the V-shape Anton had made of his and coated himself in her honey. "Do you need my mouth there, huh?"

She moaned a little louder. Sounded like a yes.

"Say again."

"Yes, please, professor."

Anton shook his head at the title but didn't get in the way of Killian getting his face wet between her thighs. He played with her breasts while Killian ate her out and tongue-fucked her. It took barely a minute before his cock was begging him to quit with the warmup and get it wet.

"Bend her over," he said to Anton. "And for god's sakes, get that bra off her."

"Bossy."

"Adie likes that." And so did Anton, not that he encouraged in the same way.

Adie made the sort of whimper that backed him up, but willingly bent over, and unhooked her bra herself when Anton wasn't quick enough about it.

"And she especially likes winning my approval by doing as she's told. Don't you?"

She dug her front teeth into her lip and wrinkled her nose.

"Don't be a brat."

She swallowed. "I'm not. I'm just wondering what getting an A+ today is likely to involve, because I think I might draw the line at both of you fucking my arse simultaneously."

Anton coughed and spluttered. "That is... Yeah,

my mind had not gone there. Yours," he said looking at Adie. "Is obvious far filthier. Also, just what sort of porn have you been consuming?"

"Just because I watch it, doesn't mean I want to do it. Not that I have... I mean, I might have, but accidentally... It's not what I seek out."

That left both him and Anton grinning and shooting her sceptical looks.

"It isn't!"

He wanted to kiss away that pout.

"So, you say."

She smashed her lips together hard and lifted her chin.

"Arse fucking doesn't have to be on the agenda, if you don't want it to be," he said.

"I didn't say that. I just said, no double dipping back there."

He snorted. Anton clutched his sides and rolled onto his back. "God, at this rate I might die of laughter."

She poked him. "I don't see what's so funny. I'm just setting sensible boundaries. It's not like either of you would be up for it either."

"Neither of us brought it up," he said.

"Have either of you even had a single cock up your arse?"

"And now the conversation comes full circle. You didn't want to know, remember?"

"Yeah, well, I take it back. I do want to know. Have you?" she asked. He didn't answer.

"What about you, professor?" She crawled to him then rose onto her knees to look him in the face and offer a sweet smile. "Has anyone ever bent you over and had their way with you, professor?"

Killian kissed her on the nose. "No comment."

"You can tell me." She drew a finger down his abs. "I can keep a secret. Go on, whisper." She turned her ear towards him. "No?" She planted a line of kisses down his abs heading towards his cock. "It won't change how I think of you."

"Adie." He shook his head, but then she circled the base of his shaft and swallowed his tip, which put him right inside his head and sent the air whooshing out of his lungs. Damn, she was good at that. He put a hand on her head to guide her and got lost in the in and out slide to and from her mouth.

"Killian likes to be forced into relinquishing command," Anton remarked, propping himself up to watch. "He won't ever hand it over willingly, but that doesn't mean he doesn't love it when you throw him off his pedestal. A good way to do that is to do as you are."

"That is such bollocks."

"It's the gods honest truth. Take my word for it, Adie. Blow him just right and the man turns to mush. He'll let you get away with just about anything."

"And what about you, Anton? What facet of your sexual make up should we scrutinise?"

"Any facet you like. I'm an open book. I don't hide who I am. I'm a sensualist. I have a problem with authority. And I think edging's a fun sport." He rolled back onto his knees as he spoke, then planted kisses up Killian's back, and on his shoulders, while his hands fanned across Killian's arse and squeezed.

"I can't decide in this moment which of you I want to get inside of more." He adjusted his cock inside his briefs.

"Well, while you think on it... Adie..." He pulled her off his cock. "Push Anton's briefs down and get him wet."

Obedient as a puppy after a treat, she peeled down Anton's black cotton shorts, then leaned into him, eyes closed. For a moment, she simply breathed in his scent. Then her tongue swiped her upper lip, and she took him right to where her hand wrapped around his base.

Damn, it was hard to hold himself in check while watching her. Pretty soon, she was back sucking him again, and within a few sucks he was tingling from head to toe.

Anton leaned in and claimed his mouth, the two of them feasted on one another's tongues as Adie alternated her magic touch between them and tried unsuccessfully to swallow them both together. He couldn't knock her willingness to experiment, and he liked the way her arse was wiggling as she swapped back and forth between them like a kid with a double cone.

He wasn't sure how the decision was made in the end. Maybe it was down to him knowing where the stash of condoms was. He rubbered up and entered her while she was still on all-fours with Anton's cock in her mouth. They didn't stay that way for long, because she couldn't keep her pleasure contained, she had to sing it out, and he loved having that evidence of her pleasure ringing in his ears.

Of course, that left Anton free to make trouble. His gaze raked across Killian's skin as he rolled a condom on and moved in next to him. They tag teamed her for a while, swapping every time she seemed to be right on the edge of coming, delighting in filling the place the other had been. "Please. I need to come. Can't take it anymore."

Killian flipped her over onto her back. He fucked her while he rubbed her clit with his thumb, fingers spread over her denuded mons. "Once you've come on my cock. Anton's going to fuck you right where I've just been, and you're going to come again on his cock."

"Yeah!" Ecstasy over the sheer possibility stretched her mouth wide into a tooth flashing grin. "Not sure if I can, but I'm more than willing to be proved wrong."

He made her come. She'd been hanging on to the cliff edge for a while already, so all it took was a minor adjustment to the angle of his hips, and her muscles were tangoing around him. He pulled out before he utterly lost it. Not the easiest thing to do. His jaw ached with the strain of it, and he had to give the base of his cock a sound pinch.

Anton sank into the wet haven between her thighs. He stretched right over her, kissing both her breasts hello, then claiming her mouth too. "You're nicely wet and willing."

"You feel nice too."

He took hold of her wrists and spread them out to either side of her. "I want to feel what he felt, Adie. I want you to come apart around me and know that

I pushed you to that point. That you want me as much as you ever want him. That—"

"I do. Anton, I do, very much."

"Cute," he remarked adopting a deliberately scathing tone. He wasn't mad. He wasn't jealous, just playacting, and a little frustrated, but he had an idea or two about how to relieve that. Anton was spread out like a fucking banquet. His long, lean form stretched over Adie's, the ladder of his spine, the arch over two perfectly formed cheeks.

"What do you say we switch things up a little?"

He knew Anton understood him, because the muscles in his arse immediately jumped, and the slow steady strokes he was ploughing Adie with became all ragged and discordant.

"You don't mind if I borrow a bit you're not using, do you Adie?"

He trailed his fingers over that upturned arse and felt the shiver roll through the pair of them. "Let's see..." He rested his thumb at the top of the channel between those two beautiful globes. Leaned in, pressed a kiss to each cheek.

"How am I supposed to hold it together for her, with you doing that?"

"Oh, I'm going to do much worse," he sighed into the other man's skin. He palmed the lube from the drawer and let it dribble over Anton's tailbone. "I'm going to get inside of you. I'm going to fuck you so that it feels like I'm fucking all the way through you and into Adie, and you're both going to hold it together until I'm ready for you not to. Now Adie, be a good girl for me and squeeze Anton's nice thick cock with your muscles. That's it. Pull him in deep. I can feel what you're doing to him. His balls are getting all taut, and there's this quiver vibrating just below his skin."

He dripped more oil, this time letting it pool over the hole he intended to make very thorough use of. Anton clenched when he touched him there. "Relax, it's hardly the first time you've had my fingers in you." He whimpered as Killian stretched him open, his trembling becoming more pronounced as he anticipated the sweet invasion of a finger, or the promised thrust of a cock. His hips jerked unsteadily. "Hold him steady for me now, Adie."

She wriggled her wrists free of Anton's hold and clasped his cheeks. "Damn, I wish I could see."

"And you will." It just wouldn't be on this occasion. Tonight, these were his visuals to feast on. His hole to abuse. He stroked downwards with featherlight strokes, basking in all the anticipation Anton held caged within. He was going to fuck him slowly. Nothing rushed. Not tonight. Nothing frantic about this. They had time. He possessed patience. When Anton opened to him, it would be a complete surrender. No resistance, his body eagerly swallowing him up.

He listened. Waited until his rasping breaths turned into snarls. Until he was sure each tickle was turning him inside out, and Adie was making frantic mewls in turn because Anton was drilling her so well.

That's when he rolled on a new rubber and got himself thoroughly slippery.

There was barely a breath of resistance to Anton's surrender, though his exclamation was sharp.

"Fuck, that's... Oh, God!"

He buried his face in Adie's shoulder.

"Is it good?"

Anton turned his face to her and spoke against her neck. "So-oo good." His breath turned shuddery. "Not going to keep it together for long. Feels like everything's connected. Shit!" he bared his teeth. "It's coming." His groans and moans grew louder. Adie's floated above, an octave higher.

Killian rode him hard, hips toiling away, chasing the clenching sensation thickening at the base of his cock, chasing something he knew was near to impossible but wanting it, nevertheless. All of them shattering together, toppling like dominoes, spilling out words of passion, of love, and bliss. In the end, perhaps it wasn't such a far-fetched dream after all. As Anton's cock pulsed, his own did the same, emptying in thick glorious spurts, while Adie's head arched back, and her mouth opened, lips drawing back over her teeth.

When he was all done, his cock no longer even capable of a twitch, he let out a satisfied grunt, then disentangled them. Much as it would be easy to roll over and drift off to sleep utterly contented, he endeavoured not to be that sort of prick. Having used them both so well, he had a duty of care. That meant clean up, and cuddles, and straightening out the bed, so the pillows weren't on the floor, and ensuring they were all hydrated.

He got as far as disposing of the condom and hunting out a warm cloth, before they pulled him back into bed between them. Anton hooked a hairy leg over his, while Adie rested her head in the crook of his shoulder.

"That was fun."

He kissed her, because he didn't have the words to describe how it had made him feel, or what he was feeling now.

Anton squeezed his hand. "You're definitely going to want to have a turn in the middle."

Adie lifted her head. "He lets you fuck him?"

"He loves it when I fuck him. It makes him fucking crazy."

"I'm right here," he reminded them.

"We know," they both said grinning at him. "And you're staying here."

"Until at least six o'clock."

Anton made an ooh sound. "What do you say we live a little more dangerously than that? How about ten past?"

"Seven," he said. "Ten past seven." His alarm heard him and confirmed that it was set. "To be on site for eight. So, if anyone has any morning play plans, requires an orgasm to set them up for the day, or anything like that, I've approximately five minutes between my shower and coffee as long as someone else sees to the suncream."

"Joint shower?" Anton cocked a brow.

"Do you think suncream will make good handjob lube?"

He didn't know and didn't reply, letting his

eyelids close instead. But call it intuition, he had a feeling he was going to find out.

~Ж~

Aloe After Sun was better.

~Ж~

Join Adie, Killian, and Anton in a bonus epilogue adventure by using the QR code below.

-ACKNOWLEDGEMENTS-

Reviving an old project is a delicate process. How much of the old to keep? How to rearrange things to fit the new narrative? How to inject the modern world (20 years on from the original narrative) into the book? So, a huge thank you to those who've come on this journey with me. Especially, to my fabulous editor, Dayna, and my proofreading peeps, Mandie & Ren.

Also, to all the readers who've made it this far. Thanks for hanging out with me and let me know if you think Sian deserves her own book.

Madelynne, September 2024

-ABOUT THE AUTHOR-

Madelynne is a New York Times & USA Today bestselling British author of angsty bisexual romance featuring bad boys who desperately need someone to love them unconditionally.

Madelynne wrote her first novel after discovering Black Lace Books in the 1990s but had to escape the Hotel California before she could dive into storytelling full time. She's been described as a cool mum, a full-time geek, and plain old weird. Some of those might even be accurate. She lives in the UK near the Welsh border, where you can find her surrounded by books and rapidly cooling mugs of decaf coffee, dogs at her feet, listening to loud music.

To keep up to date with her releases, join her newsletter using the QR code below.